THE
CURRENT
Between US

KINDLE ALEXANDER

The Current Between Us

WARNING
This book contains material that maybe offensive to some:
graphic language, adult situations.

Trademark Acknowledgements:

 Dedication

Suzette Pylant and her team in the Dallas Madd offices, this book wouldn't have been possible without you. Thank you for always standing beside me, being the calm in my sea of unexplainable hurt – even today.
I'll love you forever.

This book is dedicated to my Kindle.
I miss you every minute of every day.
I love you beyond reason.
I'll see you soon.

Aidan, for you!

A portion of the sales of this book will be donated to Madd – Dallas.

The thing no one ever seems to consider about drinking and driving, you aren't on the streets alone. You're a risk to everyone when you decide to make that decision. Please choose wisely.

Chapter 1

A flash lit the bedroom an instant before the roar of thunder shook the small brick home. It couldn't have been much past three in the morning and instantly the house plunged into complete darkness, the electricity taken out by the storm raging outside. Trent Cooper rolled over in bed, kicking the blankets off his feet as he looked around. Seconds later, he heard the sounds of little feet hitting the floor, pounding on the hardwood as they ran toward his bedroom. In the next instant another pair of feet struck the floor. Now, both were heading his way. Pushing himself up on his elbows, he lifted his head and pulled the covers back, waiting.

"Daddy, Daddy, I'm scared. Can I sleep with you?" Emalynn, his almost-four-year-old daughter asked as she piled onto the foot of the bed and raced up into his arms. Her older brother, Hunter, wasn't far behind. Both children landed squarely on his chest.

"Daddy, I think that was more than thunder," six-year-old Hunter said, burrowing under his arm.

"Hunter, it's just the clouds bumping together. You're fine and safe." As Trent spoke, another loud crash hit. At the same moment a flash of light lit up the bedroom again. Emalynn let out a scream to rival the storm outside. She wrapped her small arms around his neck and buried her face in his shoulder. If it were even possible, Hunter moved in closer, gluing himself to Trent's side. Their little bodies trembled in his arms.

"Shhh, guys, I've got you. You know I'm not gonna let anything happen to either one of you. It's just a thunderstorm. It'll move over

1

fast, I promise. Come lay down beside me. Hunter man, tell Emalynn what your mom used to say about these storms."

It took a minute to get both children to release the tight grip they held on his body and another minute to lay everyone down and get the bed covers over them. He talked the entire time to keep their attention focused just on him. "Hunter, listen to me, son, tell Emalynn what your mom used to say."

"She always said that was Daddy in heaven trying to get our attention," Hunter finally said, his big green eyes focused on the window as he slid his body down next to Trent. The bait seemed to work for Hunter, but not Emalynn. She only released her hold on his neck to wrap herself around his chest, her death grip firmly in place. He angled an extra pillow behind his head and laid back, ignoring the powerful storm outside.

After a minute, Emalynn poked her head out the top of the covers. Her green eyes searched his face as she inched her way up his chest until she could again hide her head in the crook of his neck. Her tiny body trembled as he gently rubbed her back with the palm of his hand.

"Emalynn, I was thinking, the super loud thunder could be both your momma and daddy trying to get your attention. What do you think, Hunter? Think it could happen?" Trent asked as Hunter added his own soothing hand to Emalynn's back trying to calm her down. The trembles slowly began to ease in her little body.

"I think so, Em. Don't be scared. It's just Mommy and Daddy saying hello," Hunter added quickly.

"See? It's not bad at all." Trent gave Em a small kiss on her head before he tried to angle her down along the left side of his body, opposite Hunter, but she would have no part in loosening her hold around his neck. Instead, she put one of her hands on his cheek and turned his face down to hers. Her sweet breath tickled across his skin as she spoke.

"Daddy, I think it's scary monsters trying to eat our house!" Em's big green eyes grew huge as she said the words, then a screech tore from her lips and she ducked her head back in his neck.

"Em, that's dumb. Monsters aren't real. I learned that in school, for sure!" Hunter said it matter-of-factly with the storm outside completely forgotten.

"Shh, Emalynn, baby, Hunter's right. There's no such thing as monsters, and do you hear it? The storm's already getting calmer outside." As if on cue, the alarm clock on the nightstand flashed back to life as well as the hall bathroom light he always left on for the kids at night. "See there? The lights are back on. The storm's leaving."

"Daddy, I want to sleep with you. I'm still scared," Em said. She let up on her hold at his throat, but again her hands were on his face, turning his head to look her in the eye.

"Me too, Daddy! I want to sleep with you, too." Hunter was in instant agreement with his sister.

"Okay, but we have to go back to sleep. We only have a couple of hours before its time to get up." Trent finally dislodged Em from his neck and got her tucked in with the covers around her.

"Can we talk about my birthday? It's in six more days," Em asked, a yawn already spilling from his tired little girl. She laid her head on his chest and ran her fingertips across his chin. For whatever reason, Em always rubbed her fingers over his five o'clock shadow whenever she got the chance.

"Honey, it's eleven more days away. Today is Tuesday and your birthday is Sunday after next. We can, if we talk about it quietly," Trent said.

"Daddy, do I get a gift this year?" Hunter asked on a yawn.

"You both always get one gift on each other's birthday." Trent felt reasonably sure they were both covered and tucked in around him. He judged the yawns as a good sign the conversation wouldn't last too much longer. Trent tugged the extra pillow from behind his head and tossed it aside as he looked up at the ceiling and waited for them to fall back asleep.

"Grandma always gave you and Momma gifts on each other's birthday, right, Daddy?" Em asked.

"Yep. Always," Trent replied.

"Is that why you do it for us?" Hunter asked.

"Yep and you two need to go to sleep."

"Wait! Where are we going for Em's birthday?" Hunter asked.

"Daddy, are we going this weekend to pick out my decorations? I want a princess birthday, I think." Em lifted her head to look at Hunter.

"No, Em. You said last night we could have the Ninja Turtles, and you would be Raphael, I would be Leonardo, remember?" Hunter lifted his head, looking back at Em.

"Daddy, I want a princess birthday." Em shot a panicked look at Trent.

"Em, you change your mind too much." The argument between the two started so fast, it made it hard to keep up.

"Hey, now, Hunter, it's her birthday. She decides without our help. We can get you something to have as a decoration, too. Lay down. I'm serious, you guys, we need to sleep," Trent lowered their heads with his hands back down to his chest. He ran his fingertips gently over both their backs, trying to lull them back asleep.

"Yeah, it's my birthday, Hunter," Em added, but another soft yawn tore from her lips before she could finish the sentence.

"Daddy, Em's teacher said we can bring treats to school to send home with her pre-K class. Can we do it? Do we have enough money for treats and me a decoration and the princess decorations and the gifts?" Hunter asked.

"Of course we have enough money for treats and decorations, Hunter. Son, we have to talk about why you're so worried about how much money we have all of a sudden. You don't need to worry about things like that." Trent smiled at the sounds of soft snores coming from both sides of the bed. He completely agreed, financial affairs were snooze-worthy as hell, and enough to make anyone crash while talking about them.

Trent looked back up at the ceiling and made a mental note to send an email to Hunter's teacher asking about his sudden concern over their financial state. Did six-year-olds think about things like that?

"Close it off and go to sleep," Trent whispered to himself, trying to stop his brain, but one thought led to another and his mind finally went there. *Dang it!*

On a normal day, it took a herculean effort to force his mind off his sister. Now with Em's birthday approaching, of course he'd think about her more. The slap of a tiny hand hit Trent in the face. An offending leg came next, racking him good. The kids were sound asleep, tossing and turning. They hit anything in their way. He sighed. Between their flying limbs and his overactive mind, there would be no more sleep for him tonight. Carefully, he untangled himself from the kids' hold and quietly made his way to the bathroom.

Trent flipped on the shower and dropped his pajama pants where he stood. He barely waited a minute before he stepped under the spray, letting the warm stream coat his skin. Even as he dunked his face under the pulsating showerhead, he still couldn't seem to let go of the thoughts. No matter how many times he played it over in his head, or how it gnawed at him, the facts never changed.

Trent finally slumped back against the wet wall and scrubbed his hands up and down his face in defeat. He wasn't going to escape the memories this year either. With a thump, his head dropped back on the tile, his eyes closed, and he gave in, centering back into that time almost four years ago.

Emalynn and Hunter's father died during his last tour of duty in Iraq, six months before Emalynn was born. Lynn took his death hard and grieved badly for her husband. Trent always worried about the toll all that stress may have taken on Emalynn before her birth. He'd stayed by Lynn's side throughout the entire pregnancy, eventually moving her and Hunter in with him. He tried to give Lynn comfort in her loss, and the stability she needed to get through her pregnancy.

Trent dedicated himself to getting Lynn strong and healthy. He took his job as big brother and designated birthing coach seriously. He studied the role for months, attending all the birthing classes, picking out the best focusing tools for Lynn's use during her labor—the photos and music were all there on standby ready to go for when she needed them. Everything seemed to be going well. Lynn pushed gently with her contractions, and each stage progressed as it should, per all the books Trent read.

Lynn had allowed an epidural this time around, instead of the natural, home childbirth she'd endured with Hunter. It had surprised him, but he hadn't questioned it. His sister, the absolute health nut, believed in the natural way of things. He hadn't questioned her decision. Instead, he was thankful she hadn't had to go through all the pain. In hindsight, he'd missed that big red flag waving at him, letting him know something wasn't quite right with the whole situation.

Sophia, Lynn's lifelong best friend, stayed in the delivery room with them. Lynn's labor was in full swing. The doctor and nurses were in place, all set to guide their new baby girl out. The room bustled with medical equipment, most hooked up to Lynn, but Trent hadn't known that wasn't normal either. He appreciated how well they were monitoring Lynn and Em. There was talk of a caesarean early on in the day, but Lynn refused it, and Trent had agreed. Why would she need a C-section? They had studied for a natural birth, planned, prepared, and ready to do this thing!

He kept hearing from all the professionals that her numbers were good. Apparently, another huge indicator the process wasn't as positive as it should have been.

Trent only had one defense for missing so many warning signs: the entire experience had fundamentally changed him. The emotion of bringing a new life into the world, being so up close and personal with it all transformed him forever. Trent connected to Em before she'd ever shown her little face to the world. When it came down to the final minutes, the doctor instructed Lynn to push carefully one last time. It was all it would take to get Em there with them. Emalynn's head popped out, Trent concentrated on her swollen face seconds before his sister gave an agonizing scream and fell back on the hospital gurney.

He and Sophia were shoved from the birthing room as the crash carts slammed past them in an attempt to save his sister, Em's mother. Later, the doctor told him, Lynn had found out about the abdominal aortic aneurysm a few weeks after learning she was pregnant. She'd kept it from her family, opting to have Emalynn before going under the knife to repair the damaged artery, but she hadn't made it. Instead, she died instantly when it burst, sending the birth into a frenzy.

To this day, it truly bothered Trent that he hadn't picked up on the clues. Now, he understood the intense grieving during her pregnancy wasn't just about Lynn's lost husband, but also the fear she faced of leaving her own children. Lynn had insisted on creating a will and went into detailed explanations on how her children should be raised if anything happened to her. She left the children and everything she owned to Trent. He had sat through hours of her coaching him on how to be a father, what her finances were and the military benefits left to the children.

Never once did Trent think he would ever use the information she forced on him. At the time, he was pacifying his grieving sister. He'd even refused to listen to any more talk of death; telling her he was done with that nonsense and life was for the living! Lynn had just smiled at him and kissed his cheek. Boy, he'd gotten every bit of it completely wrong.

Trent missed Lynn. She'd been his best friend. They were the only children of a single, older mom who'd spent her life devoted to them. Trent was the oldest, but not by much. Lynn came along eleven months after his birth. The only time they were apart were the years they spent in college when Lynn met Aaron, got pregnant, and married him within a few months after their meeting. Aaron focused solely on his military career. Trent saw it as Aaron putting as much space between him and Lynn as he could, but he never said anything about her marriage. He had just been glad she moved back closer to him.

Emotion choked him as he turned and beat his forehead gently against the damp tile. Trent tried hard to hide all of this from the kids. Childhood should be filled with fun memories, snapshots to take into their adult lives. Frustration coursed through him as he grabbed the bottle of shampoo at the same moment the pungent aroma of coffee filled the steamy air of the shower. A smile spread across his lips, helping to pull him from the melancholy of his thoughts like nothing else could. Rhonny was already up and making coffee.

If there could be a silver lining to the dark cloud surrounding his life at this time of year, it centered right in on his live-in nanny. Rhonny classified as his dream come true and he thanked the good Lord for her every single day. He wouldn't have survived the last four years without her. She had come in as his first and, as it turned out, only interview for the nanny position.

Em had been barely a few weeks old, screaming in the middle of a major crying fit when Rhonny came through the front door. He remembered the moment as if it happened yesterday. Completely out of his element with the non-stop crying baby in his arms, he had opened the front door utterly flustered. There stood Rhonny, all Brazilianly beautiful and the breath of fresh air he needed in those dark, dark days. She took Em from him, calmed her down almost instantly, while explaining she was the oldest of eight children. She came with bottle, diaper, and play time experience down to a science. She could even cook a meal or two and turned out to be everything he needed. He hired her on the spot and she started that very afternoon.

All these years later, they had a solid working relationship, which he honestly considered to be more like a family than employee to employer. Their only complication: Rhonny was part of the study abroad program and graduated from college next year. They were already working on the visas needed to keep her in the country, but who knew how it all would turn out, and it worried him. The government didn't seem overly interested in how Rhonny worked her way into a necessity of his life or how the kids needed her with them.

Trent dried himself quickly and swiped the towel over his bathroom mirror before tossing it over the shower door. Daily grooming never took him too much time, and the coffee called out to his soul, speeding his process faster than normal. Not wanting to wake the kids in the other room, Trent kept the freshly grown stubble on his face, but brushed his teeth and ran a comb through his short light brown hair. He scanned his gaze over his hair, then his face, and took the moment to stare at the bright green eyes looking back at him in the mirror. They were one of the only traits he shared with his sister.

Tall, muscular, and thick, Trent played football all the way through college and kept the build into his adult life. Lynn stayed short, petite, and blonde. If she ever developed a true muscle on her body, he never saw it. These eyes and their smiles were the only things they shared as adults. Em and Hunter shared them too. Now, his stared back at him all red-eyed and exhausted.

Trent slapped himself hard on the face. The jolt surprised even him, but it did the trick and woke him completely. The goal was to keep this awake thing going for the next sixteen or so hours ahead of him.

Leaving both his image and all the mental self-reflection behind, he turned to his closet. The best renovation he'd made to this house involved relocating the door to his closet and placing it in his bathroom, instead of the bedroom. It afforded him more privacy. Trent pulled on his blue jeans and T-shirt before quietly making his way back into the bedroom to pick up his work boots by the bed. The kids slept as he tiptoed out the door and down the hall where all three of their rooms were located. He continued the silent tiptoe all the way to the kitchen at the other end of the house. Sizzling bacon filled the air, competing with the strong smell of coffee. Both made his taste buds water.

"You're up early. It's barely five," Trent said quietly, placing his shoes on the kitchen floor by the table. He made his way to the oversized sock basket in the laundry room directly off the kitchen. He and Rhonny hated matching socks so it never seemed to get done. Instead, they piled high in a laundry basket causing them to dig through it regularly trying to find matches.

"I know. The thunder woke me. By the time I got up here, the kids were already out of bed. I supposed in your room," she said quietly, standing at the stove, turning the bacon in the sizzling pan. Rhonny occupied the basement all by herself. The space was small, but held enough room for a shower, a bedroom, and a small office area. He gave it all to her when she'd accepted the job, moving his office into the garage to give her more room.

"Yeah, I don't think the first clap of thunder ended before they were already there, climbing up into bed. It pretty much ended sleeping for the night," Trent said, sitting in a chair at the table, angling his socks and boots on.

"I figured. It's why I started breakfast early. I have an eight o'clock final this morning and I need to study. But I can take the kids to school before I go, if you need me to. I didn't get your text until too late last night about my schedule for the next week. It's why I didn't text you back."

"It'd be great if you took them. I have a nine o'clock walk-through and I need to get the crews out. I'm behind on some blueprints I need to bid on. I should be able to make a big dent on the estimate before the guys get here." Trent mentally ticked off his to do list as he adjusted his feet in his thick steel-toed work boots. Rising, he made his way to the coffee pot, pouring himself a cup. He pulled another cup from the cupboard and served up a second mug for Rhonny. She used all those sweet creamers, doctoring the taste, so he pushed the cup closer to her before turning and propping himself against the kitchen counter and taking a long drink.

"It's the only early test I have for finals this week, so I should be able to take them to school the rest of the week, too. Oh, but remember, I have LSAT classes starting next week. I need to be there no later than six. I can call Auntie Crazy, if you're gonna be late. Or meet you somewhere, just let me know. I'm also going to Milwaukee this weekend. I'm leaving early Saturday morning, but I'll be here the next weekend. I told Em I would stay for her birthday, if it's okay?"

"Of course, it's okay. Thank you for planning to be here on your day off. I know she'll be excited. I can't believe she's already turning four. We're supposed to go on Sunday to pick out decorations." Trent took another long drink of the hot coffee. He could feel it slowly doing its job of getting him moving for the day.

"Oh man, she's so gonna love that. Did she stick with Tinkerbell?" Rhonny asked, looking over her shoulder, her long brown hair swinging with a twinkle in her eye.

"Heck, no, that was three decisions ago. She just told me it's a princess party now," he said, chuckling a little before drinking down the rest of his cup.

"That's funny. It'll be interesting to see what she finally decides on. Whatever it is, I'm sure it'll have lots of hot pink in it." Rhonny turned back, pulling the bacon from the skillet at the same moment the toast popped free from the toaster.

"I know, right? She was so wishing that pink Barbie kitchen table was made big enough so we could have one in our kitchen," Trent said absently, pouring another cup before turning to head through the laundry room to the attached garage.

"Here, take this with you," Rhonny called after him.

"Oh, sorry… I'm already working those plans out in my mind. Thanks for breakfast," Trent said, took the sandwich, and without another thought of the birthday parties and pink kitchen tables, he opened the garage door to his makeshift shop to begin working on the blueprints.

Chapter 2

"Sid, I don't care if you agree with retirement or not. It's here, live with it. You can't entice me with leads anymore. I'm done and it's four in the fucking morning, man. Damn it, Sid, sleep for once," Gage said, interrupting his rambling editor and letting all the irritation of being awakened bristle through the few sentences he'd spoken since the phone call began. A yawn tore across his lips as a crash of thunder rumbled outside. An unexpected groan sounded from an unknown bed partner, reminding Gage someone still shared his bed from the previous night's activity. *Damn, how did I not get rid of him before now?*

"Just tell me when I can expect the last story? The higher ups are breathing down my neck. It's been years since you promised this one, Synclair. If it's the last piece, we need to strike while the iron's hot," Sid growled vehemently. Gone were the years when Gage begged Sid to air his work. Now he was a sought after commodity working with the largest names in the broadcasting industry.

Most of the time Gage liked Sid, and he knew he owed the man; it was the only reason he didn't shop this last report and promised it to Sid straight out. Sid was the first one to take notice of the complexity of Gage's photos and the depths he went to in order to find the entire story, not just accept the obvious answers to help conclude the broadcast. With Sid's help, Gage turned into an international success, making his photo and video investigative journalism the standard to be reached in present day news.

"Buddy, it's close. Don't push it. I'm not ready to talk about it, and I haven't asked you for a dime. You're supposed to be grateful I'm giving this to you to air, remember? I gotta roll. I'll see you at the grand opening. We can talk more then," Gage said, trying to adjust his eyes, and force his mind to remember who he'd brought home last night, and why the fuck he'd brought him home at all.

"I think you just gave me a back handed bribe," Sid said. Gage could hear it worked and gave a smile.

"You know it was, bye," Gage agreed, disconnecting the phone with a swipe of his finger across the screen. He continued working the phone using the one finger until he found the number he wanted. With one last run across the screen, he dialed the number and brought the cell to his ear.

"Galaxy Cab," a dispatcher answered.

"Hi, I need a cab, ASAP to South Halsted and Eighteenth Street, 2100 South Halsted. The ride will be waiting at the front door, no need to honk. I'll double the fee if you get here in the next five minutes," Gage said, then listened to the operator confirm his request. The bedcovers moved. He heard the shifting of the blanket as the guy left the bed. The brand new wonder mattress stayed true to its word, he hadn't felt a stir the entire night.

"I'm guessing that's my exit. Well… it was a great night. I'll leave my number for you here on the desk. I would love a repeat to free your willy," the guy said, his accent thick. He scribbled something on the dresser while laughing at his own little joke. As Gage watched, he thought he might have remembered this one claimed to be a male model from Cuba, or perhaps, Guadalajara. Hell, he really had zero idea. Honestly, Gage didn't remember much from the night before, but he rarely did much talking in these kinds of situations.

Gage lifted up on his elbows and searched the dark room for the guy's clothing, wanting to help him along a little faster. Pieces of clothing were plucked off the floor and Gage sat up, pushing his hair off his forehead. As another lightning strike illuminated the room, he got a good look at the naked body standing across the bedroom. That glimpse told him everything he needed to know about this one. Spanish accent guy was a good looking dude with a super tight bubble butt and a long, thick dick…too bad Gage didn't do repeats. The room shook with the crash of thunder following that thought.

"There isn't a need to leave the number. I won't use it," Gage said, rising from the bed. He stood there, nude, pulling his wallet from the nightstand beside him and handed fifty dollars to the guy who came to stand in front of him, T-shirt in hand.

"This is for the cab ride," Gage said, and the guy pocketed the money with a smile.

"I live around here. No need for a cab. I'll be seeing you around, sexy." He winked, pulling his T-shirt over his head while turning on his heel and prancing out the bedroom door. Gage grabbed his phone, a pair of jeans off the floor, and followed along behind him. The guy was already down the stairs and halfway across the gallery as Gage struggled into his jeans while trying to keep up. Through the big windows in the front of his new gallery, he saw the taxi lights waiting at the curb. The rain poured, drenching everything outside.

"This is going to be a spectacular art gallery, the real deal. Everyone's excited you decided to open here," Spanish guy called back as he opened the front door.

"Thanks, are you sure you don't want a ride? It's raining pretty hard out there," Gage asked, coming to stand behind him at the front door.

"Yeah, I'll take you up on it," he said and stuck out his hand for more money. Gage fished his wallet out and handed him another fifty dollar bill, which the guy instantly pocketed.

"Adios," he said, running out into the rain in the opposite direction of the taxi. Gage watched him dart across the road and race down the street under the cover of the awnings until he couldn't be seen anymore.

Forced to run bare footed and bare chested out into the rain to pay the waiting taxi driver, Gage chuckled at the guy leaving him. He sure had a way of picking them! At the very least, if the guy only intended to take the money, he could have run out here and told the driver he wasn't needed. Gage had met plenty of guys just like that one throughout his life. He actually preferred them to the many others he came across. With guys like thick Spanish accent there, it never got messy and always involved a quick, gratifying fuck with money usually exchanging hands. Meaning his money into their hands before they were out the door, never to be seen or heard from again.

Gage handed the driver another fifty and ran back inside completely drenched from head to toe. He didn't look back outside, but slammed the door and twisted the lock in place. No lights lit the gallery. They hadn't bothered turning any on. He reached over to flip the switch as he squinted his eyes preparing for the glare when nothing happened. No wonder it was so dark! They'd lost electricity or he guessed they had. No way to know for sure in this building. His electrical contractor sucked. A no-show for the last several days and he had avoided all of Gage's phone calls. It could have just been the electrician's shoddy work keeping the light off so he glanced back out the front windows and didn't see any lights down the street.

As if by some sort of cosmic cue, the electricity blazed to life, throwing the entire gallery into light causing him to squint his eyes for real. When his eyesight adjusted, the sight greeting him caused a chuckle as he stood there several minutes looking around his gallery. He'd spent a lot of time in his adult life in the middle of utter destruction, whether it be manmade or at Mother Nature's hand. The chaos of this remodel reminded him of those places he'd worked in over the years. The only difference was that here he could visualize the final plans taking shape and coming together just fine.

As far as he cared, the place looked great, even with the walls newly taped and bedded, scaffolding laying everywhere, broken trim pieces, nails, screws, boxes, and dust covering everything…yeah, but they were right on schedule. It was all going to be fine. The Art Gallery's grand opening loomed only a week away. The invitations had already been sent with RSVPs coming in daily. And regardless of how it all looked at the moment, this place would be complete and dazzling within the next seven days, ready to welcome the world.

Remarkably the only complication in the remodel came with the electrical contractor. He'd fired him to keep the fast moving, steady pace he'd paid both his arms and a leg to achieve. The schedule didn't allow for anyone to put them behind. It took less than a few hours to find a new electrical contractor, and this new contractor was young and eager, ready to put the time in to finish this remodel on schedule, starting today, or so he'd been assured.

Since Gage grew up in a family of construction workers, he knew firsthand how shady subcontractors could be with their empty promises of timeframes and deadlines. It was the main reason he spent every single day and night here, pushing and threatening every worker who came through his door. He required them all to be accountable to him for their portion of the rebuild and he rewarded them when they achieved each deadline. He never lived his life on empty promises and he wasn't going to allow his art gallery modifications to turn out the same way. At thirty-three years old and already retiring from the only job he'd ever wanted to do, Gage demanded things run on time in order for him to have some semblance of a normal life in his future.

This gallery was a little risky. He'd chosen to locate in Chicago's South Side, his hometown, rather than in some trendy part of New York City. The opening of his gallery fell strategically close to the breaking news of his final investigative report. It's why the push to finish this remodel came so quickly. Both his gallery debut and the airing of his last report were designed to catapult him into regular reporting on CNN or *60 Minutes*, but from behind the desk, not in the field. Having the gallery to run and a desk broadcasting job to anchor would be monumentally easier jobs than running through the underbelly of every third world country, trying to piece together how crappy people truly were to one another.

Gage jogged back upstairs to his personal living quarters to prepare for the day. He took a quick shower and wiped the mist from the mirror with his wet towel. Always comfortable in his own skin, Gage stood completely naked, looking at himself in the mirror.

His eyes resembled those of a much older man. He'd seen too much in his need to stand on his own two feet. He'd also spent a lot of time trying to make his facial features more rugged to hide the feminine features he'd been born with. In the beginning of his career, no one had taken him seriously, discounting him, time and time again, because of his pretty boy good looks. He grew past tired of always being told he would be better off modeling or acting than trying to be taken seriously as a photo journalist.

Inner personal drive and nothing more forced him to make people take notice of his work. Ten years later, he had a dark tan from years of working in the sun and blond sun streaks running through his sandy blond hair. He'd always kept his hair length close to a buzz cut. It helped with the itching when there wasn't a bath readily available for days at a time, but now that he was back to being a regular citizen again, he'd decided to let it grow. He kept it a little longer in order to do some of those cool, slightly disarrayed hair styles so popular today.

Moving his hands through his hair, he got the look he liked with a little bit of gel and a little bit of the blow dryer's help. He decided to keep the five o'clock shadow, which always made his features look more masculine, and he did a quick trim job on the growth to keep it neat. His nose seemed a little too wide to him, but no one else ever seemed to notice, and there was just nothing he could do to hide his lips. They were big, full, and wide, spreading easily into a smile. Gage's reputation categorized him to be no nonsense, a total hard ass. That irony meant that most people in his life didn't know how much he loved to laugh and smile.

He decided on jeans and a white with blue plaid, lightweight button down. Gage flipped on the lights to his bedroom, dressing in front of his mirror. He left the shirt untucked and unbuttoned at the top and at the bottom. Gage stood tall and muscular with a solid six pack. One he got from real work, not the gym. He'd carried his own equipment during every report throughout all the years, but his body looked more like a swimmer's, lean and long. Nothing about gallery or desk work gave him the workout necessary to retain any sort of muscle. If he intended to maintain this body, he needed to reconsider the gym option.

He added a few accessories to finish off the look before checking his reflection one last time in the mirror. He liked real clothes and spent a fortune on them once he'd gotten back in town. He packed his closet full of casual, easy wearing clothes. He loved the surfer guy look of today, but he also grooved on Prada's spring collection, buying every piece shown to him. The khaki shorts, T-shirts, and work boots he wore in the field were never going to find their way back into his wardrobe again. He liked color and style, something he didn't know he liked until he'd done without it.

He took the stairs back down to his office located to the right of the front doors. He chose an ultra-cool design and spent the most money on the walls of his office. They were newly synthesized sound and bullet proof smart glass panels. They darkened with a simple touch of the remote control. He loved the look of them and would press the buttons only to watch them darken during the long boring hours of watching the construction men work. The glass panels, along with his security staff, helped make his workplace secure. His office turned out to be his own little panic room, right there in the front of the building. *How cool is that?*

He took a seat behind his chrome plated desk and booted up his laptop. He flipped on CNN by remote control, but his gaze was drawn to the street. The rain had come to an end and the morning barely began to make its presence known. The outside windows in his office were the same glass panels, but the panels opened to the street for those times Gage felt trapped. It was one of the only drawbacks to returning to the real world. He loved wide open spaces, for the breeze to blow across his skin as he worked.

He released the security on the window beside him and opened it to let the fresh smell of rain fill his office. The breeze this morning blew crisp and a little chilly. The rain must have blown in a small cold front as it drove through this morning. Chicago in May could go either way weather-wise and you never really knew what to expect or how to dress for it.

The only other drawback he found to retiring lay in the photo frames now scattered across his desk. All of his family stared back at him. His mother had brought these photos by yesterday to help remind Gage he needed to spend more time with them. One of the pictures sitting in front of all the others must have been more of a dig than a reminder. His entire family stood in front of the building which housed their family-owned business. He was the only one not there to stand in the photo.

The Keurig sat strategically close to his desk, within easy reach. He leaned over, clicking the button on. Within seconds the faint rich smells of coffee filled the room, dominating the earlier scent of rain. With an effort, he forced his mind off his family and back to the schedule lying on his desk. From now until the grand opening his schedule looked packed with appointments, meetings, and contractors. The laptop went through its motions and finally dinged to let Gage know it waited for him.

He pulled up his email and market reports, hating them both with a passion. Throughout the years, he pretended to be electronically dumb merely to avoid replying to the many messages and reports sent his way. Today turned out better than expected, every email in his inbox dealt with his last investigative report. He gave a big smile at the screen. This investigation held every bit of his interest, more than anything else these days. After six long years in the making, at a cost of several hundreds of thousands of his own personal dollars, it really looked to be coming to an end. Gage footed the entire bill and as the story grew, he knew this would be the pinnacle of his career.

In the beginning it was all about the hunch and then over the years as the pieces fit together, he knew, he needed to end on this story. It became a go-out-on-top-in-a-blaze-of-glory kind of deal, because he definitely didn't see it getting any better than this from a news reporter's stand point. Some of his top employees knew portions of the story, but no one knew the whole thing. Gage did all his own videotaping and photo work. He never left it to anyone else, because that was where the story always came from. The thousands and thousands of photos taken were reviewed over and over again until the pieces came together and the interview questions were formed.

Gage sifted through the messages in the inbox until he found his director of security's latest email. He pulled it up and launched the latest video on his subject. They were in surveillance mode now. The target found and watched, twenty-four/seven. A smile crossed his lips at the images he saw. Regular plastic surgery over the last couple of years, small nips and tucks here and there with ever changing hair and eye color, had made it a challenge, but they'd finally made a positive ID. Now they were fully in undercover mode and infiltrating the area.

As Gage sat there watching, his palms itched to be on site doing this work himself, but he'd become too famous, too recognizable; forced to sit on the sidelines, he watched from a distance. It killed him, but nothing was worth the risk of getting recognized while undercover and blowing the entire operation.

Even not being there, Gage made sure he still held all the control. He watched every detail closely, calling the shots from this laptop. He viewed the videos and photos over and over again, exactly like he did while in the field, piecing it all together. With a little more patience, he would be moving in, blowing the doors off this guy and all those supposedly civilized countries paying him to do their dirty work.

After only having the dozen or so aliases the guy used around the world, Gage recently stumbled on his birth name, Ahmed Abdulla. Abdulla was a professional and his attacks weren't about any religious or political view; it was only about the money. Once hired, Abdulla could successfully move from country to country, changing his look, his speech, and his alias while creating a new documented past, then infiltrating the different militaries across the world. He could strategically place himself where he needed to be to get the job done while always falling just under the radar.

Only on a stroke of luck had Gage even caught on to Abdulla. It came in the way of a missing person from one photo frame to the next, and now, after all this time, Gage had this guy within his grasp. Constant surveillance would track Abdulla's every move, but they would have to stay completely hidden until Gage was ready for the next phase.

If everything played out as planned, they would expose Abdulla by airing this report sometime in the next ten days to two weeks. And Gage would be all up in the middle of it, bringing Abdulla's name and face for the entire world to see. The United States military would be scrambling, but he would give them enough lead to get them in the general area before he broke the story. If he told them too much, they would take the story, pulling him out of it, and no way would he let it happen.

Gage kept his eyes trained on the monitor while leaning over to take the coffee cup from the maker, and then took a long drink. The hot brew burned its way down, giving him the jolt he needed. After watching the video in its entirety, he sent a few quick emails and made a few notes, moving the video to the corner of his screen in order to watch it all again later.

The sun lifted fully and he heard a truck pull to the front of the building. It was already seven in the morning. The crews were arriving, ready to start their day. Gage checked his calendar again, the new electrical contractor would be here around nine and he palmed his phone to alert him of the time. He couldn't afford any more mess ups and changed a couple of things on his schedule to be available when the new electrical contractor got there.

Chapter 3

The Coop Electric double cab pick-up truck pulled to the front curb of The Art Gallery, the name pretty much said it all. From what he'd been told of the area, he now sat parked in the newest, most trendy part of Chicago. It wasn't all that long ago this area of town was considered straight up hood, but over the last few years the city of Chicago dumped tons of money and tax incentives in to help revitalize its South Side. From what he could see, it worked. All along the walkway, bistros and cafes were littered in between several vintage book stores and coffee shops. He saw several high-end, ultra trendy retailers were also opening up shops, changing the whole feel of the area.

The drive wasn't too many miles away from his house, yet a world of difference existed between here and his little neighborhood in Overland Park. Today's traffic hadn't absolutely sucked, and he'd gotten to the job site a little bit early. Trent tugged the rearview mirror down and worked his fingers through his hair, making sure it all lay down close to the way it should. Then he checked his teeth for anything lingering from breakfast. He realized then he forgot to go back inside and shave after the kids woke up this morning. *Damn!* The need to give a good first impression had him quickly weighing his options.

Ten minutes early didn't leave enough time to run to the local drug store and do a quick shave, but this was a new general contractor to him, one he'd been trying to get his foot in the door with for years... *Shit!* Trent looked hard at himself. He didn't have much more than a five o'clock shadow and many guys purposefully wore their beards like this... *but dammit!*

He'd finally won a bid with Layne Construction, and he wasn't stupid, this would be the trial job to judge his performance. Nothing too big, but fast-paced and they'd be watching him closely. If he could pull this off while doing a good job, it might work his little electrical contracting business fully in the door of Layne and turn the tide for his baby, Coop Electric. It might even get him out from underneath doing so much of the day-to-day electrical work himself and would definitely help keep the receivables steadily coming in.

One last look in the mirror brought him to the decision to ignore the stubble on his face. Being on time should be more important than what he wore on his face... *Right?* Forcing it all from his mind, Trent jumped from the truck and took a look down, making sure his short sleeve button down stayed tucked into his new blue jeans and everything lay just right with his clothes. He grabbed his clipboard and phone as well as the estimate he'd given when bidding this job before giving a kick with his foot to slam the truck door. He pivoted seamlessly, turning in a full circle to open the truck door again. He grabbed a pencil and tape measure before making his way to what he thought might be the contractor and a very nicely dressed woman standing at the front doors. They looked to be in a deep conversation.

"Hi, excuse me, I'm sorry to interrupt. I'm Trent Cooper, Coop Electric. Are you Roger McCall?" he asked and fumbled with the items in his hands, trying to free his right hand for a quick shake.

"I am. Nice to meet you, Trent," McCall said, never fully taking his eyes off the woman in front of him, but stuck out his hand and shook Trent's.

"It's nice to meet you." After releasing MaCall's hand, he automatically made the same offer to the woman standing beside McCall when he didn't appear willing to make the introductions.

"I'm Jacquelyn Ballinger, The Art Gallery's new curator," she said, shaking his hand. Trent could see he'd interrupted a moment. He could tell from the look on her face it wasn't necessarily a good moment. Turning back to McCall, Trent held in his laugh. McCall's expression screamed hell bent on finishing the private conversation. The poor man wasn't picking up on a single clue the lady laid down that she wasn't interested in continuing whatever it was they'd been discussing.

21

"Ms. Ballinger, it's nice to meet you. I don't want to interrupt. I'm just here to do the walk-through before we begin work Thursday morning. Sir, I can get started and report back on anything I see different than the specs," Trent said, moving around them to the front door.

"Yeah, that would be great. We have a couple of minor changes to Jacquelyn's, I mean Ms. Ballinger's, office. I'll get with you in a few minutes, Cooper." The project manager looked like any typical foreman for this area. Older, receding hairline, hard Northern accent, and a beer belly requiring suspenders to keep his pants up, but it sure looked like he tried hard to suck that gut in to impress the lady.

Jacquelyn Ballinger on the other hand looked to be in about her forties, polished, sophisticated and by the look of the suit she wore, very accomplished. He didn't see it happening between the two of them and if this job weren't so important to him, he might even let McCall know he aimed too high with her, but instead he kept his mouth shut and balanced everything in his left hand to open the front door to the studio.

Massive structural changes were already underway inside the building. The gallery looked large and spacious, almost completely open. A vaulted cathedral style ceiling was taking shape above and jewel-toned colors were already splashing out from every corner. There looked to be a maze of display walls standing about seven feet tall in the center of the room, but none reached the high ceiling being prepared above. A small office sat to the right and a stunning ornately carved spiral staircase ran along the far right hand back wall, up to the second floor. The molding design on the stairwell looked like a perfect match to the design being added to the ceiling above.

Fast paced understated how quickly this place had come together. Trent walked farther in, immediately switching into electrical contractor mode. A frenzy of activity swirled around him; there wouldn't be any room for delays or errors. If one step faltered, it could create an entire jobsite delay, and clearly, by the look of the place, no money was being spared in getting this remodel completed on time. Initially, he'd been told the electrical portion of the remodel would be minor. His bid called for more cosmetic repairs than anything else. Every wall in the room required electricity, and the specs showed it to already be in place, but as he walked through the maze of walls, he could see it wasn't there on many of the inside walls.

He'd seen this before. These buildings were old and went through a series of remodels over the years. Electrical power could only come to the center inside walls two different ways: either from the ceiling or through the floor. Based on the concrete floor markings some had power, where others didn't. He worked through the possibilities in his mind. At this point, to get it added now meant they would have to go through the floor since the walls didn't reach the ceiling. The floors were already being primed for tile, meaning they would need to do this part of the job right away; first thing in the morning. Trent made a series of notes on his clipboard as he continued thinking it through, running a mental list of needed supplies as he jotted down his notes. It would add to the work load, but totally manageable and it could possibly be something the owner declined to do. He'd need to point it out to McCall as soon as possible.

The ventilation contractors, the dry wall specialist, and the painters were already hard at work. He could hear what he assumed were the heat and air people beginning to work on the roof. The current lighting looked terrible, but those changes were coming. Pendant fixtures were to arrive tomorrow and would be hung all over the room. Looking up, Trent scanned the ceiling closely and counted off. From this angle, it appeared like the ceiling people did an adequate job at leaving room for his men to work with minimal damage to the new woodwork. *Bonus!*

Anchoring his clipboard under his arm, Trent tested connections and made several notes on which walls absolutely didn't have electricity. He did the measurements on a few walls, deciding what could be pulled together in the least invasive ways. Other than the center walls, the specs seemed pretty dead on for this middle floor. He needed to check the electrical panel, make sure the amperage load was correct to pull all this electricity together and then check the air and heating systems voltage. If they were all right, he would let the project manager know about the inside walls and his work here would be done. The only thing left to do was to show up tomorrow and work like demons over the next eight days to complete the job on time. Holding his clipboard in one hand, Trent checked the building layout page. He found the panel in the basement. He scanned the page again and found the door leading to the basement across the room.

"Are you my new electrical contractor?" A smooth, masculine voice asked from behind. Trent turned his head over his shoulder to see an extraordinary pair of slate blue eyes staring back at him from a few feet away.

"Yes, sir," Trent said, turning completely around. He stumbled about mid-turn with his hand stuck in mid-air as he automatically went to shake hands. The man standing in front of him was none other than the legendary photo investigative journalist Gage Synclair, and Trent went dumb.

After the first moment of seeing Gage and losing all ability to think, everything began crashing through his mind all at the same time. He realized this must be Gage Synclair's new gallery, the one he'd read about online. Trent watched every report Gage ever gave and read every article written by the guy. Gage was a *Time Magazine*, *60 Minutes*, and CNN Special Reporter. Hell, his DVR currently sat filled with Gage's latest interviews and Special Reports. How could he have missed this being Gage Synclair's building?

Gage stepped in closer and Trent could only stare. The guy stood easily six foot two inches tall, an inch or so taller than Trent. His hair was longer than he ever remembered seeing it, but still short and looked a tamed, wavy blond. His eyes were deep slate blue, his skin a golden dark suntanned, and Gage wore an easy smile, with some of the fullest lips he'd ever seen. Gage Synclair looked extremely handsome in print and photos, but to see him in person shocked all of Trent's senses. It took another second for him to understand Gage Synclair's mouth moving.

"I'm Gage, this is my place. I'm guessing you're the electrical contractor?" He thought Gage may have repeated himself, but he wasn't one hundred percent certain. After another long pause and a bigger grin spreading across Gage's perfect lips, Trent finally answered.

"I'm a huge fan. I know all of your work and bought your books. I've followed your career for years. I knew you were putting up a place. I just didn't know this was that place," Trent rambled, tumbling all his words out. Gage still held out his hand with his eyebrows rising as Trent continued to speak. And still Trent stood there a minute more before accepting the handshake. "I'm sorry, I'm just a really big fan and at a complete loss for words."

"Thank you. You're very good on my ego, I'm certainly glad someone follows my work. They do put food on the table. Perhaps we could start with your first name," Gage said, his gaze never leaving

Trent's as he continued to stay spellbound under the weight of the most perfectly blue eyes he'd ever seen.

"Trent Cooper," he finally said as the handshake continued.

"Well, Trent Cooper, it's certainly my pleasure to meet you," Gage said as his smile turned to a slightly crooked, sexy grin. The look on his face changed, and Gage took on a knowing expression and advanced another small step closer, still never releasing his hand. Reality came crashing back as Trent's heart picked up a beat. He found himself a little breathless and off balance as he stood in the middle of a job site with a partial hard-on building in his jeans, acting like a teenage girl over her teeny bopper crush. To top it all off, the foreman and most of the sub-contractors were all within seeing distance of where they currently stood close together.

Trent never hid he was gay, but he also never put it out there while working. There were simply too many homophobes in the construction industry. A long time ago he decided to keep all parts of his world separate from one another. Em and Hunter were always first on his mind. They were the main reason for keeping work, dating, and them all separated, to make sure nothing ever got complicated. It was what his children deserved. Pulling his hand from Gage's hold, he forced his eyes away and cleared his throat. It still took a minute more to look back at Gage and even then, he couldn't meet those arresting eyes.

"I'm the electrical contractor. I was heading down to the panel box in the basement. I also need to check the inventory levels and check out the roof. Don't worry, my men will be starting Wednesday morning as scheduled. I only need to get everything lined out. Make sure we're clear on the end result and go over a couple of things I've found," Trent said it all while looking at Gage's forehead, wondering why he kept rattling on about schedules and check lists...He never did that.

"Mmmm, well, Trent Cooper, I could certainly tag along, show you around. I saw the site foreman has a thing for my new curator. You might need a tour guide around the building," Gage said. Trent could feel Gage's eyes still on his, but he never lowered his gaze to test his theory. Luckily, before he could respond Gage's phone began to ring at his belt. The guy palmed the phone and answered within a second, but Gage still looked directly at Trent.

"Gage Synclair, hang on a minute," Gage said into the phone before lowering it and covering the receiver with the palm of his hand.

"I regret I must take this call, Trent. I'll catch up in a bit." Gage finally turned his head away and spun around on his heels. A small trickle of sweat began to work its way down the side of Trent's face as he watched Gage in almost a slow jog, trying to get to his office before he spoke again into the phone. He could only catch something about Mexico before Gage closed his office door.

If he remembered correctly, Gage worked on one last case, something he'd started a few years ago. Since Trent followed every story so closely, he found himself in a fierce internal battle. Part of him needed Gage to leave him alone, he wouldn't have been able to hold out for too much longer before he started gushing, but he also loved the intrigue of investigations Gage put together. No one else dug as deep or found the loopholes Gage found while investigating a story. Whatever called him away may have something to do with his last investigation and wouldn't he absolutely love to know what it might be.

After a minute, he forced himself to focus solely on his surroundings and turned from the spot he apparently rooted himself to. He reminded his legs how to move across the floor and walked straight to the basement door. His head and eyes stayed trained on the door knob, not looking at anyone else in the room. Suddenly, he dropped the clipboard in his hands low to cover the bulge he just realized he sported in the front of his jeans.

From the very moment he met Gage Synclair, the room narrowed in on him until the heat of the moment dripped down his face. Gage stunned him, making it impossible to see anything other than the man who stood in front of him. Then just as quickly, the room popped back open, pulling everyone there back into this minute. Hell, for all he knew everyone in this room, gay or straight, could have responded the same as he did when meeting Gage freakin' Synclair. Of course he wouldn't be alone in the awe he felt.

Trent took the side stairs, two at a time, down to the basement, relieved to find no one there. Every one of his thoughts stayed centered on how hot Gage truly was in person. He walked straight to the panel box, opened the door, and looked blankly at the black breakers staring back at him. Chiding himself for how quickly he lost track of his reason for being there, he pulled his clipboard forward and lifted the pages attached to the giant silver clip at the top. On the inside of the steel clipboard, his kids had taped photographs of them all with sweet words of love scribbled on them. He always carried this clipboard and when times got hard, he flipped the pages up to help focus him back on why he did what he did. It did the trick and he forced his mind back on the job. He did a mental sweep over the breakers, the sizes and the brand. *Fuck!*

The old, outdated panel box stared back at him, mocking him with its low amperage. Of course, it wasn't the size or brand as outlined on the specs. It would have made this job way too easy if it were. Taking a deep breath at this jewel of a find, Trent squared his shoulders and mentally calculated the voltage this box would reasonably hold in its current state and knew in his heart it wouldn't be good enough. How in the hell did he get to be the first one to discover this huge problem in the remodel?

He tapped his pencil on the clipboard, going over his math of the voltage in the current panel box one last time. A deep pent up breath finally released, one he hadn't realized he held. Things for this job just fell into place too smoothly. He should have known nothing could be that easy. A panel replacement would seriously mess up the schedule for completion. Hell, maybe that was why he got the job in the first place. This kind of pending disaster would need a scapegoat and who better than the electrician?

Going between the panel box and his paper, Trent made notes and tallied the estimated amperage needed to run this place effectively based on average daily usage. Damn it! No way would this current box hold everything. The air conditioning alone would trip the lights and the office might not ever work properly. The city would never allow a final permit with this current box still in place. Fuck this was going to cost in both time and money.

"From where I'm standing, an electrician looks to be a very sexy job...all those tool belts and hard hats. How does one go about becoming an electrical contractor?" Gage asked from directly behind Trent. Trent could feel the guy's breath running along his neck. It startled him; he hadn't heard Gage coming down the stairs or across the room. To have him simply materialize like this shook him to the core, and his body reacted with a jolt, hardening quickly back to painful degrees. He kept his eyes on the clipboard, only closing them for one long moment, before opening them again, staring down, but seeing nothing.

"It's a family deal. My father was an electrician. Union," Trent responded in almost a croak. He lowered his brow and narrowed his eyes, mouthing the words he'd just said, wondering where such a stupid response might have come from. He scribbled on the clipboard, went over a few of the numbers with his pencil, but it was all a charade masking the sexual tension rolling through him. Finally, he lifted his head to stare blankly at the breakers in the panel box. If this were the pickup it felt like, Gage would have to make the first move. No way could he give back the sexy banter or the hot come on lines needed to seal this deal.

"Mmmm... You own your own business?" Gage asked. No mistaking the step in the guy took or the hard dick slightly pressing against his ass. The sensation sent goose bumps prickling up Trent's arms and his heart picked up several beats, beginning a slow steady thumping in his chest. He stood cornered with no place to hide, so he didn't try, but leaned toward the panel box, needing distance between them. Trent flipped through the pages of his clipboard to the pictures of his children and begged his brain to remember why he stood there! *Everything has a separate compartment in my life for a reason. Remember that reason. Don't blow it now, Trent Cooper.*

"I can take care of what's going on in those brand new Levi's of yours, handsome. There's a bathroom attached to my office. Meet me there, it's discreet." Trent felt Gage's hand snake across his hip, slide down the front of his jeans, and moments passed before he remembered to breathe. His eyes closed at the feel of the graze Gage gave his rock hard dick. And then both of Gage's hands slid down over his ass, gripping each ass cheek. It took him a minute to speak and when he did, he forced the images of his children into his mind. The strength of his voice surprised him.

"I'm not interested. I don't roll that way," Trent said. Saying it aloud somehow gave him the continued strength to step out from under the mind-blowing touches and turn back around to face Gage.

"The panel box is gonna be a problem. I need to check the units out on the roof, but it's not gonna be big enough to hold all the power you need. It's also not what was on the specs given to me. This one will only hold up to about a hundred and fifty amps. You need at least half more. It's also extremely outdated." With each word said, Trent turned back into the professional he berated himself for not being since first meeting Gage Sinclair. As he spoke, the basement door opened above. The curator now stood at the top of the stairs, poking her head down. Trent's eyes darted up, making eye contact with her, relieved they were no longer alone. If Gage would have made another move, his resolve would surely break and this would be a far different game he played.

"How was this missed? Or perhaps a better question might be, does it have to be done now?" Gage asked. He also turned his head to follow his gaze up the stairs, before turning back to Trent, confusion clear on Gage's face.

"If you're able to get a green tag during the final inspection from the city, I'd be shocked. Regardless, it won't hold through the opening. Something will blow, tripping something else. Everything electrical won't be able to work together."

"Shit! Where's McCall? Jacquelyn, could you get McCall for me" Gage said over his shoulder, acknowledging the curator for the first time. "What's it going to take to replace it and keep everything on task?"

"I need to look closer at your schedule. Right now all I can say is it's gonna take time and money. We'll pull a special permit for this. I've got to check the roof and the wiring. Depending on what I find, the electric company has to shut off the power and let us replace it. The city inspects the work, then gives the go ahead back to the power company to turn it back on. Here, let me show you what we're talking about." Trent pulled his clipboard forward to show Gage the numbers he'd worked up a few minutes earlier. "Here's the simple math of it. This column's the estimated average amp usage you'll need to run this building every day based on the equipment I've seen. At the very best case it's two hundred, probably more like two twenty-five. Your current box supports up to one fifty."

"Shit, how wasn't this caught before now?" All the sexual tension between them left as quickly as it came. Those sexy, steamy hot blue eyes were turning into shards of ice shooting daggers as he spoke. No way did Trent want any part of where those daggers might land.

"Mr. Synclair, the plans are showing a bigger box here. I'm not sure who drew up these specs… but yeah, it should have been caught before now… I guess it's past blame time. Even if we did a temporary to get you through the opening, you're gonna have to take the time to replace this thing. I can try to call in favors, I have a few, but I first need to see what I'm working with upstairs and outside before I talk to anyone."

"So what's the best possible time frame on this?" Gage asked.

"Off the top of my head, and best case scenario, my part can be done overnight. It'll be a solid eight to twelve hour job, but we can get our part done in one shot. It's the city and power company who'll require time. I may have a connection in the city who might work closely with us. I don't know, though, it's asking a lot in such a short time. Let me get up on top, see what I'm looking at and make some calls. It won't take me long. I'll find you when I'm done and we can talk pricing and timeframes," Trent said as McCall came through the basement door.

"I'll be in my office. McCall, I need to see you," Gage didn't say anything more, but took off up the stairs and out the door, Roger McCall at his heels.

Chapter 4

Trent paced the outside sidewalk in the front of the gallery, treading a solid path back and forth on the small walkway beside his old pickup. He'd called his men, all his suppliers, and the city, trying to come up with the best possible solution to get this panel change completed as soon as possible. Roger McCall all but abandoned him after what he supposed was a solid chew out by Gage Synclair. The large glass panels separating the office from the rest of the showroom hid nothing as Gage lit into McCall's ass. He didn't let him out for a good twenty minutes. McCall immediately left the jobsite, spouting something about 'informing corporate' as he tore his ass past Trent, and hadn't been back since.

Trent worked out possible solutions to the time frame as he continued to check the blueprints now spread across the hood of his truck. His head journeyman grumbled over the idea of an all-night, Saturday evening panel change and then a full day of work the next day, but he reluctantly agreed with double overtime pay as enticement. Trent called Sophia next to beg her to watch the children since Rhonny already had out-of-town weekend plans. She lived up to her reputation as Auntie Crazy when she agreed to his request but insisted he lied to her and really planned a hot sex date instead.

The supply company kept him on hold while checking pricing and availability of the different panel options. It had already been eight of the longest minutes of his entire life! This forever hold pattern completely pissed him off. They were taking their sweet time and every minute that ticked by felt like dog years. To top it all off, even after all this aggravation, his fucking hard-on still wouldn't settle the fuck down. Interesting how his super easy morning of everything falling into place took a huge nose dive, skidding him slowly and painfully across the concrete floor. Already, the anxiety of this job was past the point of dumb, and it hadn't even officially started yet.

His stomach let out a loud angry grumble of protest. He looked down at his watch. How could it already be a quarter to one in the afternoon? What he'd intended as a quick check in had turned into almost four hours already, and this stop was so not on his to-do list for the day.

Trent forced himself to calm down and stop pacing. He leaned his butt back against the side of the truck and took several deep, relaxing breaths. He listened to the terrible hold music for a minute while turning his face up to the sun, closing his eyes, letting its warmth coat his skin. He refused to think about this job for the next couple of minutes as he waited on hold. Instead, his thoughts strayed back to his conversation with Auntie Crazy and the next terrible topic in his life.

Trent couldn't even remember the last time he got to partake in real sex, which must mean it was quite a while ago. Even thinking hard, he still didn't come up with much. Shit. A year ago? Hell, maybe even longer. The bottom line, he needed to have more sex if his response this morning were any indication. It just wouldn't do for him to be out in public reacting like this on a regular basis. He didn't want to go back into the life of random, meaningless sex. Okay, he needed to rephrase that thought. He absolutely could go back to a life of frequent, random sex, but that life usually started after ten at night, and being a single parent, he went to bed around nine. Sometimes, if he got lucky, it would be more around eight thirty when he hit the sack.

Before his sister died, Trent was all about the meaningless sex. He could stay up all night, doing whoever presented available. Back in the day, he would get off work, clean himself up, and immerse himself in Chicago's club scene. He totally lived the stereotypical life of a single gay man. Sex and more sex. He got laid all the time. Then he'd been given responsibility of the kids and everything had changed. He'd had to stop being that guy, and shit got more serious. He took the responsibility to heart because he owed it to Hunter and Emalynn to be there and be the father they needed.

When Emalynn, only a few weeks old, had gotten sick, he'd had the shit scared out of him. He'd loaded up both kids and taken them to the hospital to have her checked out. The staff had given him grief over providing care once he told them he was her guardian, not her father. Social workers got involved; making it a giant fucked up mess.

The next day, he called his attorney and started the paperwork to make them legally his so they would never have to go through all the problems again. But that step changed everything again. In Trent's mind, a guardian's job was a way different thing than a dad's job. He understood how crazy that sounded, but it was true. Being a father meant setting an example, and that didn't include leaving them at home all night while he partied it up in some random gay club.

Trent had tried dating. It made perfect sense in his mind. He needed to find a committed relationship. He stupidly put self-imposed sex restrictions on his dates, requiring more than one date before allowing himself release. There would be no more random one night stands. And he'd stuck to it. Then again, only a couple of times over the last four years had he found anyone willing to go on more than one date. He did get to have sex a few times during, but it ended pretty quickly after Trent had to cancel a few dates because of a sick child.

Interestingly enough, he found if he were into the ladies, his plan would have worked. Single men with children drew women in like flies to honey. At least once a day some random female would hit on him when he towed his kids around. Funny though, the children weren't the same magnet to gay men and the restrictions which came along with being a single father kept him from being in the circles needed to meet people like himself or to do the things he liked to do. Like go out to dinner, see a movie, or take an overnight stay away.

He dropped the back of his head against the truck with a thump and kept the phone parked at his ear, listening to the beat of the music coming through the speaker, his foot tapping out the rhythm. He thought it might be some Bee Gee's classic disco remake, and he let out a huff as he realized how pathetic it was that he knew the tune so well he could tap it out with his work boot without conscious thought.

Images of Gage came back to his mind despite all his effort to stop them. Never had he been in a situation quite like this one, and without question, pulling away from the swipe of Gage's hand down the front of his jeans had cost him dearly. He wasn't sure his dick would ever forgive him for turning that down.

If he were being honest, Trent was fine with his life and fine with his lack of sex. He totally bought into the theories of a bigger purpose and a greater good. But Gage Synclair was just too fucking hot. He loved the stories Gage created with his camera. To have Gage Synclair rubbing on his dick, propositioning him with a quick round in the closest restroom truly shocked the shit out of him. The whole thing was beyond incredible. It actually ranged more in the ridiculously unbelievable category of life.

Seriously, how did Trent not say 'screw the big picture' and go in the bathroom to fuck the guy's brains out? Trent sighed. He knew the reason. Nothing was worth jeopardizing what he built with the kids or their future. Not even fifteen minutes alone with the super-hot, apparently gay, celebrity Gage Synclair sucking him hard. And boy would he make Gage Suck. Him. Hard. Who knew what Gage's preferences were, but it would have been required to have those lips on his dick for a certain amount of time.

"Mr. Cooper, thank you for holding. I've got the information you need," the nasal tone of his supplier interrupted his dangerous thoughts. Shaking his head, he forced himself back into the moment to take down the quote on parts.

Focus Trenton Cooper. *You need this business to support your babies all the way through their lives. Getting caught with Gage Synclair would ruin it all.*

Gage listened carefully to Trent's researched explanation, and completely ignored his project manager sitting in the chair beside Trent. "The cost will be around forty-five hundred dollars. My company can do it Saturday evening and through the night. My supplier's able to work with me on anything we need, no problem. I can have guys out here at six that evening, and I'll be here as I can, and stay through the night. Twelve hours should give us the time to pull new wire and replace the box. We can temporary it in. The city will come out first thing Monday morning, I've been assured. Now, ComEd says they'll work with us. I'm not so sure of that, but the temporary power should provide for the crews on Monday until it's all taken care of." Trent sat there, all business, drawing out his plan to keep this remodel on schedule.

"I've spoken with the city and ComEd personally. After we agree on things here, I'll have them call you. They'll be on standby Sunday for your call when you're done, regardless of the time. The only thing I ask, I need you personally to stick around until everything's complete on all ends, to be available to make whatever changes they need," Gage said directly back to Trent, sitting back in his desk chair, flipping a ball point pen through his fingers while watching the sexy electrical contractor look impressed with the strings he'd pulled. Gage absently wondered if this Trent Cooper might be so impressed, he'd go ahead and give Gage a quick pity suck to help relieve the hard-on he'd sported since first meeting him four hours ago.

"Wow. All right. That's no problem for me," Trent said. Nowhere in those eight words could Gage find even a hint of the suggestion: *Meet in the bathroom, and I'll suck you...*

"If we do all this, the project will stay on track, correct?" Gage seemingly ignored Trent's comment. Between the power company and the city, this little panel change snag took more money than he cared to think about in order to have them all on standby this weekend.

"Yes, as long as it's a reasonably easy switch. Based on what I'm seeing, it looks like it will be. I can keep you briefed the entire time," Trent replied.

"And this is absolutely needed?" Gage asked. He'd already verified it needed to be done. He wondered if he were still asking these questions so he could keep his eyes on the hot Trent Cooper. His voice seemed to soothe Gage, like a balm over his severely irritated heart... *Where the fuck are these thoughts coming from? He's just a guy, an apparently straight guy. And how did I get that so completely wrong? I never get that wrong.*

"Yes, absolutely," Trent said with a strong nod in confirmation.

"What if I got a second opinion?" Gage asked, hoping he looked like he contemplated all of Cooper's answers as he again wondered why he asked questions he already knew the answers too. *Perhaps the clues are hidden in the way Trent Cooper nods.*

Gage focused back on the Trent's head bobbing, certain the motions would look similar if he sucked Gage hard. A smile tugged at his lips as he realized he'd make sure the head continued to nod throughout this entire conversation, just for his own perverse pleasure. If Gage were bold, he'd get up, walk around the desk and drop his pants. Then Trent wouldn't have to do anything, but open his mouth to answer Gage's questions and nod... Trent would deep throat him over and over...

"Please feel free. Just let me know as soon as you can," Trent said. Gage just let the comment go, reminding himself it wasn't the invitation he wanted it to be, and he honestly barely even heard the rest of what Trent said after 'please feel free'.

"McCall, this should have been caught earlier," Gage's voice hardened, cutting his eyes to the man sitting next to Trent. He'd magically shown up seconds before Trent came in to have this conversation. It pissed Gage off even more when he realized he lost his few minutes alone with Trent and he then promptly ignored McCall until this moment.

"Agreed," McCall replied back, staying quiet for a minute. After a pregnant pause of Gage just staring McCall down, he turned his head back to a far more pleasing view. Trent was a stunningly attractive man, with all those good boy looks. All except the small growth on his face and Gage found he wanted to rub his cheeks against those sexy whiskers just to see what they felt like... Gage let his eyes travel lower down Trent's massive chest. It must be forty-six to forty-eight inches... hmmm... And since he already took these bold steps of examining Trent's body, he let his eyes scan lower to the still partial hard-on rockin' those hot new Levi's. God, he wanted that hard-on to be focused on him.

Reluctantly, Gage knew he needed to let the meeting end, but damn he liked the idea of having this one hanging around his gallery. He loved watching Trent's thunder thighs walk up and down the sidewalk, right outside his office window. He'd watched Trent adjust himself over and over, trying to get comfortable. Whatever had made Trent so hot and heavy shouldn't matter at this point, but Gage found it's all he could think about and again wondered if he should offer help in relieving the burden he carried in his jeans.

After at least a full minute of staring, Gage saw McCall lift his gaze for almost the first time since coming in here and Gage adjusted his stare to look directly at the project manager, hoping he looked like he contemplated his electrical options, not ogling the electrician in front of him.

"All right then, let's move forward. How do you take payment?" Gage asked, leaning forward in his chair, reaching to pull his checkbook from the side drawer of his desk.

"Half now, the rest upon completion," Trent said, his gaze never wavering, but Gage wasn't quite sure Trent looked him straight in the eye. It seemed he might be looking at his nose… Gage again sat there a minute, staring at the young man sitting across from him, trying his best to figure him out.

Gage never got it wrong! Trent must be gay or at least bi-sexual. Surely… Jacquelyn was a beautiful woman, but at least twenty years older than Trent. She had been standing on the porch when Trent arrived and also while he paced outside, but she wasn't in the gallery when Trent grew hard at their first meeting. Trent's reaction was obvious and immediate, and Gage experienced it in a seriously major way. Hell, he hadn't stopped thinking about it since it happened and clearly his body still wanted relief, ASAP. Something this strong didn't happen often, and for Gage, it never happened where he wasn't able to find immediate release with the guy.

Now, they sat together in his office. Trent sat across from him, making something close to eye contact, talking things through as if it were the most natural thing in the world to be half erect, fighting a full hard-on for most of the entire morning and doing nothing about it. Maybe it's how straight guys lived their lives but it certainly wasn't how he lived his life. Mr. Hot and Sexy sat across the desk from him, not blinking an eye at the discomfort he may or may not be feeling.

Regardless of the guy's sexual orientation, he clearly wasn't interested in finding his release with Gage, and that, for some reason, bothered the hell out of him. Maybe Trent was in a committed relationship. The jealousy snaking through his heart at the thought came out of nowhere. *And what the hell is that about?* Gage didn't even know how to process jealousy. Was it truly jealousy? He'd never been jealous of anyone a day in his life.

Putting aside the jealousy, a raging hard-on, being gay or straight, and every electrical problem in this place, this man in front of him clearly wasn't interested. He'd said as much earlier. Well, all right then! Gage would leave it alone. He would find someone else to help take care of this bulge between his legs. After all, Gage had found this morning he lived in the right neighborhood to find a hot male model that would be ready to spend time with him. Right now he had a bigger more immediate problem: where in the hell did he leave off in this conversation? Hmmm…

"I understand they're expecting you downtown for the permits. I'll have my person call you in the next few minutes. I need your number please, Trent. You'll also handle the power company from here. I'll give you my contact's information. Please call them today and work out the details. McCall, I suppose you will let the others know what we're doing, so no one is stuck in the middle of something important when the power is cut, correct?" Gage said, jotting the numbers down for Trent.

"Yes, sir," McCall said and looked up at him again for the second time this last hour.

"Then, I think I'm done with you, McCall. Take care. Trent, I'll have your check ready in a moment. Hang tight," Gage said, dismissing the project manager. Gage wrote the check, never looking up as McCall left the room. Out of the corner of his eye, he could see Trent stand and move behind the chair, in a clear attempt to put more space between them.

"Will you be monitoring the work personally?" Gage asked again for the second time in the last few minutes. He stopped the stroke of his pen halfway through writing the check. He looked up at Trent and his heart bounced around in his chest. He found it difficult to breathe properly. Trent stared down at him, the connection jumped out very clearly there between.

"Yes, sir, I will," Trent said. Now they were all the way back to 'yes, sir'. He didn't like it at all. Gage couldn't stop the pitter patter of his heart, and Mr. Yes Sir over there put as much distance between them as he could.

"What're your qualifications?" Gage asked, laying the pen down. He already knew the answer to this question. He'd checked out every contractor himself before they were brought in, but he stalled to keep Trent in this room.

"I'm a master electrician," Trent said, his voice not quite as strong as before. The simple reply gave Gage just what he needed to help break the tension forming between them since McCall left the room.

"Mmm…" A smile tore across his lips at the thought of this man in front of him being his master. Yeah, he could see Trent was well-qualified to hold such a position. His phone rang disturbing the perfect image playing in his mind. He finished the check, tearing it at the perforated edge, but didn't hand it to Trent, instead looked down at the caller ID.

"I need to answer this, hang on." Gage answered without waiting for a response. "Gage Synclair, can you hold a moment? Good. Thank you. Hang on." He put the call on hold, before turning the full weight of his stare back to the hot-number in front of him. A smile tore across his face as he chuckled at the one-liners he kept coming up with all day long about Trent Cooper. It seemed to be a pattern forming where the guy was concerned.

"So, Saturday evening at six, and you'll handle the city and the power company?" Gage asked still chuckling to himself.

"Yes, sir," Trent said, his knuckles turning white as he gripped the chair in front of him. Good, he shouldn't be the only one living in this hell between them.

"And your crews will move forward on the remodel tomorrow?" Gage asked, knowing the phone call held for him. It was the every two-hour check-in from the field operations in Mexico. He needed to take the call, but he didn't want Trent to leave him.

"Yes, sir," Trent said again.

"I'm Gage," he said, with a little too much snap in the two words, and he could feel the smile leave his face.

"Got it," Trent said, and again Gage got the impression Trent stared at his nose, not his eyes. He checked the urge to run his hand over his face to see if anything might be on there to cause Trent to become distracted.

"You could say it," Gage said, surprised by his own words.

"Yes, Mr. Synclair..." Trent said, and Gage watched him bite his lip. Gage's hips rolled forward involuntarily, and he almost came right there, watching Trent's tongue dart out over the soft skin of his lips. "Gage, we'll see you in the morning."

"Perfect. I like the sound of it," Gage said. "I have one last question, do you wear the beard all the time or are you a clean shaven kind of guy?"

"I, ah...the storm woke me, and I...yeah, I shave every day," Trent said, stumbling on his words. The look on Trent's face made it clear the question confused him.

"I thought as much," Gage said. He didn't stand because he didn't want to scare Trent away with the solid tent in his pants, but instead lifted the check and both telephone numbers toward Trent who leaned in to take them. Then Gage did the most stupid thing of all, he offered his hand. The handshake they shared caused his heart to slam into his chest and his stomach to flutter, but he squelched it down. This man across from him wasn't interested, and there were plenty more who did. Forcing his thoughts back to the phone call, Gage answered it again before Trent even turned away from him.

"Update me," Gage said as the door closed behind Trent.

"Secure line?" one of Gage's Mexico leads, Manuel, asked back in a thick Spanish accent.

"It is," Gage said.

"I'm in," Manuel said, his normally craggy voice held a hint of excitement.

"In the mission?" Gage asked, wondering if he'd heard the words correctly.

"Yes!" Manuel hissed, clearly proud of the accomplishment.

"Excellent work! Have you made contact?" Gage asked. *Could it seriously be this easy?*

"No, I will. I'm following him now. It's too open and unsecure here. I've got to watch it, this isn't making a lot of sense," Manuel said in a hushed tone.

"Yeah, I'm aware. Keep your guard up. It's rarely this easy, something isn't right. And we're still positive on the ID?" Gage asked. He sat back in his chair, staring off at nothing in his office as he thought over the possibilities.

"Did you see the videos?" Manuel asked? All the exuberance from earlier was gone. From years of working with Manuel, Gage knew the guy didn't play, he was already strategizing over his next move.

"Yeah," Gage said.

"Me too, it's a match, Mr. Synclair, down to the missing finger. I gotta go." The connection rustled as though Manuel shifted the position of the phone against his face. "They're on the move." Manuel disconnected the call.

Gage laid his phone on the desk and sat back again in his chair, this time staring out the glass windows into the gallery. Interesting how his hard-on completely deflated with talk of the loser, Abdulla. Hell, loser wasn't the right word. Loser gave the guy too much credit.

He was garbage. Gage covered lots of terrible people over the last ten years who did lots of dreadful deeds, but this guy was the worst of the worst, and now he'd secured two clear positive IDs on Abdulla in the little rundown, thought-to-be-abandoned convent mission in Mexico. It meant they were truly closing in. Bringing Abdulla to justice would be worth everything it took to get here.

Chapter 5

Trent drove his pickup through the tree-lined street of his neighborhood with the window rolled down, letting the gentle breeze coat his skin and enjoying the golden sunset on that late spring evening. He lived on a street where most of the houses were custom built about thirty years ago. He waved at his neighbors as he turned down the long drive that led to his back yard.

The gate sat pushed open, waiting for his arrival. Both Emalynn and Hunter were playing in their custom built jungle gym with Rhonny sitting in her normal spot on the patio, studying from one of her textbooks. Em saw him first and took off running from the swing set straight to the truck, but Hunter soon overtook her smaller stride. Everything became a race to the little guy. It didn't matter he beat an almost four-year-old, he loved winning and called it loudly.

"I win! I beat you, Em!" Hunter declared, tagging the truck with his hand while looking over his shoulder at his sister.

"Daddy, I wasn't racing. He didn't really beat me," Em said, finally making it to him as he got out of the truck.

"I know, baby. Hunter's just at that age," Trent said, shutting the truck door. Rhonny sat on the porch laughing as he scooped Em up for a big wet kiss on the lips. Hunter wrapped himself around Trent's leg, giving him a tight hug and Trent reached down to rub his little boy's head as they began to make their way to the back porch.

"Why do you always say I'm at that age, Daddy?" Hunter asked, walking alongside him.

42

"I say it because it's what the parenting books say. At this age, he'll do this. So I just say it back to you when you do something they say you will do at this age," Trent said, looking down at Hunter's upturned face. Both the children looked at him with their huge green eyes that seemed to reach out to his soul. He ran his hand over Hunter's short, dark hair. From Em's position in his arms, her soft wavy ash blond curls, wisped around her face and tickled his cheeks. It broke his heart to think about cutting her hair so it grew long, curling down her back.

"Oh, Daddy, did the book say I could do this? Because I learned this at school today," Hunter said, dropping down to do a very sloppy, but successful front roll in the grass.

"Good job, man. You know, I don't think it said you could do it until you were seven," Trent said as Em began bucking in his arms to get down.

"Daddy, I want to do it! Please!" Emalynn dropped straight down, landing on her feet, bending her head down to the concrete driveway.

"Hang on, Em, let me help you. Come to the grass, you'll hurt your head on the sidewalk." Trent moved to the yard where they played together until complete darkness, about forty-five minutes later. Em got the hang of the front roll, while Hunter worked on his back rolls and handstands. The whole time Trent spotted them both, making sure neither got hurt. He even executed a couple of sloppy front rolls himself to the excitement of the children.

"Daddy, Rhonny and I cooked dinner. Hunter helped too. I'm hungry," Em said, coming to stand by him while he hung on to Hunter's feet as he performed another handstand.

"Yeah, good point, Em. You two need to eat. It's already seven-thirty. Dinner, bath, bed. Yay!" Rhonny said from the porch where she'd continued to read while they played.

"No, boo!" Hunter called back, but the night had come on quick. The late May evening air grew crisp. He could see the goose bumps springing up on Em's arms.

"Come on, Rhonny's right. Let's go inside, you two. I have paperwork and you two have to go to bed. I need sleep. Sleep without arms hitting and legs kicking me. Any idea who it might have been, Hunt?" Trent asked, grabbing Em up in his arms and herding Hunter into the house.

"Emalynn," Hunter promptly replied which started a whole new round of arguing over who could have kicked him last night.

"Step up here and wash your hands, then sit at the table," Rhonny said, beginning to warm parts of the dinner. The small round oak dinner table sat four comfortably and the places were already set with plates, napkins and silverware.

"Daddy, I made the salad and Hunter made the green beans. Rhonny made the chicken," Em said, pulling her stepstool to the kitchen sink to wash her hands.

"It looks delicious, honey," Trent said, grabbing the milk from the refrigerator. He poured their drinks while Rhonny placed the food on the table. Hunter and Emalynn made fast work of washing up and then raced to the table.

Although technically Rhonny's time off, she stayed with them for dinner that night. The usual "how many bites of this do I have to eat" and "can I have more" of anything sweet on the table ensued. After dinner, everyone helped with kitchen cleanup and then came bath time. Em and Hunter still bathed together at night, although Hunter showed signs of independence, talking about needing to have his own bath. Teeth were brushed, hair combed and dried, pajamas on, and bedtime stories read. Rhonny stayed through the whole process, and it helped to have an extra pair of hands.

When Rhonny gave her time for free, she usually bailed about halfway through bath time, but not tonight. She stayed the entire way through until the end of story time, when both kids were asleep. Trent shut Hunter's door about the same time Rhonny pulled Em's door to, and they quietly walked together down the hall toward the living room.

"It gets them to bed earlier when you help. Thanks for sticking around tonight," Trent said quietly.

"It's my pleasure. I have something to talk to you about," Rhonny said, stopping in the kitchen when Trent started toward his office to finish his paperwork.

"What? And after the day I've had, you aren't allowed to tell me you're quitting." Trent looked back over his shoulder, his weariness from the day finally catching up with him. Before he crashed completely, he needed to finish the bid he'd worked on this morning. He stopped at the expression on Rhonny's face and turned completely toward her. She appeared nervous, jittery. He stepped closer to her, narrowing his eyes in concern.

"No, I'm not quitting. I love you guys. But I do have someone I want you to meet," Rhonny said, squaring her shoulders, resolve hit her brow. He could almost see her straightening her spine before she said anything more and that confused him that much more.

"Okay. Is it like playing your dad or something like that? Do I need to bring the rifle in the house? Give him my most mean look?" Trent said, a grin tugged at the corner of his lips, loving the idea of practicing the tough dad routine before Em started dating.

"No, silly, I have someone I want you to meet for you. It's one of my professors. I found out today he's gay. He's super-hot. All the girls like him, and he's totally single." Rhonny gave a nod of her head at the end of her declaration as if that settled the matter.

"Rhonny," Trent hedged.

"No, now listen. I'm completely serious. I know you don't go out much, but you need to. Auntie Crazy's going to start setting you up on blind dates. I'm not supposed to tell you, but she's serious. She got so excited when she thought you were going out with someone this weekend, and I agree with her, Trent, you need to get out of the house more. You need to relax, and having a good time wouldn't kill you. We'll both babysit and work it out with each other to be here more," Rhonny said.

"Sweetheart, I appreciate the offer, and tell Sophia, I appreciate her, but I'll ask when I need help in that area. Blind dates just sound torturous. No offense to your professor, but yeah...no..." Squinting his eyes, he gave a grimace thinking over the idea of meeting someone out in public he'd never seen before and being forced to spend the evening with him. *What a whipping!* "Yeah, really, no, not interested, Rhonny."

"Look, let me snap his picture tomorrow in class. I'll text it to you. Will you please not shoot it down without a look at him? He's hot, Trent, and you two would be super-hot together. The girls would die when you two walked by. You know all my friends want to go out with you; they don't care you're gay. They want to be the one to *change* you," Rhonny said it all while turning and walking out the kitchen toward her basement apartment. She sauntered away with a little swagger she did when she thought she was funny. She'd made those absurd remarks before, but they never failed to catch him off guard. He chuckled at her silly friends, who were all ten years younger than him. Mere babes in the woods compared to his "old man" status, especially counting the last four years.

After three hours of running totals, checking and double checking his numbers, Trent felt like the latest electrical proposal to hit his desk was finally done. The only problem, the basic, everyday bid shouldn't have taken this long to work out. He knew this information like the back of his hand, yet hours passed while he got all the way through it.

The catch in his spine as he stretched out his back couldn't be a good sign. He labored for hours over this proposal, finding mistake after mistake in his numbers. The job would be big, but not the biggest he'd ever done and certainly not the hardest. The contractor also used him exclusively, so how hard should this have been?

Over the years, he'd sat at this old desk in this old worn out leather chair for more hours than he could count, working on his business. For the first time in his adult life a sense of restless unease washed over him, making him tired. The fatigue ran deep in his bones, clouding his ability to think straight. With a shove of his palms against the edge of his desk, he rolled back about a foot and rubbed his hands over his face, before pushing them through his short hair. On a huff of his breath, he picked up his laptop and his numbers-filled scratch paper to finish this proposal in the comfort of his bed. He'd sat there long enough for one night.

His house was small, maybe fifteen hundred square feet, and he made his way through the garage, then the house, flipping off the lights and making sure all the doors were locked on his way back to his bedroom. Like every night, he looked in on the kids through the crack in their doors and both were sleeping soundly. His room sat right across the hall from theirs and he quietly pushed the door closed until only a crack remained, just like theirs. Over the years, he'd trained himself to be a light sleeper, wanting to be able to hear if they needed him in the night.

Trent laid his laptop on the nightstand before straightening the bed covers where they remained a mess from kids the night before, and then he flipped the covers back, readying them for sleep. He tossed his remote control in the middle of the bed and undressed. After a quick shower, Trent dried himself quickly and pulled on his Sponge Bob pajama pants, the ones Em had given him for Christmas, and finally made his way back to his bed.

Trent dropped down heavily on the bed, sitting on its edge. He looked at the laptop, and released a big sigh. His hands came to rest between his legs as he decided unsettled might be a better word to describe what went on inside him. He would chalk it all up to Em's birthday, but this year, for some reason, it seemed a little harder to bear. He missed his sister. He missed their time together and he missed her as his friend.

If he were being honest with himself, it also didn't help he couldn't get his mind off how totally hot Gage Synclair was in real life. Dear God, could the man look any better? Hell, he knew the answer to the question: *No freakin' way!*

Embarrassment stained his cheeks and replaced unsettled as the major emotion running through him. Trent rubbed his face hard with his hands and then rubbed his eyes harder trying to push the memory of meeting Gage today out of his mind.

Trent couldn't get a good feel for whether anyone had noticed his behavior this morning. No one appeared to, or at least if they did, they didn't treat him any differently, but he just couldn't be sure. The site foreman stayed too taken with the curator to notice. Of that, at least, he was reasonably confident. But, the curator totally picked up on it if all the little smiles and winks she tossed his way all morning were any indication.

Dropping his body back on the bed, he watched the ceiling fan above for several spins before he repositioned, sliding up against the headboard, and placed the laptop in his lap. The alarm clock on the nightstand shined brightly; half past midnight. In about three hours, he'd have been awake close to twenty-four hours, and being sleep deprived wouldn't help this crazy emotional state he seemed to be taking on. He tucked an extra pillow behind his back and booted up the laptop, thinking over Rhonny's offer from earlier.

Maybe he should try a blind date. He *could* use the sex, but not with a professor. Trent wasn't smart enough or trendy enough to date a college professor. What would they ever have in common? But maybe he should have Rhonny be on the lookout for someone or maybe he should hear Auntie Crazy out on who she'd pre-qualified on her list of eligible guys. She would certainly have someone up her sleeve waiting to be pulled out for him. She always did, but even thinking it caused a pit to settle in his stomach. No way could he trust Auntie Crazy to come up with anyone suitable to date, no matter how much she claimed to have the perfect guy. Her tastes leaned toward flamboyant, colorful, and gaudy as hell gay men. He couldn't even consider going there with her. It must have been sexual desperation causing him to wonder about her choices right now.

Shaking his head at his own insane thoughts, he opened the proposal template—a simple fill in the blank form in Word—and he began typing the numbers into the fields. But Gage Synclair kept running through his mind. What Trent wouldn't have given to take Gage up on his offer. To have pounded all that tension out in the bathroom this morning may have put an end to his day-long misery and all the uncertainty coursing through him. His dick still stood half erect from Gage's hand brushing down over it, but seriously, it may have been the best moment his cock ever experienced... *Gage Synclair touched my dick!*

Which brought on a much bigger reveal, Gage Synclair was gay or at least bisexual. Who would have known? He'd watched all Gage's specials, read every book and article written. Gage's reports were intriguing, interesting, uncovering more to the world than any other media outlet he followed. Gage regularly corresponded on PBS, CNN, and CBS. He'd even watched the last interview Gage gave on YouTube no less than ten times over the last three or four months. Gage had announced clearly his plan to retire from field work, but the speculation said Gage might get his own show, move into broadcast journalism. In all the time he'd followed the stories and career, Trent had never picked up anywhere Gage was gay. He would have remembered something like that, but he'd also never inquired about it either. How did it not ever occur to him to think along those lines?

"Daddy, I need a drink of water." Hunter's quiet voice startled him out of his musings as the boy poked his head through Trent's bedroom door.

"Okay, buddy, can you get one from the bathroom?" Trent asked as Hunter rubbed his sleepy little eyes with his fist.

"Yes, I'll be quiet," Hunter said, still standing there.

"Okay, good boy, then straight back to bed," Trent said, and Hunter finally turned, leaving the room. He listened for a minute as the sink turned on, then little footstep sounded until he heard the small squeak of Hunter's mattress. It turned out to be just the perfect distraction he needed to push all thoughts from his mind and set him back on task.

Trent forced himself to finish the proposal and send it off in an email. By the time he got it all done it was close to one in the morning. He closed the lid and placed the laptop back on the nightstand before turning off the lamp, plunging the room into darkness. He reached his hand around the bedspread for the remote and turned on the television. Since every Gage special was saved on his DVR, he went through a couple of screens to find the latest interview. It started with Gage's face filling his screen and it wasn't but a minute more before sleep took him under with images of Gage as the last thing he saw.

Chapter 6

Gage sat kicked back in his chair, watching the goings on in the gallery out the side window of his office. His eyes stayed focused on the electrician who stayed on his knees, pulling wire through a new plug on one of the random showcasing walls. The tool belt made Trent's worn Levi's ride low on his hips. The T-shirt he wore shifted under the flex and strain of the muscles in his back and arms. All that bulked up, muscled goodness had to be built by pulling wire and lifting the heavy boxes of equipment he'd watched Trent lift all day long for the last three days.

From this position, Gage could almost see the very top of Trent's pretty, perfect ass. He could definitely see the waistband of his tighty whities. Dear Lord, he desperately wanted those jeans to drop a little lower so he could see a small peek at the sexy ass taunting him. Gage determined, after hours of watching Trent this morning, the guy rocked a solid bubble butt, and boy did he love a nice, tight ass.

At this point, seven hours into the day, he could think of nothing but Trent and as Gage propped an elbow on the desk, dropping his chin in his hand, he wondered what the hell was wrong with him? It had to be the rejection. People obsessed over rejection, and he clearly obsessed over this man in front of him.

People referred to him as being super good-looking and gay men were generally an easy pickup…and besides, his gaydar was strong. He knew attraction when he saw it. When choosing his next sex partner, Gage would go into stealth mode, easily picking off the most interested and setting his sights on him. He never failed, but now he was clearly off his game, so he sat in this office and worried, because he definitely wanted Trent, the electrician. Actually the want overrode the worry by about four to one.

As he sat there, lost in Trent Cooper's hot as hell ass, he realized true fear. It scared the hell out of him to think he might not ever get to bury himself deep inside this man, who sat on his knees, taunting the hell out of him right now. To make everything a hundred times worse, Trent never looked his way, not one single time. Gage knew this with absolute certainty because anytime Trent came within fifty feet of Gage, he sensed him. Picking up Trent with this weird mental connection apparently only he shared.

Trent Cooper pushed his senses into overdrive. Gage knew the moment Trent pulled up in the morning and when he drove away in the evening. Whenever Trent left the gallery, a sense of loss overtook Gage, only to be relieved when the man returned. Now they were at the end of day three and that Synclair intuition—he'd named it while mocking himself this morning in the bathroom mirror—told him clearly Trent Cooper was connected to him in some higher power kind of way.

Gage always focused on the task at hand. The only tasks of any significance now were this opening and the report of his life. He should have been working like a madman, reviewing everything on the case he'd built against Abdulla, because the story now was falling together at an incredibly fast pace. The gallery remodel ticked away on schedule, maybe even a little ahead of schedule. It truly appeared the opening and the assignment would hit completion right on target. But instead of going over everything one last time, all he could think was how fitting would it be to close one door in his life and have another immediately open.

Gage could see himself finally settling down into a relationship. It wasn't something he'd thought about before meeting Trent, but it made sense to have a regular sex partner in a town you lived in. People did it all the time. Gage could also see the benefits of finding someone to have on his arm when needed. The problem with his line of thinking, why in the world were his thoughts on a long term relationship with a straight man? *How fucked up am I?*

Gage cut his gaze down to the list his curator had slid on top of his desk minutes earlier. It only held his attention for a second before his eyes lifted back to Trent's ass. To add icing to Gage Synclair's cake, his fantastic curator looked to have already filled the gallery calendar for special showings, by someone famous, at least once a month for the next year. The Art Gallery already got big press around the world and the VIP list for the grand opening next week grew every day. His mother's friend Oprah, only minutes ago, sent her attendance response, as well as Michelle Obama, Katie Couric, and Anderson Cooper. The media would certainly turn out, and the night would be covered if for nothing more than to gain such easy access to the numerous A-listers moving about. The grand opening was going to be spectacular.

Gage adjusted himself in his leather-bound desk chair, kicked his feet onto the desk, crossing his ankles, and laid his head back on the head rest. Trent still worked in front of him, and Gage's eyes were still trained on his hot ass. Trent lifted his arm to wipe the sweat from his brow, using the small arm sleeve of his T-shirt. It was a move Trent did quite a bit. Did Trent even realize he did it or was it an unconscious movement? And, the better question: *why do I care?*

Gage knew why he thought of boyfriends and commitments. Being back home, having his mother on him every day. It was all the things his family always wanted for him.

A grin tore across his face. The plan for the afternoon required patience and dedication, but he knew if he waited long enough he would get a glimpse. Trent sat back on his heels, rubbing his upper arm over his face again, wiping the sweat from his brow. The motion moved his jeans lower, pushing the underwear down, showing an enticing curve of his ass and the sexist butt crack Gage thought he might ever have seen in his life. It was quick, but as Trent rose, the denim slipped lower giving him a visual of a good inch to inch and a half of the crack before Trent yanked his Levi's back up by the belt loops and tucked his shirt back in, covering himself completely.

Gage felt rewarded and denied all at the same time. A man with a body like that should be required to never wear clothing anywhere he went. If he had his way, Trent would be sporting his tool belt and perhaps those work boots and nothing else, while on his knees, working hard at sucking Gage's now always hard dick. He would make sure Trent worked up a good sweat because at this point, after three days of an insatiable hard-on, Trent would be on his knees, facing one way or another for quite some time.

Hell, Gage had gone out last night trying to find someone to relieve this hard-on, but when it got down to it, he actually turned a couple of guys down. His dick turned into a fickle beast. Once it came time to relieve this tension, his dick had no problem lying down. It seemed only one person could take care of his hard-on. The one person who didn't want anything to do with him.

Trent's phone went off and Gage watched him answer it. A smile spread across his handsome face. Trent turned his head toward the front windows. Like normal, Trent kept his eyes averted from this office. The guy never looked toward the office. It was like the office didn't exist. His gaze swept to the window at the front of the gallery, and the smile grew bigger as he walked toward the front door. Something just lit up the man's world, and with sudden interest, Gage needed to know what that something might be.

If something made Trent this happy, he found he wanted to try and repeat the action, to keep that smile on Trent's face every day. Gage narrowed his eyes and lowered his brows. *Where did that thought come from?* Confusion at his own reaction stopped Gage for a moment before he swiveled around in his chair to see a perfectly put together female with a long slender body and long dark hair, walking up the sidewalk with two beautiful children.

The sun shone brightly and the temperature climbed to somewhere in the low seventies, making it a beautiful day outside. Gage's windows were still open, a nice breeze blew, birds chirped and the sounds of the neighborhood filtered inside his office. As long as they didn't get too far up the sidewalk away from his office, Gage would be able to hear the conversation. The woman lowered her phone, so did Trent as they approached. Gage stood, going to the window to watch a little more closely. It sure appeared this might be Trent's family. Dread set into Gage's heart like nothing he ever experienced before.

How had this never occurred to him in all of the time he spent watching this man over the last seventy two hours? Married with children... Something caused Gage to reject the thought immediately. Trent didn't wear a wedding ring, but lots of electrician's didn't wear rings. B*ut if Trent was mine, the guy would wear my ring every day to prove to the world he was taken.* And Gage took a small step back from the window, shocked by the thought. *Where did that come from?* He *never* thought in terms of long term commitment or marriage, and here he was thinking just that about someone completely unattainable.

"Daddy, look what I got! It's my birthday dress!" The little girl ran toward Trent who never stopped walking toward the woman and children. The little boy tore out after the girl, easily running past her.

"I win," the boy said, tagging Trent's leg.

"Daddy, I wasn't racing," the girl said with a frustrated, pronounced little whine in her voice as she reached Trent. Gage smiled, remembering doing the very thing with his younger brothers and sisters. The need to win, to be the best, happened to boys his size.

"I know you weren't, Emalynn. You look very pretty," Trent said, effectively taking the frown from the little girl's upturned face, and she twirled around, letting the dress fan out around her. The woman finally made her way up to the three of them. She playfully frowned, looking over Trent before placing a careful kiss on his cheek.

"You're sweaty and dirty," the woman said.

"Yeah, hazards of working. So what're you guys out doing this afternoon?"

"We went shopping for my dress and had ice cream, then decided to stop by to show you," the little girl said.

"That's nice, honey. You look very pretty in your dress," Trent said and turned back to the woman. "I should be home soon, off in about an hour. Does it fit your schedule?"

"Yes, perfect, and I can cancel if you need me too," the woman said.

"No, I should be fine. I've got a crew that can stay," Trent said.

"All right, guys, tell your dad bye, he needs to get back to work."

"Bye, Daddy!" the boy said, reaching to hug Trent. Gage watched Trent lower to hug both the children, careful not to get the little girl's dress dirty, and he got kisses. Trent rose, lifting his white T-shirt by the hem, and lowered his head to wipe the sweat from his brow. Now that was an unexpected treat, one Gage was glad he stood there eavesdropping in order to see. The guy's stomach muscles were hard and defined. Even learning the object of his desire dared to have a stunning wife and two gorgeous children couldn't stop Gage's mouth from watering. Listening to the remainder of the conversation took a backseat as Gage thought about licking his way down to the hard package he'd felt on the first day they'd met. When Trent walked back inside, Gage watched the woman work the children into the car seats and drive away.

Married? With children! Trent Cooper, the man he wanted above all others was married with children. Gage Synclair sat ogling a married man with two children. In what world had that ever happened before? And the bigger problem seemed to be that none of it mattered to his raging hard-on. When Trent lifted his T-shirt, showed off his hot, sexy chest, Gage's dick sprang harder to life. It wasn't the pesky half aroused he'd stayed most of the day, this one turned solid in demanding need, leaving nothing to the imagination. His curator chose then to interrupt him.

"Gage, I need approval on something. I'm not sure it's a good idea or not," she said. Gage turned his head toward her, keeping his body averted as she stuck her head in his office, but he didn't see her at all. He stayed focused on needing to take five minutes in the office bathroom and relieve this desperate hard-on.

"I'm sure it's fine, Jacquelyn. Whatever you think is best," he said, dismissing her and moving toward the restroom.

"You keep saying that," she said. She came fully in his office, crossing her arms over her chest, leaning against the wall in her super tailored business suit.

"Because I mean it." He stopped at the bathroom door, finally growing a brain, and realized the rudeness of walking into the bathroom and closing the door in her face as she spoke.

"Okay, I'll book toilets on parade at Christmas for a three week run," she said, completely straight faced. Gage stood there, berating himself for spending the last three days focused on the sexy, married with children, electrician haunting all his thoughts. He had ignored everything else around him. After this session in the bathroom, he needed to focus on work, back on the topics more important to his immediate life.

"Earth to Gage," she said, and shut the door to his office. "Gage, look at me. I've known you for forever, you have never been this distracted. What's going on with you?"

"Jacquelyn, I don't know," he said, finally looking at her. What could he possibly say? Nothing, because nothing about this made any sense.

"Gage, talk to me," she tried again. "Your mom noticed it last night at dinner. She called me this morning, wanting me to find out what was going on. I'm not supposed to tell you, and I wouldn't tell her, I just see it, too. Something's up."

He stared at her for a long moment, then ran his fingers through his hair in an exasperated grunt. "Jacquelyn... I don't even know where to start, and I honestly don't want to talk about it at all."

"Well, when you know where to start, I want you to know I'm here for you," she said, lifting from the wall and opening the door.

"It's fine. I'm fine. It won't last too much longer, I'm sure. I honestly think it'll just resolved itself," Gage said, following her lead to end the conversation and walking fully into the bathroom. "And truly, whatever you think is best on what toilet issue we have." Gage winked at her before shutting the door and yelling through the wood, "I do somewhat listen."

Chapter 7

A burst of cold water slapped his face and the chill helped shock his system awake. Trent cupped his hands again under the running faucet, tossing more on his face, trying to force the fatigue from his mind. After another splash of water, he scooped up several handfuls and ran it through his close cropped hair. His face dripped, and he kept his eyes closed, reaching for the paper towels he knew were sitting close by to dry off before rising to see his reflection in the mirror.

This nightmare job turned out to be the worst job in the history of all jobs, and if it weren't for his children, he would have ditched it, cutting his loses and saving his sanity after the first day. Everything he put his hands on fucked up in some way, making the whole experience tougher, more difficult, and much longer than he ever anticipated. Already out an entire extra salary he'd never accounted for in the bidding process, Trent couldn't blame anyone but himself. He'd had no choice but to bring in someone to clean up the mess he made as he worked and to keep him from fucking anything else up.

To top it all off, there was no real reason for it. Well, no reason other than he needed to have sex in the worst possible way, and any time Gage appeared in his vicinity, which seemed to be all the fucking time, he became a bumbling mess of nerves. Why did Gage stick around every day, all day like he did? Owners were never this involved. It's what they paid the general contractor to do.

After the first walk-through on Tuesday, Trent made the decision to avoid Gage at all cost. He couldn't even look at the guy without getting a raging hard-on. Gage tried to speak to him, asking questions about his progress on the remodel and his only strategy seemed to be the failsafe plan of sticking his cell to his ear, pretending to be talking on it and avoiding any conversation at all cost. Then it got to where he'd walk in and out of the building with his cell stuck his ear for fear he might get in a situation where he needed to say hello or goodbye to the guy. God forbid that ever happened. Seriously, though, what wealthy, successful, progressive site owner held such a part of the daily operations of his business? None! Trent had landed straight in hell. And the worst part, the sexiest man on the planet was down to earth enough to be a part of his own life. Under different circumstances, he could see them as possibly becoming friends. None of the owners he'd worked with would have stayed up all night, with no electricity, checking in on the progress made on the panel change. Gage came down at least every thirty minutes, checking in. Damn, but all Gage's involvement only helped in making Gage so much hotter to Trent.

Apparently the rumors running around the site were true. Gage did intend to live upstairs, above the studio. Seeing Gage professionally dressed was a stunning figure, but a casual Gage dressed in sweatpants and a tank caused his heart to stop beating, multiple times, and his hard-on to demand his attention. Trent had broken out in a cold sweat the minute he lost focus on his plan to keep his eyes averted at all cost and looked up to see Gage standing above him, at about the angle he would need to be to take the guy's dick into his mouth. It was all so much bullshit on how his body immediately reacted to the site of Gage standing there. He'd immediately retreated to the bathroom, in the middle of the panel change, to jackoff before he embarrassed himself in front of his entire crew. *Fuck*! How unprofessional was that crap?

In spite of Trent's erratic behavior, they finished the panel change in just under thirteen hours. Daylight was just making its presence known, around seven in the morning, and his men were loading up, preparing to leave as he stood in the bathroom, hiding. The city had been standing by and gave a green tag on his work, which allowed the power company to do their magic and turn the power back on. He just needed to wait and make sure it all worked before leaving. The other contractors would be arriving soon, and he prayed everything was installed correctly because he needed to get the hell on up out of here as soon as humanly possible.

After finger combing his hair back in place, Trent retucked his shirt while forcing himself to man up and stop hiding. He needed to get back out there, face the situation. His guys were gone to get a few hours' sleep, before needing to be back here midday, working their scheduled shift. Auntie Crazy made plans for today, Rhonny was headed to Milwaukee, and his children would be waiting for him. Trent needed to focus, and stop acting like a teenage girl. Today would be shopping for birthday party decorations and getting the kids ready for the week, nothing more or less than his normal life. He looked at himself critically in the mirror and pointed a finger at the image staring back at him. *Act right*, he mentally chided, before his phone rang.

"Daddy, it's me," Emalynn said before he even got a chance to say hello.

"Em, I was just thinking about you," he said. Well, he'd sort of been thinking about her.

"Daddy, we put breakfast in your truck. Aunt Sophia said we couldn't bother you to tell you, so I called from the car. When are you coming home? Should I be ready to go look at my decorations?" Emalynn said it all on one breath, her excitement for the upcoming promised shopping trip bubbling over the connection.

"We'll go right after lunch, I promise," Trent replied, finally stepping from the bathroom. He could hear Sophia asking for the phone and then the radio got louder in the background.

"All right, Trenton Cooper, I saw the hottie in the window again. Start talking, mister," she said.

"My name is Trent. It's never been Trenton, ever in my life, and you saw nothing but the owner. Thanks for the breakfast," he said, coming to stand in the middle of the gallery, but kept his eyes averted from the office. He turned his back to the office windows in order to ensure he couldn't look that way.

"Are you sure he has nothing to do with how strange you've been acting?" Suspicion laced her words.

"I haven't been acting weird, just busy, nothing else. Well, I'm tired, that's all. Waiting for the power company to do their thing so I can pick up the kids and go shopping. You know how much I love shopping," he said, then waited to see if he successfully changed the subject.

"Do you need me to stay longer today? I can cancel my plans and go with Em and Hunter to get her decorations," Sophia asked.

"No, I promised I would take her, let her look all around. I was thinking maybe I could take a nap first and then we could go," he said.

"Tell Daddy I've been thinking Dora the Explorer decorations," Emalynn called out from the backseat. He could hear her voice loud and clear over the music playing on the radio.

"Whatever you want," both Trent and Sophia said at the same time, causing Trent to smile.

"Trent, let's go back to the guy who was looking out the window? He's pretty hot. He looked familiar to me," Sophia asked. All Trent could do was roll his eyes to the ceiling. *Here we go.*

"His name is Gage Synclair. He's the reporter guy. His office is right by the window. It's his gallery we're working on," he said.

"Trent, he's gorgeous. Oh. My. God, you love his work! You have all his DVDs. That's what's wrong with you. It's him!" The power company truck pulled up in front of the gallery, saving Trent.

"Sophia you're way off base, and I have to go. The power company's here," Trent started to move toward the front door.

"Trent, he's gorgeous. You two would be great together. How hot would that be?" Surely she didn't expect him to answer her question.

"You're so not even in the ballpark of being correct, Soph. I gotta go." Trent didn't wait, but disconnected the phone before he could hear anything more and met the power company at the front door.

"He's taken a vow of silence," Gage's first onsite contact, Javier, said into the phone.

"A vow of silence? Like he isn't speaking at all?" Gage asked, completely confused by what he'd heard.

"Yeah, and he spends lots of time with the highest bishop, the leader here," his contact said. The weak signal faded in and out, and Javier's accent so thick, made him harder to hear and understand.

"Is this a set up?" Gage asked, although he'd talked himself out of that as an option weeks ago.

"If it is, I can't find it," Javier said.

"Yeah, neither can I. So, he's found religion?" Gage asked.

"It's looking like it. I must go. I'll check back tomorrow if I can." The line disconnected, and Gage ended the call on his side.

This one threw him for a surprise, and he leaned forward in his chair. With a few swipes on his keyboard, Gage brought the live video feed back up on his computer to watch in real time, like he'd been doing for most of the night and all of the day. They were in the La Popa Basin, located in Mexico, an obscure location in a tiny abandoned sixteenth century Christian mission. Men from all over the world stumbled there every day, joining the cult-like teachings of this pseudo-religious throw back of the Christian church from hundreds of years ago.

They all wore long, dark robes, their heads cleanly shaven, and no shoes on their feet. Hours and hours were spent in silent meditation, only to then go into hours and hours of lecture-style teachings of how old religious values of a simpler, yet darker, time in our history, got it right all those centuries ago. The teachings went just shy of promoting the massacres of earlier centuries, changing course in mid-teaching, making it all about the Lord's love. Gage listened and came to the conclusion this was some sort of vigilante-meet-Gandhi kind of place and still undecided which side might prevail in the end.

The best Gage could determine, the mission looked like a recent start-up and appeared strategically planned, with abundant hiding places in the mountains surrounding the old cathedral-style buildings. The most undesirable men of the world flocked there and the drug cartel still ran Mexico, but the teachings of this mission's underlying goals were to take back their country to a more wholesome time. These newly trained clergy were coming to help in the cause. Perhaps building a small army to fight the drug cartel? Time would tell. For now, Gage knew only one thing for certain: Abdulla spent his days there, on his knees, with no sign of interaction with anyone.

If Abdulla had a target in the mission, it never made itself known under the constant surveillance. Gage's gut told him Abdulla fully bought into this new religion he got himself into, because he could have easily taken them all out the first day he arrived and no one would be the wiser. None of Gage's contacts found any sign of weapons on the property.

A vow of silence…well, wasn't that convenient. By all accounts, it looked like Abdulla might be having a change of heart or at least conscience, but Gage rejected the thought as quickly as it came in his mind. *Come on, asshole, show me what you're up to.* Why hide in such a remote, uncivilized area? Gage chuckled at his thought. The question actually answered itself: hiding. But who else might be looking for him? Gage's pursuit had been utterly discreet. Abdulla may have contacts reporting back to him, but one of the reasons it had taken so long to nail this report down were the lengths Gage went to in researching Abdulla. He never spoke with anyone directly associated with the guy. Gage worked his way through interviews with the grieving and hurt, those people left standing after Abdulla demolished their lives on his quest for power and money.

Gage focused on the screen again, watching the newsfeed come through in less than desirable conditions. The video looked grainy, and slightly off focus because of how they hid the device in the room. Abdulla sat on the floor with his legs crossed, meditating now for the last seven hours. He never moved from his spot, nor did he open his eyes. He remained in this position, praying silently. His mouth moved, but no words issued forth.

Under normal circumstances, Gage would have sat right here with Abdulla, watching each minute pass, trying to find the discrepancies, but today he found every few minutes his eyes wandered back out into the gallery, looking for Trent and each time he would have to remind himself Trent had left hours before.

Last night, Gage stayed up watching these videos courtesy of a generator in his bedroom and office. The panel change went on beneath him, the construction stayed loud all night, and Trent's presence affected Gage. He could sense him there, within reach, but completely untouchable. There wasn't much sleep happening when all his body and mind wanted were for him to be right down there in the middle of Trent's mess, watching the guy work.

Gage made the trip downstairs, under the cover of checking on progress, about every thirty minutes. On about the third trip down, Gage realized Trent wasn't clueless to him, but purposefully ignored him. Those were two vastly different things.

The night then became a game to Gage. He dropped in, over and over, putting himself in Trent's way. He'd chuckled as he'd watched Trent fumble through the chance meetings, dropping his tools, pulling the wire a little too hard, or bumping into things as he took the widest distance around wherever Gage stood. Trent never looked his way, and when forced to, he focused on Gage's forehead. Surely it meant Trent wasn't as unaffected as he pretended to be. Could it be Trent was a closet homosexual or maybe a closet bisexual? But Gage rejected that thought immediately; Trent didn't seem like the kind of guy who messed around on his commitments. Maybe a late in life homosexual, now stuck with a wife and children.

Even with those thoughts, nothing helped him find an outcome where he could get inside Trent's pants without looking like a big ass perv. So, just as he had last night, Gage forced his eyes and attention back to the screen, back to something he could work until the outcome landed in his favor. He sat back, getting comfortable, and prepared to sit there for the next several hours watching Abdulla breathe until he slipped.

One minute, he sat watching the video, the next the gallery plunged into total darkness. Gage looked around the gallery and every laborer working came to an abrupt stop. The air conditioning guys came from the basement door, heading toward his office.

"We blew a breaker," one of the two said.

"Did you reset it?" Gage called out through the open office door.

"It's not resetting," the other replied.

"No one leave! Let me get Coop Electric out here," Gage said, jumping up from his desk and making his way toward the door. He knew he needed to make it clear no one could leave before every one of these guys loaded up and hightailed it out of there for the night. He palmed his cell and dialed the number he'd saved after their first meeting about the panel change. He stood outside the office door, blocking the way to the front in case anyone made a run for it.

"I have a couple of generators around back for those who need something right away," Gage said as he listened to the sexiest masculine voice he thought he'd ever heard answer the phone. He couldn't stop the silly grin from spreading across his face or his heart from thumping wildly in his chest. Both were reactions he shouldn't be having, especially since his aggressive remodel had come to a complete stop due to lack of electricity.

"Trent, it's Gage Synclair."

Trent popped the top and chugged a double shot espresso while weaving through the exit doors of their crowded local grocery store. Past the point of exhaustion, a yawn ripped free from his lips, clearly to prove the feeling. The few hours' nap he'd planned for when he got home this morning never fully materialized. Emalynn couldn't contain her excitement and bounced off the walls. She couldn't let him sleep for more than five minutes before bursting in, asking if it was time for him to get up yet.

After about the third interruption, he finally forced himself up and got them ready to go. The first stop sent them straight to Party City, where they spent an hour and a half going through row after row of decorations, letting Em look at everything before she decided on a Barbie themed party, which happened to be the center display when they first walked in the door. As Rhonny suspected, every piece was saturated in hot pink, which fit Emalynn perfectly. Hunter chose the Hulk party plates and balloons for his place setting, officially making his children as different as two could be. With all that, and a hundred dollar bill later, they were out the door of Party City, loaded down, ready to decorate.

The next stop pointed them in the direction of the neighborhood bakery down the street from their house. Em got to taste three different cakes before deciding on a chocolate cake with buttercream icing, just like she always preferred. Of course his little girl talked the decorator into making the entire cake hot pink with Barbie's face drawn on top matching her decorations. Their third stop for the afternoon, a quick hair cut for Hunter. And the fourth stop, the local grocery store for their weekly groceries. It took them about an hour in the store, most of the time spent navigating through the masses of people, before they were able to check out and get the heck out of dodge.

Em sat in the front of the cart like normal, and against his better judgment, Trent let Hunter talk him into walking outside the cart, holding the sides with his hand. Trent only needed to remind him about thirty times to hang on to the side and not get distracted away. Emalynn chatted her little head off the entire time about all the selections she could have made at the party store and why Barbie was the very best. The benefit to Em's chatter, she never really required him to talk back to her. She could hold the entire conversation on her own, never feeling the least bit slighted if he didn't respond. Hunter, on the other hand, needed constant watching for fear he might wander off if something caught his eye.

As they made their way outside, Trent squinted in the bright sun. He pulled the cart to a stop. The parking lot was jammed packed with cars everywhere. He needed the minute to remind himself where he may have parked. Spotting the truck, he pushed them forward and got about halfway through the parking lot when his phone began to ring. He palmed it from his belt, moving them out of the way of any oncoming cars so he could answer.

"Hunter, I said hold on to the side. You're gonna get hurt, son," Trent said when Hunter bent down, looking at something sparkling in the sun, lying on the ground beside them.

"Sorry, Daddy, I forgot," he said, looking over his shoulder, taking the side of the cart again, but he turned back, keeping his eyes focused on the ground. By the third ring, Trent finally looked down at the phone screen and hesitated, not recognizing the number.

"Daddy, can I add the Barbie doll to my birthday list? She's so beautiful," Em chatted on. When she didn't get his attention right away she began to tap her hand on his arm. "Daddy, you aren't hearing me."

"Hunter, get out of the street and hang on to the side of the cart or you have to get in the basket. Em, hang on, honey." Trent thumbed the phone connection open on the fourth ring. "Coop Electric."

"Trent, it's Gage Synclair." After a momentary pause as Trent registered what he heard, his heart plunged to his feet right before it slammed back into his chest. "Did I catch you at a bad time?"

Everything came to a stop in the middle of the fast-paced parking lot. Emalynn sat in the basket looking at him, her mouth moving, but he heard nothing she said. He reached down and grabbed Hunter by the back of the collar, pulling him up, keeping a tight hold on his shirt to draw him in closer. He never let go of the back of Hunter's shirt and centered into the call.

Trent waited another heartbeat, then two before he answered. "No, is there a problem?"

"Actually, yes. Our AC breaker is tripping and taking the lights with it. They came this afternoon to test the units and the breaker isn't holding. Now, they won't reset," Gage said.

"All right, and my guys have already left for the day?" Trent asked.

"Yes, a couple of hours ago. The ceiling guys are scheduled in tonight and the AC needs to be tested first," Gage said.

"I'll get someone over there," Trent said.

"Thank you, Trent," Gage said.

"Thank you... I mean, not a problem. Wait, goodbye," he fumbled all over himself and finally disconnected the call, standing there a minute looking down at his phone before the blare of a car horn forced him back into reality.

"Shit," he muttered, pulling Hunter along while pushing the cart farther aside. They had stopped behind a car needing to back out of its space.

"Daddy, you said a bad word," Em said, watching him closely. Hunter also stood, staring up and back at him. Both kids looked a little uncertain as to what was actually happening. Trent looked around the parking lot, trying to get his bearings. He saw his truck parked only a few spaces away and for some reason relief flooded at the thought of finally getting to the vehicle.

"Come on, guys. I need to get you in the truck. I have a work emergency," Trent said. Hunter stayed stuck to his side, Trent never let go until he finally bent down and scooped Hunter up, under one arm, holding Hunter like he held a football. He tugged his truck keys from his pocket and hit the unlock button.

"Climb in, buddy. You too, Em," he said, lifting her from the cart, placing her inside the truck. They could handle their own car seats, but both sat there looking at him until they climbed to the back window of the truck, and watched him dump their groceries into the bed. His brain went ninety to nothing and he palmed his phone again to check the time. It was already four thirty in the afternoon. His crew had worked all night, then all day. This fell strongly into the asking too much category, but he dialed, John, his lead journeyman electrician.

"Yo, boss man," John said, answering the phone.

"Hey, what's going on?" Trent asked.

"Havin a party in the back yard! Whew, man, you should stop by. Bring the kids. I have my kids this weekend. I have plenty of beer. Stop by, man."

"What? You have your kids this weekend? I wouldn't have asked you to work last night," Trent said, and stopped pacing the length of the truck to drop his head on the side of the bed with a thump. No way could he ask John to go.

"Nah, man, it's cool. The old lady watched them, they're going home soon anyway," John said.

"How much have you had to drink?" Trent knew the answer, but prayed for a miracle.

"Not too much, man. A six pack or two," John said. "What up?"

"Nothing, you stay with your family. I'll see you tomorrow," Trent said.

"Cool, stop by if you can, man."

"Thanks, I'll talk to you later." Trent disconnected the phone and braced his head in his hand. So much for miracles. It only left Trent to do the emergency work call. His pacing started up again, walking the length of the truck and back again. He called Rhonny, but she'd barely left Milwaukee with hours to go before she got home. The phone call to Sophia went to voice mail. He didn't leave a message. She had talked about a big date this afternoon, and he knew in his heart he couldn't interrupt her. She'd been too excited.

"Daddy, we're in our car seats." Hunter's head popped out the open truck door and jarred Trent back to them.

"Guys, I have to go to work," he said, looking in the backseat to make sure they were buckled in right before shutting the door and climbing in the driver's side.

"Boooooo!" It was an extended boo, lasting until he got in and started the truck.

"And even more fun for you two, you're going to have to come with me." He feigned excitement as he spoke, backing out of the parking spot.

"Yay!" they yelled back at him.

"No, yay... You have to be quiet and super good. There's too much dangerous stuff there, and they're painting. You have to stay out of everyone's way and it's gonna be a little dark. I'll give you a

67

flashlight and stay close by, but you must be good. Can you do that for me?" he asked, looking in the rearview mirror at each of them before pulling out onto the road.

"Can I take my new Hulk with us?" Hunter asked.

"Me too, Daddy. I want to take my Barbie," Em piped in.

"Will you promise to be good and sit still, doing everything I tell you to?" Trent asked, navigating onto the highway.

"Yes, sir," they said in unison. They always tossed in the 'sir' in an attempt to show they were good.

"No arguing or fighting. Promise me," Trent said.

"Yes, sir." Again said together.

"Daddy, if we're good can we go to McDonald's for dinner?" Hunter asked.

"Yes, but only if you're good," Trent said.

"Yay! We get to go to McDonald's!"

Chapter 8

Trent made good time, but it still took forty-five minutes to get to the jobsite. They made a quick run by the house to unload the groceries, have a potty break, and grab an electrical breaker from his inventory. The drive to the gallery went fast, no traffic anywhere along the way. He pulled the kids from the backseat, grabbed his tool belt and an extra flashlight from the toolbox in the bed of the truck.

"You remember how you have to act, right? Very good, very quiet, and do not touch anything," he said, buckling his tool belt in place.

"And we get to play at McDonald's?" Hunter asked.

"And you get McDonald's if you're good," Trent said, taking the breaker from the seat and scooping Em up in his arms.

"What about those hard hats, can we wear those?" Hunter asked, causing Trent to smile as he backtracked to the truck, digging in the back for two hard hats.

"Yes, sir, Hunt-man, good call, buddy," Trent said. He found two, placing them on the kid's heads. Trent ushered the two of them inside the building and looked immediately into the office, relieved when he didn't see Gage. Keeping Em in his arms, he took Hunter by the hand and ate up the distance between the front door and the basement to the panel box. He all but drug Hunter along, trying to get out of the main gallery room before Gage showed up. It was dark in the basement. He left the door opened to filter in light and flipped on his flashlight. Once he got to the bottom of the stairs, he sat them both down on the last step from the bottom.

"Sit right here. Don't move, I have to work right over there. Do you see? No more than ten feet from you," he said, pointing the flashlight in the direction of the panel box. "Keep your flashlight on and I'll be right here with my other flashlight, okay? I won't leave you at all."

"You made it," Gage said. They all turned to see him coming down the stairs. Of course, he looked gorgeous in the dark slacks and dress shirt he wore today.

"Mr. Synclair, these are my children, Hunter and Emalynn. Today's my nanny's day off," Trent began, trying to make excuses, but Gage cut him off.

"No, it's not a problem. Thank you for getting here so quickly," Gage said, coming to stand directly behind the children. He took a seat on a step above them and placed a hand on each of their upturned heads, smiling down at both of them as Trent spoke.

"It's probably nothing more than a bad breaker. I know the amperage is right, the feed's good or it would have already shown itself. I need to check the connections and a couple of other things just to make sure, but it shouldn't take too long. We'll be out of here soon," Trent said, and for the first time in days, he looked Gage straight in the eyes. It helped to have the kids there between them, it took some of the pressure off. Trent knelt down one last time to again tell the kids to stay put while he worked.

"Hi, you two, I'm Gage, why don't you come up to my office with me? I have paints, crayons, big rolls of paper. My nieces and nephews say it's all really cool stuff. You can paint and color, while we wait for your dad to finish, and you won't be stuck on this step the whole time. You can bring the flashlight, but I have windows in my office. It won't get dark," Gage said, looking at them, then up at Trent.

"Can we, Daddy?" Hunter asked.

"I don't want to put you out, Mr. Synclair. They've done this before. They'll be fine," Trent said.

"It's not putting me out at all. I offered and it'll speed things up for you. The AC people are waiting," Gage said, helping the kids with their toys. "We'll be in my office. I'll leave the front office door open for you. We'll stay in the front of the office. I'll keep them safe."

"Daddy, can we?" Hunter asked again while Gage stood to his full height waiting for him to answer.

"Be good, guys…on your best behavior and manners. I'll just be a few minutes. Do what Mr. Synclair says and don't touch anything you aren't supposed to," Trent said.

"Yes!" Hunter cheered enthusiastically. Em being a little more reluctant stayed seated. "Em, come on! He has paints!"

"I have lots of pink paints. Do you like pink?" Gage asked. He bent down again, getting more on her level.

"Yes," she answered quietly.

"Then come up stairs with me and I can show them all to you," Gage said.

It took a minute and Em looked up at Trent for confirmation. When he nodded his head, she finally rose and held up her arms to Gage.

"Em, walk…" Trent began, but Gage cut him off.

"No, it's fine, I got her. You get my AC people happy. We'll be upstairs."

"Paint or colors? I have both," Gage said, putting Em on the floor as he walked into his office, heading straight to the credenza in the waiting area. He opened a cabinet and pulled out a large box filled with every type of paint, color, and coloring book imaginable.

"You guys can sit at the table," Gage said, walking past Em to place the box in the center of the small conference table. He pulled out two of the heavy oak chairs and helped Em, then Hunter, up into them. He pushed the chairs closer to the table, where they scrambled up on their knees to be able to see and reach better.

"I have a little bit of everything here. After all it is an art gallery. What's your preference?" he said, dumping the contents of the box directly onto the table, letting it scatter around for them both to see.

"Paints! And the Hulk! Em likes colors," Hunter said, pulling a Marvel coloring book and paint set to him.

"Colors!" Em said, affirming Hunter's selection for her, but she waited, her sweet little face smiling up at him, waiting for him to give her what she wanted.

"Okay, Emalynn, do you like princess, or fairies, or Barbies?" Gage asked, shifting the different books in her direction. He handed her a boxed set of colors, letting her open the lid and see all the different shades available to her. Em chose the Barbie coloring book and began instantly searching out a page. Gage went to a sink, pouring water in a cup for Hunter. He ripped off several paper towels, ready for any spills.

"How come you have all these colors?" Hunter asked, never taking his eyes from the page he'd selected. He began to work the brush in the lines on the page. Gage sat down between them, placing the water at the top of Hunter's area and the paper towels around the glass.

"Hunter, use all the brushes you want, you don't have to use the same one over and over. It'll help you keep the color exactly like you want them on the page. Cool?" Gage said, and grinned as Hunter turned toward him with the biggest smile ever. His smile looked exactly like Em's, which looked exactly like their father's and it completely took his breath away.

"To answer your question, Hunter, I have lots of nieces and nephews who stop by all the time. I learned to keep them busy or they get bored and loud," Gage said, turning his attention to Em, coloring away in her book.

"My daddy says we get loud, too. Do you have daughters or sons?" Em asked, concentrating hard on her page, choosing the colors exactly how she thought the page should look. He loved the intensity she used in judging which color should go where.

"Nope, not any," Gage said, leaning over and pointing to a color Em might like to use for the sky.

"Are you married?" Hunter asked, still concentrating hard on his painting.

"Nope, not yet," Gage said, placing a couple more paint brushes out for Hunter. The boy took him seriously when he said use a new brush for every color. Six used brushes were lying on the paper towels already.

"Are you going to get married?" Em asked. Gage smiled, feeling a little double teamed by their shooting questions about such a personal topic.

"Maybe someday, if I meet the right person," Gage said, and showed Em another color she might like for the grass on the picture.

"Oh! Em just picked out Barbie birthday decorations. I knew you would pick Barbie, Em," Hunter said. He kept talking and painting, never taking his eyes from the book. "Her birthday's next Sunday. It's the day our mom died, but we don't talk about it. We just talk about Emalynn's birthday. Right, Em?" Hunter asked, and Emalynn nodded her head, looking through the colors, finally picking the pinkest of the pink for the dress. Gage watched the kids closely. They were talking of their mother and her death, keeping it all very casual. The words reached out and touched his soul, hurting his heart. He wasn't sure what to say.

"It's the day we came to live with Daddy. I was just born," Em said, working the pink back and forth on the page, coloring the dress in. For one of the first times in his life, Gage didn't know how to respond. Their mother must have died giving birth to Em, and it broke his heart. He looked back and forth between the two of them, judging their reaction to what Em had just said.

"Do you like living with your dad and step mom?" Gage finally asked, needing to say something to fill in the desolate quiet after the kids dropped their little bomb. For the first time since she started the coloring, Em looked up, concentration clear on her face, but she looked confused.

"We don't have a mom," she said. Hunter jumped right in to explain.

"We have Rhonny and Auntie Sophia. Daddy calls her Auntie Crazy because she tries to make Daddy go on dates with her friends, and he doesn't want to. But we can't call her that, she makes us call her Auntie Sophia," Hunter said. They both stopped coloring and were looking at him, questioning his question. He wasn't sure why it seemed an odd question to them, so he went for a different angle.

"How old are you going to be on your birthday?" he asked.

"Four," she said back, staring at him.

"How old are you, Hunter?" Gage asked, turning to him.

"I just turned six," he said, and they were both quietly staring at him.

"So that's first grade?"

"No, I'm in kindergarten. School's out soon and I'm going to be in first grade. My teacher says I'm smart enough to be in first grade though. I can read, want me to?" Hunter didn't wait, but began sounding out words from the coloring book he'd chosen.

"He isn't very good at reading," Em said and turned her attention back to the coloring book.

"I am too! Daddy says I'm very good," Hunter shot back, anger filling his words.

"Wait, hold up. I think you did great, Hunter. Keep going, Em, try this color, too. Look, let me show you. See how this is a little lighter pink than the one you're using? Color this one like this," Gage said, making several shading strokes on the page and Em's eyes lit up in response.

"I can do that." Em picked up the color and began copying his stroke in earnest, awe lighting her features.

"Daddy's taking us to McDonald's when he's done," Hunter blurted out, giving up on the reading.

"He is? You sound lucky," Gage said, picking up the paint brush, handing it back to Hunter. If he could get them back working their papers, maybe he could get them back on the subject of their father.

"He said it was our reward if we acted good," Hunter said. He took the brush, keeping his eyes focused on Gage.

"Did we act good?" Em asked. Again they were both looking at him and not their papers which were his target goals.

"I think you're acting great," Gage said.

"Do you want to come to McDonald's too, because you're acting good, too? And it's lots of fun," Em asked, her face back to an excited glow.

"I don't want to get in the way," Gage said, smiling back at her. Her invitation was so sweetly offered, he couldn't help but run a hand down her long hair, while the lights shot back to life in the gallery.

"You should come to McDonald's so daddy has someone to talk to. Then we can play longer," Hunter said.

"Yeah, you should come so we can play longer," Em said, nodding her head. "Will you come?"

"I guess I can do it to help such a worthy cause," Gage said, laughing at their excitement.

"Okay, you guys, clean up your mess. Let's get out of Mr. Synclair's hair." Trent said, coming into the room, not looking at anyone as he began loading up the spilled box with the coloring books from the table. "You're back up and running. There was a faulty cell in the breaker. You're replaced and everything's running fine. You can call me if anything else happens and I'll be right back out."

"Daddy! Mr. Synclair's coming to McDonald's with you," Hunter said, folding up his coloring book and dumping the paints back in the box.

"I'm Gage, Hunter. Call me Gage," he said, picking up and dropping all the paint brushes into the water to soak. At the same time, Trent answered the kids.

"No, he doesn't want to come to McDonald's, guys," Trent said, working the colors in Em's box back into their spots. Gage gave Trent kudos. He worked fast, never looking over at him, trying hard to get them out of the office as quickly as possible.

"Daddy, he said he wanted to come so you wouldn't be lonely sitting there," Em said. She gave up helping Trent and sat back in the chair trying to explain why Gage needed to go.

"Honey, no, he doesn't want to go to McDonald's," Trent said. He finally dumped everything left on the table into the box with no care to it at all.

"I would love to go to McDonald's. I've never been," Gage said. It caused Trent's eyes to pop up to look him straight in the face.

"You've never been to McDonald's?" Trent asked. His hands stopped in mid-wipe, where he had taken Hunter's paper towel to clean off the table.

"No, not once, and apparently I've had a neglected childhood. Hunter and Em offered, I accepted. So it looks like we're off," Gage said, not giving Trent any more room to exclude him. Gage pulled Em's chair back and she bounced off. Hunter wiggled out of his, both heading toward the front door of the gallery.

"Guys... You haven't finished cleaning up," Trent said to their retreating backs.

"Leave it, I'll get it later. Let's go," Gage said, looking back over his shoulder as he walked into his office to grab his wallet and car keys. The workers were here for at least another three hours; surely he would be back before their shift ended.

"Are you riding with us?" Em asked Gage from the front door.

"I have the work truck, guys," Trent said, and Gage could see the inward groan he gave at their question. He bet Trent worked hard in his mind, trying to find a way out of Gage going. No way would he give on this. Trent stayed a complete mystery, especially after what the kids told him tonight. He needed answers, and maybe those answers would help Gage put this guy to bed. Okay, not the best choice of words, but he knew what he meant.

"How far is it?" Gage asked.

"I know of the one in Oakland Park, where we live. It's about fifteen minutes away," Trent said, stepping out the front door of the gallery. He grabbed on to Hunter's shirt so he didn't dart out to the truck and get lost in the people walking the street.

"Then I'll meet you there. Let me check things out in here, let them know I'll be back," Gage said as the front door began to close between them.

"See you there, Gage," Em said right before Trent scooped her up in his arms and turned away to his truck. He laughed at the look of discomfort all over Trent's face. He must have thought Gage wasn't looking. Clearly Mr. Hot and Sexy didn't realize Gage was always looking. Watching this man, coming up with little names for him, was turning into his favorite past time. Whatever. The discomfort served Trent right, Gage had been uncomfortable all week and Trent needed to know the feeling.

Chapter 9

What the hell just happened? Gage freakin' Synclair is going to McDonald's... with me... and my children... What. The. Hell? Trent's mind couldn't wrap around the mere idea of the crazy notion let alone focus on the more important issue; how in the hell could he completely ignore the only other person sitting at the same table with him? Oh, this was so not going to be good!

To make it all a hundred times worse, he'd been awake for twenty-eight hours. He coasted on no sleep and both his body and mind were strung out, completely exhausted. Trent sighed before reaching back to pull the seatbelt forward. Once secured, he glanced down at his lap. His fucking dick, which should be exhausted too, was already half aroused from merely being in the same room with Gage. One more of those hot, sexy looks Gage tossed his way and he would, without a doubt, be sporting a straight up, tent-building hard-on through the entire McDonald's experience. How could he possibly explain that one to the man sitting across from him?

The bigger, more pressing problem for right now, he knew the fatigue showed on his face, making his eyes red and swollen. He looked at himself in the rearview mirror and saw little lines showing under his eyes. He looked terrible, and why should it matter to him? Dinner with Gage hadn't been in his game plan for the evening. How did he let this happen? Turning on the ignition, he looked back to make sure the kids were buckled up. He'd been in such a state of distressed mental anguish over Gage's plan to meet them at the restaurant that he didn't remember getting the kids in the truck, but they appeared to be perfectly secured in their usual seats.

"Guys, listen to me. You can't just invite people to go with us like you did. You have to talk to me first. Hunter, you and I have had this discussion before. You need to remember and talk to me first. I don't want this to happen again, do you understand?" Trent said, while pulling the truck from the curb out into the street. Neither Em nor Hunter responded, and he looked back in the rearview mirror again. Both their little eyes were lifted to the mirror staring back at him. With the look on their faces and the silence coming from the backseat, he knew he must have said it too harshly. They thought they were in trouble.

"I'm sorry, Daddy," Em said first.

"I'm sorry, too," Hunter said immediately after and they both fell back into silence.

"Just remember for me, okay?" Trent said. His eyes were back on the road, but he took his hand and rubbed it over his face, frustrated with himself for making the kids uneasy. Technically, they really had done nothing wrong.

"Yes, sir," Hunter said quietly.

"Yes, sir, Daddy," Em said, and he looked back in the rearview mirror to see Hunter sitting with his hands in his lap, his head bent down, and Em's little bottom lip quivering. She hated being in trouble. They both hated it.

"Honey, it's okay. You're both okay," Trent said, reaching a hand behind the seat, ruffling Hunter's hair. He couldn't reach Em.

"Daddy, we just wanted to play longer," Em said, those big tears finally spilling out of her eyes.

"I know, baby. You're fine. It's okay," he said and wondered how in one minute he scolded them and the next he comforted and apologized to them for being angry. They drove the rest of the ride in silence. Trent focused on a mental game plan for getting through the fast food dinner. He racked his brain until it finally dawned on him in a relieved thump of his heart. He'd watched everything on Gage Synclair. What was he so worried about? Quickly he ticked off a list of worldwide topics they could talk about. He could ask Gage's opinion, get him talking, and keep him talking, about the state of the world. If he paced himself, stayed on his game, maybe he could kill the hour with no harm, no foul, and move them out the door.

"Daddy, he beat us here," Em said, her eyes darting to the rearview mirror meeting his. He could see the uncertainty in her eyes and hated he'd put it there.

"It's okay, baby. Let's go say hi, and you two can play." Trent pulled the truck in the closest parking space to the front doors and got both the kids out on his side of the truck. Hunter tried hard to show his independence, refusing to hold hands across the parking lot.

"Daddy, I want a cheeseburger with no pickles or mustard," Hunter said.

"Can we get ice cream?" Em asked. He supposed the remorse of the situation faded as they almost bounced toward the restaurant.

"We can, if you're good and there's no fighting," he said, his eyes trained on Gage who stood a few feet away on the sidewalk by the front door. Gage watched them approach, his smile spread as the kids bounded toward him and that smile cost Trent. Gage seemed genuinely pleased to be here with his children and Trent had to force his heart not to connect with the thought.

"I wanted to wait to enter my first McDonald's so you two could show me around," Gage said to the kids.

"Is this really your first time here?" Trent asked, keeping his eyes averted while getting the kids inside.

"I think I might have had McDonald's in Indonesia, but I can't be absolutely certain. It may not have been a hamburger. It's always hard to tell what you're really eating on that side of the world," Gage said, following them inside. His wonderful, brilliant children took over and grabbed Gage's hand, guiding him to the indoor play area. If he could have high fived them for occupying Gage, he would have, and Trent followed along behind them as they guided him through the maze of tables.

"Come on, this playground is the best!" Em called out, already kicking off her shoes.

"They have real video games, too," Hunter said, dragging Gage along with him.

"Well, then, how can we wait another minute," Gage said. A grin spread across Trent's lips watching his children's excitement. The sun hovered over the horizon, beginning to set. The overhead lights popped on inside the playroom. The play area swarmed with kids jumping, playing, having fun, but as they got closer Trent could see quite a few parents corralling their children as though preparing to leave. It wouldn't take long before the room thinned out.

"Would you like something to eat?" Trent asked, trailing behind them.

"Just a soda," Gage said over his shoulder, his crooked grin in place. The smile always seemed to settle squarely in his pants, bringing on the full hard-on he'd been trying to avoid. Gage was sexy as hell on his own, but watching him play with his kids became almost too much. And then his heart strings stirred, oh dear, that couldn't be good. Shoving his hands in his jean pockets, he discreetly adjusted himself and stared after them. It took a moment for him to realize he stood looking at nothing but the swinging playroom door. The kids had Gage inside, showing him everything they could do.

Trent went to the counter and ordered food, getting a couple of sodas for him and Gage. He carried the tray to the playroom where several families still sat, eating or waiting for their children. He could see some of the adults eyeing Gage, maybe a bit of recognition, but none spoke to him. Gage stood off to the side watching Hunter as he climbed to the top of the elaborate indoor play yard, disappearing in one of the multiple tubes connecting everything together. The novelty of a captive audience, having Gage there to show off in front of, had begun to fade as Em and Hunter made friends inside the enormous play set. It never took long.

"You don't really have to stay," Trent said, walking past Gage to an isolated table in the far corner of the room.

"No, this is all very exciting. I may have to bring my nieces and nephews here at some point. It's amazing how a set of cubbies for children's shoes are just fascinating to this younger crowd," Gage said, following behind Trent to take a seat at the small table.

"I know, right? They pick those cubbies with critical care, don't they?" Trent asked, pulling the happy meals from the tray, getting the kids juice boxes ready.

"Yes, absolutely, and Emalynn dared to pick the wrong cubby. Good thing Hunter's an expert cubby picker," Gage said, taking the offered soda as Trent moved the tray from the table.

"Yeah, Hunter tries hard to make sure he takes care of Em, no matter how loudly she rejects his help," he said, chuckling while opening his straw. So far, the first five minutes seemed to be going fine. Trent found enough to occupy Gage in conversation while opening the kid's food. He was also able to keep his eyes averted, focused on other things, without making it look obvious. High five to him for the first five minutes!

"Taking care of his sister is the sign of a true gentleman in the making," Gage said. Trent couldn't help but laugh straight out loud at that one.

"Yeah, except he can't stand to let her win at anything she does," Trent said, finally sitting down, taking a seat across from Gage.

"Well, I think that just makes him a man," Gage said, turning fully to Trent at the table. The full force of his gaze had Trent fumbling a little with the simple task of opening the kids' food.

"You're probably right," Trent said, turning away toward the tubes, scanning the playground, listening and looking for both heads darting around. Silence ensued between them, but it wasn't bad and he still avoided purposeful eye contact. He thought over the list of questions he'd come up with on the way over, trying to decide where best to start.

"Listen, Trent, I only barged in on your family time tonight to apologize," Gage said. Hunter chose that moment to barrel up to the table.

"Daddy, where's my drink?"

"Right here, Hunt... Hey, man, slow down, some." Hunter gulped half his apple juice before turning to leave. Hunter stopped though and pivoted back around as quickly as he'd come.

"I have a new friend," Hunter said, his little chest heaving.

"That's good, buddy. Go play," Trent said. It's all it took to have Hunter dashing off, back into the playground.

"I'm sorry, what were you saying?" Trent asked, keeping his eyes on Hunter until he disappeared into one of the giant tubes.

"I was just apologizing," Gage said, but not saying anything more.

"What could you possibly have to apologize for?" Trent asked, glancing over to Gage. His confusion caused him to lose focus, throw him off his game, and he didn't guard his expression or the location of his gaze. He looked Gage straight in the eyes and... it wasn't terrible.

81

"The other day, when I met you... we got off on the wrong foot. I misread some... things. I shouldn't have hit on you like I did. I'm not sure what I was thinking. I guess I wasn't thinking," Gage said and took a drink of his soda. A grin formed as Gage kept his stare trained on Trent's. Trent felt his cheeks heat in a small blush. After a minute, he looked around to see who might be close by or may have overheard, but they were alone on this side of the playground.

"Really, it's fine, I was flattered. I just gave up the lifestyle when I got the kids. Plus, I never mix my personal life with business, not in my industry. Construction's too packed with homophobes. I don't hide, I'm happy with who I am, I just don't flaunt it. I try to keep all the different parts of my life separated. I tried hard to not bring the kids tonight to work with me, but I couldn't find anyone to watch them. I really try to keep everything separate from each other," Trent said. He rambled a little as he spoke, but hoped enough pieces were there to cover it all.

"So you are gay?" Gage asked. He looked confused, and again Trent looked around making sure they weren't in hearing range.

"Yeah, I am," he said, but Gage still looked confused.

"What lifestyle did you give up?" Gage asked.

"The quickie... that meaningless moment. When my sister left me Em and Hunter, I decided I needed to be the best role model I could be. I'm gay. Totally gay, but I can still be responsible and morally sound, if that makes any sense. Back then, I thought I would turn it to relationships. You know, find someone to share all this with. I was so happy and still am, but I was naïve. I thought I could find someone who would want a monogamous relationship, someone to date. Yeah, I laugh about it now. Women are totally into the kids, but guys can't hang so well. I get it. This is a whole lot to handle," Trent said.

"Daddy, where's my drink?" Em came to the end of the table, interrupting their conversation.

"Right here," he said, handing her the ready juice box, and she drank it down quickly.

"When do we get ice cream?" she asked, placing the empty juice box on the table.

"After you eat, which needs to be soon," he said.

"Three more minutes?" she asked, with no concept of time. Three minutes could be three hours if he wasn't careful.

"Okay, three more minutes, and tell Hunter, too," Trent said, grinning down at her upturned, smiling face. She didn't wait, but took off running back to the play tubes.

"See? It never stops with them. It's a lot, I get it," Trent said, turning back to Gage. Amazed again, he sat there easily holding the guy's gaze without going into panic mode. Yay, him! It was a small, but thorough, accomplishment after the last few days of hell.

"Just a minute, I have so many questions. Are you saying you only date?" Gage asked, his brow narrowed like he tried to figure out some complicated math equation.

"Yes, I guess so. I don't do the random moments at all anymore," Trent said.

"Then go out with me," Gage said. It wasn't really a question, more an answer given to him and it effectively silenced Trent who only stared back at Gage. After a minute, Gage gave his charming grin and added, "I must say, I would have liked a solid yes, but silence is better than a no."

"I…" Trent moved his mouth, but nothing more came out. He hadn't expected that turn of events and continued to stare at Gage, bewildered. But the slow steady pound of his heart picked up a beat, and the solid arousal hardened tighter in his jeans. Finally, he pushed his gaze up, away from Gage, focusing on the wall behind him, trying hard to regain his ability to think.

"I can see I need to do better. I honestly don't believe I've ever asked anyone out before, but it can't be hard and I do understand the benefits. Let me start over. Trent, please do me the honor of allowing me to escort you to dinner. Dinner's what you do on a date, right?" Gage asked. He lifted his finger to Trent's chin and pulled his head down to where their eyes met again. "There you go. I'm right here. What do you say to dinner with me, Trent?"

"I would say I don't mix business with pleasure," Trent said.

"Well, then, you're fired. Now have dinner with me," Gage said with a chuckle. "No, really, have dinner with me. Say yes, it's just dinner," Gage said, his elbows were now on the table and he leaned in closer to Trent. "And before you say no, again, technically your business is with Layne Construction, not me, so there is no real mixing going on," Gage added. Trent hesitated still, but Gage had a point. He did work for Layne, not Gage. After a long pause with Gage staring at him hard, he finally answered.

"All right, I'll go to dinner with you," he muttered, still shocked to the very core.

"Great. I'll take that yes, and say, how about tomorrow night?" The grin spread easily across Gage's lips, making Trent absolutely certain he sat looking at the most handsome man on the planet.

"My nanny has class every night this week, I think." He stayed transfixed on Gage.

"I might be able to send my housekeeper over," Gage suggested.

"No, I'm sorry, I need to know the person who watches them. Let me check with Auntie Crazy, see what she's doing, hang on." He palmed his phone on Gage's chuckle.

"I heard about that name from the kids tonight. Is she a sister?" Gage asked.

"No, my sister's best friend, they grew up together," Trent said, flipping through his contacts and sending Sophia a quick text message.

"Hunter and Emalynn are your sister's children, correct?" Gage asked.

"Yes, my sister passed away when Emalynn was born. Their father died right about the time Lynn got pregnant with Em. He was military. My parents are gone, so they came to me. I legally adopted them. It's why they call me Dad." Trent's phone rang with Sophia on the other end of caller ID. Of course she couldn't have just texted back.

"Hello," he said.

"Is this for a date for you? I can come right now?" The tension of sitting across from Gage, compounded with hearing the desperation in Sophia's voice, caused Trent to laugh at her question. The volume on his phone was up high in order to hear in the playroom. With a glance up, his suspensions were confirmed, Gage heard it all.

"No, not now, just one night this week," he said.

"Tomorrow! Trent, see if she's free tomorrow night," Gage said.

"Is that him, are you with him now? Is it the gallery guy? Oh my god, he's so freakin' hot, Trent, you lucky boy!" Trent looked up, horrified, and Gage leaned in closer to the phone before he spoke.

"Tell her, indeed, it is the gallery guy, unless there's more than one? Then I think I'm entitled to know who my competition is so I may fire him," Gage said while looking straight at him. Trent didn't say a word, just held the gaze and listened. It sure sounded like Gage flirted with him, and for the second time tonight his heart connected to Gage, doing another strong pull toward the guy. Being flirted with soothed his nerves and made him smile. Trent hadn't realized until that minute how much he needed someone to flirt with him, someone to want to be with him.

"Oh, Trent, he sounds sexy as hell. Tomorrow! I can babysit tomorrow. Tell him right now, I can be there right after work!" she said.

"Tomorrow it is, then. It's been a pleasure talking to you, Auntie Crazy. I can't wait to meet you," Gage said into the phone, leaning all the way across the table now. Trent never said a word.

"I'll bring clothes and spend the night. I can leave for work from your house. You can stay out late," she added.

"It's a work and school night. I'll be in early." He finally got something out to add to the conversation. At that point, Gage leaned far across the table. His full lips were still spread in a big, arresting grin, his slate blue eyes sparked with amusement.

"I'll still stay there. It will be easier. So what time? Never mind, I'll just come right after work. When does Rhonny leave?" she asked.

"She has class at six, I think," he said, and it took everything in him to tear his eyes away from Gage to check on the kids playing.

"I'll be there somewhere around six tomorrow evening. And Trent... Yay! He is so yummy! Good job! I'm high fiving you right now! Trent, listen to me! Get laid! Don't wait! Do you hear me?" With that Gage laughed and Trent disconnected the call.

"See why I call her Auntie Crazy?" he asked.

"I think her points may have merit, with a definite solid outcome theory," Gage said, wiggling his eye brows, making them both laugh.

"Let me get the kids to eat, it's getting late." Trent called them down under strong protest. When he finally wrangled them to the table, they all sat together talking about the playground slides, and the new friends they met tonight as they ate their dinner. When it was time to leave, Gage walked them to the truck, stayed with his back leaning against the bed of the truck with his arms crossed over his chest while Trent got Em and Hunter buckled in their car seats. With nothing left to occupy him, Trent shut the door to the backseat and turned to Gage.

An awkward silence fell between them as they stood staring at one another and Trent felt the stain of a blush heating his cheeks again.

"I enjoyed tonight, thank you for letting me tag along," Gage said quietly, tucking his hands in his slacks pockets.

"I can't imagine how you enjoyed this." Trent replied, and following Gage's lead, he tucked his hands in his pockets.

"I'm looking forward to tomorrow night, Trent," Gage said, taking a step away from the truck, backing out into the parking lot. When Trent didn't reply, Gage gave a quick wink, before turning and heading to his car. Trent tracked him the entire way, feeling breathless, and warm all over. When Gage turned back to him, before getting in the driver's side, he lifted his hand in a small wave.

"Me too," Trent finally said, watching Gage pull out of the parking lot.

Chapter 10

Work started bright and early Monday morning, but something about clearing the air with Gage made everything a little less complicated in Trent's life. The job definitely got better, he seemed to make far fewer mistakes, and didn't quite have the problem of meeting Gage's direct stare today. The heavy weight of the last few days lifted, and in its place a sense of contentment settled.

One thing he did notice, Gage seemed to stare at him quite a bit today. While Trent had stayed vigilant on his avoid-Gage-at-all-cost regime, he never noticed how much Gage might be looking at him, but today, every time he turned around, Gage's eyes were on him.

On his knees, Trent worked the wiring to the wall sockets his crew had installed on Sunday afternoon. Remarkably, everything managed to stay on track, even with the unexpected electrical panel change. It said a lot to Gage's involvement with the job. As he tucked the wire into the socket, his phone vibrated at his belt, alerting him to an incoming text. He sat back on his heels, palming his phone to see an unknown number. He clicked the message to read it.

Your ass is what my dreams are made of... it looks good bent over like that. It's driven me crazy for five straight days. I thought you should know.

Trent read the message and looked over his shoulder to the glass walls of Gage's office to see him sitting at his desk, feet kicked up on the corner, staring at Trent. Gage's sexy grin was in place and he winked at Trent.

I'm sorry, who is this? Trent teasingly texted back, and then turned back to finish screwing the cover over the socket. As he moved to the next socket his phone vibrated again, alerting him of another text.

As I suspected! I'm sure there are many men paying homage to that tight ass of yours. I'm your date for the night and I need your address to pick you up.

He didn't look back at Gage this time, but texted back quickly.

I can meet you, just tell me where.

He didn't get a second before a new text came in. *Oh no... I'm picking my date up this evening. I asked, you accepted, it's the proper thing to do. What's your address?*

Trent replied back quickly. *Really, it's not necessary. I can meet you.*

Sexy, and that's just one of the many names I've come up to describe you over the last five days...don't make me come out there and force your address out of you. Just tell me where you live. I made dinner reservations for seven. Sports coat required. I should pick you up no later than six thirty.

Trent couldn't help but love the little name Gage used on him. The last few years battered both his heart and ego pretty badly, but Gage had already begun to mend those broken pieces, without even realizing it, healing his soul from the inside out. After a second, he allowed himself another quick look over his shoulder. Gage still sat in the same spot, his eyes focused on Trent and the grin spread again across his lips. His heart tripped. Oh dear God, Trent was in over his head. A call came through to Gage's office. Trent watched him pick up the phone on the first ring. After a minute, Gage rose and shut the office door.

Then the windows darkened, blocking anyone from seeing into the office. Those moments happened several times a day, and they were all so mysterious. Only once, in passing, did he hear any mention of anything related to a possible report. He assumed all this secrecy went along with the investigation. It was how he imagined it would all go down, the private conversations, held in out of the way, remote locations. Wrapped up in thoughts of double agents and secret missions, Trent worked until jarred back to the real world with another incoming text.

Your address… still waiting. Well, the text blew the image Trent was forming of Gage posing as James Bond, hiding in some seedy back room gathering his information through extreme interrogation tactics. He texted his address with the disclaimer he could absolutely meet him anywhere and finished working the sockets in the main showroom.

He saw glimpses of photo's matted and framed, being placed around the room for hanging. They were beginning to arrive daily, and he heard the official grand opening was scheduled for Thursday, three days from now. After today, they were moving upstairs to finish Gage's personal space and then on to the basement to rough it out for storage, both would be done by the end of the week.

Gage stayed locked up in his office for the rest of the afternoon, and Trent decided to take off a little early to get a haircut. On a whim, he swung by Men's Warehouse and picked out a new suit, something a little more modern than the years old versions hanging in his closet. As he drove home, the early rush hour traffic didn't bother him like it normally would. Every one of his thoughts stayed centered on Gage. His anticipation levels were all in overdrive, and he knew the pull his heart felt wasn't a good sign. He tried hard to rein in the runaway thoughts of future dates or of the times he and Gage might take the kids to the park, or to the movies.

Those daydreams were dumb, and he knew the intensity of this emotion coursing through him was all one-sided. He also knew the signs of already being too emotionally attached. He lectured himself on keeping it casual and easy going. Gage wouldn't stick around for any real length of time. But damn, fantasizing came easy after seeing how well Gage handled his children. It did something special to a man's heart to watch his love interest help his son open a ketchup packet or wipe food from his daughter's face.

As he pulled into the driveway, Trent grounded all his flights of fancy. He would keep it casual tonight. If this were his one night with Gage, he would enjoy the evening and hold it as a fond memory. Exactly like his dinner at McDonald's last night.

Regardless of what the future held, Em's birthday inched closer, and if he played his cards right, he could keep his mind occupied long enough to get through the day without the funk that usually followed.

Em, Hunter, and Rhonny were at the kitchen table doing homework when he walked in with his new suit over his shoulder. The kids jumped down from their seats, running toward him, both hugging a leg before he could make it too far out of the entryway. Em's homework consisted of coloring and she brought the page with her for his inspection.

"Daddy, I'm drawing this for Mr. Gage because Rhonny said Auntie Crazy's watching us so you can see him again tonight. I'm doing what he told me to do with the colors. I don't have two pinks though so I used green and pink," she said, shoving the hair out of her face as she spoke.

"Very nice work," he said as she grabbed the paper back and ran to the kitchen table.

"I have to finish before you leave," she said, crawling back on the chair in the kitchen.

"How was your day at school, Hunter?" Trent asked. The little guy still hugged his leg. "You okay?"

"Thomas said his dad was stronger than my dad, and he could beat you up," Hunter said. It caught Trent's attention and he looked down at Hunter a little closer seeing the worry on his brow. He knelt down on one knee, keeping Hunter in the circle of his arms.

"Did he say why he says that?" Trent asked.

"No." Hunter offered up nothing more as a response.

"How did you respond to Thomas?" Trent asked, hooking his finger under Hunter's chin, lifting his worried face to where he could see his eyes.

"I told him you were stronger and had bigger muscles and you could beat up his dad," Hunter said, his voice growing with conviction as he spoke.

"Well, son, that's one way to answer his question. What happened then?" Trent asked, trying to hide the relief he felt. He worried about the gay thing when it came to the kids; he didn't want them to be targets of harassment.

"The teacher told us to stop, but, Daddy, I know you can beat him up. Your muscles are bigger than all the dads in my class," Hunter said seriously.

"Hunt, I don't want to fight anyone and I think those other dad's feel the same as I do," Trent said.

"I knew you were gonna say that, but you can still win. I know!" Hunter said, apparently done with the conversation as he turned and ran back to the table.

"Hi, Rhonny, I'm going to get dressed. I'll be out in a little while," he said to Rhonny. Her textbook was open, but her eyes were on him and Hunter. She smirked as they spoke, clearly she'd already heard this story from Hunter.

"Rockin' haircut, Trent. Lookin' hot and I agree, your muscles are bigger!" Rhonny said. He didn't even turn back around to look at her because he knew the wiggly eyebrows and suggestive looks he would see.

"Thanks… I'll be out in a little while," he said, making his way down the hallway and shutting his bedroom door behind him.

Manscaping took much longer than Trent remembered. He'd spent almost an hour making sure everything was shaved, combed, plucked, and tucked in the right way. His hair took the most time, and he wondered how such a short, easy cut could be so cumbersome to fix, but he followed the stylist's direction to a tee and it turned out pretty well. Rhonny had come into his room about thirty minutes ago to do a visual inspection before leaving for class. She worked a minute with his hair, fixing a few problem areas that didn't do what they were supposed to do. Auntie Crazy texted to let them know she was running late but was close by, and both Em and Hunter were on his bed, watching Sponge Bob, chatting nonstop, all excited about his date.

"You look nice, Daddy," Em said as she started to jump up and down on the bed.

"I want to cut my hair like yours," Hunter said, standing up on the bed to see himself in the dresser mirror. From the angle of the mirror, they were able to stand side by side. "Can I get my hair like yours?"

"Sure, on your next haircut, okay?" he said, sitting down on the bed to put his shoes and socks on. Both children came to sit beside him.

"I told Gage about Sophia being Auntie Crazy. He said I could call him Gage," Hunter said. "Did you shine your shoes?"

"Yes, sir, I did. After you went to sleep last night," Trent said, standing up and turning to the kids. They were so sweet and very excited for him.

"I think I need a kiss for encouragement," he said, and they both jumped back up on the bed, giving him two giant, wet kisses as the doorbell rang.

"Daddy, he's here!" Em shouted, climbing off the bed. Hunter jump forward, racing down the hall.

"Let me get my suit jacket," he called out after them. As he took his jacket off the hanger, he heard Sophia at the door.

"It's Auntie Crazy and Gage together," Hunter yelled down the hall. He could only imagine what Sophia might say if she got the chance to get Gage alone. If they arrived at the same time, it gave her the chance. Hunter and Emalynn were clearly bouncing off the walls. He could hear their shoes pounding on the hardwood floor. On a deep breath, he shrugged his suit jacket on and walked over to his dresser's mirror, adjusting the open collar of his shirt under the jacket. He chose to go tieless tonight, and after one more scan, he decided he looked as good as he possibly could. It wasn't Gage good-looking, but he looked the best he could and turned away, forcing himself to lose the nerves and get out there to face Gage.

He rounded the corner of his room, listening to the kids talking over each other in order to get Gage's attention. Sophia stayed quiet, which was incredibly odd, maybe even a first. As he stepped out of his room, he saw all four of them standing inside the entryway. They all turned toward him as he walked down the hall. Sophia stood all doe-eyed and the kids were overly excited. Em held Gage's hand, her colored sheet of paper in his other hand, and he realized he needed to make this fast and get them out of the house before his family ran Gage off.

Gage looked stunning as Trent knew he would. He wore a soft black suit which matched his build perfectly as if the suit were made specifically for him. In contrast, he wore a tieless white French cuff dress shirt, the collar left open by three buttons. The cufflinks were some sort of black stone. Trent always thought of Gage as ruggedly handsome. His reports took him to some of the most remote parts of the world. He worked hard, spending hours and hours in the sun, resulting in his dark, deep suntan and blond sun streaks all throughout his hair, but the suit he chose to wear tonight accented and transformed him into a proper, polished gentleman and Trent's heart did another little flip.

Gage's eyes were focused on Trent, but Emalynn chatted away, telling Gage a story about something and it gave him a minute to just be lost in Gage while walking down the hall toward them. When he reached Em, he placed his hand on her hair and she stopped talking as he stood there a moment holding Gage's gaze.

"You look extraordinarily handsome tonight," Gage finally said, and Trent tucked his hands in his slacks pocket to give them something to do. He could have sworn he heard a female sigh right before a picture snapped causing them both to break their stare and turn to Auntie Crazy.

"Sorry, I promised Rhonny I would capture the moment when you first saw one another. She almost skipped class tonight to see this! She should have, it was greatness." Auntie Crazy snapped another picture.

"Daddy, can we ask Gage to come to my birthday?" Emalynn asked, looking so excited at the idea. "I asked you before I asked him. Isn't that what you said I had to do last night?"

"We'll see, Emalynn," Trent said. All he could do was smile down at his little girl's upturned face. She looked so excited and proud of herself for remembering his directive this time. "And… Yeah, I think we should be off. No more pictures, Sophia," Trent said, moving to the front door.

"I have to get one more. I promised, Trent," Sophia said, angling the camera to her eye. Gage let out a laugh as Trent rolled his eyes and turned to the door.

"I would apologize, Gage, but this seems to be my life," Trent said, opening the front door for Gage. Both children and Sophia followed along behind them.

"There's no need for apologies. You have a charming home and family, Trent. Goodbye everyone. Sophia, it was a pleasure to meet you. Emalynn, finish the lovely drawing for me. You're doing a great job. Hunter, goodnight, buddy," Gage said before walking out the door.

"You all are staying in this house, and put the camera down, Sophia. I'll be back later. Call me if you need me." Trent shut the door in their faces before they could make a run for it and follow them out, but Sophia quickly opened it again, snapping another picture from her phone.

"*That's* it, I promise," Sophia called out and slammed the door back shut. Gage's grin grew as they heard footsteps in the house racing to the front window. He heard Hunter going wild with muffled oohs and ahhs, but Trent stayed focused on watching the front door to make sure no one else came out. After a minute, he turned back to Gage who stood on the porch, close to the steps, with his hands in his pockets, and his crooked grin still on his face.

"I'm sorry. It's no wonder there are hardly any second dates. They don't know how to act right at all. I'll have to work on it," Trent said, moving closer to Gage.

"I think they're charming and love you very much," Gage said, staying rooted in his spot in front of the steps leading down to the sidewalk.

"They do love me, but I think charming is a nice word for wildly inappropriate and crazy as hell," Trent said, coming to stand right in front of Gage. He would have led them down the steps, but Gage didn't move. He stayed there, blocking the path.

"It's all fine. I was nervous when I came in but they're so comfortable and easy to be around, they helped settle me down," Gage said. The breeze blew gently, with a bit of a nip in the air as the night grew dark, yet Trent didn't feel any of it. Gage's words confused him and his gaze went immediately to Gage's face, searching. He couldn't wrap his mind around how Gage could possibly be nervous. And then Trent's own anxiety struck him in full force, he could feel the need to fidget and ran his hand down the front of his lapels before he dropped his hands back in his pockets, matching Gage's stance as he stood directly in front of him.

Gage stood, quietly staring at Trent, with his fist clenched and tucked in his slacks pockets in order to keep from reaching out to touch the man who had haunted him for last six days. Trent looked exceedingly gorgeous in every way—from the toned, buff body, to the hard, chiseled face and all the way down the brand new suit he wore so well. Tonight, something about Trent seemed to call straight to his soul and he knew that from the minute he pulled into the driveway. Gage had panicked a little sitting behind the driver's seat. His breath hitched as he looked over the small suburban house. Without question, he knew if he went through with this date it wasn't going to be the usual one night stand; he'd be connected here and yet he'd still opened his car door and walked the steps to the front porch.

Trent's family met him with excitement, and he loved watching Trent interact with them. He could tell Trent tried hard to be the man of the house, but his family came with too much personality to do such simple things as follow a few well-placed rules.

"You're nervous?" Trent appeared surprised by the thought.

"Mmm hmm, I've never dated anyone. I've actually never been on a date; not that I can remember anyway. This is a first for me," Gage said, still not moving, only standing there watching this stunning man in front of him.

"Well, you're doing great. I never would've guessed this is a first for you," Trent said.

"Mmm... Well, let's see, I scheduled dinner at Sapore di Casa. I thought we would start there, then maybe dancing if there's time," Gage said, watching for Trent's reaction.

"I should probably be home early tonight. I have a crew starting at six in the morning. I've got this bear for a boss on a remodel I'm working," Trent said, a hint of a smile tugged at his lips and Gage laughed.

"Well, then, we better be off. I moved our reservations back a little. Oh and from here on out, I get the doors. I asked you on this date—had I waited for you to ask I would have been a very old man— since I did the asking, I get the doors. And I pay the bill tonight. No question or fight about it, got it?" Gage said, he loved this new look on Trent's face. He loved when Trent smiled, but this look of pursing his lips together, his brow narrowing while forming his reply, was absolutely one of the hottest looks he'd seen, and he stepped in closer, losing the debate going on inside him. His eyes focused on Trent's lips as he spoke.

"It's only right. You can do it when you do the asking. I find I'm looking forward to ending this date. Your lips have been foremost in my thoughts since I first laid eyes on them," Gage whispered, slowly leaning in.

"Daddy, go so we can watch you leave." Emalynn stuck her head out the door seconds before Gage made lip contact for the first time with this man of his dreams. Trent's breath rushed out, sliding like a balm over Gage's face, and he turned his head to the front door.

"Em, go inside and tell Sophia to stop making you do things like this," Trent said. He turned back to Gage, worry set in his eyes. "I'm sorry."

"No, don't be sorry. We do need to get going. Besides, anticipation's an enticing reward in getting you home early," Gage said wiggling his eye brows with a gleam in his eyes. He stepped away as he extended his arm for Trent to lead the way. Trent gave a smile, and if he was interpreting correctly, looked a little disappointed by the interruption as he walked forward and then down the steps. The smile, though, completely melted any part of Gage's heart which remained his. He loved Trent's smile and vowed again to see it there more often. As he followed behind, taking the few steps down, Trent spotted his car, stopping in his tracks.

"Oh my God, it's a Ferrari, Gage. You drive a Ferrari? You drove a Prius last night..." Trent said. The night was full-on and they stood in a darkened area of the walkway leading to the driveway. It gave Gage the opportunity to step forward and brush his hard-on against Trent's ass. He wrapped his arms around Trent's waist and slid one hand down the length of his body to see what might be going on inside his slacks. He wasn't disappointed with the feel or the slight roll Trent's hip gave into his hand during the brief touch.

An intake of breath pushed Trent back further against Gage's chest, more into the circle of his arms, and Gage breathed in Trent's scent while running his nose along his neck. Gage didn't move or blow it off as an accident. Instead, he tightened his arms, pulling Trent even closer to his chest. Judging by where they stood, Gage didn't think they could be seen from the window or the front doors because he couldn't see the children or Sophia.

Finally, after so many long agonizing days, Gage got to hold this man in his arms, and he couldn't bring himself to let go. His heart pounded in his chest. He could feel Trent's heartbeat matched his own. Gage stood slightly taller than Trent, but not really enough to matter, and he bent his nose in, allowing it to make contact with Trent's skin, before running it up into the back of his hair. Gage smiled when Trent finally lifted his arm to hold his head in place, sliding his fingers into the ends of Gage's hair.

"I love your scent. You'll have to tell me what it is so I can make sure you never run out," Gage whispered into his hair. He could feel Trent wanted him as much as he wanted Trent. After days of trying to convince himself this would never happen, it felt so good to finally have this one in his arms.

Trent stayed quiet. After a moment he turned his head, giving a sideways glance back at Gage. He used his hand in Gage's hair to pull his face closer in. The moment their lips touched, Gage thrust his hips forward in such need, and Trent pushed his ass back, grinding their bodies together. Gage licked out immediately, wanting in Trent's mouth with a desperation he'd never experienced before in his life. Trent slowly turned in his arms, opening for him and then deepening the kiss. Gage surged his tongue forward, welding their mouths together. Trent was impossibly intriguing and incredibly hot. He plunged his tongue deep inside, basking in the taste of this man in his arms.

Gage wrapped himself around Trent, sliding his hands up under his suit jacket, pulling Trent fully against his body. The kiss was hot, but tender, and went on for several long minutes. Both were rigidly hard, brushing their cocks against one another. It was the most erotic kiss of his life and Gage had had some kisses. Never had one turned him on like this stolen kiss in a darkened neighborhood of a Chicago suburb. He wanted this man. God, he wanted him badly, but he wanted Trent long term. The thought of wanting this man for many years to come stunned him and made him feel like a happily drowning man.

Gage slowed down, forcing himself from the kiss, until he pulled free enough to place small nibbles along the outside of Trent's lips. He could feel Trent's desire to take the kiss deep again, but he held off, wanting to do this right because Trent tried so hard to be that kind of man, the kind that did things right.

"I've wanted your kiss for days, and dear Lord, I wasn't disappointed. Thank you," Gage said in a whisper into his ear. He pulled back slightly, unable to bring himself more than a few inches from Trent's jaw and neck. "I have something to look forward to in bringing you home tonight."

"We could skip dinner," Trent began, his voice husky and deep with need. Gage stopped and forced himself to push back to where he could at least look at Trent.

"I find I need to do this right by you. It's a strange place for me to be, so let's not question it. Let's just get in my car and drive to our reservations. Now, you were saying something about my car, do you approve?" Gage said, stepping back, but keeping his hand in Trent's. It took Trent a minute to answer, and when he did, he looked over his shoulder at the car.

"It's a Ferrari. I was going to offer we drive my truck, but you drive a Ferrari. Is it yours?" Trent said, turning back from looking at the car, entwining their fingers tighter together. Trent didn't seem to want to let him go either.

"Of course, it's mine! Who else's would it be?" Gage asked and only released one hand to walk past Trent, taking him to the car.

"I don't know, but it's a Ferrari." Gage was pleased to see how excited Trent acted over the car. He'd hoped to impress him when he brought it out tonight. As they made their way out of the shadows, Gage saw Trent's kids still stood peering out the window. He could see their excited faces. Trent and Gage turned to wave at them, until Sophia finally shooed them away from the window, closing the curtain.

"They're an incredible family," Gage said, opening the car door for Trent.

"I know, they're just excited," Trent said, allowing Gage to usher him inside the car

"I'm glad they're excited. So am I." Gage reached in before shutting the car door and turned Trent's face up to him, quickly kissing his lips. He stayed close as he spoke. "It cost me to pull away from your kiss back there, Trent Cooper... It was about the hardest thing I've ever done. I'm not sure it will happen too many more times. Be ready when you ask again," Gage said, looking down at Trent's upturned face. He didn't wait for an answer, but shut the door firmly before making his way to the driver's side.

Chapter 11

No matter what he'd seen around the world nothing compared to Chicago at night. The huge sky scrapers were lit up against the dark backdrop of the lake, drawing people in like flies to honey. The city looked alive and full of life. Because it was Monday night, the traffic stayed light the entire way in. Trent was quiet for most of the ride. His hand entwined with Gage's, even as he shifted the gears pulling on and off the highway and down through the city's streets. Comfortable silence surrounded them, and they listened to the local rock-n-roll station. Every so often he or Trent might say something, but it never grew into a full blown conversation.

When Gage had dressed for the night, he'd told himself he would take things slow, keep it casual, and end the date with the traditional first kiss, but like everything between the two of them, nothing went as planned or stayed casual. He already felt a deep connection to Trent and couldn't help but kiss him, just like he couldn't help but hold his hand now. He needed to touch Trent. His life seemed to depend on the occasional absently-given swipe of Trent's thumb across his knuckles. Besides, it was appropriate to take Trent's hand; after all, they'd shared their first kiss. It was done and out of the way. Completely and devastatingly sweet, it made Gage long for so many more just like it.

Gage was so caught up in the sheer romance of this date he refused to allow Trent to take the night away from him by moving it straight to sex. He liked the idea of taking Trent out on the town, giving him time away from the children without an obligation of anything more. Gage wanted to spend his time and his money on Trent tonight, wining and dining him. The feel of Trent's hand in his made him feel strong and worthy. He never wanted to let it go. That thought led to another. Gage found he loved everything he knew about Trent Cooper and how very unexpected was that?

"You look very nice tonight," Gage said, weaving through traffic.

"So do you," Trent said, giving him a sideways grin and effectively stopping Gage's heart.

"I didn't think I could like your look any more than those low lying Levi's, but you proved me wrong." Trent turned to him, giving a grin and perhaps even a small blush darkened Trent's cheeks. A blush. How long had it been since Gage saw one of those? It sent his heart slamming in his chest and he jerked his eyes away, swallowing back the play of emotion tugging at his heart. After a minute or two, he brought their joined hands up to his lips and kissed Trent's knuckles.

"Your grins touch my heart," Gage said, expertly navigating the streets of downtown Chicago only as a man who grew up there could. Trent didn't know his family owned the building they were headed toward as well as many others in this city. Gage never shared this information with anyone and certainly had never used his connections to impress another. He pulled the car into valet parking. "I hope you like Sapore di Casa. It's the only place I knew with complete certainty we would have a quiet atmosphere so we might talk and get to know one another."

"Mr. Synclair, good evening, sir. It's been a while," the valet said, opening his door.

"Hi, Harry, you're supposed to call me, Gage. How many times do we need to go over this?" Gage said, stepping from the car, watching as they opened Trent's passenger side door. *Damn, I wanted to get his door...*

"At least once more, sir," the valet said. Gage chuckled at his family's valet who'd serviced their cars for well over thirty years, virtually all of his life. Gage never stopped, but rounded the car to Trent, ushering him inside through the front doors of the property.

He liked Harry and would normally have stayed a minute to get caught up on his life, but he worked in stealth mode right now, trying to keep his family out of their way for a little while longer, to keep Trent in the dark as to who his family was in this community. Besides, who knew what his parents would do if they found he contemplated settling down and dating, living a normal life, but certainly it would include them being in his personal space, and he wasn't ready to share Trent with them yet. Hell, all this emotion coursing through him was new, and he couldn't comprehend the feelings going on inside him, but their kiss sealed the deal, firming his resolve to figure out where this might lead.

The doors to the skyscraper opened automatically. This particular building held an entire world within the structure—shopping on the first several floors, office space on the next, and living spaces to the top. The building hopped with shoppers on the main floor, and security gave him a nod as they passed by. Gage moved quickly again, taking Trent's hand, moving him along at a fast pace to the bank of elevators leading to the top floors.

"Trent, have you ever been to Sapore di Casa?" Gage asked, trying to find something to say as he hit the elevator button and waited for the doors to open. He usually went through his secured entrance on the fourth floor, but that would be a dead giveaway as to his ties to this building.

"No, I haven't, but I've heard of it. I almost got the bid on the electrical if I remember correctly. I think the contractor doing your gallery is the one who did the work on the restaurant," Trent said, dropping his free hand into his slacks pocket.

"They probably did, it makes sense. I eat here regularly, at least every time I come home. It's cozy, has a good feel, quiet, and I love the chef," Gage said, scooting Trent into the first elevator doors sliding open. Gage pressed the appropriate floor at the top of the building and turned back to Trent. Their fingers were still locked together. The hold felt so natural. Gage's concentration had been focused on getting them inside the building unseen by any of the regular staff or his family, and he'd forgotten for a minute that he finally had Trent within his grasp. He'd neglected this opportunity for too long, and immediately corrected his mistake by stepping into Trent's personal space, a smile tugging at the corner of his lips.

"I want to kiss you again. Would it be too big a scene to kiss you here in front of the others?" Gage said, four other people filled the small box. As luck would have it, all four got off after a two-story ascent, not riding the other fifty or so stories up with them. Gage didn't hesitate and took the opportunity of privacy, pushing Trent back into the corner, his lips on Trent's in a matter of seconds. Trent opened immediately for him, spreading his legs apart, drawing Gage in as the kiss deepened to a frenzy. Gone was the sweetness of the last kiss, to be replaced with a hunger building inside both of them. Gage's hard-on punched forward at the flavor of the sweetest lips he'd ever tasted. Trent kissed him as if they were made for one another. There were no awkward moments. They were fluid as if they had done this for years.

The kiss lasted until the ding sounded to announce their arrival at their floor. So many times Gage rode this elevator thinking it to be the slowest one in the history of all elevators, but tonight when the bellhop to the restaurant stood outside the elevator door, clearing his throat, Gage knew he got it wrong. He needed to talk to maintenance about slowing it down for any future dates he might have with Trent. Gage pulled from the kiss, but not the embrace.

"Your kisses undo me," Gage said. He was rewarded with Trent slowly opening his eyes, a dazed glassy look staring back at him. Trent didn't let him go, but pulled Gage tighter against his body, grinding his hips into Gage's.

"Is that you, Mr. Sinclair?" the bellhop asked discreetly.

"Yes, Johnson, and we're coming, right, Trent?" Trent looked around, startled. Gage could see the moment he realized where they were and what ended the kiss.

"Come, let's have dinner," Gage said, taking a step back, but he still kept his back to the bellhop. His rigid cock raged. He took the moment to adjust himself and button his suit jacket together before he turned. Gage ran a hand down his front, making sure nothing stuck out too badly and looked back to see Trent do the same.

"I like your reaction to our kisses, handsome," Gage said with a wink. The beeping on the elevator began in earnest, which meant Johnson forced the elevator doors to stay open.

"Sure you do, until I completely embarrass you by stepping out of the elevator with my dick sticking straight out," Trent whispered. He looked up at Gage as he pulled his clothing together. The stain of the blush was back on his cheeks and Gage chuckled at his words.

"I assure you, it wouldn't embarrass me in the least. Actually, quite the contrary, I believe I would love it because everyone here would know I brought on this reaction in you and you were mine. No one else's for the picking," Gage said. The words were uncensored and completely caught Gage off guard after he spoke them. Johnson looked surprised, his eyebrows lifted, and his gaze shot straight to Gage, then to Trent, before he diverted it downward.

It seemed every time he put his lips on Trent, a new round of possessive, caveman thoughts came barreling to the forefront. He'd never cared whether anyone he brought chose to leave with or without him. Actually, if he were being truthful, he never brought anyone anywhere, so to care if they left with another would mean he needed to care enough to bring someone with him. Mentally forcing himself to slow it down, Gage extended a hand, letting Trent walk in front of him. The bellhop kept his eyes averted, but a smile wreathed his face until they were off the elevator.

"Would you like me to escort you to the restaurant, Mr. Synclair?" Johnson asked.

"No, Johnson, I know the way. Thank you," Gage said.

They took a long hall to the end and then turned to the right. There were a couple of steps down to two large glass doors. Gage insisted he get the doors, and Trent allowed him, which he loved. Gage liked this role and in an evening of many firsts, he knew he wanted more nights where he opened the door for Trent. They were staggering thoughts to a confirmed-for-life bachelor, but since birth, once he got something in his head it was going to be just like that and apparently both his head and his heart wanted Trent beside him.

He gave his brain a good talking to as he walked up to the maître d. They were only on the first of many steps involved in dating and relationships. Although in his mind, they were already an old married couple. Many more steps needed to occur before he let Trent in on his plans to be his one and only.

"Good evening, Mr. Synclair. Let's see, you aren't sitting in your usual table, tonight..." The maître d asked, looking over the table chart on the stand.

"Jean-Paul, I think we would like something along the back wall tonight, looking out over the lake," Gage said, looking back at Trent who stood gazing around the room. Gage couldn't judge his reaction, but he hoped Trent was impressed.

Jean-Paul only nodded. "Follow me this way, gentlemen."

The restaurant looked busier than he expected it to be for a Monday night, but the table he chose earlier in the day while making the reservation stayed vacant and waiting for them. Located in the far right hand corner of the restaurant, it gave the best view of both the lake and downtown Chicago. As instructed, Trent was seated where he could easily see both. Gage did the maître d's job and pulled the chair out for Trent. He saw the move startled Trent, but he sat, allowing Gage to push the seat forward from behind. The table was small and intimate, keeping them close together no matter where Gage chose to sit, but he took the seat directly to the left of Trent. Jean-Paul handed each one their menu and began reciting the specials of the evening.

"Tonight's specials are the Veal Chop Alla Armani and the Bistecca Alla Zorich. Mr. Synclair, your usual bottle of wine?" he asked.

"Yes, thank you, Jean-Paul," Gage said, looking up at the maître d as he gave a slight bow and left. His eyes lowered to Trent, who opened the menu, a confused expression came over his features as he scanned the page, causing Gage to chuckle.

The menu was written in Italian or so Trent assumed. Of course, no prices lurked anywhere to be found. He lifted his gaze and looked out along Lake Michigan. The sheer opulence overwhelmed him. As long as he'd lived in Chicago, he'd never witnessed anything quite like this. He knew it existed; big money makers were scattered all over Chicago, but he'd never been invited to anything near as nice.

The tables were spread out with four or five feet between them. Not anything like the restaurants he frequented, where as many tables as possible were shoved in a room, turning over every thirty minutes. Every table here seemed to be placed for privacy as well as viewing advantage. To his left, the city sparkled in the night for as far as the eye could see, and from the right, the lake waved and rippled under the constant glow of the moon.

On a whim, he turned in his seat, looking back over the restaurant and a dreadful thought occurred to him. He'd only brought a hundred dollars with him tonight and who knew if there was any room on his work credit card. Every bit of the supplies bought for Gage's gallery had been purchased on his company card. The American Express edged dangerously close to maxed out, at least until any of his receivables came in. He'd been so absorbed in Gage, it never occurred to him to grab his debit card or checkbook from the truck before coming out tonight. Gage mentioned something about paying, but he couldn't and shouldn't let him do that.

It would be more appropriate for him to buy Gage's meal. After all, Gage was technically considered his client. Trent turned back in his seat and lifted the menu again, studying it hard. Surely to God his meal wouldn't be over a hundred dollars, even in such a fine place. But what if it were? What were his options? He scanned the menu, trying to decipher anything that might look like a price. The only option he could see, he would have to call Sophia, and ask her to bring him his debit card and wouldn't that be totally embarrassing? He could feel the heat of a blush coming to his cheeks as those thoughts caused his brow to narrow even further.

"Do you read Italian?" Gage asked, drawing Trent's attention back to him.

"No, not at all," he said, but bit his lip as the answer dawned on him. He should order something simple. A salad or maybe an appetizer, surely even in a place like this neither of those would cost over a hundred dollars.

"You sure look like you're trying to," Gage said with a wink.

"No, I was trying to decide how hungry I am. I think something simple. Maybe a soup," Trent said and lowered the menu, placing it carefully on the place setting beside him.

"Ahh, Trent, I think you should try the special tonight. It's a marvelous dish from an extremely sought after chef. I remember doing a tour in Italy and running across him back when he first started out. I'll never forget the extraordinary meal he cooked for me. It didn't take too long to get him here. His filets are the most tender you have ever eaten. Please allow me the opportunity to order for you. If you aren't hungry, you can just taste it."

Gage said it all while reaching across the table to place the menu on top of his before reaching over to retake Trent's hand, lacing their fingers together. Gage rested their joined hands on the table before starting the slow, sensual rub of his thumb along his skin. Gage's thumb reached in and gently caressed his palm. A small electrical current shot up his arm and landed in both his heart and his dick with every swipe. Before things went much further, and he lost all his ability to think straight, Trent decided to try honesty.

"Gage, I'm not sure I brought enough money to cover this meal. I don't know what I was thinking. Well, I know what I thought... I thought we would be at the Chili's close to my house and then back home within a couple of hours. It didn't occur to me we might come downtown. It should have, but it didn't," he said, and the blush in his cheeks grew hotter with each word he spoke.

"Babe," Gage said, leaning in closer to him as the waiter came forward with a wine bucket to sit beside Gage. The waiter went through the steps of opening the bottle of wine with a friendly smile in place. Gage sat back, pausing so the waiter could complete his task.

"Hello, Mr. Synclair. It's a nice evening out. Will you be having the special, sir?" the waiter asked while working the cork out of the bottle and pouring one glass, allowing Gage to test the wine first.

"Yes, I do believe we've decided on two specials please." Gage took a sip of the wine, savoring the taste. "And the wine's perfect." The waiter poured another glass for Trent, placing it in front of him. As the waiter looked at him, the warm smile he gave Gage was gone. Something close to animosity radiated from the young man's face before he looked away. Trent recognized that look. This waiter had spent time with Gage, probably recently if the guy were this upset by Trent's presence.

Gage took up the conversation again once the waiter retreated from the table. "Babe, listen to me. I invited you out. I did the asking. This is my date to pay. You invited me to your McDonald's last night. I let you pay and never said a word. I also let you get the doors. Now it's my turn."

"A Coke is a way different thing than a menu with no pricing, Gage," Trent shot back.

"That may be, but it's still where I chose to bring you. You're my date tonight," Gage reiterated, sitting back in his seat, picking up his glass of wine with his free hand and taking a long drink.

"All right, I can't see how I have much of an argument, but the next time is mine, if there is a next time. I have a change in subject though. You were with the waiter who served us, but I can tell by the look on your face you don't even remember, do you?" Trent asked.

"Of course, I remember...well, I try to remember... Do you remember all your times?" Gage asked. He never released Trent's hand and sat there looking perfectly relaxed.

"No, I guess I don't, but you haven't been back in town for more than a couple of months," Trent said.

"Hmm... Yes, that's true..." Gage sat forward and placed his wine glass back on the table. He leaned in toward Trent drawing their joined hands up for a small swipe of a kiss across Trent's knuckles. "Let's talk about how you've followed my career. It may help in rebuilding my confidence back to my fragile heart. You've given me a good run, Trent Cooper. I was convinced I lusted after a straight married man. I do believe you'll have to spend some time making it all up to me in the very near future."

He watched as if the world were in slow motion. When those lips caressed his hand, the sensation sent his heart slamming wildly in his chest and his skin tickled under the touch. After a small pause, he finally asked, "You thought I was married?"

"Yes, your Auntie Crazy came to the gallery with the kids the afternoon before the panel change. Since my new favorite pastime includes watching you do anything and everything, I saw you all outside. I must confess I eavesdropped on much of the conversation while you were outside. I could hear them calling you Daddy. You're all a very pretty family. The kids look like you, Emalynn especially. I would have no idea they weren't your natural born children. You must have resembled your sister," Gage said.

"In some ways I do, she had a lighter complexion and naturally blond hair. She was a little thing, people thought we were twins when we were younger, but our differences were more pronounced the older we got. Hunter looks more like his dad while Emalynn looks just like my sister. I have pictures of Lynn when she was little. You can't tell them apart except my sister was blonder than Em," Trent said.

"You're a lucky man. The children are great," Gage said.

"I feel lucky most of the time, and I'm glad to be here with you, tonight. I'm glad it worked out. I was afraid you weren't gonna show. My last date met the kids the night before we were to go out and then he didn't show. Well, we planned for me to pick him up, but he wasn't home when I got there. They can be a handful. Hunter's at the age where he's picking at Em a lot. It can be a lot to handle. I think Em's about to start the *why* phase. Why is the grass green? Why is the sky blue? Everything is why," Trent said, abruptly stopping in mid-sentence once he realized what he just rambled on about. He'd talked to himself about keeping the kids out of any conversations tonight. They were on a date, no one wanted to be dragged down by more of his children's stories or his past dating debacles. Trent stopped the flow of words, and sat back in his chair, taking his wine glass with him. He kept his hand linked with Gage's, but looked out into the night, staying silent, not sure how to recover the conversation.

"My nieces and nephews all went through that stage. The oldest has to be ten now. The youngest must be two. There are eight of them. They're a loud mess when they get together. My brothers and sisters are a fertile bunch. I've watched them during our family holidays and always thought I would rather take a month in Haiti before I could imagine raising a child in today's world. But now, I have to admit, you make the job look very appealing," Gage said.

The compliment startled him, and he shifted his eyes immediately back to Gage, trying to figure out what it meant. He knew what it sounded like it meant, but surely not. The waiter interrupted them again. "Your dinner, Mr. Synclair."

The waiter never acknowledged Trent, but placed the plates in front of him. There were two large plates filled with food and his stomach let out an approving growl.

"Good, you're hungry. I thought you might be. I didn't see you take lunch today," Gage said and brought their joined hands back to his lips for another kiss, before he let go.

"Is there anything more I can get you?" Gage looked over at Trent first, then back to the waiter who had become distantly polite and nothing more than professional.

"Perhaps another bottle of wine, but nothing more, we're fine." The waiter reached for the bottle of wine, but Gage beat him to it, and topped off Trent's wine glass before they began to eat. Trent almost felt sorry for the guy as he retreated. His eyes stayed on Gage, and Gage never seemed to notice.

The dinner amazed, exactly as Gage promised. The meat seemed some sort of pork, slow cooked with lots of care. There were pasta dishes, salads, vegetables, the plates never stopped coming and their conversation never waned. They spoke of Gage's job, of his travels, and of which special reports Trent liked the most. At some point during the meal they removed their jackets and became more comfortable at the table. The conversations flowed naturally between them with no lulls as they sat and ate.

"I should be paying for my dinner," Trent said, taking his last bite.

"Handsome, I should be paying you for being such good company," Gage said. The waiter walked up at that moment, knowing instinctively when he could remove their plates. Gage kept the wine close by, topping off Trent's glass every so often throughout the meal and again before he relaxed back in his seat, reaching for Trent's hand once again. This time the caress became more finger play than actual hand holding. Gage ran his fingers through Trent's, extending each one, while constantly running his thumb up and down his palm.

"Your babysitter isn't on a time restriction tonight, is she?" Gage asked.

"No, Sophia's spending the night, but Rhonny will be home by eleven at the latest, if she wanted to leave," Trent said and looked out into the night, then around the room. They were alone, and Trent had no idea what time it was. "I guess it's close to ten now."

"I think so. Actually close to eleven by my watch," Gage said.

"Really?" Trent asked, surprised, and arching his brow. Gage was so comfortable to be around that he'd lost all track of time.

"Mmmm... the night has flown by. You're good company," Gage said.

"Thanks, but I'm afraid that's you. You have such an interesting life. There's so much to talk about," Trent said.

"Those are my thoughts on you." Gage's wide smile lit his whole face. "So tell me, this dating rule you started... I suppose it means no sex on the first date," Gage asked, staring at him as he spoke.

"In theory, it does," Trent said, his eyes never left Gage's, but his heart did pick up a slight beat. He wanted nothing more than to end this evening having sex with Gage Synclair.

"I've told you, I find I want to follow your rules. Give you the kind of a relationship you want, but a thought occurred to me a little while go," Gage said, but Trent interrupted him.

"Gage... I appreciate this effort, I do, but you don't have to say things like that. It's all right..." Trent's gaze never wavered from Gage. He simply lifted his hand, silencing Trent.

"My thought," Gage said, lifting an eyebrow, picking up exactly where Trent interrupted him. "This should technically be considered our second date. I do believe you invited me to McDonald's last night. I accepted and we went, so in my book, it was a date. So my question to you now, wouldn't this be our second date?"

"I see where some might say yes," Trent said, a smile spread across his lips.

"Good," Gage said. With no delay, he rose, pulling Trent with him. Trent went for his wallet while Gage gathered their suit jackets, handing Trent his.

"It's taken care of Trent. They bill me. Come, let's go back to my place," Gage said, stepping away from the table, holding a hand out for Trent to walk ahead of him.

"I thought you were in overnight construction mode, I'm not sure it's good for us to go back there," Trent said, stepping in front of Gage, questioning. Gage took the opportunity and closed the distance between them; his arm snaked out, hooking around Trent's waist as they stood there, chest to chest in the empty restaurant, looking at one another. He could feel Gage's arousal pressing into him, but checked the urge to rub up against it. Just barely.

"It is in overnight construction, but I have another place close by. You need to come with me and not argue. I'm finding it very hard to not push you back on this table and press those sweet lips to mine, again. I've never been more envious of a fork in my entire life. Now follow me, it won't be long," Gage said, grabbing his hand and taking the lead, guiding him through the empty restaurant.

"Should you check in at home?" Gage asked as they walked together to the elevator.

"They should all be asleep now. Let me make sure no one called." Reaching in his suit jacket he pulled out his phone, checking the messages. The only one he'd received came from Sophia, letting him know they were all sleeping in his bed, leaving him to sofa city for the night.

"Johnson, we need to go to my place. Is everything good, Trent?" Trent glanced up from his phone to see the bellhop holding the door open for him. When they were all in the elevator, Johnson pressed a button a couple of floors down and rode down with them.

"You live here?" Trent asked.

"Sometimes… It's been a base over the years. Johnson is anyone home this evening?" Gage asked.

"No, sir, not that I'm aware. There was a benefit away if I remember correctly," the bellhop said, keeping his eyes trained on the doors of the elevator, never looking back at Gage or Trent.

"Thank you," Gage said and turned to Trent, never releasing his hand. "Is everything good at home?"

"Yes, they're all asleep in my bed. I get the sofa when I get home tonight," Trent said, but stayed unsure as to exactly what was going on around him. Gage dodged the question of where he lived, but the bellhop clearly knew him. And who were the others Gage spoke of?

"Thank you, Johnson, and no one needs to hear of this," Gage said, extending a hand, anchoring the other to the small of Trent's back, guiding him to walk out the elevators first. Through a sideways glance, Trent thought he may have seen money exchange hands from Gage to the bellhop. The elevator opened to what looked like a hotel hall, but there were only two doors Trent could see and possibly a hall farther down. As Trent turned back to question Gage further, Gage's predatory gaze hit him and the man took a stalking step forward.

"Absolutely, sir," Johnson said as the doors shut behind him. They were only two floors below the restaurant.

"Where are we going?" Trent asked, backing away from Gage, panic filling his mind—panic that had nothing to do with that predatory stare, and everything to do with these living arrangements. Gage was already so far above him with just his worldly experience, but if he lived here, no way could he ever be in Trent's league. Trent had let his heart rule tonight, and he feared pieces already belonged to Gage. He knew if he attempted to name these feelings coursing through him where it would lead... *No!* He wouldn't let himself think it. Slowly, he forced some of the mental walls broken down tonight to slide back in place.

"My place... I told you," Gage said, stepping forward again seeming to like the chase Trent inadvertently started.

"You live here?" Trent asked. His heart began to pound in his chest at Gage's expression. This man looked so sexy, too sexy, and Trent's breath caught in his throat. He took a small step back as Gage reached out and pulled him forward, but he kept a hand between them, holding Gage away from him.

"I do, well, I have throughout the years whenever I'm home. I'm moving to the gallery, having my home base there. Now, I do believe there's way too much talking going on and not near enough of those sweet lips on mine, gorgeous," Gage said. Breaking through the barrier of Trent's outstretched arm, Gage wrapped his arms tightly around Trent's waist, tugging him in, chest to chest.

"Is this like a penthouse?" Trent asked, letting himself be brought forward, but he dodged the first kiss. Living in buildings like this, on floors this high, driving Ferrari's were for the extremely wealthy. He wanted Gage. He wanted to be fucking him right now, but another obstacle between them made its presence known. Gage was loaded and Trent was nothing more than a blue collar worker. He and the waiter upstairs were the same guy and his heart dropped as another wall fell into place, protecting him.

"No, of course it's not the penthouse." Gage glanced around the place as if trying to figure out what Trent saw that he didn't. "It's just an apartment. Why all these questions? I can see by the look on your face you're putting all those barriers back up. I just can't understand why when all I'm focused on is your lips being back on mine. Let's go for whatever this is happening here between us. I've never experienced anything like this before, and I can see no reason for you to distance from me. I won't hurt you, I promise." Gage pushed Trent up against the wall as he finished his speech. A ding sounded from the elevator at the same moment Gage placed the palm of his hand on Trent's cheek, circling around to his neck to draw him in for a life-altering kiss.

Gage pressed the length of his body securely against Trent's, and he was unable to do anything more than splay his hands across Gage's back and pull him in tighter, wrapping his arms completely around this man as he opened for the tongue thrusting forward. Trent was lost as Gage dived deeper inside his mouth, kissing him with a hunger and passion he'd never experienced before.

Chapter 12

"Hey, Gage, as hot as this show is you're putting on out here in the hall, you should remember you have a room. It's just down the hall and to the right," an unknown voice said. Gage pulled only inches away, looking back over his shoulder. Trent cocked his head around to see the guy standing behind Gage. The newcomer was a striking man who looked very much like Gage, maybe not as tall or as good looking, but still formidable in his own right.

"Little brother... discretion. We've discussed this in the past," Gage said.

"No, that was Garrett... I'm Gary... It's hard to confuse us, because I'm four inches taller than him. By the way, Mom's on her way up... and you're welcome. You owe me because I would have enjoyed *that* show," Gary said, chuckling. Gage moved quicker than Trent thought possible, ushering him down the hall to a random door. The hall looked very much like a hotel, but the door was unlocked and Gage opened it to one of the most luxurious homes he'd ever seen.

"Damn, Gage, this place..." Trent said, taking several steps inside the multi-level apartment with an open living area and floor to ceiling glass windows running all along the far wall, looking out over the city. He'd never seen anything like this and turned in a complete circle.

"No, no... I just got you alone. Just me... Focus just on me." The doubt was back in Trent's heart, and it must have shown clearly on his face. He took a step back again, needing space between them, but Gage would have none of it, stalking forward with purpose, drawing him back in while wrapping him tightly in his arms.

"It's you and me. Nothing more." He lowered his hand as he spoke, palming Trent's rock hard cock, and began to massage. The sensations dueled with those of his insecurity, and Trent became a drowning man, completely in over his head. The internal fight for which emotion would dominate his heart caused an ache as he closed his eyes and rolled his hips into Gage's hand.

When this night ended, if he let himself get any more emotionally involved, he'd be in the same position as the waiter. There could be no future with this man who held him, rubbing him so enticingly. They lived two completely different lives. Hell, his entire house would easily fit inside Gage's living room with room to spare. Trent would become the next forgotten someone in a sea of forgotten men, but in his heart, Trent had known all this from the beginning, and the dull ache in his chest increased at the thought. Trent broke his well-placed rules, and they were there for a reason. Even now, there would be consequences, but from this point forward he resolved to make it only about the sex, and he needed desperately to have sex.

"Trent, look at me. Nothing's changed. I can feel you want me, and dear God, I want you. Let me take care of you," Gage said in deep husky voice filled with need. As Gage spoke, he thrust his hips into Trent, their cocks rubbing against one another. The hand never stopped caressing his rock hard dick. This seductive grind became too much, his need too high, and Gage watched him closely. Gage seemed to know the moment Trent gave in, because he leaned in, slanting his mouth over Trent's, thrusting his tongue back into his mouth, and Trent met him greedily. The hesitation vanished, now everything stayed all about the sex. Trent matched the thrust of his hips, ramming himself further into Gage's hand, and pulled him even closer to deepen the kiss. Gage began to work his belt off and Trent helped, allowing his pants to drop to the floor with his underwear following quickly behind.

Gage's knees hit the floor seconds before he took Trent into his mouth. The slick steel of Trent's cock slid easily inside as if made to be there. He took him deep, all the way down his throat while he created an immediate gentle sucking. Gage trailed his fingertips up the inside of Trent's muscular thighs to cup his sac, rolling the balls round in his palm as he gently mashed them together.

"Fuck, Gage, that feels good," Trent groaned, his hand sliding over Gage's face, Trent's fingers caressing his cheek, jaw, and neck. Trent's free hand tangled into Gage's hair urging him on, rolling his hips, moving back and forth into the wet mouth. Gage brought the tip of Trent's broad head to the edge of his lips and groaned as he sucked him back deep inside, letting Trent deep throat him, going as far as he could go, savoring Trent's taste.

Over the last week, watching the bulge in Trent's pants, Gage decided the guy was hung, but what a treat to finally get this big, thick cock in his mouth. It turned Gage on like nothing ever had before. His own dick strained against his slacks, and the sounds Trent made caused him to drip with anticipation of what might be coming his way. Gage lifted his eyes to Trent's face as a new soft moan escaped his lips. Trent's hips began to solidly move in the rhythm Gage created with his mouth, and Gage forced himself to relax, taking Trent deeper down his throat.

Trent's eyes remained locked on his cock sliding in and out of Gage's mouth. The intensity in his expression caused Gage to grip the base tighter, work him harder, and increase the tempo with his mouth. The reward came as Trent's eyes rolled to the back of his head and his soft moan grew louder, letting Gage know he did everything just right.

"I can't take much more… it feels too good…" Trent said, and Gage picked up the pace, sucking him harder and deeper, moving in quick aggressive strokes. He moved his free hand to Trent's ass, holding him in place. He massaged Trent's ass, slipping between his cheeks, fingering the tight rim until he slid one finger slowly inside, all the while keeping up the sucking caress on Trent's cock.

"It's been too long, I'm coming…" Trent pleaded and tried to push back to free himself, but Gage held tight, sucking him hard. He wanted to taste this man. Trent's balls tightened and he bucked his hips, fucking Gage's mouth. Gage could only hold the pace as Trent took over completely. Within seconds the orgasm came, spilling out and down his throat in wave after wave of hot release. Gage stuck with it all the way through, milking Trent, making sure he got the last drop before releasing him.

While still on his knees, Gage took the moment to free Trent of his shoes and help him step out of his slacks. Gage rose, climbing up

Trent's body, keeping a tight hold of the man. Dazed was a good look on Trent, one Gage wanted there on a very regular basis. Trent rolled his head back between his shoulders, letting out a long pent up breath. Gage held on tight, feeling like if he let go, Trent's knees might actually give out.

"You were made to be in my mouth," Gage said, whispering in Trent's ear, running his nose along Trent's neck, into his hair. He breathed Trent in, relishing the taste of this man still on his tongue as he gave Trent the time he needed to recover for their second round. And no question about it, there would be a second round.

"Mmm," Trent murmured. It was all he got back as Trent straightened his head and opened his eyes, giving Gage a dazed expression and a small smile before he lowered his head, resting his forehead on Gage's shoulder, and whispered quietly, "Really good at that, thank you."

Gage reached between their bodies, pushing Trent's suit jacket off his shoulders. He never let go of Trent, but tossed the jacket in the direction of a living room chair a few feet away. He began to unbutton Trent's dress shirt with one hand from the bottom up. When Gage worked his way up to the top button, he reached both his hands up to Trent's face, gripping the sides of his head and brought Trent's face up, their eyes locking.

"You're built. I knew I saw a six pack under those work clothes you wear... I'm not finished with you, yet. Not by a long shot," Gage said, crushing their lips together, thrusting his tongue deep into Trent's mouth. Trent met him stroke for stroke as he began to pull Trent through his house to his bedroom. The only thing Trent still wore was his dress shirt and he made sure to discard it along the way.

The kiss never broke. Gage lost track of his way, stumbling into a random chair or wall, but they finally tumbled into the master bedroom. Trent made clumsy work of freeing Gage's belt and shirt, pushing the shirt down his shoulders, but forgetting to release the cuff links at his wrist. Gage didn't make it easy for Trent, refusing to remove his tongue from his mouth. On a frustrated sigh, Trent broke from the kiss, but Gage took advantage of the opportunity, pushing the male back onto his bed.

The drapes along the back wall were open, allowing the moonlight to stream in from the floor to ceiling windows covering the length of the bedroom. Gage's only concern focused on the man lying on his bed. Trent naked was a glorious thing. His long, muscular, hard, maybe a little brawny body appealed to everything inside Gage. Trent was perfect in every way, and Gage watched as he grew hard again, recovering quickly, exactly the way Gage wanted him. He watched the cock coming alive under his inspection, and smiled in what he thought of as his most wicked grin.

"You're gorgeous, Trent. You look very good lying on my bed," Trent pushed himself up farther on the mattress until he reached the pillows and hooked an arm behind his head to watch Gage undress. Trent's eyes stayed on him while he pulled his belt free and unbuttoned his slacks, letting them drop to the floor. His underwear followed, allowing his rigid length to spring free with beads of moisture already forming in anticipation of the naked man lying on his bed.

"Which way do you prefer? I'll go either way," Gage asked, moving to the bed, but not yet climbing on. Instead, he stood at the end, looking down at Trent while removing his cufflinks.

"I'll go either way, too," Trent said, and his dick jerked as he said the words.

"I want to see you better, Trent. The moonlight isn't enough. You're sexy as hell and you've tantalized me all week." Gage walked around the bed to the nightstand and pressed the switch, bringing the lamp to a soft glow. He carelessly tossed the cufflinks on the bedside table.

"But what do you prefer? Tonight's about you," Gage said. He finally tore his eyes from Trent's body, reaching a hand inside the nightstand drawer to draw out a small bottle of oil along with several packets of condoms.

"I prefer to bottom," Trent said in a deeply husky voice. Trent pushed himself to the center of the bed. "But I'll go either way, if it's your preferred way."

"It's been awhile?" Gage asked, letting his shirt slide off his body and drop to the floor, before crawling in beside Trent on the bed. A blush actually came to Trent's face at the question and he turned his head away as though formulating an answer. No matter how much Gage loved the blush, no way would he have any of this turning away business! Gage wanted Trent's eyes on him all night long. He hooked a finger under Trent's chin, bringing his face up to meet his. "Look at me, handsome, my eyes are up here... that's it, now, Trent, I want you so badly, but I want this right. We need to get you ready. I want nothing more than to be buried deep inside you, but I don't want to hurt you. We need to take the time to get you ready."

On those words, Gage flipped the lid to the bottle of oil, coated his fingers, and clicked the lid closed with his thumb. He absently tossed the bottle aside, keeping it in reach, before leaning down and capturing Trent's lips again. His tongue dove in, while his hand dropped low to gently massage Trent's rim and ass. He was tight, but Gage knew that already from fingering him before. Gage deepened the kiss, glad he took the time for the blow job; it would help in relaxing Trent.

The kiss continued, along with the massage he gave, and Trent reached up, snaking his fingers back in Gage's hair. Then he wrapped Gage in his arms, with one strong arm pressing their bodies together, mingling their cocks against one another. The entire time, Gage worked Trent, inserting one finger, then two, stretching and massaging him until his hips began to roll with the movement of Gage's hand. The kiss deepened with the sexy sounds of encouragement. Gage realized in a shocking moment, sex did seem to mean more when there were feelings involved, and Gage's emotions were most definitely involved. The connection between them was undeniable. He craved this to the depths of his soul. Gage wanted it to be right and perfect for Trent; therefore, he refused to rush, no matter what his cock might want at this moment.

Trent urged and begged him on, too, reaching low to grip Gage's dick. His hands were magic and just what Gage needed. Each touch landed straight in his heart escalating the emotions he couldn't define. Trent began to stroke him in earnest, moving up and down with just the right amount of pressure until Gage thought he'd explode, but he held fast, determined to take his time. He reached for the bottle of lubricate again, quickly snapped it open, and poured a few more drops directly on Trent's ass as he added his third finger.

Trent bent his legs and tugged, pulling Gage on top of his body, locking him between his knees. He begged Gage to take this further, but Gage kept his hand between their bodies massaging him, hitting all the right spots over and over. Trent had already completely recovered from his first orgasm of the night, but another threatened to undo him again quickly.

"Now… I need you now…" Trent pleaded.

"I want it to be good for you," Gage said, panting. His own cock begged him to move this along, but he held off, working Trent the entire time.

"Please, baby, I'm ready... I'm so, so ready..." Trent said, stroking Gage, while pushing him down by the cock, positioning him between his legs. "Now, please, I can't wait!"

Gage took over. He grabbed the oil again, drizzling several drops directly onto his cock as he positioned himself. He slid his hand through the lube, coating his dick while rubbing his broad head around Trent's wet, relaxed rim. Beads of moisture pulsed out in small bursts with each swipe he made. His breath caught in his throat, he was beyond ready for this moment. He slowly began to push forward. Gage closed his eyes as he eased the head inside the tight ring of muscle. The sensations took his breath away—Wait! He wasn't wearing a condom. How could he have forgotten? *Shit! Goddammit!* Gage jerked his eyes open and up to Trent's who looked back at him with such a look of anticipation it floored him. He lurched forward on the bed, but Trent grabbed at him, getting in his way, wanting to hold him in place.

"Condom! I need a condom!" Gage struggled free of Trent's hold, reaching far across the bed to the nightstand, fumbling with the packets. Several fell to the floor, but he managed to get one in his hand, lifting it as if he'd grabbed the million dollar prize at the bottom of the pile. Trent helped him position himself back between Trent's knees in a matter of seconds. His overwhelming need to be in this man caused him to be clumsy, and he fumbled the packet, but Trent lifted it to him and helped him put the condom on, coating it with the oil.

They worked together, and when done, Trent lifted his head, bringing his hands to Gage's face, kissing him. Only a small swipe of the tongue, but it settled Gage, calmed him, and Trent smiled as he lowered back to the bed. Gage positioned himself again and slowly entered, getting all of his broad head inside. Trent was tight, but very ready, and Gage's breath rushed forward, escaping his lips in the deep anticipation of the moments to come.

"You already feel so good," Gage said on an exhale while Trent laid back, letting an enticing moan escape his lips. Trent arched his body, lifted his ass by the heels of his feet, pushing Gage's cock farther down. That action was all it took. Gage slid in, anchoring his arms around under Trent's knees, lifting Trent's legs for a better position.

Inch by delicious inch, he moved deeper inside. It took everything for him to take it slow, but he wanted this to be as good for Trent as it was for him right now. His heart pumped wildly in his chest. Gage closed his eyes and ground his teeth together to fight against his need to take this man lying beneath him, to violently buck his hips and fuck him. His release hovered close to the surface, barely contained as he slid completely inside.

They both held completely still. Gage opened his eyes with his breath panting and sweat trickling down the side of his face with the exertion he used in keeping control. His eyes met Trent's and his heart lurched from his chest. This man was his. Trent Cooper was made for him. He released Trent's legs and they wrapped around his waist, encircling Gage. Trent's heels dug into his ass, his thighs clenched around his hips forcing him to move back and forth. Gage fell forward, catching himself on his elbows, tangling his fingers into Trent's hair and never stopped moving into this man who so deliciously surrounded him, encouraging him on.

Gage wanted to say the words coursing through both his heart and head. He loved this man in his arms. He'd never before made love to another, and it was perfect, better than anything ever before. Gage's rhythm broke and his hips slowed as his thoughts registered, staggering him. His movement became erratic, and he lowered his head in the crook of Trent's neck, breathing him in, taking a moment to gather his wits. He let this scent fill his soul, knowing it would always be there with him from this moment on. Instead of saying words that shouldn't come this early in their relationship, he reached down and placed a simple kiss on Trent's lips.

"Am I hurting you?" he whispered and pulled his hips back, bringing himself almost completely out of Trent before gently sliding back in when Trent's heels pushed at his ass.

"No, it feels good," Trent panted, giving the soft kiss back, but he rolled his head back, again arching his body forward when Gage slid out and back again.

"I like it hard," Trent whispered, his head still back against the pillow. Gage pushed out and thrust forward again with a little more force.

"I'll come," Gage whispered, dropping his head in the crook of Trent's shoulder, and he pushed back and forth again, grinding his teeth together trying to hold off with each thrust of his hips.

"I will, too," Trent groaned out, digging his heels into Gage's ass. Gage rose, anchoring himself on one arm and dug his knees into the mattress. He never stopped the flow of his hips, but picked up the pace, moving faster into Trent. He needed to give Trent the hard fucking the man wanted, but dear God, he couldn't hold back, he was already so close. He pistoned his hips and slid his hand down between their bodies to grip Trent's cock.

Trent reacted with a deeper moan, tightening the grip his arms and legs held around Gage. His lover's muscles strained, and he bucked his hips at the same time his heels dug hard in Gage's ass, helping drive Gage farther inside on each thrust. It became a tortured bliss. Gage began to stroke Trent to the same rhythm created by their hips. They were hard, fast strokes and Trent called out unintelligible words of encouragement while digging his heels harder into Gage's ass.

Trent gripped the duvet in his fisted hand seconds before he arched his back and thrust his hips against Gage. Burst after burst of creamy white pumped out onto his chest. Gage released Trent's cock and grabbed the headboard, gripping it with all his strength, but nothing held off the release building inside him. Trent was just too hot to watch and it felt too good. Gage bucked his hips forward and came with a force he'd never experienced before. His release continued, wave after wave, until there was nothing left.

With an effort, he managed to fall and push himself to the side, just missing Trent's chest as Gage's face buried in the pillow. He panted, his heart raced, and Trent's legs stayed wrapped around his hips, holding him inside. His ankles must have been crossed because the hold was still tight, even in this awkward position they laid in. Gage tried in vain to get a hold of himself to move, but Trent took care of that for him. He anchored his big beefy arm around Gage's body and pulled Gage on top of him, wrapping him tightly in his arms.

"We'll clean it up in a little while," Trent whispered, Gage securely tucked in his arms. He slid his legs down, keeping them wrapped around Gage until their feet tangled together. Gage had never touched anyone after sex, let alone held them, but he wrapped his arms around Trent, laid his head on his shoulder, and listened as Trent fell asleep in his arms as if it were the most natural thing in the world.

"You were perfect tonight," Gage whispered. Trent didn't stir, and he smiled, lifting his head to place a small kiss on Trent's shoulder. *I want this... I want you, like this...* He watched Trent sleeping. His own heart finally slowed, and his breath became normal, but he still just stared down at this beauty in his arms. Trent was at his most vulnerable, his features softened and his short hair spilling across his forehead. Trent Cooper was the most handsome man he'd ever seen. Gage wanted this moment, every single day. He wanted to fall asleep in Trent's arms and wake to him every morning. He wanted their nights filled with moments of love making, very much like tonight. "I want you to be my date at the gallery grand opening and I want you to say yes to me."

His heart felt complete and connected to Trent's like it never connected to anything before. No question in his mind, they'd made love tonight. Gage couldn't believe it had happened to him. He made love for the first time in his life, and it was to the man he loved, the perfect Trent Cooper. Resting his head back on Trent's chest, he laid there listening to him breathe and spoke quietly, telling him everything in his heart.

"These feeling I have for you are so strong. I've never had them for anyone before you. It's a little scary... but I simply don't run from fear, Trent. It's not who I am. I run toward it and I know now without question you're the end of this road. I want you. I want to be with you. I don't want you to keep me at bay... but I also do understand how lonely your life is... Trent, I get the reason for your compartments... I get it's a safety mechanism for you. I also get how let down you've been. Okay, for you, I'll try to take it slow, but it's not who I am. Just don't push me too far away. Let's do this... me and you..." Gage whispered it all, so quietly Trent's breathing never changed. He laid there sleeping, and Gage lay with him, praying it would all work out for them.

Chapter 13

Startled awake, Trent jerked open his eyes to see Gage propped up on one elbow lightly placing kisses on his lips. He still held Gage tight against him. Even in sleep, his arms were securely wrapped around the man, not letting him get too far away, and Gage seemed perfectly content in his embrace. Bonus for him!

"Hi," Trent said sleepily, giving Gage a soft kiss back, then let go with a deep, satisfying yawn.

"Hi, handsome, you snore. Not terribly, kind of softly, but it's still a snore," Gage said, resting his head on his hand his eyes scanning Trent's face.

"I like the little names you call me," Trent mumbled, still half asleep. Gage smiled and leaned in for a light kiss.

"Good, I seem to like to use them on you. You know, you're a perfectly made man. Everything about you is captivatingly sexy to me. I've thoroughly enjoyed you being here in my bed. I could get use to you here with me. Please know in no way is this a blow off, buts it's a little past four in the morning. I'm not sure what time the children wake up, but do you need to be there when they do?"

"Shit, it's four already?" Trent pushed up quickly, looking around for a clock, shocked to see it read a quarter past four in the morning. "I have to go. Shit! I don't even know where my phone is… What if they tried to call me?"

Trent untangled himself from Gage's hold and rose from the bed. Gage stayed in the same position, his head in his hand, his body bare, gazing at Trent as he moved about the room searching for his clothing. As an afterthought, he glanced down at his chest, rubbing a hand absently across his heart, realizing at some point Gage must have cleaned them. His heart gave a tug at the simple gesture of having someone take care of him. Trent ignored the need coursing through him, pushing him back in bed with the hottest man he'd ever seen laying there so seductively, just staring at him.

Instead, he let responsibility lead his actions. With an effort, Trent forced his head away from the super sexy Gage Sinclair and followed the trail of his discarded clothes into the living room. His slacks lay where they were dropped on the floor right off the entryway. He dug in the pants pocket, palming his phone, and checked for messages. Only one text from Rhonny showed on the screen from about midnight. It cost him time off his life waiting the two seconds for the message to come up on his phone. It simply read, *Everything is good here. You stay out as long as you want. I'll call you if we need you.*

"Is everything okay? I should have thought to bring your phone to bed with us," Gage said from behind him. Gage slid his body along the back of Trent's, wrapping his arms around his waist, kissing his neck before placing his chin on his shoulder.

"Yeah, it's fine, Rhonny's got everything under control. I should have thought to bring the phone to bed. I never forget things like that," Trent said, keeping his phone and pants in one hand, while sliding his other arm up, tangling his fingers in Gage's hair.

"I want to think it was because you were so taken with me you couldn't think straight. Don't tell me any different. Let me have this moment," Gage said, bringing his hand up to Trent's chin, pushing his face back toward Gage. He thrust his tongue forward as their lips met. The kiss lasted several minutes with his body stirring to life, before Trent developed a conscience and pulled away.

"I need to go, it's late. The kids will be up in about an hour or so," Trent said, turning in Gage's arms to hold him tighter. They stood bare chest to bare chest now.

"I was asking you a question when you fell asleep. Do you remember it, or do I need to ask it again?" Gage asked. Trent stayed silent, trying to remember anything they might have discussed. Nothing came to him. He didn't remember anything after tugging Gage closer to him.

"Ahh, well, I can see I need to ask again, and I'll have to work on my after love making repertoire. I don't want to bore you to sleep again."

"You didn't at all, I'm always—" Gage stopped him in mid-sentence.

"I was teasing, you were perfect, and I loved you falling asleep in my arms. This has been a night of so many firsts, this being another one. Now, Trent, pay attention, here I go again. I would like you to be my date to the gallery grand opening. Now before you say no, spouting all the separate parts of your life, I have to tell you I didn't invite any of the contractors involved in the rebuild and I would love for the children, as well as Rhonny and even Auntie Crazy to attend with us for a little while. I know Thursday's a work and school day, but we can have the children come for a little while and leave. I'll take you home when we're done. I have to leave Friday for a few days and I would like to see you again before I go. What do you say?"

Well, that was unexpected... Gage's date for the gallery grand opening... as in, see him again three days from now? Gage confused him completely. He narrowed his eyes and lowered his brow, trying to make sense of it all. Gage wanted him to be his date for the gallery opening? None of this made sense. "I'm not sure what to say. Honestly, I really thought this would be a one night stand."

"Well, did you not hear what I told you in bed?" Gage asked.

"Apparently not," Trent shot back quickly, as confused as before. They were still standing in each other's arms, nude in the living room, as though it was the most natural thing in the world to do.

"Hmmm... Well, it's your loss, but I meant every word I said. Now, what do you say about Thursday?" Gage asked.

"I think..." Trent started and chuckled. Gage stood before him nodding his head yes as Trent spoke. The kids would love it, so would Rhonny, and they never got to get out of the house together like this. Having them exposed to art and the artistic culture couldn't be a bad thing. Slowly Trent responded, thinking through it all as he spoke.

"I think it sounds good, very good. I think the kids and Rhonny would love it. She might even ditch class for the chance. Sophia's at month end with her job, I'm not sure she can break away from work to go, but I'll ask her if you're sure," Trent said, and a clock chimed in the room, reminding him of the time.

"I have to go. I'll need to call a cab," he said, stepping out of the circle of Gage's arms, pulling his slacks on, buttoning them up.

"Absolutely not, I'll drive you," Gage said, and padded back across the floor to his bedroom.

"I don't want to put you out. I should have met you in town," Trent called after him and put on his shirt where he stood.

"No, this is the way we're doing things. Besides I'm finding I like this old fashioned way of dating. And we agreed, we're dating, we said it in bed, and I made you nod your head in agreement, so you're stuck with me. I'll be picking you up from here on out," Gage called back to him.

"I like the sound of all that. I can't imagine I would have argued much, had I heard it," Trent said, smiling as Gage came back in the room wearing a pair of blue jeans, a T-shirt, and holding sandals in his hand. Trent slid his shoes, then his suit jacket, back on.

"I like the sound of it, too. I didn't want to risk it, so I asked while you were sleeping and helped you nod in agreement. It was a tough move to do. I didn't want to wake you. You've had me on a big, merry chase this last week. I won't be risking much where you're concerned," Gage said as he dropped his sandals on the floor and toed each one on. Trent placed his socks and underwear in his jacket pocket and looked around the room as Gage spoke. His newfound confidence slipped a notch or two with the sudden memory that this down-to-earth Gage was beyond wealthy. To think this could be any sort of meaningful relationship, which might actually work for long term, would be an error in his thinking. He'd be wise to remember it before his heart got too far out of control.

The clock blinked two in the afternoon and Gage reached over to flip the Keurig on. The lack of sleep last night finally made its presence known. Up until now, the silly smile he wore and the happiness in his heart overrode the fact he didn't sleep at all the night before.

After he dropped Trent off, he returned to the gallery, where the work crews were in the midst of a shift change. He got the latest update on their overnight progress. Gage went into his office, caught up on all the surveillance videos and several photo logs sent overnight, and then watched the live feed for several hours. Abdulla wasn't doing much more than sleeping, eating, and meditating all day and all night long. Gage found it all incredibly interesting, though somewhat boring to watch. Abdulla must be the most wanted, unknown man on the planet, and he currently sat in a mission on his hands and knees praying. Praying for what? For the hundreds, maybe thousands, of lives he tortured and sacrificed over the years? Or the women, who at his hand were stolen, kidnapped, sold, and repeatedly raped for nothing more than money in his pocket? Probably not those things. His evil deeds ran too deep, and he liked himself too much to just give it all up on a prayer.

Nothing in Abdulla's recent background indicated he'd found God in any way. Him being there had to have meaning. But what? The background reports on the priests, bishops, and other clergy in the mission were coming back indicating none had any sort of documented past. Gage spent hours thinking over the possibilities, but nothing made any sense at all. After becoming frustrated with piecing together the meaning of Abdulla's presence, he switched to planning for his upcoming trip. His flights were booked, his equipment being prepared, and his on-ground transportation ready. He scheduled Tuesday and Wednesday the following week as tentative reporting days, and notified Sid under the condition of extreme confidence to find him time for a breaking news special report. It gave him five full days on location before he began the report. He could check out the surrounding cities, hit some local bars, and see if he could find anything out on why Abdulla chose this path before he broke the story.

Next on his long to-do list, he placed a phone call to his buyer at Nordstrom's. Gage arranged to have the Cooper family outfitted for The Gallery's grand opening. The buyer, who he'd known since grade school, thoroughly questioned him about the purchase. Asking all the questions he knew his mother would ask her once she spread this information around. Who were these people, why did he do it, and if he were willing to donate to her latest cause to keep this quiet from his family.

Of course, Gage gave very little information away, just his open credit card to get them all ready for the evening as well as to donate a sizable amount to Doctors without Dolce, or whatever she pushed this week. But he gave two stipulations on the deal. First, take the price tags off everything they showed Trent and the kids. Second, the entire process needed to be done in Trent's home. He didn't want Trent or Rhonny to know what store provided the clothes.

He'd witnessed Trent's reaction to his penthouse and it wasn't good. Several walls dropped between them as Trent glanced around his living room again before they'd left this morning. Trent had shut him out and it was an almost tangible feeling. He'd fought the urge to defend himself, to tell Trent this wasn't really who he was as a person, but he couldn't explain it without bringing his family into the mix, and he certainly wasn't ready to have that conversation with his skittish new boyfriend.

Ahhh... new boyfriend... his boyfriend... Those words had never entered his vocabulary before, but he liked them, liked them a lot when applied to Trent Cooper. But he didn't want to have to continue breaking the walls down every time they were together. Gage wanted to move this relationship along, not start from the beginning over and over again.

Trent walked through the gallery with one of his electricians and the movement caught Gage's attention. They stopped at a lighting fixture where Trent used his hands while talking to the other man. Gage watched him for several minutes before he picked up the phone and called Trent.

"Coop Electric," Trent said without looking at caller ID.

"You're sexy dancing like that. We should have gone dancing last night. I would love to hold you in my arms, swaying back and forth... Mmmmm... And the club I frequent has excellent semi-private bathrooms," Gage said, smiling as Trent turned toward him, then quickly away.

"Hang on a minute," Trent said and dropped the hand holding the phone to his ear. "I have to take this. When you're done out front, come in here, tighten all these fixtures the way I told you," Trent said before lifting the phone back to his ear and turning toward the front windows. He stayed in Gage's view, but with his head turned away.

"I've arranged for a friend of mine to dress you guys for the grand opening. Now, I see you about to open your mouth and tell me no, but let me finish. She can come to the house when Rhonny and the kids are home and let them pick out some things. Then come back and get your measurements for a tuxedo. Unless you have a tux, then it's just for the kids. Now, go ahead and tell me no, I'm prepared," Gage said, watching Trent the entire time he spoke.

"Gage, you aren't buying my children something to wear. I'll take care of it," Trent said.

"Oh, really? And when will you do this? I have you working night and day until Thursday. No way you have the time. Now bring on the next argument," Gage said.

"I work it out all the time. I'll work this out. Thank you, but no." Trent turned to look at Gage as he said it. Gage wondered if he realized he'd turned to stare at him in the crowded gallery foyer. Gage stared back at Trent, pleased to not be hiding this between them, but he could see the stares Trent got.

"I like talking to you better when you're sleeping, you don't tell me *no* as much," Gage said.

"You know you keep referencing our conversation while I slept. At some point you're gonna have to tell me what you said and what you think I agreed to," Trent said, coming to stand right outside the front of the office. He was relaxed now, smiling, and the absolute hottest man Gage ever laid eyes on.

"I will, I promise. The next time I'm buried deep inside you, I'll tell you. As a matter of fact that may be another time I can ask you questions, you give me lots of yeses then, too," Gage said, giving Trent a wink and grin back. Trent just stood there, staring at Gage, the bulge in his pants growing more pronounced with each word he spoke.

"I'm hot for you, Trent Cooper. I can't get last night out of my mind... I loved making love to you," Gage said, his voice turning husky as he spoke.

"Me too," Trent said, very quietly.

"Good, I'm glad. I can't wait for the repeat. Now, back to this matter of the children's clothing. I have already paid. This is a longtime friend who needs this sale. Emmie and Rhonny will love having their new clothes brought to the house. Please say she can come tomorrow at three. If you need her to come here and measure you, she can or she can come back tomorrow night, handsome. Now say yes," Gage said, nodding his head to encourage the appropriate answer.

"Only if I can pay her directly or pay you back," Trent said.

"Deal," Gage said immediately.

"I don't trust that quick deal," Trent said. Gage laughed out loud. "Think you know me so well already? Well, you do, but you've agreed. What's Rhonny's number? I'll get Ladonda to call her directly and then call you to set up a time to be measured," Gage said.

"I'll text it to you, it's in my phone. I should go, I'm on a strict deadline," Trent said, lifting a hand to wave at him.

"Goodbye, sexy. I'll talk to you later," Gage said, disconnecting the call. Trent stood there a minute more, smiling, then turned and left the room completely oblivious to everyone staring at him and Gage. He couldn't force the grin from his face either, so he just dropped his head and began to type an email to the buyer, giving her Trent's number and Rhonny's when the text came through a few minutes later.

Unsure what small children ate for dinner, Gage parked his Prius in the front of the Gourmet Haven grocery store and hightailed it in to the gourmet dinner section. The lines for both the deli and the pre-made dinner counter were long, packed with people just getting off work. Gage did a wide sweep around the displays looking at all the food. The specials for the evening were roasted lamb and bacon wrapped asparagus or spinach, feta, artichoke salad. Both looked good to him, but he wasn't sure Em or Hunter would really like any of it after watching them go crazy over those chicken nuggets the other night. On second thought, if Trent's kids liked McDonald's he wasn't sure Gourmet Haven would be on their list of acceptable food choices. Reaching for his phone, he stood in front of the counter and decided to forgo the surprise of bringing dinner over. Instead he called Trent.

"Babe, I'm standing in Gourmet Haven, and I can't decide what Emmie and Hunter might like to eat. Oh, and what're you doing? Can I bring dinner over? I miss you already," Gage said, still looking over all the selections of gourmet dinners while trying to decide.

"I'm cooking dinner now and you don't have to come over, you have to be exhausted, Gage. I don't expect to see you every day," Trent said. Gage could hear all the activity in Trent's house. The TV blared, the kids were talking and the water or something ran in the background, maybe from the washing machine.

"Okay, well how about if I bring a pie or cake... Kid's like all cake, right?" Gage said, pivoting on his heels to the bakery down the aisle.

"No sweets before bed. The sugar hypes them up, but you can come over if you want. There's enough for you. I'm making grilled chicken, some sort of bagged rice deal, and fresh green beans they won't eat," Trent said.

"I don't want to be in the way, Trent, and Lord knows I have more than my fair share going on. I just missed my boyfriend and the things you promised me last night, but I don't want to mess up the flow of your night. I only wanted to spend a couple of hours with you before the crews finish up tonight and I need to be back to lockup," Gage said, walking through the double automatic opening doors back out into the parking lot, forgoing the plan.

"You know, you keep bringing this up. At some point you're gonna have to tell me what we talked about while I slept," Trent said. His voiced lowered until Gage practically had to shove the phone inside his ear to hear Trent speak.

"Are the kids right there," Gage said, climbing inside his car.

"Yep," Trent replied quickly.

"Can they hear me?" Gage asked, starting the car and then backing out of the spot.

"No..." Trent said.

"Well, you agreed to let me lick that tight ass of yours next time we're together," Gage said, grinning as he pulled out into traffic, heading toward Trent's house.

"I did not," Trent said, chuckling.

"You did, that was right after you agreed to be my boyfriend," Gage said.

"Boyfriend, huh? I think we need to make a new rule. When I'm sleeping, no talking," Trent said, and called out to the kids to settle down.

"No way! I told you, it's the only time you say yes. Well, it's not the only time you say yes; if I remember correctly, you called it out several times while I had you in my mouth... I'll be there in about ten minutes, babe." Gage disconnected the call, not waiting for an answer. No one in his circles would believe this side of him. He'd always been considered hard, focused, and stern with his career, and since he lived only for his job—before meeting Trent—that was how he lived his life. Now, he couldn't keep the smile off his face or the teasing banter from rolling from his lips. Whatever! He'd gotten an invite to dinner and he was spending time with his boyfriend. The night suddenly looked up.

"Trent, make him stay until I get home! I can't believe I'm going to miss him again. This is so not fair!" Rhonny said, actually stomping her foot with her books in her hands and her backpack slung over her shoulder.

"We'll see. Last night was a long night; he couldn't have slept much, and he was already at the gallery when I got there," Trent said.

"Then I'm not going tonight. I'll stay here," Rhonny said, this time with a very distinct whine in her voice.

"You have to go tonight, Rhonny. You're taking off Thursday night and we need you to do well on the LSAT, it'll help you stay in the country longer, honey," Trent said, turning off the grill and lifting the lid. He took each piece off the hot grill, balancing it on the plate in his hand. "You need to get out the door now. You're already gonna be late and remember the woman from the department store will be here tomorrow after school, so come straight home."

"I'll remember, but promise me you'll see if he can stay," she said, not budging from the spot.

"I will, now go, you're late already!" No sooner did he say it than the doorbell rang. He could hear the kids landing on the hardwood floor of his living room as they bounced off the sofa, running toward the front door.

"Daddy, he's here, he's here!" they both yelled out to him as if he couldn't hear the doorbell.

"It looks like you stalled long enough and he made some seriously good time," Trent said, juggling the patio door with his hands full and Rhonny right on his heels as the kids answered the door.

"Gage!" Em said, launching herself into his arms.

"Well, this is a great greeting. How are you today, Emalynn?" Gage asked, heaving her up in his arms, putting her on his hip. Gage only had eyes for Em as she answered his question, but he reached down and cupped Hunter's head with his hand. The gesture tore at Trent's heart strings. Gage seemed to genuinely like his children and it lured him closer to Gage, more so than anything else could have.

"I'm good. Daddy's in a good mood and said we can watch SpongeBob tonight while we go to sleep," Em said, her excited face turned, beaming in Trent's direction.

"You're lucky," Gage said, following Em's gaze to Trent who now stood in the entryway. "Hunter, how're you tonight?"

"I'm good," Hunter said, staying beside Gage in the doorway.

"Guys, let him come in," Trent said, breaking the spell weaving around him at seeing how pretty a picture the gorgeous Gage Synclair made while talking to his children. Trent took the door handle, ushering Hunter back inside. Gage dropped Emalynn back to her feet, and they both ran close to Rhonny. All three of them watched Gage as he came inside the house.

"Thank you for letting me come by. I missed you," Gage said, walking in the front door. He leaned in for a light kiss on Trent's lips. The click of a captured photo sounded in the background as Emalynn giggled the sweetest little laugh at the quick peck. It drew both their eyes toward Rhonny and the kids.

"Sorry, Sophia would want me to get this moment for her," Rhonny said, looking down at her phone, sliding her finger across the screen, Trent assumed to text the photo. He was horrified, but Gage seemed to love it and walked over to Rhonny.

"You must be Rhonny. I'm glad I didn't miss you tonight before you went to class," he said, holding his hand out to her.

"I am, and I'm so happy you got here this quick. I've heard so much about you," Rhonny said, her biggest grin in place.

"Me too, about you, Rhonny. Thank you for holding down the fort last night and letting me keep Trent out later than we originally planned," Gage said. Trent came from behind and placed the chicken on the kitchen table, only a few feet away. He watched Rhonny's reactions, grinning until he finally chuckled. Gage had that spellbound effect on people, and Rhonny's grin proved she wasn't resistant to his charm.

"Trent needed to get out of the house. It's been too long," Rhonny said. Trent immediately interrupted her. No way did he want this to turn into a poor Trent never got out of the house conversation. A worldly guy like Gage Synclair wouldn't be interested in a guy who couldn't find a date. Especially if everyone kept reminding Gage how easy it was to resist the current man he chose to spend time with!

"You're going to be super late. You have to get going," Trent said.

"Did the buyer contact you about tomorrow?" Gage asked, keeping his eyes on Rhonny.

"Yes, we're meeting here at three tomorrow afternoon. Thank you for helping out in that department. I wouldn't have known what to wear," Rhonny said.

"Anytime. Only make sure you pick something you like and can wear again or not, whatever you want," Gage said while tucking his hands in his pockets as he spoke. Gage had done it again, drawn Rhonny back into him, looking at her as if she were the only person on the planet who mattered to him.

"Rhonny, *go!*" Trent said, jerking her out of her haze.

"I am, *old man*! Bye, everyone," she called out, causing them all to laugh as she took off out the front door.

"You two, wash up. Dinner's ready," Trent said, but neither child budged.

"Is Gage staying for dinner?" Hunter asked.

"Yes, now go wash up," Trent said to the sudden cheers. They tore past him into the kitchen, Em trying to get to the sink first. He could hear their stepstools scraping on the floor. For the first time since Gage arrived they were momentarily alone, and Gage took full advantage of it, stepping in to Trent, wrapping him in his arms.

His head descended immediately, hovering above his lips as he breathed in Trent's scent and whispered quietly. "You were amazing last night. I thought about you all day. Just one kiss before we go in there." Trent opened for him, meeting Gage's tongue halfway until they were sliding and swirling together. The kiss was intense but brief, ending as the stools scraped back to their place in the kitchen. Trent kept Gage in the circle of his arms when he would have pulled away.

"Thank you for coming out here tonight. You have to be exhausted. Feel free to bail whenever you want," Trent said, looking Gage directly in the eye. Before, he'd always found a way to avert his gaze because Gage's stare reached out and touched his soul. But now, after watching this whole exchange in his front room, he seemed to crave those feelings, wanting the connection Gage seemed happy to give him and his family.

"I'm not leaving until I get some sofa time... It's been twenty years since I made out on someone's couch, and I think it was probably with a girl so it doesn't count at all. That's changing tonight," Gage said, pulling free of Trent's hold as Hunter and Em came around the corner.

"Daddy made my favorite tonight. Chicken and rice! Mmmm, it's so good! Gage, you're gonna love it," Em said.

"Can Gage sit by me, Daddy?" Hunter said.

"No, by me!" Em said.

"Stop it, you two. You'll scare him off before we even sit down. Get up at the table. I'll get your milk," Trent said, stepping away and herding them to the table. "Gage, you can have Rhonny's spot. Guys, show him where to sit."

Chapter 14

The table was set, loaded with the dinner Trent cooked. Gage took his seat in Rhonny's spot with both Em and Hunter on each side of him at the small table. Trent filled the children's glasses with milk and did a quick inventory of possible drink options. He stood at the refrigerator door looking over at Gage.

"I have a Chardonnay, probably something Sophia left. I have Heineken, Bud Light, tea, and water, what would you like?" Trent asked.

"The Chardonnay sounds good to me," Gage said.

"Got it," Trent said. He grabbed a Heineken and the Chardonnay bottle, pouring Gage a glass in his dollar store wine glasses. He made a mental note to pick something up a little nicer in the near future. Trent placed the milk glasses on the table in front of Em and Hunter and handed Gage his wine before he took his seat.

"It's not much, but I hope it's good. I'm not gonna lie. I'm not a super good cook," Trent said as he sat, scooping spoonfuls of rice and green beans on the kids' plates.

"Daddy, just three green beans," Em said.

"No, let's do four," Trent negotiated back. "It's close enough to your birthday for four."

"No, it's the rule, Daddy," Em said, pushing one of the four green beans to the edge of the plate.

"It smells wonderful and green beans are my favorite," Gage added, and after a minute, he smiled as Em pushed the fourth green bean back with her others on her plate. Trent put a chicken breast on each plate and started with Hunter as he began cutting them up in small bites for the kids to eat. Gage watched him for a minute, then took Em's plate and followed Trent's lead, cutting the pieces for Em. Dinner stayed pretty much like that through the course of the meal.

It surprised him at how easily Gage fit into his family. After last night, he'd tried to push Gage mentally away as best as he could. Making Gage something fun to play with until the socialite got tired of playing with the regular folk, but Gage transitioned between the worlds easily. There was no awkwardness as they sat in his small, outdated kitchen, and conversation flowed easily. The kids settled down with their excitement of having someone over and fell into their normal, comfortable conversation, as well. The whole thing pleased Trent, and he pretty much thought his kids were about the most well-mannered, easy to be around children in the world.

"Do you like my daddy?" Hunter asked Gage.

"I do, very much," Gage replied, looking up at Trent, giving him a wink.

"Why?" Hunter asked.

"Hunter," Trent began, but Gage cut him off.

"No, it's a fair question. I like him because he's smart, funny, handsome, and very strong. He can lift..." Gage said, and Hunter cut him off.

"He's the strongest dad in my class and he has the biggest muscles. He can beat up all the other dads. I know it," Hunter said, looking straight at Gage. Hunter's face remained serious as he spoke.

"Hunter," Trent said again, completely reevaluating the whole perfect kid theory from a few seconds ago.

"I'm sure he could. I watched him working today and he can lift very heavy things," Gage said. Hunter started to speak, but Em turned to Trent, a huge smile on her face.

"I told my teacher at school that my daddy's in love and gonna get married. Daddy, did you decide if Gage can come to my birthday party?" Em asked. Trent stared at her for the briefest of seconds just blinking, having no idea how to respond to the first part, so he chose to ignore it and concentrated on the second part of what Em said.

"Em, baby, you're supposed to ask me in private, with no one around. But I don't think he can come this time. He has to go out of town this weekend, right after the grand opening we're all going to," Trent said. Em's excited face fell with disappointment in her eyes as she looked back at Gage.

"Sweetheart, my plans might change. I *might* be able to be back early Sunday. If you can get me invited, I'll try to come, but please don't be upset if I can't be here," Gage said, tossing a green bean in his mouth.

"Daddy, please! In private, please say yes!" Trent kept his eyes on Gage, surprised. This was completely different than what he and Gage talked about last night. "Of course, you're welcome to spend the day with us, but be warned, it's an all-day deal. Em has us going to lunch, a movie, skating, and ending at Chuck E. Cheese," Trent said.

"I'd be honored to be there. Just please promise me not to be disappointed if I can't come. My flights might not work out right. Promise me and if I'm not here, we can all go out for the day when I get back," Gage said.

"Yay! Gage is coming to my birthday, Hunter!" Em yelled across the small table and did the happy dance in her booster seat.

"Em, he said *maybe*," Hunter said from across the table.

"Em, settle down and eat, your dinner's getting cold," Trent said, tapping the side of her plate with his fork. She did and managed to get all four of the green beans down, showing Gage every time she ate one.

The television played quietly in the background as Gage sat on the oversized, slightly outdated sofa waiting for Trent to get the kids to sleep. He reached over to the coffee table and grabbed the remote control, muting the volume in order to hear better as the children tried to talk Trent into letting them stay up a little while longer. Hunter was the negotiator and Em the closer. They double-teamed Trent with such success, he wondered if he should bring the Chicago Police Department out to learn their negotiation skills.

Hunter successfully bargained for both he and Em into Trent's bigger bed, with the bigger, better television, and got a full fifteen minutes more of cartoons before the television turned off for bedtime.

Trent tried to get them down, but they were wound up. Gage could tell his presence added to the problem tonight. The kids wanted to stay up, be with the company in the house and Trent was determined they were to stay in bed and go to sleep. Gage laughed because it seemed the three of them shared a common goal. They all wanted back in here until Gage left for the night.

After a minute more of listening to the bedtime exchange, Gage got up and went back into the small kitchen to begin washing the dishes from their dinner. Apparently the Cooper family ate dinner together at the kitchen table every night. Hunter wasn't so keen on that plan; he explained how his friends got to eat dinner watching television, but Trent made them sit together as a family and share their day.

It seemed dinner time also came with cleanup time because the kids celebrated not having to clean the kitchen tonight. This little family ate together every night, and then cleaned the kitchen together afterward before getting ready for bed. They did it all like a little team, which made this scenario another on the long list of reasons endearing Trent to him, driving him deeper inside his heart.

Now, as he looked down at the dirty dishes in the sink, he admitted he wasn't an expert on this whole dish cleaning thing, but surely he could clean these dishes without making a bigger mess. He looked around the kitchen and spotted the few things he needed. There wasn't a dishwasher, but a dish rack sat to one side, soap and sponge on the sink. He took a couple of steps forward to the sink and saw a disposal and then spotted the switch he thought might turn it on. Okay, well maybe he did have this...

Filling one part of the sink with water, he began the process of washing the dinner dishes. He dumped the food in the disposal, relieved when the switch turned on the device, and dish by dish, washed their plates, cups, and silverware. It didn't take long, and surprisingly, it wasn't the terrible chore he always thought it would be. There was actually something appealing in knowing he helped Trent in the heavy load he carried.

"What are you doing?" Trent asked from behind Gage. "No, don't do that. I'll get it later. No really, Gage. You're our guest, stop..."

"I'm on the last dish, and I believe it's only right, you cooked, I'll clean," he said from over his shoulder, but Trent would have none of it. He came to him, taking the dish from Gage, handing him a hand towel for his wet hands.

"No, really, please just stop. I'll do it after you're gone. There's something terribly wrong with *the* Gage Synclair in my house, doing my dishes," Trent said, rinsing the dish and placing it on the rack before sticking his hand in the sink and pulling the plug up, letting the dish soap run down the drain.

"I thought we were past all that," Gage said, wiping his hands with the towel, staying close to Trent, but turning around, leaning back against the counter. His eyes were glued to Trent's face, but the man wouldn't look at him as he sprayed the sink down and began putting everything away. "Trent, answer me. I thought we were past all this…"

"It's gonna take some time. It's hard to walk in here and see you at my sink, in this old, small kitchen, knowing where you live, what you do for a living… I think my house is the size of your living room," Trent said. He fished in a drawer and pulled out another dish towel to dry his hands and matched Gage's stance, leaning back against the sink. "Are you sure you really want to try and date? We come from such different places."

"We aren't so much different, not really. Not on the things that matter," Gage said, folding the towel in his hands and placing it on the counter.

"Oh really?" Trent replied. He turned to face Gage, crossing his arms over his chest, cocking an eyebrow.

"Sure. We both have a love of family. Although I hide my love from my family, I still adore them. We both have a need to be self-made men. After meeting you, meeting your children, I'm finding out I think I might want a little boy of my own someday who will declare to the entire world my muscles are the biggest and I can beat up all the other dads, or maybe a little girl who will smile up at me as if I have conquered the world just by coming to her birthday party," Gage said, turning to face Trent who stayed looking at him, a smile spread across his lips.

"You don't understand, I could take ninety-nine percent of all the dads at Hunter's school," Trent teased, grinning as he said it.

"I don't doubt it for a second. Remember, I've seen you naked," Gage said, stepping forward, turning toward Trent to place himself between his legs. He wrapped his arms loosely around Trent's waist

140

and felt rewarded when Trent did the same. "I wanted to do these dishes. I enjoyed dinner immensely. Please don't make light of it or make it something less. You're single-handedly restoring my faith in parenting. I'm in awe of you, baby," Gage said and lifted his hand to stop Trent from speaking.

"Shhhh, Trent, listen to me. You think I'm something... well, I truly think you're something. You're honor and integrity every single day, all in the way you carry yourself. I've never seen anyone like you... I didn't really think it existed in this world. As I stand here in your arms, you make me feel special knowing someone like you would pick someone like me to spend any time with at all," Gage said, looking Trent straight in the eye. He slid his hands up Trent's chest, trailed fingertips along his neck, and used his thumbs to keep Trent's head in this position. Gage wouldn't allow him to turn his eyes away as he placed a kiss on Trent's sweet lips.

"Gage, you don't have to say these things," Trent said, but he pulled Gage in closer, kissing him again.

"I'm being completely honest with you, and if I come to your house and do your dishes, just let me. It's the least I can do," Gage said, taking his thumbs and nodding Trent's head. "Well good, you agreed, and I've found another way to get a yes out of you. I was afraid I would have to put you to sleep before we ever spoke again!"

"Well, if you want to do something, my garage is an inventory nightmare. Feel free to jump in and clean it up anytime you want." Trent lifted a brow, biting his lip in the most adorable way to hide his smile.

"Oh really? The garage's your office, right? Did I hear that at some point?" Gage asked.

"Yes, it's my office and the shop where the guys come every morning. The neighbors love me," Trent said, smiling big now.

"Show me," Gage said, stepping away from Trent, but entwining their hands, pulling Trent forward.

"It's a mess. You don't want to see it," Trent said, having to be moved step by step.

"I wanna see. You get to see where I work," Gage said, proud of his argument.

"So not the same thing," Trent said. They were now standing in the middle of the kitchen, Gage cocking his head to look through the laundry room at the garage door.

"Show me, babe. Is it through here?" Gage asked, pulling Trent toward the door.

"Yes." Gage pulled Trent along through the laundry room, where he noted the laundry basket full of unmatched socks, to the attached garage. Gage walked down a couple of steps as Trent flipped on the overhead lights. The garage seemed almost as large as the house, and from this angle, it was definitely an add-on. Gage hadn't noticed it while being out front. The room was packed with shelves, filled with tools, boxes, ladders, wire, connectors, everything an electrician could possibly use.

Directly across from the laundry room door sat a large desk with several chairs scattered around it. Gage knew Trent put the desk right here to be able to see or hear anything coming from the house. The back wall consisted of two large rolling warehouse doors, along with a normal back door off to the left. Gage walked around Trent, stepping out into the garage as Trent stayed close to the laundry room door.

"You run your business from out of here?" Gage said, taking several steps around the room, looking at all the different equipment laying everywhere.

"Yes. It makes it easier on the kids. I had a shop, but gave it up. My neighbors hate it, but I can get the guys started in the morning and end the day with paperwork, and all that while the kids are able to sleep in their own beds or play in their rooms. It's easier on all of us," Trent said, watching Gage closely. He wasn't sure what Trent expected of him, but he walked to the back door and moved the curtain from the small window. He saw a giant swing set, one of those wooden, homemade deals, an above ground swimming pool, a huge sandbox, and a large covered patio.

"Your backyard is huge," Gage said, opening the door, walking through. Trent either had to leave the spot he stood rooted in or be left alone in the garage. The moon shone brightly, lighting Gage's path outside as he walked into the backyard. What he couldn't see from the window was a tall wooden fence surrounding the property and a reasonably organized pipe rack sitting to the side. Several large wire spools were also stacked against the fence close to the pipe rack. A chain length fence surrounded the electrical equipment. Gage assumed it kept the kids out of there, unharmed and safe.

The driveway reached all the way around the house, back where trucks could easily load and unload from the giant warehouse doors. The wooden fence had a huge gate currently closed and locked with a chain and safety lock in place. The light from the garage dimmed as Trent shut the door behind him.

"One of those first days after I met you, you pulled one of those heavy spools of wire off your truck. It was honestly about the hottest thing I think I have ever seen," Gage said, then turned back to the play area of the yard not waiting for Trent to answer. "Did you build this?"

"Last year," Trent said and came to stand beside Gage who now stood in the middle of the backyard. Trent's hands were in his jean pockets.

"When do you fill the pool?" Gage asked.

"I will this weekend. I've been getting it ready, it won't take long to fill it," Trent said.

"I would have loved this as a child," Gage said, walking to the play set, gripping his hands on the ladder, stopping short of climbing up the steps.

"Me too," Trent agreed as he followed behind Gage at a slower pace.

"They're lucky to have you." Gage turned back to face him.

"I'm the lucky one," Trent protested, watching Gage.

"I'm lucky to be here with you," Gage said and took the steps separating them until he wrapped his arm around Trent, pulling him to his chest while leaning in for a slow soft kiss.

"I envisioned making out on the sofa tonight, but the moonlight might be just as good," Gage said, watching the stunning man in his arms as he spoke. His heart swelled with love and romance, everything he wanted with Trent. He didn't speak, but leaned in sliding his tongue across Trent's lips, trying to gain access. The kiss started slow but quickly turned demanding and Gage couldn't seem to get close enough to Trent. He held him tightly, pressed together from toe to chest, nothing separating them.

Trent seemed to innately understand and agree. He pulled Gage tightly to him, slanting his mouth, opening wide and taking everything offered. Several minutes passed as they kissed in the backyard under the moonlight.

Gage pulled Trent's T-shirt out of his jeans, pushing his hands inside the thin cotton material. He needed to feel Trent's skin against his. Trent threaded his fingers into Gage's hair, turning his head farther to the left to help reach the far depths of his mouth. Trent kissed him as if he were making love to him, and it was everything Gage wanted from the world right now. Several more minutes passed before Gage tore his mouth free, trailing kisses along Trent's jaw, neck, and up to his ear.

"I want you so badly. When I came here tonight, I just wanted to spend time with you. Nothing could keep me away from being here with you. But you're so damn sexy, Trent. Your chiseled jaw, this strong chin, your emerald green eyes, the smile... Dear God, I love your smile," Gage said, holding Trent's head between his hands, placing small kisses all along his face as he spoke.

"You're the beautiful one," Trent said and slid his tongue forward between Gage's slightly parted lips. Trent thrust his hips up, driving his hard-on against Gage's own rigid dick. Gage met the movement with one of his own, making sure Trent knew how much he was wanted. It only seemed to heighten the kiss as Trent devoured him, pulling his shirt free of his jeans, roaming his hands over Gage's back and then sliding one to the front, shoving it down over his swollen cock, while the other arm kept Gage locked in the embrace.

"I want you," Trent said into the kiss, dragging breath deep into his lungs. Trent didn't pull back for long, but latched himself on to Gage's neck, nibbling and licking the way up to his ear.

"You know I want you, baby," Gage said, bringing his palms to the front of Trent's chest still under his shirt, running them over the hard muscles of his stomach. He pushed his fingertips down into Trent's jeans. Gage brushed the tip of Trent's cock as he leaned his head back, giving Trent's lips and tongue full access to his neck. He was so turned on, so ready, he rolled his cock into Trent's hand and ground his jaw together to keep the urge at bay to take this further. When Trent's tongue plunged into his ear, Gage's hips pitched forward, bucking several times, and he lost complete control in that moment. He gripped Trent's hips, digging his fingers into the hard muscle, trying to hold himself together as his own hips rocked back and forth into Trent's hands.

"Baby, I can't take it. You have to stop," Gage said, leaning his ear into the kiss. Every one of his actions encouraged Trent to do more. Trent didn't stop, but thrust his tongue forward again, then sucked Gage's earlobe into his mouth.

"You liked that?" Trent whispered. The sexy sound of his voice sent shivers running down Gage's body, causing his legs to buckle. Gage forced his eyes open and hung on to Trent for his life. Trent kept him up, but Gage needed to gain some perspective, fast.

"You have to stop. You have to." Trent didn't. Instead he ground his rigid cock, into Gage's swollen, thick arousal and thrust his tongue back into Gage's ear. Gage panted as he tried to speak and pushed himself away from Trent, stumbling backward several feet. His hands were extended out in front of him to keep Trent away and his legs were weak, barely able to hold him up. Gage panicked, his gaze was wild and he dropped one hand to the front of his jeans to see if he'd actually come on himself. Shocked to find he hadn't. Trent moved toward him, like a predator after his prey. His intentions clear, he wasn't done, but Gage stepped away again, keeping his hand out.

"It's too much. I can't risk your kid's still being awake and me standing in the backyard coming on myself," Gage said, his hand still out, keeping Trent at arm's length. What he said finally registered, and Trent flipped his head to the window at the corner of the house. It was dark and quiet.

"They're asleep, but I need to check. Shit! I'm sorry, Gage," Trent hissed in a voice a little louder than a whisper. Trent ran his hands through his hair; he panted for breath much like Gage.

"Shit! Let's go back inside. I'll check on them," Trent said. He took a step back, again running his hands over his face, then through his hair, the ends standing straight up. After the gesture, Trent looked back to Gage and pointed a finger in his direction.

"You make me forget things, no one has ever made me forget," Trent said.

"Yeah, well, I thought I just came on myself, so back at ya, babe," Gage said, keeping his distance, but grinning at the knowledge his Trent had become as undone as he had.

"Come on, this door will be unlocked," Trent said, walking several steps ahead of Gage. His body still hadn't calmed down and he wasn't risking coming anywhere within reach of Trent until things changed inside him.

Making out on the couch was everything Trent remembered it to be from high school. After he checked on Em and Hunter, he and Gage took up residence on the sofa, necking like two schoolboys. Neither of them took it too far, but still, it was hot as hell. Trent loved lying on the sofa with Gage in his arms, kissing him like tomorrow didn't matter. Trent barely heard Rhonny come through the living room, and with her ear buds in her ears, she apparently hadn't heard them either. She let out a terrified scream, piercing the house.

"Rhonny! *What*? It's just me!" Trent said, bolting upright. He and Gage couldn't untangle themselves fast enough before the overhead light on the ceiling fan brought the room to full glow.

"*What the hell*, you scared the crap out of me, Trent!" Rhonny yelled.

"Daddy," Hunter called from the bedroom, his voice scared.

"It's okay, Hunter. It was dark and Rhonny didn't see me. I scared her," Trent called out. Both he and Gage were up and off the sofa. Rhonny stood trembling, clearly terrified. He tried hard to diffuse the situation as Gage grinned like he got caught with his hand in the cookie jar. Gage stayed close to the sofa, tucking his shirt back inside his jeans.

"Daddy, Em and I are scared," Hunter called back with Em seconding his comment.

"I'm coming," Trent said, and he could see both their heads sticking out his door down the lit hall.

"I need to go. You go take care of them," Gage said.

Rhonny finally got her wits about her. "I'll get them back in bed, Trent. You say goodbye, but I think you need to leave the porch light on Mister! You scared me to death!" Rhonny said, grinning, and then turning back to the kids.

"Your daddy scared me bad!" Rhonny said, shooing both the kids back into Trent's bedroom.

"Can you walk me out?" Gage asked, taking a step toward the front door. The moment created a slight awkwardness between them, and Trent smiled ducking his head. This felt very much like getting caught by your parents doing something you shouldn't be doing. Trent got to the front door first and opened it for Gage. He stepped out onto the porch and Trent followed. The lights were off. Gage took a couple of steps forward before turning on his heel, startling Trent at the abruptness of the movement. Instead of walking down the steps, he grasped Trent by the hand and led him to the railing.

"I have something to say... I should just leave. I have so much to do to get ready for Thursday. It's just fucking hard. I want to spend all my time with you. You've become everything I think about. I can't focus on this grand opening; I can't focus on my report. Only you. You're every one of my thoughts and I know we have forever. I don't have to rush this, but it's not my nature to *not* rush it." Gage paused in his flow of words. Both Trent's hands were now in his and Gage held on to them tightly.

Trent tried to sort out the words being flung at him, to understand what Gage was really saying, and after a couple of moments of Gage standing there scanning his face, Trent narrowed his eyes, lowered his brow, and bit his lip. Trent wanted to say he understood. He'd experienced all those same things, but fear kept him quiet. Words like forever scared the crap out of him because he wanted those exact same things with Gage. At some point, Gage would get bored, everyone always did, and if Trent didn't keep some perspective and rein these emotions in, it would hurt too badly when Gage left.

"Give me something... anything to let me know I'm not alone in this, Trent. I get you're reserved, and extremely cautious, and I understand I'm balls-to-the-wall, but I need something... anything..." Gage pleaded.

He didn't know if he could say the right words, but he did lean in, slanting his mouth over Gage's, and kissed him again. It wasn't the soft romantic kisses on the sofa, but more like the hard kiss they'd shared in the backyard. Gage melted into Trent, and he wrapped his arms around Gage, threading his fingers in his hair. Several minutes passed before they broke to come up for air.

"We're so different," Trent started, but Gage stopped him, placing his hands on Trent's lips.

"What's in your heart, Trent? Am I alone in this?" Gage asked, and he wouldn't release Trent's gaze. Desperation poured off Gage as he waited for the answer.

"You're not alone, Gage." Trent whispered the confession, and somehow, by saying it out loud, a few of the walls he'd built around his heart crumbled. Gage smiled and reached out to kiss his lips lightly.

"Good, it's enough for now," Gage said and captured Trent's lips with his.

Chapter 15

"I think we're good. I'll go ahead and green tag you today, *if* those voltage changes were made out front. Where's your electrician?" The inspector asked during the final walk through of the remodel. Gage, the inspector, and Roger McCall were upstairs in Gage's living area, taking the last tour around. Tomorrow was Thursday, the big grand opening, and at this point, there was no time to get it wrong. They were down to the last few steps before Gage could declare victory.

"I believe he's in the bedroom, hanging the last ceiling fan," McCall said, and in unison they all three turned toward the bedroom. Gage stayed through the entire walk-through, although he missed a scheduled call in from one of his guys, but he left nothing to chance. The foreman couldn't be trusted to get anything right. It was truly a wonder they were on schedule at all, even with him and his father breathing down everyone's neck.

As they entered the bedroom, Gage's eyes went immediately to the ladder in the middle of the room, where Trent stood, working. The bed was pushed aside. His tool belt hung on his hips bringing his jeans down low, almost showing a peek of that sexy butt crack. His hands were above his head, holding and mounting the heavy fan to the ceiling. The muscles in his arms and back strained under the exertion he used to hold it all in place. Gage forgot everything else going on around him and stood there watching Trent's T-shirt stretch tight across his back. He prayed those jeans would magically fall to his ankles while he stood right here.

"Cooper, when you get done, I need a minute," the inspector said. Trent didn't turn around and didn't startle, he continued to work and replied back.

"Almost done," Trent said, turning the base plate, locking the fan into position. He released his tight hold, but stayed in the position, making sure the ceiling fan remained secure before he made his way down. The apprentice electrician standing under him closed the ladder and cleaned up the floor as Trent dropped his tools back in his belt and walked toward them.

"Yes, sir," he said, shaking the inspectors hand in greeting.

"I need to check the sign voltage out front. They're gonna have to raise the sign, but I'm passing it today on the contingency everything we've talked about today is done by the first of next week." As the inspector spoke, Gage stood there silently watching Trent. All his attention focused on the man in front of him. He watched as Trent raised his arm to wipe the sweat from his brow onto the short sleeve of his T-shirt. Trent stood with his back straight, his hands on his hips, his legs spread apart and those jeans still riding low because of the tool belt. Gage loved this look Trent sported. Trent stunned him regularly with that ruggedly hard yet gorgeously-made male thing he had going on. Gage was completely lost in this man.

He forced his eyes down to his feet as he felt his body harden. He needed to gain perspective fast. Hell, his body still hadn't recovered from last night. Gage never went without sex when his body raged with such a need, but sex had never been about love before and now it seemed like the only thing that mattered.

"Mr. Sinclair, did you hear me?" the inspector asked.

"No, I'm sorry, I didn't," Gage said, looking up at all three of them staring at him.

"We're going downstairs to talk to the sign people. I'll release the building. Make sure that sign gets raised before next weekend, or I'll have to shut it down again," the inspector said.

"Not a problem. Thank you," Gage said, and turned to Roger McCall who stood beside him. He held out his hand as he watched the inspector and Trent leave the room together. "Thank you for your part in getting this done on time, it hasn't been easy. Please make sure the sign gets moved. I'll be out of town for a few days which will be most of next week."

"Yes, sir, we'll do it Monday morning, first thing," McCall said. Gage nodded, but didn't really listen. Every part of him centered into every part of Trent, and he listened to Trent's work boots stepping down the stairs. Trent led, the inspector followed. Then he heard the door to his private area open and close, taking Trent away from him. Gage felt the loss immediately. It became an almost tangible emotion as if he could reach out and touch it. *God, I have it bad!*

"I'm going downstairs to get some work done," Gage said, and he didn't wait for McCall to answer, just left, taking the stairs down two at a time. It shocked him at how much he liked seeing Trent in his bedroom even if it was work related. Possessiveness rushed over him as he realized how badly he wanted Trent with him all the time, not these few minutes here and there, but all day, every day. Gage was the quintessential free spirit, roaming as he pleased. He'd never needed to have someone with him all the time. As he hit the first step down, he pulled his phone from his pocket and sent the object of his desire a text.

There's an outlet out in the bathroom connecting to my office. When you get done, can you come check it out? Gage typed the message and hit send. By the time he made it inside his office, a text came back.

"When I finish with the inspector. Give me a minute."

A minute worked perfectly, Gage didn't need any more time. He darkened the windows in his office, blocking out the rest of the gallery and went into his personal restroom. The small room came with a sink, commode, and a full length mirror. He pulled off his dress shirt, leaving on his white undershirt. He unbuckled his belt, pulling it free, and hung it on the same hook as his dress shirt. He unfastened the button to his slacks and lowered the zipper some, leaving his pants open, but still up on his hips. Gage couldn't resist the need coursing through him and reached low, bringing both the zipper and his underwear down as he gripped his raging hard-on and began to stroke.

The side drawer held several condom packets and a small bottle of oil. He placed them both on the counter, flipping the top open within easy reach. He tore the condom packet open, and decided to stop short of putting it on. Desperation ran so deep in his soul, it kept his hand moving, sliding up and down on his own dick, praying Trent would hurry. The knock came on the end of his thought.

"It's Trent," Gage heard through the door.

"You alone?" Gage asked, moving to the door.

"Yeah?" Trent replied, sounding more like a question. Gage opened the door, pulling Trent in by the T-shirt he wore.

"You're such a tease," Gage growled, pulling Trent to him, reaching for those sexy lips with a demanding urgent thrust of his tongue. He kissed Trent like he did last night in the backyard. It conveyed everything held deeply in his heart. Trent startled, but reacted in kind, pulling Gage to him, opening wider for the kiss. Gage couldn't move fast enough. He kept Trent in the kiss, but lowered his hands, working the buckle of his tool belt free. Trent lifted his hands to Gage's face, holding him in place as he began to ravish his mouth. The force of the kiss caused Gage to stumble back and Trent dominated him as the tool belt hit the floor in a loud thump.

"Your pants…" Gage pushed Trent back until he hit the sink, regaining the dominance of the moment.

"I want you so fucking bad," he said in a whispered growl as he took a predatory step forward. Trent worked the button of his own jeans, shoving them down, freeing his already hard cock. Gage gripped it and began to stroke, his own cock jutting out, begging to be touched. He leaned into Trent, reaching around with his free hand to grab the condom packet.

"You're driving me insane," Gage said. "I can't think of anything but you anymore." Gage slid the condom on in one quick movement with his free hand, never stopping the stroke on Trent's cock.

"Gage," Trent said in a breathless whisper while pushing his pants down further to his thighs.

"Take off your shirt," Gage said, flipping Trent around.

Gage reached around to grab Trent's dick at the same moment he poured several drops of oil onto his throbbing cock. His every intention was to stroke Trent as he prepared him from behind, but Gage lost his mind when he pushed his finger inside Trent's tight rim.

"No, don't wait, do it now…" Trent groaned. Gage looked up in the mirror, seeing Trent's beautiful masculine face reflecting the same deep desire he held in his heart. Trent dropped his head between his shoulders, reaching back to Gage's cock, positioning him to enter. Trent thrust his hips back, driving Gage inside. It felt damn good to be put inside this man. No one had ever done anything similar to him before. Gage gripped Trent's hips, holding him still as he bent forward dropping his head on Trent's back.

"Don't move, babe... Please don't move," Gage begged, desperate. He panted, his load threateningly close to exploding in the tight confines of his lover's body. Trent didn't listen, though, he thrust his hips forward then back again against Gage. Trent lifted his head, pushing them both upright, and laid his head back on Gage's shoulder. The sweetest of moans escaped Trent's lips, and Gage couldn't hold back any longer; he rocked back and forth, burying himself again and again inside Trent. His hips jerked and his release built quickly. He closed his eyes, leaned slightly forward, wrapping his arms around the male who now gripped the sink tightly in his hands. Trent's head again lowered, hitting against the mirror. Deep unintelligible words poured from Trent and encouraged the pounding to continue.

Gage thought he heard Trent working himself and for a split second he realized he should be stroking his Trent, but his orgasm crested, and he curled his hips forward as he closed his eyes and let his seed shoot out of him. The sensation was so perfect, so right his legs almost buckled out from underneath him. He wrapped Trent in his arms, bringing him back against his body. Gage's arms wrapped tightly around Trent's chest, holding him as close as he possibly could. Trent rested the back of his head on Gage's shoulder again, and his breath continued to pant. Gage's heart hammered and the earth fell out from under his feet, and then his knees did buckle.

Something happened in that moment. Something magical, something beyond anything Gage had ever experienced before. He couldn't name it, but the feelings made him gasp for breath from the sheer force of their weight, as if his heart physically left his body landing straight into Trent's hands. Trent was his and held his heart completely captive. He loved this man. He loved him as completely as he ever loved anything and his future stood right here, encircled in his arms. The pure emotion of the moment forced him to confess this love. It gave him no choice, but when he opened his eyes, Trent lifted his head. The gaze meeting his in the mirror was filled with fear. It wasn't what he expected to see. It wasn't the love he'd thought they had just shared. Trent was afraid, unsure and unsteady. Gage held his tongue, not saying what his heart demanded he say. Instead he said the next most important thing.

"Did you come, too?" Gage asked, not breaking eye contact in the mirror.

"Yes." Trent said. There seemed to be a lot of unsaid things flying between them.

"I should have done that. You felt so good, I lost my mind for a minute," Gage said, tightening his hold on Trent, leaning his chin on his shoulder.

"No, it's good, it didn't take much," Trent said. Gage stood there, staring at him as his now sated, limp dick slipped from Trent. Gage wasn't ready to let him go. He couldn't see how he was ever going to loosen his arms from the grip they held on this man. Trent kept their eyes locked and lifted his arm, placing it along Gage's, linking their hands together as he continued to hold him.

"I still should have stroked you off," Gage said quietly, and *I love you* he thought to himself.

"It's all good. And I think I even made it in the sink. I'm guessing there isn't an electrical problem in here," Trent said, neither seemed to want this moment to end.

"No, the currents running between us feel great, don't you think? You did what I needed you to do," Gage said with a smile.

"I need to get back out there. The site owner's a tyrant of a guy, kind of a diva, and added a whole back patio electrical upgrade, even as we're pushing to finish the main specs on time," Trent said in little more than a whisper. Gage smiled, kissing him softly on the shoulder, smiling at the shiver the small kiss gave Trent.

"I won't be able to see you tonight. I have crews in here decorating, bringing furniture and setting up the tables for tomorrow. I have to inspect the hangings myself. I'm sorry I won't be able to drive out to your place. And I know I wasn't invited to do so, but it doesn't seem to be stopping me," Gage said, his chin still resting on Trent's shoulder.

"It's okay. I don't have to see you every night. I'm not that needy," Trent said.

"Well, apparently, I am that needy. I already miss you," Gage said.

"You don't have to say things like that, Gage," Trent said. The fear and insecurity were back in Trent's eyes, and Gage lifted their joined hands, turning Trent's head to his so he could look him directly in the eyes.

"I'm not that nice of a guy to just say things for your benefit. I'm actually holding so much in I want to say. I don't like the fear in your eyes. I'm finding I would rather cut off a limb than see you hurt in any way. Trent, baby, can't you see it? You mean everything to me. No, don't pull away. I'll leave it there for now, but we're going to have this talk sooner or later. I can't hold it in much longer," Gage said. He leaned in to place a soft kiss on Trent's parted lips, but the insecurity still stayed in Trent's eyes.

Gage didn't wait for him to reply, he didn't want to hear what Trent might say because he doubted it would have anything to do with what mattered to him. He pulled the condom off and grabbed a hand towel to clean himself. He kept his eyes on the task he performed, but saw Trent cleaning up the sink, then pulling his pants back in place. Maybe Gage had read Trent wrong. Maybe it wasn't fear, maybe Trent wasn't feeling everything he felt. He'd put Trent on the spot last night, then again today. This could easily be one-sided. Isn't that how these things normally went down? Trent's T-shirt lay on the floor by his feet and Gage scooped it up, holding it hostage until Trent looked at him.

"You're making me insecure, Trent. I wasn't going to push you, and I'm still not, but tell me if you're as interested in this between us as I am before my runaway heart goes much further," Gage said, forcing himself to stay still, keeping the amused fake look on his face as his heart hammered in his chest.

"Gage," Trent couldn't hold the stare. Instead he paused looking down and Gage lifted his hand behind Trent's neck, tangling his fingers in the short strands.

"You don't have to say it," Gage whispered into his ear. He hated pushing him. He wished he hadn't said anything. The silence was answer enough. Just like always, he pushed at everything too much, too hard, and he needed to better read the signs Trent gave. His silence spoke volumes.

"I'm scared. It's a hard time for me. Em's birthday, my sister's death," Trent said, never looking up at Gage.

"Shhh... It's okay, baby, I shouldn't have asked. I'm not sure where this need for constant validation keeps coming from," Gage said, resting his forehead on Trent's head. He closed his eyes at the pain he heard in Trent's words and at the pain now coursing through his heart at the rejection. He was alone in this with Trent, and it hurt deeper than anything ever hurt before. Alone, alone, alone. And no matter how many times he thought it, it didn't make it easier to absorb. Trent lifted his head and raised a hand to Gage's face, holding his jaw in place as they looked one another in the eye for several long seconds.

"I'm in…in for whatever this is between us, but when it's over, I'll be okay. Whenever it is and if it's tomorrow, I'll be okay. I don't want you to feel obligated to stay with me in any way," Trent said.

"Good, I'm glad you're in. Me too," Gage said. Relief struck his heart, staggering him again. A smile spread across his lips, and he reached his head in to kiss Trent's lips, but he was denied when Trent pulled back. *Why does he keep distancing from me?*

"It's important to me that you know I don't want you obligated to me. Just tell me when we're done. All right?" Trent asked, keeping his head back.

"I honestly don't see it happening, Trent," Gage said, watching him closely. Right then Gage decided Trent was one of the most stubborn men on the planet. Nothing penetrated, no matter what Gage said or did.

"Just say you will," Trent replied.

"I will, but what if this is forever? What then?" Gage asked, back to pushing Trent, but taking on the same defensive tone Trent used on him.

"I honestly don't see it happening, Gage." Trent used Gage's words back on him and grabbed his shirt from Gage's hand, pulling it over his head while dodging Gage as he ducked down and grabbed his tool belt. He walked out of the bathroom and across the office. He never looked back, but right before he left the office, he ran his hand over his hair, making sure it wasn't sticking up, and then ran it over his face, letting out a long frustrated sigh. Gage watched him square his shoulders and leave the office. At some point, Trent would have to admit what they were doing. Gage would get a commitment out of the man sooner or later.

The single beep sounded seconds before Trent's phone began to vibrate on the nightstand beside his bed. The rattling jarred him awake and his eyes flew to the small alarm clock beside the phone. One thirty in the morning. Who would text him this late? Trent rose from bed, reaching up to turn on the lamp before palming his phone. This was the first night this week he got to bed at a decent hour and his brain seemed a little resistant to fully waking. Groggy, he rubbed the sleep from his eyes and opened the message. A smile formed as he saw Gage's name on his phone.

Are you up? Gage texted.

I am. Everything good? Trent sent back.

Yes, did I wake you?

No, I was awake, Trent typed, yawning as he hit send and lay back down on the bed pulling the pillows up behind his head.

Then why was your house so dark before I sent the text? Gage countered.

What? Where are you? Trent sat straight up in bed and texted back.

In your driveway.

What? Trent sent while getting out of bed and walking out into the hall quietly tiptoeing toward the front door. Four rapid fire messages set the phone to buzzing like angry bees in his hand.

Time got away from me tonight. I missed talking to you and I had an overwhelming urge to kiss you goodnight. Can you come out? I'll make it quick, I promise. And don't change. Come out like you sleep, but if you're wearing a shirt take it off. I love your bare chest. I envision you sleeping with a bare chest. Gage texted back.

As quietly as he could, Trent opened the front door to see Gage's Prius sitting in the front drive. The headlights were off, the car sat idling quietly. Trent ran his hands through his hair, hoping it wasn't standing straight up, and opened the screen door, shutting it quietly behind him. The breeze blew gently, sending a slight chill across his skin. His entire neighborhood was dark and the moonlight guided his path down the front steps to the sidewalk. He wasn't wearing shoes or a T-shirt, his pajama pants hung low on his hips. He first stepped up to Gage's side of the car bending at the knee as the window rolled down.

"Hi. Can you get in for a few minutes?" Gage asked. Trent looked back at the house, checking everything before he stood and walked around to the passenger side of the car.

"What are you doing here? You have to be exhausted," Trent said, climbing in the front seat. He didn't get to finish his sentence before

Gage had him in a lip lock, pulling him into his arms. It only took him a second to catch up. He met Gage's long lazy stroke of the tongue with one of his own. Only pulling away to catch his breath. He'd been caught completely off guard, and forgot to breathe. Gage stayed with the kiss, trailing down his neck, over his shoulder then back up, placing soft kisses on his lips.

"This is one of the busiest times of my life and you're all I can think of... Trent... baby," Gage said between kisses.

"Me too," Trent whispered, taking Gage's lips again with his own. Gage kissed him thoroughly and completely one more time before inching back a little, but staying close and taking Trent's hands in his.

"Did you take the shirt off or sleep bare-chested?" Gage asked.

"Bare-chested," Trent said with a smile.

"Good, that's the way I dream it. Did the department store come out today and get you ready for tonight?" Gage asked. He brought Trent's knuckles up for a quick kiss as he spoke and it warmed Trent's heart as he watched Gage's lips on his skin.

"Yes, but, Gage, seriously, I should've paid for it. They told me when we were making arrangements they would let me pay, but once it was over they wouldn't let me. I tried to send the stuff back, they wouldn't allow it. You shouldn't be buying our clothes," Trent said, with Gage still only inches from his face, and he reached in kissing Trent's lips softly again.

"Shhh... I told you, it was a favor to me. I got some great deals you wouldn't have gotten. Did Rhonny and Em like their selections?" Gage asked.

"Are you kidding? I'm not sure either of them took their dresses off for the rest of the night. Em might still be wearing hers to bed and Rhonny looks like some kind of exotic supermodel. I had no idea she could look like that. I'll be playing dad all night, I'm sure," Trent said.

"Good! What about Hunter? Did he pick a suit? What did he pick?" Gage asked. He seemed genuinely excited.

"Black and white, like mine," Trent said, smiling.

"Good. You'll all look stunning. I'm glad. You deserve it," Gage said, kissing his knuckles again.

"I'll pick you up about six tomorrow night. The opening begins at seven. We need to get there on time," Gage said.

"I can drive us. You don't have to come out here," Trent said.

"No, I want to. I have a special car for the kid's tomorrow night."

"Gage, you're doing too much." Trent shook his head no as he spoke.

"No, I'm not, Trent. Please just let me do this," Gage said.

"The kids won't be able to stay too late. I need to be able to take them home early, and you can't leave your own grand opening to take us home."

"I thought I'd have a driver bring Rhonny and the kid's home early. You can stay with me for the evening, right? I want you to be there with me, by my side, through the entire night. I know it's asking a lot. There will be so many people coming and going all night. The RSVPs are up to five hundred guests," Gage said.

"That's great. Isn't that great?" Trent asked.

"Yeah, it's only my work on display tomorrow night. No one else's; I'm just surprised." Gage laid his head on the side of Trent's seat, staying within the confines of Trent's personal space.

"I'm not surprised. You're a big deal, Gage."

"I don't know. We'll see what the sales turn out to be. I'm not so sure, but The Gallery looks good, so much better than I dreamed. Thank you for doing so much," Gage added, smiling again.

"It's my job. You paid me to do it," Trent said.

"No, I watched you. You were careful with everything, making changes as they were needed. The panel box alone should have set us way back. Thank you," Gage said again.

"I was glad to do it, but I need to get back inside. If Em or Hunter wakes…"

"All right, one more kiss," Gage said, wrapping his arms around Trent, pulling him forward for the kiss. This time Gage took his time and Trent melted into him. The kiss reached out and touched his soul like the man sitting next to him did every time he did these unexpected things. When they parted, Trent knew some of his soul was left behind, given to Gage during the kiss. Trent tried so hard to keep Gage in his place. Keep him at arm's length, but it wasn't working. In just a few days, Gage made his way solidly inside his heart and could own it if he wanted it.

"Be careful going home," he said, smiling when he finally opened his eyes. Gage still right there in his face, coming in for another soft kiss.

"I will. Thank you for this afternoon and for coming out tonight," Gage said, kissing him again on the lips.

"I'll see you tomorrow." Trent's hand was on the door handle when Gage pulled him back for one last soft kiss.

"Goodnight, handsome. Dream of me, I'll be dreaming of you," Gage added, grinning that sexy smile.

"I will. I'll see you in the morning," Trent said, opening the door and sliding out. Gage didn't leave until he got safely inside the house, with the door shut and locked from the inside.

Chapter 16

"Daddy, my socks match my dress," Em said, walking into his bedroom completely dressed, her hair bouncing with soft curls. Sophia had come by to help tonight. She'd brushed Em's hair until it shined, then used hot rollers giving it an extra lift, or so they told him in great detail as the rollers were being put in her hair. Her little dress was pink satin organza and both her lacy socks and shoes matched perfectly. "I want to get married in this dress. I think I look like a princess, Daddy."

"I do too, Emalynn. How's Hunter doing?" Trent asked, tying his tie in the mirror.

"He's coming. Auntie Crazy is brushing his hair with gel, and he's making faces in the mirror," Em said, standing very still in the middle of the room to avoid wrinkling her dress.

"I bet he is," Trent said, pushing the knot up and laying the collar down.

"Knock, knock," Rhonny said from the doorway. Trent turned and stopped what he was doing, not at all prepared for how striking she looked in her new clothes. He usually saw her in jeans, a T-shirt and her long hair tied in a knot on top of her head, now she stood in front of him as a glamorous supermodel ready to take on the runway in the navy blue, deep V-neck sequin evening dress. She looked way too sexy and all his parental instincts kicked in.

"Rhonny you look beautiful, too!" Em said and jumped up and down.

"Do I, squirt?" Rhonny asked.

"*Yes!*" Em said.

"You do look very pretty. I feel like a protective father. Where's my shotgun?" Trent teased, sort of.

"Oh, whatever! And you're looking pretty good there yourself, Dad! You too, little Emmie," Rhonny said.

"Yes! Daddy looks pretty, too!" Em said, beaming up at him. She was about the cutest, sweetest thing he'd ever seen, and she couldn't contain her excitement about the night.

"Guys, look how handsome Hunter looks," Sophia said. Hunter walked past Sophia, wearing his suit with the tie knotted perfectly and his hair gelled in place. Hunter barely moved as he walked forward, so not to mess up his hair. Trent grinned. He looked very handsome all made up. They all did and he chuckled because everyone now stood in the middle of his small bedroom staring at one another.

"Hunter man, you look great! Now does anyone need to go to the bathroom before Gage gets here?" Trent asked.

"No, Auntie Crazy made us go," Em said.

"Well, that's some good lookin' out, Sophia," Trent said, giving her a high five as the doorbell rang.

"He's here!" Em shrieked, her little heels clicked on the hardwood floor as she ran to the door.

"So much for them remembering our talk about being quiet and good tonight," Sophia laughed as Hunter hightailed it out of the room, still trying to move his head as little as possible as he speed-walked to the door. Rhonny followed Hunter to the living room.

"You look nice, Trent," Sophia said as he shrugged on his tux jacket. "I'm glad to see you happy."

"Thank you, I am happy. Nervous about it all, but I'm trying to go with it," Trent said, looking in the mirror one last time.

"You should, he seems into you," Sophia said, propping her shoulder against the door frame.

"Which doesn't make any sense," Trent said, adjusting his dress shirt before he picked up his wallet and phone from the dresser.

"It makes every bit of sense!" Sophia started, but Trent effectively cut her off.

"Are you sure you don't want to come? It's not too late."

"No, I have to go back to work. It's month end. I just wanted to help get everyone ready and take pictures."

"Thank you, Sophia. The kid's look incredible. I wouldn't have been able to pull it off without your help," Trent said, and he could hear Gage's voice in the hallway.

"Daddy, come on. Gage is here and has a surprise!" Em yelled down the hall.

"It's so good to see them excited like this," Trent said softly as he approached Sophia.

"Trent, they're great kids. You've done such a wonderful job." Emotion high in Sophia's voice, she reached out to hug Trent, kissing him lightly on the lips. Em's shoes clicked on the hard floor, running his way.

"Go, Trent," Sophia whispered, smiling with tears in her eyes.

"Daddy, come on," Em said, pulling at his hand.

"Em, you have to settle down," he said, taking her hand and letting himself be pulled from the bedroom. The minute he stepped out into the hall, his eyes made contact with Gage. The sight took his breath away. Gage looked stunningly handsome in his tuxedo. His perfect blond hair looked newly trimmed and neatly in place. His face appeared freshly shaven, and the black tux looked made for his body. He was the most striking man Trent had ever seen. A slow smile came to Gage's lips, transforming him into a man more handsome than he was a moment earlier.

He forced his eyes away from Gage to his family. Em made it back in front of Gage, beaming with excitement. Rhonny stood close by, her hand on Hunter's shoulder and Hunter looked up at him, standing so quietly still, his hands in his slacks pockets and a smile on his upturned face. Trent's eyes darted back up to Gage. Emotion swelled in his heart. This time of year was usually such a hard time to manage for them. They all tried to put on a brave face as Lynn's death loomed over them. Now, in a few short days, Gage took away all that pain, giving them something fun and hopeful to have in their lives. Trent forced himself forward, willing himself not to let the emotion coursing through him show on his face. Instead, he hoped Lynn was here with them now watching them with as much pride as he felt so deeply in his heart.

"Good evening, you look stunning, Mr. Cooper," Gage said, reaching for him, bending in for a sweet soft kiss.

"Thank you, you look handsome," Trent replied, his voice cracking a little as he spoke. He turned his eyes away quickly, afraid they were betraying the emotions running through him. "You all look really nice."

"Daddy, let's go! Gage has a surprise for us outside." Em squealed.

"Yes, indeed I do. Let's be gone," Gage said with a smile and took the few steps back to the front door, opening it wide. The kid's went first out the door, then Rhonny and Trent followed. The kids got to the first step and stopped, before dashing out, forgetting they were dressed up. Rhonny did about the same thing, but Gage pulled Trent back for another soft kiss.

"You look, gorgeous. I knew you would, but yet again you've captivated me, body and soul, handsome," Gage whispered after the kiss.

"Daddy, it's a limo," Hunter yelled.

Trent could hear Sophia behind him snapping pictures, and the kids were back up the steps, pulling him out into the yard. His eyes registered the long black stretch limo in his driveway. A driver stood outside the far back door, waiting on them, and most of the neighborhood stood outside watching to see what was happening in their little piece of the world.

"Go, Trent, I want to get the kids' faces," Sophia said behind him. He looked back and Gage was shutting the front door. A giant smile plastered across his face. The kids raced across the yard, looking at the car from every angle. When Trent made it over to the car, the driver opened the door.

"Good evening, sir," he said.

"Wait, I want pictures. Em, Hunter, come stand with your dad and Rhonny in front of the limo. Gage come get in the picture," Sophia said, her camera up to her eye, angling the shot. The driver closed the door and stepped out of the picture, smiling indulgently. Gage stepped down from the front porch with a giant grin. He came from the side, moving his way in next to Trent.

"I want a copy of this photo, Sophia. You guys should see it from the inside," Gage said, smiling as she snapped the picture.

"It's so big, Gage," Em said, her little facing beaming up at him for the next snap of the picture. "Thank you for letting us ride in your limbo."

"It's a limo, Em," Hunter corrected her.

"Limo," Em repeated, but never took her adoring eyes from Gage.

"This is my pleasure, Emmie. Now let's get these pictures done so we can get inside," Gage said and scooped Em up in his arms. She hooked her arm around his neck for several more rounds of photos, before Trent stopped Sophia. The driver reopened the door. The kids got in first and the oohs and ahhhs were so loud the adults laughed and were joined by the neighbors standing closer now.

Rhonny scooted in next with about the same reaction. Sophia came to them, standing outside the car, ducking her head in at Em and Hunter's request. She took a couple more photos of Rhonny, Em, and Hunter inside the car before she rose, facing both Gage and Trent with tears swimming in her eyes. Trent knew the emotion, they shared it. Gage reached down to take his hand as Sophia came in to hug them both.

"Ignore me. Just go, I'm really happy. Go!" Sophia said, taking several steps back, waving Trent off before lifting the camera again to snap more pictures with tears streaming down her face.

"Babe, we have to go," Gage said, looking between Sophia and Trent. Trent worried about leaving her alone in such an emotional state. At times like this he missed Lynn the most.

"Go, Trent. I'm just very happy, I promise," Sophia said and retreated again. "Go on, so I can get you guys leaving."

"Sophia, please email me the pictures," Gage asked and offered up a hand to Trent encouraging him into the car. Trent slid inside with Gage's hand on his lower back. Gage followed close behind. Emalynn was in straight up awe, touching everything. He and Gage sat along the back seat, while Rhonny sat on the side of the limo and Em and Hunter sat facing them in the front.

"Look, Daddy, it's wine chilling. Rhonny said it," Em pointed to the two buckets filled with ice.

"Very cool, Em. Hunter what're you thinking about all this?" Trent asked. His son loved anything mobile, and Hunter's big eyes searched the entire place although he stayed cool, calm, and collected, sitting back in his seat, his hands in his lap. Unusual behavior for Hunter.

"I like it," he said, his eyes fixing on the neon lights surrounding the roof of the car. They started down the street. Em and Hunter both went to the long side window where Rhonny sat, looking out. Their friends in the neighborhood still stood outside watching them pull away and Em and Hunter ate it up, waving at everyone as they drove past.

"Rhonny, you look lovely tonight. What a great choice in gowns," Gage said, pulling one of the two bottles chilling in the champagne buckets.

"Thank you for all of this, Gage," Rhonny said. Em moved to sit beside her.

"Thank you, Gage," Em said, finally scooting back on the seat, and placing her hands in her lap.

"No thanks necessary, sweetheart," Gage said, pulling the cork on the bottle. "I got you and Hunter sparkling white grape juice so we can all make a toast." Gage poured two crystal champagne glasses, with not more than a swallow in each one for Em and Hunter. Then poured three glasses of champagne, handing one to Rhonny and one to Trent, before pouring the last one for himself.

Trent kept an eye on Em, but Hunter held most of his attention. His little boy seemed to be changing in front of him. Maybe this was part of growing up. As he continued to watch Hunter, it occurred to Trent that Hunter mimicked his moves and mannerisms. Hunter sat quietly, his suit jacket unbuttoned, one hand in his lap, the other carefully holding the champagne glass, and he just watched Trent. A smile tore across his face; it amazed him how such a small gesture filled his heart with unbelievable flattery and warmth. His Hunter was trying to be like him. He winked at Hunter who winked back, both eyes closing in Hunter's sweet wink back to him.

"I have a toast to make," Gage announced to everyone. They all turned his way as he raised his glass.

"I believe people come into your life for a reason and as important as this night may be to me, having you all here, sharing it with me makes every moment of it better," Gage said. He lifted his glass higher. "So this toast is for you, Hunter, Em, Rhonny, and Trent. Thank you for being here with me tonight."

Gage extended his hand and everyone followed his lead. They clinked their glasses together and drank from their crystal champagne glasses. Gage turned on the radio, showed Rhonny how to find the music, and the children went immediately into investigation mode, turning on every light, the television, and touching all the neat gadgets the limo offered them. Rhonny soon went into texting mode, snapping pictures and sending them to her friends and family. She snapped pictures of everything from herself, to the kids, to Trent and Gage together, even proclaiming everything was now documented on Facebook. Trent stayed quiet, his champagne glass in his hand, watching his family as Gage moved around the limo answering all of Hunter and Em's questions. Gage stayed patient with Em and Hunter through it all. After a few minutes, Gage made it back to his seat beside Trent and took his hand, bringing it to his lips for a soft kiss on the knuckles.

"You didn't have to do all this—" Trent chuckled at the look on Gage's face when he started the sentence. He changed it up in mid-thought and re-stated it. "Thank you, we're very grateful. Everyone looks really nice."

"I like that response so much better," Gage said, leaning in a little closer and sniffing. "I like your scent. I need to know what you wear. Are you nervous?" Gage asked, staying close to Trent's face. Gage's eyes seemed to focus on his lips, waiting for him to answer.

"A little," Trent said.

"Don't be, you'll be fine, I promise." They made great time to the gallery, staying somewhat on schedule even in the traffic surrounding the building. When they were about five minutes from the front door, Gage pulled them all together.

"Listen, guys, here's what we do when we get out of the limo. Hopkins, my head of security, will be standing right by the car door. Rhonny you step out first, Hopkins will be there to help you. Take his hand and stand up, but stay close to the car. Hunter, you go next and then Hunter you stand by the car door and take Em's hand, helping her out, okay?" Gage explained, and Trent chuckled at the three sets of big eyes just staring at him, soaking it all in.

"The area's roped off, but we have so many big names coming, they've already sent messages to me that the press cameras are lining up. I want you to walk straight up to the front doors. I want you to look up, with smiles on your faces. Just look and focus on the front doors. The flashes won't blind you so badly. My security will stay with you the entire way, even inside until your dad and I get there. Trent, I want you to walk up with me. I'll get out first and then help you out. Got it, everyone?" Gage asked, nodding his head, smiling, clearly trying to encourage them on, and they all sat there staring back at him, not one of them smiling or saying a word.

"Got it?" Gage asked again, lifting his brow this time, but the silence continued.

"Do I need to go over it again?" Gage asked as they waited for their turn in a long line of limos in the front of the gallery.

"Maybe I should go with them," Trent added, looking at the kids. They seemed to be getting smaller by the second.

"I would like you to walk with me, Trent. I want the world to know I found you," Gage said, gripping Trent's hand a little tighter. Gage's last words seemed to bring Rhonny out of her haze.

"I can get the kids up there. We'll wait inside for you," she said, and he watched Rhonny trying to regain her confidence.

"We can do this, right, guys?" she said, lifting her hand for a high five, but it took a second for each child to lift a hand for a half-hearted high five. His Hunter and Em were nervous and it showed on their faces. A few seconds later, they pulled to the front of the building, and they were all quietly staring out the darkened windows. Gage was right, the cameras were lined up, the night already dark, and the excitement filled the air with everyone outside wondering who might be in this limo. The side door opened, and after a brief pause, everything clicked into gear.

"Rhonny, you first. Hopkins is security. He'll stand there with you, then walk you all up," Gage said as a hand came down into the car. "That's him. Now remember to smile for me, and keep your head up." Rhonny did as instructed and Gage smiled proudly back at Hunter.

"Hunter, man, you next, then Em. Remember to smile. Let me see your smiles." Gage waited for them to smile before continuing. "Now keep them just like this until you get inside," Gage instructed. Hunter climbed out of the car, and then helped Em do the same. Trent leaned his head over and watched them walk into the building. Em almost pranced as she walked up the carpeted runway, and he couldn't help but smile even with all the nerves running through him.

"Em's a natural," Gage said, watching them closely, too. "Okay, Trent baby, I'm getting out. I'll stand and button my jacket, then put my hand in for you. I know you can get out on your own; it's more of a symbolic gesture. I'll keep and hold your hand the entire time while walking slightly ahead of you. We don't stop. We keep walking forward. Hold your head up, smile and stay with me no matter where I go, okay? These cameras aren't here for me, but for the celebrities coming tonight. This is just the first time I've ever brought anyone to anything; someone may be interested. Good?" Gage didn't wait for him to answer, but kissed his lips quickly and got out of the car. Trent followed as instructed and prayed the heated blush he felt wasn't visible on his cheeks quite yet.

Gage reached a hand into the limo. Trent took it and stood, but couldn't help but look down. The flashing blinded him. Trent fumbled at buttoning his jacket, but got it done, and Gage stood in front of him blocking everything for a moment. He whispered a quick word of encouragement, but Trent couldn't hear over the questions being hurled at Gage from the photographers and reporters mobbing the runway to the door.

"Is this your boyfriend, Mr. Synclair? Is this why you're retiring? Were those your children?"

They were still by the limo. Gage leaned in closer and whispered loudly in Trent's ear, "Let's go, handsome. Take my hand, look at the front doors, and smile your charming smile. You know the one you give when you forget you're keeping yourself at a distance from me."

It caused Trent to look up and meet Gage's gaze. "There we go, now smile... Yes, perfect. Let's go," Gage said. He took Trent's hand, leading the way to the gallery. Gage looked at the crowd and waved, but Trent didn't, he walked forward, a step or two behind Gage, keeping their hands together. His face focused on the front doors, and Em and Hunter's little heads were stuck in the window, watching him walk up. When he saw them, they waved, and he couldn't help but smile bigger as he made his way through the reporters and photographers. His children were so excited watching them walk up.

"Daddy, they took your picture, too!" Em said, running the few steps to him when Gage opened the door and propelled him through first.

"That was crazy, wasn't it?" Trent said, placing his hand on the back of her head. He looked up at the completed gallery, unprepared for the elegance. One of Gage's photos, the shot he loved the most hung right up front. It was the only one unveiled in the studio. Gage had snapped the photo of children playing in a natural spring while covering the tsunami in Sri Lanka. Destruction lay all around them in the background of the photo, but the children's faces held genuine delight in the spraying water raining down on them. It sank in a little more who Gage Synclair actually was in this world.

Trent looked down at Em's smiling face and then looked back at the photo. If he were ever going to have a framed photo of Gage's, this would be the one. It took a minute, but he realized Hunter was tugging on his jacket, and he looked down again.

"Daddy, I walked with my head up and smiled like Gage told me to," Hunter said. Hunter stood close to Gage now and they were still in the doorway, cameras still clicking away.

"I'm very proud of you, Hunter. You did really good. Em and Rhonny, too," Trent said, but he turned to Gage. "That's my favorite picture out of all the ones I've ever seen."

"Thank you, it's mine, too," Gage said, giving him a small smile. "Come this way. Let me get you three on the back patio with my family. You'll enjoy the whole experience more that way."

Chapter 17

Gage ignored all requests for his attention and ushered them to the back patio. A gentle breeze blew and although the night was completely dark now, the area was reasonably blocked in and climate controlled. The festively decorated patio splashed with color shooting out from every corner. The understated elegance of the main room evaporated, and in its place a decidedly fun, easy, and definitely casual area for gathering took shape. Trent couldn't believe the transformation now that the decoration and patio furniture had been added. Gage had done an outstanding job pulling it all together. A string quartet played in the corner, quietly filling the night with music, drowning everything else out. A small buffet took shape along a side wall and a mobile bar resided in the back of the patio.

The area was already packed and he'd seen many of these faces on local television. Everyone in the room seemed beautiful and well put together. Nothing about the occasion appeared new to them. They were at home in the elegance of what they wore. Gage escorted them directly to one table in the front of the patio and began to make quick introductions.

"Mom, Dad, I would like you to meet Trent Cooper and his family. This is Rhonny, Em, and Hunter. Trent, this is my mom and dad, Connie and Jack," Gage said, but glanced up sweeping his arm around the room at the many faces staring at them. Judging the looks they received back, Gage apparently took everyone off guard with his introduction. Many of the eyes looking at them traveled down to their joined hands, then back up at Trent, speculatively.

"Trent, this is my brother, Garrett, and his wife Natalie. This is Gary, you might remember him from the other night. This is Ginny, my sister, and her husband Kent, and Ginger, my sister, and her husband Stephen. These are all my nieces and nephews." Gage went through them all quickly and efficiently. There were at least ten children all ranging from four to twelve. Gage held firm to Trent's left hand, which left his right hand free to shake his father's hand.

"It's a pleasure to meet you," Trent said. Em came to stand closer to him, wedging her hand in between his and Gage's, until Gage was finally forced to let go so Trent could hold her hand. Hunter came in close, too, wrapping an arm around his leg. He didn't blame them; they weren't shy children by any stretch of the imagination they were just tossed into too many big situations at once to process all these inquisitive faces. And by the look of it, Gage's family tried to acclimate to a new set of events as well; they appeared as surprised to meet him as he was them. Gage's mother followed her husband's lead and stood, tentatively shaking Trent's hand.

Gage took after his mother. She stood tall, elegant, and blonde. They shared the same eyes and lips. His father was darker and their other children shared more of his looks. Still, no one said a word. They all stood there staring at one another.

After a long uncertain moment and Gage's acknowledging chuckle, it became obvious to Trent that Rhonny was the complication in this scenario. They didn't know what to make of her. She stood beside him, staying quiet, but her hands rested on Hunter's shoulders. Gage picked it up first, and his chuckle turned into a full laugh.

"Trent, honey, my parents never know what to expect from me... Mom, Dad, this is Rhonny. She's a firm member of Trent's family. She's also the children's nanny," Gage said, and Trent couldn't help the small laugh at the relief clear on his parents' faces.

"Ahh... Trent, let me start over. It's such a pleasure to meet you," Gage's mother said, with the others stepping forward. Em and Hunter were sucked into the fold with the children and Gary, Gage's youngest brother, zeroed in on Rhonny.

After getting through all the hand shaking and introductions Gage interrupted them. "I have to get back out there. The guests are starting to arrive. I hoped Rhonny and the children could stay out here with you, have dinner, play, and be more comfortable."

"I can stay here with them while you take care of business," Trent said immediately. Through all the hand shaking, Gage retook and never let go of his left hand, but Trent began to pull free now.

"I would really like you by my side tonight. If you're comfortable leaving them out here," Gage said, keeping hold of Trent.

"I'll be here with them, Trent. I promise to keep an eye on them," Rhonny said. Trent glanced over to Hunter and Em, already absorbed in playing with the other children. They didn't even notice they were being talked about. The whole idea of standing by Gage's side tonight, playing host, made Trent a little nervous. Gage looked so eager, Trent steeled his nerve and tried to jump in, hoping not to embarrass Gage too badly.

The evening whirled by in a blur. Trent greeted guests for the first hour. Then the official opening launched, unveiling all of Gage's photos. Attendants stood by each photo and pulled a dark curtain off the frame. Gage's curator, Jacquelyn, looked elegant and regal, selling her way through the gallery. The big names everyone waited for arrived, adding the glitz and glamour to the night. Gage kept Trent by his side all evening, introducing him to everyone. When it came time for Gage to give his speech, he even tried to get Trent to come up on stage and stand by him, but he drew the line there. Instead, he stood off to the side, alone, waiting for Gage to finish. After a few minutes, both Gage's mother and father came to stand beside Trent.

"Your children are adorable... and fine. I see you poking your head around, keeping an eye on them. My oldest granddaughter has the littlest ones upstairs in Gage's apartment coloring," Connie said quietly as Gage finished his speech.

"Are they in the way?" Trent asked, quickly looking over at Gage's mother. His father stood beside her, his arms wrapped around his wife, staying quiet, but listening to their conversation.

"No, they're fine, I promise. She has them tucked away happily playing and I'm sure making a mess of Gage's place. My littlest granddaughter, Mirabella, is only a few months older than Emalynn. They are cut from the same cloth. Rhonny's with Hunter and the boys. I do believe Gary is quite taken with her and is there, too."

"She's a good girl, ma'am," Trent said immediately about Rhonny.

"I can tell. You have a nice family, Trent," Connie said, giving a reassuring smile.

"Thank you." Trent's eyes were drawn back to Gage as he left the small platform.

"You're the first person Gage has ever brought for us to meet," Connie added. Trent stayed quiet, watching Gage shake hands with a dozen more patrons. "We've worried for him. He's so stubborn and independent. Always going to make it on his own."

"He has, too," Trent said, keeping his eyes on Gage, trying to figure out where this conversation might be headed.

"Yes, he has, and we're very proud of him."

"Gage has always been gay. When did you decide you were?" his father abruptly asked. He said it with no real aggression, just wanting the information. *Now* he understood the conversation. Trent smiled. The parental protective claws were coming out. Trent knew them well. He played both mother and father to his children and was absolutely sure he would be asking these same questions if he were in their shoes.

"I've always been gay, sir," he responded back, looking Jack straight in the eyes.

"Were you married to their mother?" Jack asked.

"Lord no, that would be terribly wrong. They're my sister's children. She died almost four years ago while giving birth to Emalynn. I adopted them shortly after. Their father was killed in the service, and our mom was older. She passed away about the time Hunter was born. It's just me and them," Trent said, turning to make eye contact with both of them as he spoke.

"Trent, I'm sorry," he said immediately.

"No, sir, no need to be, I get it. I'm a parent now, too. I'm the electrical contractor on this job. Rhonny is my nanny. I found her a few weeks after Emalynn was born. She saved me because I had no idea what I was doing. We've all been together since. I haven't known your son long, and believe it or not, I held out. I don't like having a bunch of different people in front of the kids, and I don't like messing with anything that will affect my business. It's how I pay for everything they need. But they actually sold me on Gage," Trent said. Gage worked the crowd, still several feet from the three of them, but diligently working his way over. Gage smiled and beamed when their eyes met as he continued to shake everyone's hand.

"You're the new lead electrical contractor on this job? You did the immediate panel change? I understand you kept this job on track for my son," Jack said.

"Yes, sir, I did, but Gage kept this job on track. He's a born project manager. It has to be in his blood. My end wasn't that big a deal, Mr. Sinclair, it's my job. Gage pulled the strings getting the city and power company out here to work with me. I wouldn't have been able to do that," Trent said.

"Son, I'm Jackson Layne. Sinclair is Gage's middle name and stage name," Jack said. Trent stopped moving his attention between Gage and his parents to focus solely on his father, the pieces to the puzzle all coming together. Gage's parents were Layne Construction, LLC, the billion dollar construction and property company. They owned the largest general contracting company in the world.

"Sir, I didn't know." He couldn't say anything else, stunned into silence. His heart hammered in his chest.

"Trent, you just keep getting better and better," Connie said, while reaching out to hug him tightly. "Welcome to the family, son."

Trent let her draw him in, but his shocked eyes stayed on Trent's father who stood back, the smile still on his face. Gage chose then to break free from the throng, coming back to Trent's side. Gage's hand landed lightly on Trent's back, but his mother wrapped her arms around him, too, dragging him into the embrace.

"You did great, son. Such a nice evening. Congratulations," she whispered between them.

"Thank you, Mom," Gage said, and leaned in to kiss her cheek, but wrapped his left arm around Trent, keeping him close. His father stayed back, chuckling, clearly watching the scene unfold in front of him.

"Trent and I have been discussing business," Jack said. Gage gave a laugh, still holding his mom close, but did venture a quick look over at Trent.

"So *there's* the reason for the look on your face. Don't be mad at me, baby. I'm not really in the family business. I didn't want it to sway you away from me with all your separate parts of life," Gage said quickly, leaning in to kiss Trent's still stunned lips.

"I didn't even guess…" Trent started, but couldn't finish.

"Gage, can we get a picture with you and the painting," Jacquelyn came to his side.

"Mom, Dad, we'll be back shortly," Gage said. With no more time for discussions, Trent got pulled away, back by Gage's side for the rest of the night.

Around ten, Rhonny appeared at his side, Gary standing close by, letting him know Em had fallen asleep on Gage's sofa and Hunter was drifting off fast. They were two hours past their normal bedtime, and Trent was actually surprised they'd lasted this long. Gage, having heard their exchange, immediately arranged for his driver to take them back home.

Trent and Gage got the kids loaded in the car with Rhonny. Gary valiantly tried to ride home with them, but settled for Rhonny's number and a promise for a date on Saturday night. Trent could see so much of Gage in Gary. Gary knew what he wanted and he worked to get it; it hadn't bothered him at all to ask for the date in front of everyone.

Trent stayed by Gage's side throughout the remainder of the evening until the final guest left. He helped in shutting down the gallery, while Jacquelyn went over the sales numbers for the night. As it turned out, Gage was a complete success as a solo artist. He'd sold every photo hanging in the gallery. They were the last to leave, somewhere around one in the morning. Security stayed around the clock now that photos hung in The Gallery, but Gage set the alarms and locked the doors before getting in the limo to take Trent home.

"I can get home, Gage. You're exhausted, I've seen your hidden yawns and you couldn't have slept more than a few hours all week," Trent said, stifling his own yawn as he got settled inside the limo. Both were already tieless, jackets discarded, neck and cuff buttons unfastened to get comfortable after the last guest left.

"I'm not sleeping when I could be spending time with you. I'm leaving tomorrow, and I'm not sure when I'll be back. Did I tell you I'm having presents delivered to Em tomorrow? Don't let her open them until her birthday. I don't know what she has so take back anything she doesn't want," Gage said, sliding into the car and shutting the door.

"Gage, you do too much," Trent said as Gage pulled him forward, bringing them both to the long sofa on the side. Gage untucked his shirt and stretched out in the corner seat, kicking his shoes off.

"I do nothing, and I feel awful I might not be there for her birthday. She invited me again no less than eight times tonight. She plans on wearing her dress again all day Sunday." Gage moved him to sit where Trent's back rested against his chest, wrapping him tightly in his arms. They hadn't been apart for more than a few minutes tonight, but Gage still wanted him in the circle of his arms exactly where Trent wanted to be.

"Is it possible to already be deeply in love with your children? They're precious, Trent. So well behaved, they were perfect tonight. You've done such a good job with them," Gage said, adjusting Trent to where his back lay across Gage so he could look at him as they spoke.

"Thank you for tonight... Hell, scratch that, thank you for coming into my life. You've made me a whole man. This night was incredible, better than I could have expected and it's all because you were with me," Gage said, looking down at him with such love in his eyes. Trent didn't respond, but leaned up and kissed Gage softly on the lips.

"Handsome... Baby..." Gage said, looking tenderly at Trent. Gage ran his fingertips over Trent's face just gazing down at him, the love so clear in Gage's eyes, shocking Trent with its intensity seconds before Gage's mouth slanted over his and he lost himself in another kiss. Gage thrust his tongue forward and Trent tried to meet him halfway while wrapping Gage in his arms. Gage dominated him, kissing him with desperation, not letting Trent get much more than a few deep moans or a swipe of his tongue in.

Gage deepened the kiss and slid his hand down Trent's chest, down the front of his slacks, gripping Trent's arousal, rubbing his palm up and down his swollen cock. Gage reached up to unbuckle his belt before unfastening his slacks button. He slid his hand inside Trent's underwear and gripped him, flesh on flesh, slowly stroking his rigid length, back and forth. The intensity of the movement and the connection he shared with Gage ran deep into his heart, knocking down every last one of the barriers he held in place. Gage held his heart and Trent wanted him forever by his side. Allowing himself to even consider the possibility caused his heart to slam wildly in his chest knowing without question he was a man deeply in love.

The skilled hand working him never stopped. Trent tore free of the kiss, burying his head in Gage's neck, stretching his long body out across the seat. A deep moan escaped his lips as Gage picked up the pace and stroked him faster. Trent rolled his hips forward farther into Gage's hand.

"I love when you touch me," Trent moaned against Gage's neck, his eyes closed and his head rolled back on the seat.

"Baby, let me come inside. We'll be quiet. I need to make love to you properly... please say yes." Gage whispered, trailing kisses up his neck, and used the arm under Trent's shoulders to pull his head closer, to plunge his tongue into Trent's ear. All Trent could manage was a deeper moan and bucked his hips forward. Gage squeezed his dick tightly, keeping the orgasm held off a little while longer.

"Listen to me. We're at your house. Let me come in. We can lock the bedroom door, and be quiet, the kids won't ever know. Let me make love to you tonight," Gage whispered in his ear. The hot, moist breath tickled, sending shivers shooting down Trent's body, and Gage again started the massage on his cock. This time stroking with purpose.

"I want more than the backseat, tonight. Please," Gage asked again, pulling his hand free and working to push Trent back into his slacks.

Trent finally registered the words coming at him, and he missed the loss of Gage's hand on his cock. He rose, keeping Gage in his arms, looking out the limo window. They were parked in the street of his neighborhood in front of his house. How had he missed that? "Damn, I didn't even realize."

"That's a compliment, now, say you'll let me come in," Gage said, moving his head back in Trent's line of vision.

"We have to be quiet, Gage," Trent said and inhaled a small breath when Gage rubbed him from the outside of his pants.

"I will, and I'll be gone way before they wake up, I promise," Gage said.

"All right, let's go," Trent said and rose off Gage. His pants were unbuttoned and it took a minute to adjust himself and straighten his clothing. Gage grabbed his jacket and tie, not bothering to right himself, but turned to a small cabinet.

"Do you have condoms and such, Trent? I can bring these?" Gage didn't wait for the answer, but dropped them into his coat pocket. Trent stayed behind a minute more, adjusting himself, and he could hear Gage talking quietly as he tucked his shirt all the way in.

"Can you have my Prius brought to me? Put the keys in the mailbox, please," Gage said.

"Yes, sir, and you won't need me any further tonight, Mr. Synclair?" the driver asked. Trent bypassed the conversation and began to walk up to the house, but Gage stopped him, grabbing his hand, pulling him back.

"No, thank you for everything tonight," Gage said to the driver.

"Good night, sir." The driver nodded at Trent and checked the back door before rounding the trunk to make his way to the driver's side. All night, Gage never let Trent stray more than a step or two away from him and they walked up to the house together hand-in-hand, neither saying a word. Trent carefully unlocked the door, opening it as silently as he could. Gage slid off his shoes and carried them in the same hand as his jacket. They snuck into the house. Trent toed off his shoes and left them by the entrance. Once the front door closed, Trent listened to see if anything awakened the children, but no one stirred.

He took Gage's hand and led him down the hall to his bedroom. He didn't turn the overhead lights on, but walked to the bedside lamp and flipped it on, before going back to the bedroom door. He carefully turned the outdated knob before silently clicking the lock into place, and then closing the door. Gage stayed quiet, walking into his room, looking around. It wasn't the cleanest it could have been, clothes were draped over an armchair, and he couldn't remember the last time he'd dusted. Gage didn't seem to notice. Instead, he focused on the contents of his TV stand which stood to the right of the foot of his bed.

"You do have my reports." Gage lifted a case as he whispered quietly.

"I told you I did," Trent said, coming to stand behind Gage, wrapping him in his arms.

"All of a sudden, I'm proud of myself. I'm glad you like them, Trent," Gage said, discarding the video while turning in Trent's arms, dipping his head for a smoldering kiss. "Make love to me, Trent. I need you." Gage's voice dripped in seduction as he trailed kisses down Trent's neck.

Trent took the shoes from Gage's hand and quietly placed them on the floor by the television. He took the jacket still in Gage's arms, first dumping the condoms and oil onto his bed, before tossing the jacket over the arm of his chair. Gage never left the circle of Trent's arms, as he stood there watching him, and Trent lifted his arms to finish unbuttoning Gage's shirt. He pushed it off Gage's shoulders and grabbed it before it hit the floor, tossing it over the tux jacket.

Tonight, Gage wore a white undershirt, and Trent lifted it up and over his head, throwing it in the general direction of Gage's other things while running his fingertips and palms over his muscular chest. Gage began to unbuckle his belt.

"Let me undress you tonight," Trent said, placing a hand over Gage's, stopping him. He took his time. Gage leaned in, trying to slant his mouth over Trent's, but he dodged it, pulling away. "No, I've finally gotten you in my bedroom, where I've dreamed of you every night since first laying eyes on you. I'm going to make this last."

"Sexy, I like the effort, I do, but I want you so badly," Gage said and pushed Trent's hands down, rubbing them along his dick. "I've been like this since I watched you walk down your hall tonight. Please make love to me, don't drag this out."

Gage's voice grew desperate, his eyes implored him to do his bidding, and Trent squeezed Gage's cock with his palm, bringing his other hand up to work the belt and button free. His intention was to take piece by piece off the man standing before him, but he found he needed to taste this hard-on in his hand faster than he thought.

When he lowered the zipper, Trent shoved his hands inside, pushing the slacks and boxers down until they fell to the ground. Trent bent low, positioning Gage's cock to make it a smooth slide into his mouth. He hadn't given Gage a blow job yet, and it had been a very long time since he'd been in this position. He didn't hesitate, though; he took Gage straight into his mouth, letting his tongue lick and slide down the hard, velvety cock in his hands. Gage let out the most delicious moan and tangled his fingers into Trent's hair, urging him on.

Trent took him deep, while slowly dropping to his knees. He could feel his throat constrict as he sucked Gage in and out of his mouth in several long, deep strokes. His fingers slid around Gage's ass and began to massage the tight rim. Trent willed himself to relax, wanting to take Gage farther down his throat and after a couple more attempts of sliding Gage in and out of his mouth, he succeeded. Trent couldn't be certain whether it was the finger he pushed into Gage's ass or the way his mouth worked him, but Gage pistoned his hips, driving his cock forward, fucking Trent's mouth until he pulled back. Trent slid Gage fully out of his mouth and took his finger from his ass while licking across Gage's broad head, lapping at the small beads of moisture gathering at the top. He loved his taste.

"Don't stop, baby," Gage groaned quietly, gently pushing Trent's head back down with the grip he still had on his hair. Trent smiled and chuckled at the urgency of Gage's hands, wanting him to do more.

"Get in bed. I want you to enjoy this," Trent said, lifting his hand and massaging Gage's sac as he spoke.

"I am enjoying it," Gage said, his hands still in Trent's hair. Trent glanced up, captured by Gage's erotically intense stare. If eyes could beg, these were willing him to keep going.

"Bed, Gage," Trent said, and sat back on his heels, unbuttoning his own shirt, pulling it off his body. He let the material slide down his arms and flexed his pecs and biceps as the material slid free. That gained Gage's attention. A smile tugged at Gage's lips as he gripped his own cock, watching Trent closely. Gage sat down on the end of the bed and pushed himself back to the headboard, his eyes never left Trent. Gage's hand continued the back and forth movement, stroking his cock as he stood, and continued to undressed.

Trent tossed the shirt on the chair and unbuckled his belt, snapping it free of the loops in one quick movement. He tossed the belt on his chair along with their other things. Next came the button to the slacks, he flicked it open smiling at the smoldering look in Gage's eyes. He paused on the slacks, deciding to save those for last and lifted each foot, taking each sock off, purposely flexing all the muscles in his arms with every tug and then tossing the socks over to the chair as well.

"You're such a tease," Gage said, but Trent could tell he thoroughly enjoyed the show.

"You said you like my chest," Trent said, lifting his eyebrows, a slow smile sliding in place.

"I do," Gage said. Trent flexed his chest muscles again, in a little show of dominance. Gage rolled his hips, shoving his dick farther in his hand. A moan slipped from his parted lips. "Trent, take your pants off."

Trent began lowering the zipper of his slacks, letting the muscles on his stomach ripple as the zipper slid down. Gage gave an approving moan at the show he put on, and Trent hooked his thumbs inside his slacks, and slowly pushed down, until they fell to the floor. He stepped out of them, kicking them up with his foot to his hand. He tossed them over the chair and turned his gaze back to Gage as he lowered his briefs and let them fall to the floor.

"Come to me, let me take care of that for you, handsome," Gage said, still working himself.

"No, this is my night, Gage," Trent said, removing Gage's socks. When they were both fully naked, Trent made a show of climbing onto the end of the bed and crawling between Gage's legs. Gage tried to bring him forward, tried to kiss him, but he evaded the attempts, moving the condoms and oil closer to him and laying his chest between Gage's parted thighs.

He gripped the base of Gage's cock while placing small kisses and simple licks up Gage's thighs toward the sac hanging below his cock. As he worked his mouth forward, Trent gently mashed Gage's balls together with his lips, sucking each one into his mouth before he lifted with a final lap of his tongue, taking the jutting cock back into his mouth. He slid Gage deep, opening his throat as far as he could at that angle, before pulling back and licking his way back up. He held onto the base of Gage's cock, stroking him, and lifted his eyes to take in Gage's reaction. He'd stayed quiet through it all, and Trent needed confirmation from his lover. Gage's expression clearly indicated his intense pleasure, and Trent reached down to place a small kiss on the broad head of the dripping cock, ready to take this man to the peak of ecstasy.

"Dear God, you're fucking good." Gage dropped his head back onto the pillow. A deep moan escaped Gage's lips, and he gripped the bedspread with each hand, fisting it tight. Trent reached for the oil and took Gage back inside his mouth; this time moving faster and using his hand to work the base of Gage's cock. He flipped the bottle open with his thumb and poured drops straight onto Gage's ass. With each pump of his mouth, Trent worked a finger inside of Gage. He could feel his own cock swelling thicker and fuller until it jerked, ready to burst with the mere thought of making love to Gage. When Gage grew hard as steel, his balls clenching, Trent stopped and moved away, grabbing the condoms and oil beside him.

"No!" Gage called out, his voice hoarse with need. His head lifted up, confusion clear in his eyes.

"Shhh," Trent said, ripping the condom package open, sliding it on his hard dick.

"Trent, suck me just a little more. I'm almost there." Gage reached for him, trying to move him back down.

"I know, but it's not time yet. I want us to come together," Trent said, crawling up between Gage's parted legs to lie down on his chest, drawing him into a demanding swirl of tongue and teeth. Trent thrust his tongue forward again and again, and Gage wrapped himself around his body, holding him tightly in place. Their hard cocks rubbed together between their bodies, and Gage pumped his hips up in one urgent thrust after another seeking relief. Trent ripped free of the tight hold, pushing himself up to his knees spreading Gage farther apart.

Gage's ass looked oil slicked and relaxed, but his face looked in pain. The agony of his own need raged through him. He opened the small bottle again, tipping it to drip straight on his dick and then poured several drops on his fingers. He massaged Gage's rim to keep the tight opening relaxed. Nothing would stop Trent from trying to give Gage the best sex of his life. He never knew he had one, but Trent had surely found a possessive side as the night continued, and all of the sudden, he wanted Gage to forget anyone before him and crave only his touch, like he craved Gage's.

He circled the tight ring of muscle and slid his thumb inside, finding the spot immediately. As he pressed down, Gage bucked his hips forward and grasped his dick while his head rolled back. Trent pushed Gage's hands away and took his cock in his hand, stroking it in time to the movement of his thumb while adding a second finger.

"Fuck, Trent, goddamn, please," Gage said in a desperate whisper.

"I'm not rushing this. I want you ready... Ready for me," Trent said and released the throbbing cock in his hand to add a condom, and a few more drops of oil to his third finger before sliding inside Gage. He added a few extra drops to his own cock, flipped the lid back closed, and tossed it to the side. He stroked his own swollen cock, coating it thoroughly before positioning himself between Gage's parted legs. Gage lifted his legs, gripping his thighs tightly in his hands to give Trent all the room he needed. Trent slowly slid inside. With each inch he worked himself in, he watched Gage arch his long back and strain his shoulders and neck, tossing his head back onto the pillow. A smile came to Gage's lips with a long quiet moan escaping.

Gage made such a gorgeous, intoxicating sight. Trent bit his lip and forced himself to concentrate.

He pushed forward, burying himself completely inside Gage. The sensation forced the air from his lungs, and his hips began moving slowly out, only to slide back in again. His breath heaved in staccato pants, his heart slammed against his ribs, and he fell forward burying his face in Gage's neck.

Gage's body stayed hard, tense, and his rocking hips met Trent's, move for move. They were fluid together. Easily becoming one and all his plans to make Gage forget all the others backfired as Trent lost himself to the man in his arms.

Trent kept a measured pace, moving in and out, back and forth, slowly making love to Gage. He reached his arms under Gage's back to grip his shoulders, keeping him from moving too far forward with every thrust he made. He ran his nose along Gage's neck, breathing in the musky cologne with the sweet smell of their sex filling the air. He lifted his mouth, placing a soft kiss on Gage's ear before whispering the words so deep in his heart.

"I love you," Trent said. Gage didn't stop the rolling movement of his hips, but forced Trent's head up by placing both hands on his cheeks, physically lifting him to make eye contact. Gage's lust-filled gaze centered in on his face, his breath panted from between those sexy lips, and he forced Trent to look at him before he spoke.

"I love you, Trent. I do, so much. I want you… this… forever," Gage whispered. Trent lowered his head, slanting his mouth over Gage's, desperate to have contact in every way possible. The kiss, like their current love making, was the most tender of his life. Gage matched him as they swirled their tongues together. His hips slowly began to buck into Gage and the movement picked up speed. Trent pulled away from the hands on his face, shifted his weight to his elbow, to reach between their bodies and stroke Gage's steel-hard cock. Gage wrapped his arms around Trent and pushed his head back into the pillow as far as it would go, begging Trent to finish this. The simple touch was all it took. Gage went first, his seed shooting up his chest. Trent held off no more than a second before wave after wave of hot ecstasy crashed over him.

He let go of Gage, trying not to fall down on top of him. The effort was futile, and he collapsed in a heap. Gage seemed ready for him though, and wrapped him back into his arms. They lay there several minutes, letting the earth slowly settle back around them. Gage recovered first and kissed his head lying on the pillow beside him.

"I want you to know I meant it," Gage whispered quietly into his hair.

"I did too," Trent whispered into the pillow, his heart finally slowing to a normal beat.

"Good," Gage said, and with a monumental effort, Trent pushed himself off Gage to lie on his back on the bedspread. He took a second, watching the ceiling fan turn.

"Hang on, don't move. I'll get you a towel," Trent said, but didn't really move like he'd planned to do. Instead, he closed his eyes, listening to Gage move.

"You're just as messy as I am," Gage said and rolled to the side of the bed, pushing slowly to his feet. He walked to the bathroom and wet a towel, cleaning himself. He grabbed a wet washcloth and wiped it across Trent. The cold water jarred him enough to get the condom off and disposed of and Gage cleaned him up there, too.

"What time do the kids wake up?" Gage asked, taking the towel back to the bathroom.

"Around six. They'll probably sleep in a little later tomorrow morning because they stayed up so late tonight," Trent said, finally rising to a sitting position, his feet on the floor. Gage came to sit beside him on the bed.

"You were perfect tonight. Thank you... I have a thought, if I set my phone for five thirty, I could be gone before they ever wake, but it would give me a few hours to sleep, holding you in my arms before I have to go out of town," Gage said.

"I hate to ask you to leave like that," Trent said a yawn forming as he spoke.

"It's fine," Gage said, following Trent's yawn with his own. "I would rather do it like that than leave now. I'll be gone for several days. I'm gonna miss you bad, Trent." Gage ran his hand up the inside of Trent's thigh.

"Get up, come get in bed," Trent said, rising to push the covers down. Gage slid in bed on the same side as Trent and pushed himself to the middle. Trent followed him in, turning off the lamp beside his bed, covering them as he slid into Gage's arms.

"I meant what I said, Trent. All of it," Gage said.

"Me, too," Trent said, again. It took them a minute to decide who would lie where, but finally Gage came across Trent's chest, tangling their legs together, tucking his phone under the pillow to silently wake him in a few hours.

"I've wanted to tell you for a few days," Gage said, not letting the moment go. Trent brought Gage's chin up, looking at him in the dark, wanting to hear this. "I've known for a while, for sure since our first date, but honestly before then. I couldn't get you out of my mind, no matter how hard I tried. You consumed me from the very beginning."

"It's the way I feel about you," Trent whispered, his voice hoarse with the emotion of his confession.

"Good, I'm glad. You made me a bit of a crazy man," Gage said, kissing his chest before he lowered his head again.

"I couldn't see how someone like you could want someone like me."

"Are you kidding me? You were the most handsome man in the room tonight, Trent Cooper. And your integrity is definitely higher than any person I've ever known," Gage said.

"Whatever, but you did great tonight. People love you, but some are scared of you, too. It was kind of funny to watch," Trent said, chuckling at the thought of all the 'Yes, Mr. Synclairs' he'd heard tonight.

"It was a good night. Since the sales were so high, I'll attract bigger artist names for shows. I can mix some of the unknowns in there to make it a good place for beginners to have a starting point, and be seen," Gage said, lifting again to kiss his chest and Trent leaned forward, letting Gage kiss his lips. "I hadn't officially come out before tonight."

"I couldn't remember ever hearing you're gay. I racked my brain about it. I thought I would have remembered hearing something like that. Why haven't you?" Trent asked.

"Because I hadn't met you, yet," Gage simply said. Trent lifted again to get a kiss, and he wrapped Gage tighter into his arms as the love of the words washed over his heart.

"Will it affect you?" Trent asked.

"I don't know. I think this last investigation is strong enough to overcome it, though. I think the merit of it will help put the focus back on the person and not the sleeping partner," Gage said.

"Mmmm... I haven't asked about this last report. I don't want to know. I like seeing it all together on TV, but is it dangerous? Your reports seem a little more dangerous each time," Trent said.

"I really can't talk about this one yet. It's a big one, but I'll be careful. Are you worried about me?" Gage asked, looking up with a grin.

"Of course I am... I guess I just came out in a major way, too," Trent said, dropping his head back down on the pillow, realizing what he'd done tonight. How had that not occurred to him before now?

"Yeah, I thought of it, but I spoke with my father tonight. He was impressed with you. He agreed to throw more business your way, make you the lead electrical contractor for this area. You won them over tonight. I knew you would. He looked around at your work, I told him about the panel change, and the project manager said you busted your ass to get it all done. He agreed, there'll be paperwork to get you signed up, but he's calling you next week to get it all finalized," Gage said, tightening his hold.

"Really?"

"Yep."

"I wanted in there," Trent said, thinking over the possibility.

"My parents like you. They loved the kids. It's funny, I've spent most of my life trying to separate from my family, prove I can do it on my own. Then I met you. You make family look appealing. They were shocked when they saw you. I hadn't told them you guys were coming. They hid it well, but they were shocked. Babe, promise to tell me if any of your customers leave you over me. I don't want you hurt in any way for standing beside me, tonight," Gage said and lifted up again to make direct eye contact with Trent. He stayed silent, not answering. Gage settled back against his chest. He knew he wouldn't tell Gage any of it. He didn't want Gage obligated to him. It would be the fastest way to run him off. He had some money saved, several jobs booked, and he was a master electrician. Surely he could keep things going, at the very least, until he found a decent job.

Gage's soft snores jarred him from his thoughts. He lifted up and moved a little to look at Gage while he slept. His features softened in sleep, those sexy lips relaxed. Even though they'd only known each other a short time, their fates had collided, and Gage had truly become everything to him. Trent had never allowed another man in this room before tonight. After a few minutes of watching, he snuggled Gage up to him a little more, and laid his head back down on the pillow, falling asleep.

Gage woke with a start when the phone vibrated under his pillow. It took a second for him to figure out where he was and another second to remember he needed to get the heck out of Trent's house before the kids woke.

Trent still slept in his arms, but they had shifted positions, with Trent's back pressed against his chest. Gage's arms were wrapped around Trent, a leg thrown across him to keep him close. He'd never voluntarily slept with another person. One too many drinks may have helped him pass out in another's bed, but he never woke touching anyone, ever. Now it was like his arms refused to leave Trent.

While he worked he would occasionally interview grieving spouses or parents. They would say thing like my arms ached to hold my husband or my child. Gage hadn't understood the sentiment as completely as he did in this moment.

He stayed there a few minutes more, listening to Trent sleep. It wasn't a snore necessarily, but a deep breathing like before, and he leaned his head in, running his nose along Trent's hair breathing him in. He wore masculine scented cologne, a spicy musk. The fragrance appealed to Gage just like the soft ends of Trent's hair brushing against his face. When he came back from finalizing this story, he planned to aggressively pursue Trent. Flowers, hearts, love poems… Whatever it took, he would do it all until enough time passed when he could legally make Trent his. Gage wanted it all now. He wanted the soul mate for life, the happily ever after. Maybe they could add a couple of other children, giving Em and Hunter a big family to pull from as they got older.

A smile tugged at his lips as he watched the clock blink five forty-five. He promised Trent he would leave before the kids saw him, but he couldn't help but to hold out until the last possible minute. With a sigh, he pulled himself silently from the bed, choosing not to wake Trent. His clothes still lay under Trent's, and he carefully watched his sleeping boyfriend as he quietly pulled on his pants and then shrugged on his shirt. He only buttoned one button of his shirt before grabbing his jacket and shoes. He lifted them with two fingers and silently walked over to the door.

The lock was set, but he'd been in the position of sneaking out so many times he knew how to release the mechanism without making noise. He held the lock button with his thumb and turned the knob. The release gave way without a loud click, and he slowly lifted his thumb. He opened the door, slid out, and shut it behind him. The house was quiet, but not quite as dark with the sun just beginning to make its presence known. He tiptoed down the hall, made it to the front entryway, opening the door quietly like he had Trent's bedroom door.

"Hi, Gage," Hunter said. It startled him and he jerked back around to see the little boy standing in the entryway, his Spider-man pajamas on, just staring at him.

"Hey, Hunter," Gage whispered back. "What are you doing up?

"I had to get a drink of water," Hunter said, rubbing his sleepy eyes. "Daddy's sleeping, should I go wake him up?"

"No, don't wake him. I… I just… I just thought I would surprise him and make breakfast for you all," Gage said, and he groaned internally as his mind rejected the stupid lie. Even a child wouldn't believe that silly gesture. Why couldn't he come up with something better?

"Can I help?" Hunter asked, the sleep leaving his face, replaced by excitement. Gage watched him closely for any sign that the boy thought something was up. *Score!* He was in the clear.

"Sure, I would like for you to, but we have to be quiet to make it a surprise," Gage said, softly shutting the door back as though he'd just arrived.

"Can Em help? She likes to cook," Hunter asked.

"I guess so. Go wake her up and be super quiet for me."

"Okay." Hunter headed off to rouse Em.

Gage prayed Trent would be okay with this turn of events. He weighed his options. He could call out for breakfast, but then the kids couldn't help. He could try to pull together something. Maybe scrambled eggs and bacon, if Trent had bacon… But he so wasn't a cook! Deciding it would be fastest to just try to put together a breakfast, he went into the kitchen and began rummaging through the refrigerator. He got a little lost digging through the different things on the shelf. He never cooked for himself unless there was no other choice, and generally only after starving for a full twenty-four hours beforehand. Those situations happened rarely, usually during a campout in some remote part of the world.

"Hi, Gage," Em said through the middle of a big yawn. He dug through the refrigerator, pulling things out, and looked around the door to see her standing there. Her long hair a braided tangled mess, and her eyes barely open. The pink pajamas with princess characters on them fit her personality perfectly. Hunter stood behind her.

"Hi, honey, you wanna help?" he asked.

"Yes, please," she said on another yawn.

"Good. I'm thinking scrambled eggs, bacon, and toast," he said, pulling the eggs out last.

"Daddy likes coffee," Hunter said.

"Okay, we'll make coffee, too," Gage said.

"I like chocolate milk," Em said.

"We don't have any chocolate milk, Em," Hunter said, walking around her into the kitchen to get his stool.

"I know, I was just sayin' it," she said, following him.

"Where do you keep the bread?" Gage asked, trying to get them moving, sensing an argument coming on. With the kids' help, he found the coffee components, made the coffee—in all honesty, he was an expert coffee maker—and then started the bacon sizzling. He assigned Hunter to making the toast, and busied Em with stirring the eggs before he poured them in the skillet to cook. The time ticked away, but Gage kept an eye on the clock as they finished the eggs.

About then, he heard Trent coming down the hall, footsteps heavy with residual sleepiness. He could hear Trent flipping on lights, and what sounded like opening the kids' bedroom doors as he passed by on his way toward the kitchen.

"Hunter, Em, it's time to get up. Hit the floor guys. Only one more week left of school," Trent said, and the kids started giggling. Gage shushed them and they stood ready for him to walk in the kitchen.

"Say surprise when you see him," Gage said in a quiet whisper.

"Rhonny, I don't even understand why you're awake, but thank God you are." Trent came around the corner, pulling his T-shirt over his head, and stopped in mid tug.

"*Surprise!*" the kids yelled, standing next to Gage. They were both on their stepstools in their respective stations, finishing up their part of breakfast. Gage stood in the middle of them, letting the worry of the moment show on his face, and he shrugged his shoulders.

"What's this?" Trent asked. Hunter hopped off his stool and ran to Trent who scooped him up.

"Daddy, Gage was coming in the front door, and I was getting a drink of water. He was going to surprise you with breakfast, and he said we could help!" Hunter's body became straight as a board as he wiggled free, done with being held.

"I made the eggs with Gage, and we were quiet," Em said, spatula in hand moving the eggs around the pan, flipping some out as she stirred. "Ooops!"

Trent came through the kitchen, looking at Gage with a very clear *what the hell* expression on his face. He bypassed Gage and grabbed a cup to pour coffee. "I think I need a cup of this before I form any more of a response. You wanna cup, Gage?"

He turned to see Gage helping Em finish the eggs and making sure she stayed safe near the stove.

"A cup would be lovely," Gage said. He poured another cup, then pulled plates, silverware, and napkins out of the cabinet.

"It smells good in here," Trent said, giving Gage the cup of coffee. "The cream is in the fridge. You shouldn't have done all this."

"It's my pleasure, handsome," Gage said, turning to give him a wink.

Trent jumped in to fix the kids' plates, pour their milk and get them settled at the table. Gage followed suit fixing his own plate and pouring more coffee before he sat. As Trent fixed his plate, Rhonny came through the kitchen door, stopping in mid-stride, looking at Gage, then Trent. Her eyes focused on the kids, then Gage, then back to Trent again. Her long hair piled on her head, held together in a messy knot, and she wore pajama pants and a tank top.

"Good morning, guys?" she said, her brow narrowing.

"Rhonny, we cooked breakfast with Gage," Em said.

"I see," Rhonny said, still looking at Trent like he'd completely lost his mind.

"Gage surprised us. He was coming in when Hunter was getting a drink." Trent left it hanging there, taking his seat at the table. He could see when the explanation made sense, and she finally turned, heading straight for the coffee.

"I see, well, lucky me. I get the morning breakfast chores off. Gage, I had a great time last night. Thank you for inviting me," Rhonny said, pouring her coffee.

"I'm glad you had a good time. I hope my brother didn't spoil your night, he seemed very attentive," Gage said, scooping eggs into his mouth.

"He was nice, I think we might go to dinner on Saturday night if Trent doesn't need me," Rhonny said, grabbing a slice of bacon and coming back to the table. She sat on a barstool, her leg bent, foot in the chair, eating the bacon.

"That's 'cause Rhonny's in love," Hunter said.

"Whatever, squirt! You better hush and eat that breakfast or I'm telling your dad you have a girlfriend at school!" Rhonny said, lifting her brow, acting like she let the secret out.

"What? A girlfriend?" Trent asked, looking over at Hunter.

"Rhonny!" Hunter yelled.

"He does, Daddy, I forgot I was going to tell you. I told Rhonny," Em said. "Her name is Holly."

"Holly and Hunter, that's cool. Is it the Holly in your class?" Trent asked his red-faced little boy. Hunter refused to speak, keeping his head down. Trent reached over and rustled his hair, looking down, trying to catch his eye. "Hunter, I don't care if you have a girlfriend. It's fine, buddy. It's normal at your age. The books said it, my man..."

"They're going to get married," Em said, and Hunter finally lifted his head, glaring at her.

"Not until at least ninth grade," Hunter said. "But, Daddy, she has to stop saying 'come here' so much. She makes me stop playing with my friends to come here and play with her."

"Yeah, girls are like that," Gage said, and Rhonny laughed.

"All right, guys, we have to get dressed. It's already close to seven. We only have a little while before we have to leave," Rhonny said. She got them up from the table, working them out of the kitchen.

"Hunter, come here a minute," Trent said, and Hunter walked around the table, keeping his head down as he came to stand by him. He wrapped an arm around his little boy and pulled Hunter in close, bending down to talk quietly to him. "Son, I'm very proud of you, and you can tell me anything, you don't have to keep secrets. I want you to have a good life, okay?"

"Daddy, I didn't want you to feel bad because I had a girlfriend and you don't have anyone. Auntie Sophia said you were lonely and you needed to go out and meet people." Hunter spilled it all out and finally lifted those big green eyes to his, worry all over his face.

"Son, how could I be lonely? I have you and Em with me?"

"Daddy, that's what I thought, too. I was right!" Hunter wrapped his arms around Trent's neck and hugged him tight, then bounded off, apparently done with the conversation. Rhonny and Em stood by the kitchen door, waiting on him.

"Bye, Gage," Hunter said, zooming from the room.

"Bye, Gage," Em called.

"Bye, guys, thanks for helping me with breakfast," he said. Em came back to give him a hug before she took off into the living room. Trent sat across the table for several long moments before Gage moved closer, taking Hunter's seat.

"You're a very good father, and I'm so sorry. He caught me at the door and I didn't know what to do," Gage said.

"You covered it well," Trent said, taking a drink of his coffee.

"He totally busted me. I waited too long to leave. I laid there watching you sleep and lost track of time," Gage said, watching Trent closely.

"You watched me sleep?" Trent asked, his grin growing with each word spoken.

"Absolutely, I'm a man in love! You're the most exquisite thing I've ever laid eyes on." Gage leaned in and gave Trent a sweet soft kiss on the lips. "I have to get going. My plane needs to leave by ten. I'm sorry to leave you with the dishes."

"No, it's fine, besides you said whoever cooks shouldn't do the dishes. Thank you for breakfast," Trent said. Gage reached across the table, taking Trent's hand.

"Thank you for last night. I loved waking up with you in my arms," Gage said, leaning into Trent again, kissing him a little more than before. Gage gave a small swipe of his tongue this time.

"I slept good, too. I didn't want to get up," Trent said, leaning close.

"Me either, it's why Hunter caught me. I'll have to do better next time," Gage said, getting up, placing his cup in the sink. "Walk me out?"

"Sure." Trent scooted his chair out and took Gage through the living room to the front door. Once on the porch, Gage turned, taking Trent into his arms pushing him to the far reaches of the porch somewhat secluded from the street.

"I don't want to leave," Gage said and leaned in, placing a simple kiss on Trent's lips. Trent wrapped his arms around Gage, tightening his hold. He didn't want Gage to leave. He wanted exactly this moment every day from now until… well, forever.

"Be safe this trip. Make it an amazing story," Trent said, feeling reasonably sure he sounded convincing.

"I meant everything I said last night," Gage said while never leaving Trent's personal space.

"Me too," Trent said. *And I want you to say it again.*

"I want to kiss you so badly, but I haven't brushed me teeth," Gage said, and Trent reached up, but Gage pulled back. Not willing to be denied, Trent grinned and lifted his hand to Gage's head before he spun him around, changing positions. Now he had Gage pressed back against the wall. Trent slanted his mouth over Gage's and thrust his tongue forward. Gage didn't resist and opened for the kiss. Trent kissed him long and hard until his dick stood wanting and his knees wobbled. Even then it took several minutes before he pulled away.

"Think about me when you're gone. No meeting any men along the way," Trent said, drawing Gage into a hug.

"You have nothing to worry about there. My guy holds my heart." Gage leaned in to kiss Trent's neck as one of the Coop Electric trucks pulled into the driveway behind Gage's Prius. His electrician could see everything from where he sat in his truck. All eyes met one another. His electrician's eyes narrowed, really taking in the scene before looking away.

"I haven't hid, I swear, but I've never mixed it all up like this. I guess I'm completely out now," Trent said, turning back to Gage trying to hide his worry.

"It's all good. They're gonna have to get used to seeing me around, Trent. I'm here to stay." Gage kissed him again on the lips and pulled free of the hold. He took the steps down, looking back over his shoulder. "I'll call you as soon as I can and let you know my schedule. I'm going to Mexico. I don't know how good my signal will be, but I'll try to stay in touch. Remember those gifts are coming tomorrow, and tell Em happy birthday for me. I really wish I could be here for both her and you, I'll try. I love you."

"I love you," Trent called after him and watched his electrician back out of the driveway to let Gage leave, then pulled back into the drive a little too aggressively. Trent kept his eyes on the guy, until he pulled past the house into the back, and he prayed everything would work out.

Chapter 18

The surveillance equipment laid spread across Gage's bed, and he looked over everything, ticking off his mental check list of needed supplies. His cameras, lenses, scores of memory cards, tripods, cleaning equipment, all terrain laptop, and back up everything were all ready to go. On the other side of the bed, his personal climbing gear, binoculars, compass, canteen, toiletries, and clothing consisting of a couple of T-shirts, shorts, socks, underwear, and bandanas scattered across the coverlet. Gage packed numerous bandanas to keep the sweat out of his eyes and the dust from his mouth.

He didn't plan on staying long. Gage added his broadcasting equipment to the gear, but in his heart he planned to do what it took to be back here for Emalynn's birthday party on Sunday. That meant he would fly back to Mexico on Monday morning to broadcast his findings from the short weekend trip.

All of this was his personal equipment, and he never let anyone handle it. This load would be heavy, but the checkpoints to the mission were reasonably secure and waited his arrival. His hidden campsite required a three mile hike through the desert of Mexico, placing them just west of the mission. They would use manmade tunnels, all carved out centuries ago, in one of the mountain ranges to be the go-between from the campsite to the abandoned convent mission tucked in a Valley between two mountain ranges. Gage had checked the forecast before he came up to pack. It looked like the temperature would be somewhere around a million degrees, making it a fun-filled, treacherous assignment all the way around.

Gage ran his hands over his face and through his hair. He needed to get this show started; time ticked away, and he was making himself late. The chartered jet sat waiting for him while he stalled because all he could think about was his sexy, hot as hell, new boyfriend... who loved him. He shook his head at the grin that wouldn't leave his face, and he silently began packing. He was a loved man...someone amazing loved just him...and it set his world on fire.

Slinging his cases over his arm, he dropped his keys and phone into the front pocket of his walking shorts and turned off the lights in the upstairs area. He trotted down the stairs and hit the door to the gallery with a kick in his step. He shut the door and set the security to his upstairs apartment and turned to see his driver, his security guard, and Jacquelyn all staring at him. At first, he didn't understand their confused appraisal of him, and then he remembered the smile that never left his face.

"I guess someone had a good time last night," Jacquelyn said, coming to stand at the front entrance of her office.

"I did, great showing last night," he said, passing her by.

"Here, Gage. I have a collection of media coverage on last night. I packed it for you to read on the flight," Jacquelyn said, handing him a large manila envelope full of newspaper clippings. "This is print media. I'm sending you an email link of all the online news feeds coming in. Your boy was a big hit last night, you two have pictures everywhere."

"Hmmm... keep me posted on that. If it doesn't die down in a few days, I want to know. Refer everything to my agent, they have some statement ready to go," he said, walking past her to the front door.

"You two were hot last night, and for the record, I totally picked up on it from day one," she called out after Gage.

"Yeah, right, whatever! Maybe you could have put me out of my misery, because I sure didn't pick it up," Gage called out, laughing, as he walked out the front door, his driver following behind him.

The chartered jet waited for him at Executive International. His driver drove him directly to the tarmac after passing through security at the gates. It took only minutes for him to board before they were on their way to Mexico. Gage pulled out his laptop, sent a couple of quick emails to his travel agent, needing to book this same flight for Sunday morning. They emailed back and forth, and for a small fortune, he'd arranged to have the plane waiting for him in Mexico at midnight,

Sunday morning, with a return flight placing him back on Mexican soil sometime after six in the morning on Monday. That would give him all day with Em, then all night with Trent. If he worked aggressively, he could broadcast by Tuesday and be home Wednesday morning.

Absently, he wondered if there were a way to talk Trent into being at his apartment Wednesday about mid-day in nothing other than his tool belt and a smile, possibly bent over working an outlet when he arrived home. The thought made his smile grow, and he pulled out his phone to bring up a photo he'd snapped last night when Trent had been unaware he'd been watching. Trent Cooper was such a handsome man. Everything about him turned Gage on. This snapshot may have been about the time Trent learned who his parents were. He breathed a sigh of relief over that situation. He'd been lucky. Gage had worried Trent would be angry with him for keeping the secret, but so far he seemed to understand.

The in-flight attendants made their presence known, bringing Gage his normal coffee and bagel. A tradition he'd started years ago and never changed. As he sat, picking at the bagel, he pulled the newspapers out and grinned. Jacquelyn was right. Every entertainment section of every major newspaper printed the story from the Associated Press about his gallery opening. The same picture ran in all the newspapers. Admittedly, it was a great picture. He stood with his arm wrapped casually around Trent's waist, introducing him to Katie Couric. They were all smiling at one another, Trent's charming grin in place, Katie looking a bit overwhelmed by Trent, and Gage laughing at her for being so taken with his date.

The article didn't give much away about Trent. It talked about Gage's opening and the small reference he made during his speech about the last report. Sid was quoted saying everything in this last report came together nicely. The only other comment the article made was a quote from Gage when he told a reporter Trent was his boyfriend and lived locally in Chicago. Gage cringed, looking at the article. In hindsight, maybe he shouldn't have said that, but pride ran deep inside him. He didn't want to hide them, but he also hadn't considered the homophobic atmosphere of construction and what it might mean to Trent's future. He laid the newspaper aside and brought his phone up to text his father.

Dad, thank you for coming last night. It meant the world for you and mom to be there. Gage sent the text to his father.

Son, I'm not your mother, you don't need to butter me up. What can I do for you? Jack Layne texted back, and Gage chuckled at the reply. His father knew him well.

I'm reminding you to get Coop Electric on as a vendor as we discussed last night.

Already done, son. They'll contact him early next week and get all the paperwork completed. Bids should come his way as early as the end of next week. Jack sent back.

Perfect, Dad, thank you. Gage sighed in relief, knowing Trent would be protected...at least professionally.

No thanks necessary. Now, this does mean I want you at Sunday dinner as much as you can be there. It means everything to your mom to have all her children there. Bring Trent and the kids. We need to get them used to our crazy crew.

I will. I'm in Mexico this weekend, but I'll talk to Trent about the next weekend for sure.

Thanks, son. Be careful out there. Let us know you're home safe.

Thanks, Dad. Gage ended the text session and placed the phone back on the table close to the laptop.

He spent the rest of the trip attempting to return emails, go over market reports, and check on the sales number from last night, but his mind stayed on Trent the entire time he worked. His silly grin stayed firmly in place.

As the plane descended, Gage palmed his phone one last time and sent a message to Trent. *This is probably the last time I'll have service for a while. I wanted to tell you bye and I miss you already. I'll see you when I can. I love you, baby. Now I've said it out loud, I seem to want to say it over and over. I love you, Trent. You've made me the happiest man in the world. Have a good day, I'll be home soon. Gage.*

The plane touched down and Gage realized he hadn't done one bit of the homework he should have done since missing most of the day yesterday. He'd spent the flight concentrating on Trent and not much more. Yet this was game time, he should have been going over yesterday's videos, reading the reports, not focused on exactly what shade of green matched the true color of Trent's eyes.

Gage needed to get down to business. There would be no time for him to continue like this. If he did, he could easily blow the whole report. Abdulla was cunning and deadly. It wouldn't just be the report he blew, but he could jeopardize his men's safety if he didn't maintain his A-game.

Gage flipped up the blind on the small window inside the plane to view the remote landing location, an old abandoned airfield now overgrown with foliage. They were approximately one hundred fifty miles west of the convent mission. Two jeeps barreled up to the plane, supposedly his ride for the next leg of the adventure.

"Sir, we just got word Manuel is here. Is it safe to lower the steps?" the captain asked.

"Ah, my ride. Yes, please do." Gage rose. The flight attendant had his bags ready, and he slung his equipment and duffle over his shoulder and grabbed his laptop before he made his way to the front of the plane. The hatch opened and the stairs descended. Gage stopped as he exited the plane, and stuck his head back inside the cabin to look at the attendant. He pointed toward the print media settled on a seat.

"Please keep those articles safe, I'll get them from you when I return." He dropped his aviators in place and ducked out the door again. The first jeep waited for him near the bottom of the stairs. They looked like a muscled band of Contra rebels waiting below. There were three fully armed men in the first jeep, four in the next, all wearing assault rifles resting within easy reach. They watched their surroundings as he climbed off the plane and stalked to the first jeep.

Manuel, the only one Gage knew by sight, lifted a hand in a silent salute, and Gage nodded, taking the last step, now fully entering Abdulla's world. He mentally shed his life in Chicago, transitioning his mind, focusing on his target. This was his career, his passion. But Trent was too good for this mess, and Gage relegated him to the back corners of his mind, going straight into investigator mode for the duration of his stay. He dumped his bags in the backseat and used the sidebar to slide inside. Within seconds of his ass hitting the seat, they rocketed out of there.

"Daddy!" Em called, climbing up on his bed, launching herself across his body. "It's my birthday, and it's time to *get up!*"

"Em, are you certain it's your birthday?" Trent asked, grabbing her around the chest, dodging all the limbs and bringing her in for a tight hug.

"Yep, *now get up*! We have to open presents," she said, pushing away from him and landing on her feet back on the floor.

"Wait, Em, I need to look at you, see if you look older," Trent said, lying back on his pillow, giving a big yawn.

"I do, Daddy, now *get up*," Em said, pulling at his arm.

"You don't look older at all, Emalynn," Hunter said from where he'd climbed onto the end of the bed.

"Daddy, get up! I'm so excited!" Em started jumping up and down and Trent looked over at his alarm clock, it was six forty-three on Sunday morning.

"All right, I'll meet you in the living room. I have to brush my teeth and start the coffee, and then we're gonna open those presents," Trent said, feigning excitement that sent Em barreling from the room.

"I'll go with her and make sure she doesn't open them without you," Hunter said.

"Thanks, Hunter, my man," Trent said, ruffling his hair as he walked by, heading toward the bathroom.

Trent brushed his teeth and washed his face. He took a hand towel and ran it over his face, then through his hair and almost wet himself when he rose to see Gage standing in the doorway of his bathroom, holding Em in his arms. Both Rhonny and Hunter started laughing at his shocked expression.

"What are you doing here?" he asked, turning quickly, slinging water everywhere.

"I just couldn't miss today. I was afraid I was getting here too early, but my driver insisted Em would be up. His children all get up at the crack of dawn on their birthdays," Gage said, Em bouncing in his arms.

"Daddy, come on! Let's open presents," Em begged. Gage put her down and she took off again to the living room. Hunter followed, but at a much slower pace.

"I'm going to start the coffee," Rhonny said, and she turned following Hunter out.

"What're you doing here?" Trent asked again, running the towel over his hair, patting it down into some semblance of order while coming to stand in front of Gage.

"How can I convince you I want to stand by your side if I miss the first big thing in our lives?" Gage asked. Trent stayed quiet, staring with an occasional blink, speechless. He'd never expected any of this, but most certainly not those words. That one sentence revealed so much more than the desire to show up for his daughter's birthday. Before he could formulate a response, Gage continued, "Exactly, you have no answer, because there is no answer. Now, how about a kiss, handsome? I flew all night." Trent leaned in, but Em tore her way between them before their lips could make contact.

"*Daaaadddddyyyy*, he came to spend the day with me and you. *Come on!*" Em pleaded. They both laughed as she grabbed his hand, pulling him along with her to the living room with Gage following closely behind.

In a place of honor sat a huge stack of wrapped gifts thanks to Gage's generosity. Em went nuts the day before when the delivery driver had dropped them off. Six packages, of all different sizes, wrapped in bright pink gift wrap and giant pink bows. It drove her crazy having to look at them all day without being able to open them. And if she couldn't open them, the next best thing was to speculate as to the contents. She must have guessed a million different things they could be, and last night, when they were decorating the house in streamers, balloons, and Barbie party decorations, she moved them all by herself from place to place trying to find the best spot for them to be opened this morning.

"Let me get a trash bag and the camera, sweet girl," Trent said, and retrieved both, before pouring coffee. Em had Gage sit in the spot of honor next to her on the couch as she opened her gifts. Hunter sat on the floor close to Em, his two gifts nearby, waiting to be opened. Gage had thought of giving Hunter a present as well, adding to Trent's family tradition.

"Did you know he was coming?" Rhonny asked while she grabbed the cream, then Gage's cup of coffee.

"No, it's a surprise. He said he might, but I didn't think he would with everything going on," Trent whispered back as they slowly made their way from the kitchen.

"I like him, Trent," Rhonny said, quietly walking back to the living room.

"Me too," Trent said, following behind her.

"Good," Rhonny teased back, giving him a grin.

Em waited impatiently for their return. Her hands were ready to pull the paper away from the first gift, and she started with the biggest gift from Gage. Once the paper was torn, the present revealed, it took all of five seconds for her to scream, jumping up and down.

"It's the Barbie Dream House! I wanted this so bad! Daddy, I wanted this!" Em cheered.

"Say thank you to Gage, baby," Trent said, smiling at her enthusiasm.

"Thank you! Thank you, Gage!" Hugs were given to everyone in the room and so started the experience for every gift she opened. Hunter gave about the same response, perhaps a little more sedate, but he was equally thrilled with his monster Lego set and duel pack action figure set. When Em got to Rhonny's gift, she opened it and everything stopped until the tiara was placed properly upon her head.

The rest of the morning passed with Trent building the Barbie Dream House, Rhonny cooking Em's specially requested breakfast of pancakes, bacon, and ice cream, and Gage who sat with Hunter, building the Lego set. Em stayed close to Trent while he worked, giving him advice on what she thought about the progress he made and playing with her new Barbies, changing clothes from outfit to outfit. The time flew by. After breakfast, they all dressed to begin the official celebrations of the day. Auntie Crazy came over and a whole new round of squealing started when she brought them presents. Auntie Crazy bought a life size Barbie, which came with a matching dress for Em. Without hesitation, Em made an abrupt wardrobe change, exchanging the dress from the grand opening for the Barbie dress. With the addition of her tiara, they were ready for Chuck E. Cheese and the movies.

It was a perfect day and each minute solidified Gage deeper inside Trent's heart. Though thoughts of Lynn never strayed too far, Gage made everything bearable, easier, and Trent fell more deeply in love with him. With his easy going and fun attitude, Gage fit his family perfectly. He played with the kids the entire time they were at Chuck E. Cheese. By the end of the day, Trent could see that both Rhonny and Sophia fell to his charms as well.

Trent didn't know how, but every time his thoughts drifted toward Lynn and his feelings of loss resurfaced, Gage would pick that exact moment to engage him, draw him out of the melancholy, and bring him back into the celebration of Em. They played together for hours, the adults right alongside Em and Hunter, and it became a competition over the tickets they accumulated from each game. When it looked like Gage might lose the battle of who won the most tickets, he broke the rules and purchased whatever the kids wanted from the prize wall. Later, as they sat in the theater watching the latest Disney film come to life, Gage held Trent's hand and leaned in a couple of times, placing simple sweet kisses on his lips. Gage seemed genuinely happy to be with them.

By nightfall, both Hunter and Em were completely wiped out. There weren't going to be the normal challenges of getting them to sleep that evening. Sophia left for home directly from the theater, and Rhonny scooted off to meet Gary for a late dinner, which left Gage and Trent to take the kids home together. Both tuckered tikes crashed on the ride home, sound asleep before they'd reached the driveway.

Trent carried Hunter inside, while Gage carried a sleeping Em. Gage hadn't been a part of his nightly parenting duties before, and Trent wasn't sure it was a good idea to involve him now, but it did make things easier with both the kids passed out.

"If you can put her in bed, I'll be there in a minute to get her in her PJs," Trent whispered, taking Hunter into his room. The boy never woke as he undressed him and put on his pajamas. As he passed by Em's bedroom door, he heard Gage talking quietly to her. She laid in her bed, changed into her pajamas, and Gage sat on the edge of her bed, reading to her. Her little eyes drifted closed again, and he knew Gage wouldn't be in there too much longer.

Leaving the doorway, he went to get Gage's duffle bag from the entryway where he'd left it this morning. He assumed Gage would be spending the night. Gage's car sat parked in the driveway where someone had dropped it off at some point during the day. As he picked up the bag, he started to put it down again, wondering if he were reading the situation correctly—maybe Gage didn't plan to stay. A sudden movement caused him to turn with a start and Gage stood behind him.

"Shit, you scared me," Trent said with a grin, putting the bag down.

"What are you doing?" Gage demanded.

"I was gonna put this in my room, then I thought you might not be planning to stay," Trent said, looking Gage over. Something was clearly wrong. His smile faded and he felt the crease begin in his brow as he tried to work through the change he saw in Gage. Gage's face was masked in anger. Trent stepped toward him, concerned at what might have happened in the last thirty seconds to upset Gage. "What's wrong?"

Gage stood there staring at him, the anger radiating in waves, but Gage said nothing. Gage finally moved, walking around him, grabbing his duffle, slinging it over his shoulder in a possessive move. The gesture clear. Nothing lost in the translation of the action, but it was still one Trent didn't understand at all. Gage put miles of distance between them in that one move. The ache forming in his heart threatened to win against the confusion crashing through his brain. Trent then noticed the framed picture Gage held.

"What are you doing with Em's picture?" Trent asked, but took a step back. Everything Gage put out to him told him to back the fuck off, so he did.

"Who is this, Trent?" Gage said, thrusting his hand forward, showing Trent the photo.

"It's my sister and her husband; it's Em's parents," Trent said, and crossed his arms over his chest. The pain there crushed him as he looked at his sister on this day, the day of her death, and up at this man who made everything better until this very moment. What had happened?

"These are Em's parents?" Gage said, turning the picture back around to look it over. A sneer formed across his face.

"Yes, Gage, what's going on?" Trent asked, almost pleaded, as he spoke.

"You tell me," Gage demanded.

"I don't know," he said quietly back, and took another step back in sheer protection mode. The man in front of him wasn't the one he'd spent the day with; this man was threatening, and he had no idea what was going on, what had upset Gage so badly.

"Who are you?" Gage stalked toward him, getting in his face.

"What?" Trent asked.

"Did you draw me here on purpose? Did you forget to put this up? Have I walked into a trap?" Gage demanded, stepping in farther, directly into Trent's personal space, just short of bumping his chest.

"What are you talking about?" Trent said and took another step back. His own anger starting to surface.

"Am I being recorded? Are you being paid? Don't fucking lie to me anymore, Trent." Gage yelled the last sentence, and Trent heard the kid's rustling in their beds.

"I have no idea what you're talking about, Gage," Trent said, glancing down the hall to see if either was up yet. A sound beeped on Gage's phone, and he finally backed off, going to the front door.

"You can tell whoever the fuck you're working with I have you completely surrounded. When I walk out this door, I'm being watched. All my men are being watched. Take me down, and it won't save him." Gage didn't wait for a response as he pushed through the door, leaving it open, and jogged to his car, the lock clicking open as he ran. The framed photo still in his hand. He took off in the car, pealing the little Prius out of the drive, and two cars started in the neighborhood, following behind him. Trent went out on the front porch and stood, staring after them. Nothing about what just happened made any sense. Why would he record Gage? Record him doing what? Trent looked out into the night, took several steps out on his porch and looked around. Was he being watched? Had Gage lost his mind? Why would he be watched?

Gage wasn't out of Trent's driveway before he had his head of security on the phone. He'd sent a Code Red via text while standing in Em's room after seeing the picture, in order for him to get out of the house as safely as possible. Code Red indicated the highest possible alert for his security team. Everyone went on lockdown the moment it was given. Over the years, they'd only had three Code Reds. Hopkins answered on the third ring, and Gage knew his entire team would be in a frenzy of work right now.

"Synclair, I'm leaving Cooper's house now, what the fuck happened?" Hopkins asked, sounding out of breath.

"No, you stay there. I want you and whatever team you have left there to stay on Cooper. Did you send the alert out to everyone?" Gage asked, navigating the neighborhood streets with more speed than he should. The anger rolling through him required he put as much distance between him and Trent as quickly as he possibly could.

"What? No, Synclair, I need to be on you. What the fuck happened?" Hopkins asked again.

"Abdulla is related to the Cooper family," Gage said, taking the ramp onto the highway, dodging in and out of cars as he drove. The two security cars behind him stayed with him, but he didn't make it easy.

"What? Gage, are you sure? This wasn't in anything we found on him," Hopkins said.

"Positive ID. I have the proof in the way of a photograph. The story I got, he's the kids father, died three years ago, no four years ago now. Photo taken with Trent's sister," Gage said. As he spoke the words aloud, his heart screamed for attention over the anger bubbling through his system. It hurt and he let up on the gas as he realized what he'd just lost.

"Do they know?"

"I have no idea. I'd have to say this is too big a coincidence. Coop Electric wasn't the original contractor on my job. The other contractor abandoned the job. He could have been put there on purpose..." Gage thought about it quickly and slammed his fist forward, punching the dashboard over the thought. "*Goddammit!* I'm fucking positive I wasn't supposed to see this picture!"

Gage tried to contain his rage and brought the car down to the posted speed limit, then off to the shoulder of the highway, throwing the vehicle in park. He ignored the blood dripping from his fist. How did Abdulla know? Where had he slipped up and not covered his tracks?

"Get immediate communication into Mexico. Tell everyone to stand down. *Do not* abandon post, just stand down, and be on alert. Hopkins, I want you personally on Trent Cooper. I want men on those children twenty-four/seven. I want someone on Rhonny and someone on Sophia. I want everything recorded and I want the files you have taken so far on the entire family in my email before I get back to my desk tonight."

"Yes, sir," Hopkins said.

"Hopkins, watch Trent close. Everything he does, I want recorded. He'll have to make contact with Abdulla now that I know. Unless Abdulla has been fuckin' watching me, *goddammit!*" Gage disconnected the call and sat in the car, staring out the window, knowing it was a bad idea to make himself an open target like this, but he didn't care. The heartsick pain caving in his chest beat anything he'd ever felt before. How could he have fallen in love so quickly? What did he really know about Trent Cooper, anyway? How the fuck had they figured out the best possible way to get to him was through honor and integrity in a motherfucking *hot* goddamn package? *Fuck!* Gage laid his head on the steering wheel. How had they known? He'd hidden his need for family from everyone, even himself. Trent had inspired feelings inside him that even he wasn't aware of? How the fuck had Abdulla figured it all out?

Gage stayed with his head bent over, his heart torn apart, and his eyes staring down at nothing until they focused on his phone. The screen saver flashed to Trent in his tux, and then faded away as the screen turned dark. Gage ran his finger over his phone and stared at the picture until it faded away again. He swiped again across the screen to find a particular number, and dialed it. Answered on the first ring. "I'm calling in every favor I've given you. Sid, I need immediate background checks on seven people. I need everything ever documented on these people."

"Go slow, and spell the names," Sid said. Gage gave the name of every member in the Cooper family and the last known addresses he knew until Sid cut Gage off.

"Wait, he's the guy you were with the other night."

"Last known address…" Gage finished giving the address, unwilling to talk about it with Sid, but his tone changed from one of authority to one of pain. Everything settled into this moment. The man he loved was connected with the man he hated most in the world. How the hell had this happened? He disconnected the call, unable to say anything more. Anger kept the tears at bay, but just barely.

Gage put the car in drive and tapped his brakes a couple of times to let those following him know he planned to leave. He pulled back onto the highway and picked up his phone for one last call.

"Dad, there's been a breach on my end. Please tell your people to be on heightened alert and tell everyone to watch it. I'll call you when I know more."

"Son, are you all right? You don't sound good."

"I gotta go, Dad. I'll call you when I know more. This is a big one, I'm sorry, please make sure your security knows," Gage said and disconnected the call.

Gage's knuckles ached from where he'd hit the dash, and he stretched out his hand before gripping the steering wheel again. He forced the pain from his mind. The love of his life worked for Abdulla. They played him like a school girl, and he fell hook, line, and sinker. Steeling his heart, he drove the rest of the way to the gallery almost numb, giving himself this time before he jumped right in the middle of Trent Cooper's ass, bringing them all down along with Abdulla.

Chapter 19

His head throbbed. Trent ran his left hand up to his forehead and leaned his head on his palm. He closed his eyes while dropping the phone in the cradle on his desk. For the first time in two days, something hurt worse than the pain in his heart. Five days since the grand opening which easily categorized as one of the best days of his entire life. Two days since Gage had stormed off in an unexplained anger. And even though it was only Tuesday, this week could easily vie for the worst in his life so far. Since the opening, he'd lost his lead electrician, five contracted jobs, and his boyfriend, but really, could he consider Gage a boyfriend after a week? No, he couldn't, but to help the pity party going on in his head he let it count. And to make everything much worse, Trent shouldered every bit of the blame. *What the fuck was I thinking?*

A bottle of Advil sat on his desk. He palmed the container, opening it while scooting back in his rolling desk chair. He pushed back far enough to reach the mini-fridge he kept behind his desk. Without looking, Trent opened the door and pulled out a Bud Light, popping the top. He dumped a handful of pills in his mouth and took a long swig of the beer, swallowing them down.

It should have been a relief to lose the electrician since he didn't have the work anymore to keep him busy, but it still ate at him to know the sole reason the man quit was because he wasn't going to work for a fag. That had happened immediately after Gage left for his trip. Happy Friday morning! By ten the same morning, the first job had canceled. When Trent saw the picture of him in the circle of

Gage's arm on the front page of CNN.com, he figured he could expect a little backlash, but love and pride had filled his heart and hope floated, replacing the fear that should have been present. He'd never anticipated his already contracted jobs might cancel, though. By eleven, he had a second cancelation. And nothing had gotten better from there. Saturday brought with it another cancelation, by email no less.

Sunday morning felt like the changing tide when Gage made everything better by showing up to spend the day with him. Now Monday and Tuesday came with his heart ruined, his kids and Rhonny walking on eggshells, and two more canceled jobs. He didn't have enough work to keep his second crew busy for more than another day or two. He figured the only reason those jobs hadn't canceled was because they were already in the final stages. And it was all because he hadn't kept everything completely separated like he'd known he should.

Trent took another long swig of the beer, thinking over his financial situation, which only caused his head to throb more. He'd put everything into completing The Art Gallery. He'd bid the job low, barely covering the cost, in order to try to get his foot in the door of Layne Construction. When he'd gotten the job, he put every one of his crews on it to complete it and hopefully impress Layne. Now as he stared at the last invoice he needed to send Gage, anger finally set in.

On Monday, he'd decided he wasn't going to invoice the last of the gallery. He would eat it and move on. He had enough work, and if he was careful, he would be okay without billing Gage and taking anything else from him. It would pay Gage back for the clothes, the limo, and the presents. They could cut ties and be done, but now, less than forty-eight hours later, he needed the money. There wasn't enough to float anything, and he didn't know how long it would take for this whole thing to blow over and business to come back his way.

Trent rose and stared at the invoice on his desk. His eyes filled with tears and he hated he had no control over it. This felt remarkably close to what it felt like to lose Lynn. He gripped the sides of the desk, digging his fingers into the wood, and closed his eyes. He strained his muscles, gritted his teeth, and demanded the tears to stop and the pain to go away. When they didn't, he raged inside, and swept the contents of the desk across the garage in one swift swing of the arm. He grabbed his chair behind him and threw it with the paperwork across his garage. *Every motherfucking thing is ruined, and I'm sitting here crying over Gage fucking Synclair.*

Stalking across the garage, Trent stormed into the backyard, slamming the door behind him. All the equipment he'd already purchased for the canceled jobs sat piling up in his backyard. He stormed to his truck, jumped in, and started it, squealing the tires as he drove it around to the backyard. He got out of the truck, slamming the door, and stalked to the back, lowering the bed. The entire time he worked at loading the equipment and material into the bed of his pick-up, he cried. The tears never stopped as he lifted everything by himself and dumped it into the back of his truck. Sweat rolled down his face, dampening his hair, and he pulled off his T-shirt, wiping it across his face, still crying. He'd been a fool. A complete fool, and now he was ruined, losing everything, all because he hadn't followed his own damn rules.

Gage sat in his office, his head in his hands, and he forced his tired brain to think. Forty hours had passed since he left Trent's house in a rage of anger and confusion. He hadn't slept a wink since he'd left, and really, with the exception of the plane ride home Sunday morning, he hadn't slept more than a few hours in the last week. Gage was exhausted and the exhaustion caused this whole investigation to take much longer than it should.

When he'd gotten back from Trent's house Sunday night, he couldn't believe he'd missed such a key part of the evidence while investigating Abdulla. Now, he questioned everything. He dug and searched through every report he'd made and still couldn't find Trent and the kids in anything on Abdulla. Then he prayed the theory 'everyone has a twin somewhere on the planet' was true and decided immediate forensic testing would prove that point.

As the possibilities rolled through his mind, it occurred to him perhaps this may be a test of some sort, or Trent and the kids, unknown to them, were planted for a reason. But he couldn't come up with any viable explanation. He'd spent two days and nights scouring everything, every note he'd taken for six long years and every file he'd created, but couldn't find anything to connect Abdulla to Trent's sister, Lynn, or any other member of the family.

The picture of Lynn and Abdulla sat on his desk, mocking him, showing him he'd clearly missed a major part of his quarry's life. Lynn married Abdulla who fathered Em and Hunter, and yet, Gage had never found a single ounce of evidence relating to those facts until he sat reading a bedtime story to little Emmie. His gaze had drifted to her nightstand, the picture set with care right in the center. He'd created such a thorough background check, but sitting in front of him on a little girl's nightstand, in a Chicago suburb of the man he'd fallen in love with was another piece to the puzzle of Abdulla's life he'd never found. It couldn't be a coincidence, but it made no sense at all.

Sid had only taken a few hours to assimilate mountains of background information on the entire Cooper clan. Gage spent Monday morning sifting through everything provided on Lynn, Trent, and Sophia. Through it all everything came back exactly like Trent told him. There were no variations from any of the reporting agencies Sid used. Lynn married Aaron Adams in Mexico, it was all clearly documented. On the surface, Aaron Adams showed the exact background Trent told him about yet there were no clear beginnings or endings to his life, which was exactly the MO Abdulla always used. Nothing indicated Lynn was anything different than Trent had shared. She and Sophia grew up together. He held pictures of a young Trent and a young Lynn all throughout school. There were also pictures of Aaron Adams, Lynn, and Sophia on what looked to be a vacation. Aaron wore his US Army fatigues in almost all the photographs.

As he stared at the vacation pictures, the evil so prevalent in Abdulla's eyes was missing. He appeared taken with Lynn, genuine affection shining through, and in those shots he could see what Hunter might grow to look like. How did the evil Abdulla father such sweet children? Could Trent really have known nothing about any of this?

Now all these hours later, Gage's gut told him the answer, and if he were honest with himself, he'd known it from the minute he'd calmed down. Trent Cooper wasn't a part of any of this. You couldn't fake all that goodness Trent had going on, but to call everything a massive case of coincidence... It was still very hard to believe.

When Gage left Em's room Sunday night, he'd grabbed a brush sitting on her dresser, which he then sent off for forensic testing. They had Abdulla's DNA on file, having gathered it through the investigation once contact was made. Gage called in favors, and rushed the initial testing, which arrived only moments ago. The preliminary finding confirmed Abdulla had fathered both children. Another complicating factor, Abdulla's alias of Aaron Adams, soldier in the United States Army wasn't registered anywhere in US military records, yet Gage remembered Trent saying something about benefits the children received from their father's time in service... Neither Gage nor Sid could find any record of monies being paid to Trent from the government.

There were clear holes in this story, many questions left unanswered, but this deep ache in his heart wouldn't give. He'd been without Trent for almost forty-eight hours. Gage hadn't called him or texted him, and Trent had done nothing to reach out to him. Though, that didn't surprise him. Trent was a proud guy, and Gage stormed off with such angry accusations being flung everywhere. But what was he supposed to have thought? Gage needed to get back there and figure out what had happened, because it seemed like his world caved in around him in those few seconds in Em's bedroom. Hell, at the precise moment of finding that picture, Gage feared for his men's lives.

Now, he needed to talk to Trent. Try to resolve these unanswered questions, but first he needed to get all his ducks in a row, and he needed sleep. When he spoke to Trent, the kids needed to be in bed or out of the house, and even then, he didn't know how Trent would take the unmistakable fact Gage was about to blow his family out of the water. Rubbing his hands over his face, he forced those thoughts from his mind. Gage rose from the desk he'd been at for most of the last two days. He needed to be at his best and right now he was too exhausted to be any good to anyone. First, he needed rest, then he would deal with security for the report he'd soon have on air, last he would deal with Trent.

"No, he's home more. Work has slowed down," Rhonny said quietly into the phone, walking into the kitchen from the living room where Em was bent over the coffee table coloring.

"Why? Is he sad?" Sophia asked.

"Yeah, but I think some jobs have canceled on him. One of his guys quit," Rhonny said, leaning back against the kitchen counter, bringing a fingernail to her mouth, chewing at it. She worried about Trent and couldn't think of any way to help him. It drove her to call Sophia.

"Really? Why?" Sophia asked.

"I don't know for sure. He doesn't talk to me about stuff like that, but I heard him outside. He was moving those big spools of wire. He does that when he's mad, and he muttered something about coming out and keeping everything separated for a reason," Rhonny said.

"Oh, that's not good," Sophia said.

"No, I didn't think so either," Rhonny said.

"How are the kids?" Sophia asked.

"I think good… Hunter's asked about Gage, and Trent told him he didn't think Gage would be around anymore. Hunter got sad, and Em cried. Trent hugged them and said he was sorry, he shouldn't have let Gage meet them yet, and he told them it was his fault about Gage, and they shouldn't worry about it. Em's at the living room table now making Gage a card with the art set he got her. She's been coloring on it all afternoon. She wants me to drive her over to give it to Gage," Rhonny said.

"Are you going to?" Sophia asked.

"I don't know. It doesn't seem right for me to."

"I think you totally should. Let dumbass see what he's so willing to give up," Sophia said, and for the first time in the call Sophia sounded angry and defensive.

"You know guys don't think like that," Rhonny said.

"What does Gary say?" Sophia asked.

"He says Gage has always been a loner, never dated anyone before. It was a big deal we all went to the opening."

"Hmmm… I don't know what it means."

"Me either."

"Poor Trent," Sophia finally said.

"I know. I think he was crying this afternoon. His eyes were really red. He said he was tired, but I think he was crying," Rhonny said, and finally bit her nail. She'd been trying to break the nail-biting habit, but all the stress in the house had her biting one fingernail, then another.

"Damn it, Rhonny. I think you need to take Em to the gallery!" Sophia said.

"I don't know…"

"No, take her. Take her now before Trent gets home. Where's Trent, anyway?"

"Hunter has summer T-ball. It starts this week. He needed cleats."

"Take her, Rhonny, right now, before he gets back. And call when you leave the gallery. Watch everything he does, from the minute you walk in to the minute you leave, I want all the details."

"All right, if you think so," Rhonny still hedged.

"I do think so! Go now," Sophia said.

She disconnected the call and looked over at the table where Em still colored away, trying hard with the picture. She couldn't decide what to do. It wasn't cool what Gage had done—whatever that was— but she really couldn't see how putting Em in front of him would do more than push him away. Staring at Em, her heart gave a small little dip. She was such a sweet little girl. Trent did a great job raising them, keeping everything bad from them. How could Gage come on so strong, then just vanish like that?

"I'm ready, Rhonny. I'm done, what do you think? I messed up some lines, but the color is the colors Gage said to use, I think," Em said, studying the picture closely.

"It's wonderful, honey," Rhonny said, coming to kneel down beside Em, staring at the picture, still not sure what she should do.

"Will you write on it?" Em asked.

"Why don't I write out what you want to say, and you copy it."

"Okay, but he might not be able to read it," Em said.

"He will, I promise. Tell me what you want to say," Rhonny grabbed a sheet of paper from the stack, and Em stopped coloring and looked up at the ceiling, thinking hard.

"I want to say thank you for making my daddy and me and Hunter happy," Em said, looking at Rhonny while biting her lip.

"Oh, Em, that's very sweet." Rhonny wrote the note putting enough space between each word to set them apart. "Write it just like this, okay? I'm going to go get my shoes and purse. I'll grab your sandals, and then we'll go."

"Okay," Em said, concentrating hard on writing each letter on the paper. When Rhonny got back, she helped Em on with her sandals and looked over the colored paper. Em's letters were too big and the space wasn't really there between the words, but she thought Gage might get it and if nothing more he might at least carry guilt for what he'd done to Trent's heart.

Gage came down the stairs from his personal living space feeling like a new man. He took a solid five hour nap. Well, he supposed it could be called a nap. He'd pretty much passed out under the stress and fatigue he'd put his body through over the last two days. The rest had helped, though. Then he took a full shower, shaved, did the whole manscaping deal, and chose his power clothing: his black Prada slacks and a black, light-weight Prada cashmere sweater. If he was going to try to fix this mess with Trent, he wanted to look and feel his best. In all honesty, Gage wasn't sure this could be fixed, but his heart begged him to try.

The special report on Abdulla was the biggest of his life. It would change the way the world saw him and solidify him as a true investigative reporter. This would launch his after-retirement career and give him a break from all the field work he'd done over the last ten years. It would also inadvertently destroy Trent Cooper and his children. Everything inside Gage rejected hurting Trent in any way, no matter how much he needed the acclaim this report would bring him. A solid war between his heart and his head waged inside his body, and when it came down to it, he needed to use his head, period. The heart was a fickle thing.

Gage stepped out into the main lobby of the gallery at the same moment his head of security and the local police chief stepped inside the front door. He'd arranged this meeting in an effort to make sure Trent, Em, and Hunter were provided adequate protection once the story broke sometime in the next twenty-four hours.

"Mr. Hopkins and Chief Sorreal, thank you for coming," Gage said, taking long strides to meet them in the middle of the gallery. There were no polite pleasantries. The chief just began speaking right where he and Hopkins left off.

"Mr. Synclair, Mr. Hopkins and I have met, I'm going to assure you we will do our best to keep this family safe, but we can't act until we know more and your head of security was incredibly vague," the chief said.

"I understand, sir. I'm sure Mr. Hopkins explained my men are there with the family now, watching them closely. It's really what we wanted you to know. The officers patrolling need to know they are there and present, just in case something goes down."

"Would you care to give me more specifics?" he asked.

"I can't right now, but I will soon," Gage said, taking on the chief's stance, legs apart, arms crossed over his chest, staring at one another.

"Then all we can do is pick up patrols and keep our eyes open for something we don't even know about. And should your men get in an altercation, we won't be able to distinguish them from the perpetrators. Everyone will be going to jail at that point," the chief said.

"It's fine. My men know what to do. They've been with me for years. Once I can tell you more, I'll call you directly. Until then, please increase the patrols around the Cooper household."

"We will, but I expect a call as soon as you possibly can. I don't like my men going in with blinders," the chief said. Gage nodded, staying quiet. This wasn't his first rodeo with law enforcement. He knew they liked to be the ones in control, but he wasn't gonna give it to them, so he stayed quiet. He went to shake the chief's hands when the front door burst open, banging loudly. All three of them turned toward the door, where Em stood looking shocked the door had opened so easily. Rhonny stood right behind her, stepping inside, checking to see if Em broke anything.

"Excuse me, please," Gage said and never looked back at the chief or Hopkins, going straight to Em. Her little face beamed when she saw him.

"I'm sorry I banged the door," Em said, rooted to her spot, which was odd for her. She usually stayed on the run; a launch-yourself-at-whatever kind of kid.

"It's fine, sweetheart," he said. Em looked straight at him, smiling, but Rhonny stood back solemn faced and wouldn't look him directly in the eye.

"To what do I owe this pleasure?" Gage asked, deciding Em was the more likely of the two to speak, and dropped down, bending at the knee, coming to Em's eye level.

"I made you this present and Daddy said you weren't gonna come over anymore so Rhonny brought me here to give it to you." Gage watched her closely as she spoke, her smile fading and her forehead narrowing at the same time pain shot through his heart at her words. It staggered him as loss filled his soul at her uncensored words. He couldn't help but reach out to her and take her in his arms.

"Did he say that?" Gage asked, bending his head to keep his eyes on hers.

"Yes," Em said and bit her lip, her brow still narrowed.

"Hmmm… Can I see what you made me?" Gage asked. Em didn't say anything, but handed him the colored sheet of paper. He looked up at Rhonny who still wouldn't look at him. She kept her eyes on Em and hovered around the little girl. He could tell Rhonny wasn't sure about being there, and he guessed he deserved it, but he absolutely hated it.

"Did you color this?" he asked as he glanced at the paper.

"Yes," Em said, looking at the paper too.

"And you tried to use the different colors I showed you. It looks wonderful, honey. I love this, thank you," Gage said, looking over the picture. He had no idea what it was supposed to be, but she clearly tried hard, and his heart did a little flip at the love it took for her to color this for him. There were words at the top, but all the letters ran together. All he could make out was the 'thank you for'… Then the rest all ran together. After a minute, he started reading it out loud.

"Thank you for… What does this say, Emmie?"

"It says, thank you for making my daddy and me and Hunter happy. Right, Rhonny?" Em asked, looking back over her shoulder. Rhonny nodded, giving a small smile, and Em turned back to Gage.

"I had to write the rest on the back." She took the paper and turned it over, showing the rest of the writing.

"You don't have to thank me, Emalynn, I love your daddy." Her little eyes bounded up to his, tears instantly filling them and his heart may as well have physically fallen from his chest with the pain he felt.

"But he doesn't think you do."

"Em, I can't tell you more. This is grown up stuff, but I promise you, I do love him very much, and I'll call him. Okay?" She nodded, but kept biting her lip, and the tears finally built enough steam to spill down her cheeks. Gage used his thumbs to brush them away and smiled at her. "Your daddy's very lucky to have you, Emalynn."

"Em, we need to go," Rhonny said from behind her.

"Can I have a hug?" Gage asked, and Em nodded wrapping her arms around his neck, squeezing him tight. He closed his eyes, loving this little hug.

"Thank you for my picture," he said into the hug and embraced her back, keeping her there just a moment longer.

"Goodbye, Gage."

"Bye, sweetheart." He wanted to tell her he would see her soon, but after he laid his findings out to Trent, he wasn't sure Trent would ever have anything to do with him again. He rose and watched as Rhonny and Em left. Rhonny waited until they got outside before she picked Em up, carrying her to the car. Em continued to cry on her shoulder as Rhonny patted her back. He'd already caused this family so much pain, and he hadn't even given his report yet. Gage kept his eyes on both of them the entire way to the car, and it crushed him to know the part he'd played in putting sad faces on those two lovely girls.

Hours passed and the night grew dark as Gage sat in his office staring at his phone. The photo he'd snapped of Trent at the gallery during the grand opening now shining as his background picture. He would never forget that night for as long as he lived or the man who'd stood by his side for the entire evening. Trent played the perfect host for him. Everyone wanted to know about him and commented on how happy Gage seemed with Trent. Gage never let him get more than a step or two away before he drew Trent back to him. It felt so normal, so natural to have Trent there with him.

Gage also watched other men staring at Trent during the opening, trying to get his attention, and he remembered the desperate sense of jealousy coursing through him with each long glance he caught directed toward his date. A chuckle escaped his lips, now, thinking about it. He'd never been jealous a day in his life, but he knew, first hand, what those sideways glances the guys gave Trent meant. Hell, he'd perfected that look, but Trent never seemed to notice. Trent only had eyes for him all night long.

Gage couldn't understand why Trent didn't see how wanted he was in this world, but thank God he didn't, otherwise he would have been scooped up a long time ago. It staggered Gage to think he might have never had a chance to know Trent Cooper. On a whim, while he waited for night to fall, Gage had downloaded the photo onto his laptop and loaded it as his screen saver. He ran his finger over Trent's lips, those perfect lips. He was stalling, delaying the inevitable. He needed to call Trent. As it stood right now, he might still have a chance to keep Trent in his life, but once he met with him tonight, explained everything, he knew in his heart they would be over, forever.

Gage's career had always been the most important thing to him. Building his own life meant everything to him. Standing on his own two feet was just a part of who he was as a person, but keeping Trent and the kids safe and unharmed had become as important as the career he'd always put above all others. The love he felt for Trent…it couldn't be placed into words. The thought of going on, without Trent, crushed his soul. He looked down at his desk, his brows coming together, and absorbed the deep pain slashing through his heart at losing such a man. He looked at the papers on his desk, holding the images of Abdulla, but all he could see were the images of Trent and his sweet children running through his mind.

Gage forced himself to stop, take a breath, and gain perspective. There was no question in his mind he would be moving forward on this case. Abdulla couldn't be allowed to continue his reign of terror; he deserved everything about to rain down on his sorry ass. He'd killed hundreds, maybe thousands, of innocent people for nothing more than money. He'd infiltrated government military structures, killing servicemen from within their own ranks. Gage couldn't imagine how those last moments had gone for the hundreds of soldiers who lost their lives at the hand of someone supposedly a comrade. Abdulla was treasonous, a blight on humanity, and charges must be filed against him, justice claimed once and for all. He needed to stand public trial for the mass genocide and destruction he'd caused around the world.

Trent, Em, and Hunter would probably need to be put in some sort of witness protection program. If it came out Abdulla had children, those children would be in danger for their lives, for the rest of their lives, from all the competing militia groups Abdulla fucked over throughout the years. Gage's need to protect those children shouted loudly from inside his heart. He'd studied these groups too closely, and to them, killing Abdulla's children, no matter how innocent they were, would most assuredly be within a range of acceptable practices when exacting revenge against their enemy.

Trent would be in danger, too, and the thought caused Gage's newly encountered protective streak to surge to the forefront like never before. He needed to keep Trent safe like he needed to breathe. The testosterone pumping through him pushed him to rip someone's head off for even thinking to harm Trent, Hunter, or Em. The aggression coursed through him required control and he ran his hands over his face, pushing back from the desk. Wars were never won by brawn, they were only won by brains, and he would do well to remember that in this case. Trent needed him to be on his A-game.

How had this happened? He'd worked this report for six long years. How had this case ended up here? His eyes glanced down at the clock on the computer, eight pm. Em and Hunter's bedtime. He forced himself to stop stalling and palmed his phone, running his finger across the screen. He wasn't going to let himself worry about the future any more tonight. The bottom line: even if Trent never wanted to see him again, he would offer his help. If Trent didn't want it, he'd secretly take care of things whether they liked it or not. Gage ignored the pain in his heart at the prospect of never seeing Trent again and dialed the number.

The first call went to voice mail. So did the second one, but Gage knew Trent always carried his phone on him. It was also his work phone and he answered it all night long. Gage picked up the gallery's phone and called again a third time, Trent answered.

"Yes," Trent's voice sounded clipped, edgy and sharp. So he knew this number, too.

"We need to talk," Gage said, trying for matter-of-fact, but feeling like he fell short. He got silence back for several long moments. So much silence, Gage looked down at his phone's caller ID to see if the call had been dropped or disconnected, but it hadn't.

"I know I asked you to just tell me when this ended for you, but you've already said it loud and clear," Trent said.

"I have?" Gage asked. Why had he asked that?

"Yes." Again Trent's voice sounded clipped and sharp.

"I disagree." No, he didn't disagree. He'd been terrible to Trent Sunday night... More silence. Trent had an incredible way of being very quiet, and yet it spoke volumes. "I need to talk to you. Are the children asleep?"

Silence again.

"Trent, I'm coming over, I'll be there in twenty minutes." Gage disconnected the call. His voice held more confidence than the insecurities racing through him should have allowed. He gathered the file he'd put together, outlining all the evidence, step by step, for Trent. At the last minute, he shut his laptop, grabbing it, too. Gage decided a boost to his confidence couldn't hurt, and snagged the keys to the Ferrari for the drive over.

Chapter 20

Trent stood in front of his bathroom mirror inspecting himself closely. He'd taken a quick shower, and dressed in fresh clean blue jeans and a polo golf shirt. He put on socks and a pair of loafers, shaved and brushed his teeth. He did everything he could do to build himself up. The only problem he could see were the red rimmed eyes staring back at him. He didn't know how to get rid of those. Hell, those eyes staring back at him reminded him of the time surrounding his sister's death. He always had carried his heart in his eyes, or so he'd been told. There was just no way to hide the pain of heartbreak.

He'd keep the house dark; that was the only option he could think of to hide his eyes. He didn't want Gage to know the effect his rejection had on him. He sent Rhonny a text message telling her Gage planned to come over. He expected this to be the breakup talk and asked her to stay hidden for a while. He then went through the house turning off all the lights he could without appearing odd. Hopefully, it would help mask him from Gage. At this point, all he had left was his self-respect, and if it looked like he spent his time being a crying mess, he wouldn't even have self-respect to get him through the next few minutes.

Trent went into the living room and took a seat on the sofa. The house seemed eerily quiet, and he crossed his leg over his knee psyching himself up for the coming conversation. Ignoring the pain in his heart, he'd let Gage say whatever he needed to say and then ask him to leave. He would walk Gage to the door, shut, and lock it before he let one tear slip down his face. In this big master plan, he decided he would allow himself tonight for a full on pity party. Tomorrow, he would wake up and begin to repair the damage done to his company by coming out so publically. What a dumbass he'd been. He would also begin looking for some part-time work to bring immediate money into the house.

Having his picture in the paper for the city to see just wasn't one of his smartest decisions. He should have thought through it better, but he promised himself he would never do anything like this again. Em and Hunter deserved someone to think with their head, not their stupid, lovesick heart. And honestly, it was beyond pathetic how in love he already felt with a guy he knew from the beginning wasn't for him. If this didn't push all the stupid, romantic thoughts from his heart, he guessed nothing ever would.

A quiet knock tapped at the front door. Trent stayed seated for a second more, steeling his heart before he rose and took the few steps to the entryway. His great plan to stay strong began to waver as he watched Gage at the front door through the frosted glass. He definitely wouldn't make eye contact. He would look at his forehead or nose, but never in the eye. He opened the door and stepped back. If he didn't invite him in, just stood right there to let Gage say what he wanted, he could shut the door and be done very easily. Gage didn't wait to be invited in, though, he stepped inside carrying a folder and his laptop, and stopped in front of Trent, too close for comfort.

"I'm sorry I hurt you Sunday night. I'll live with the fact I did for the rest of my life. It was unfair of me, but I was very confused with what I found. It's not an excuse, just what happened, and I'm very sorry," Gage said, taking an additional step into his personal space. It occurred to Trent perhaps Gage didn't understand the meaning behind personal space because he always did this. He stayed so close Trent could feel every breath Gage took.

"It's fine, Gage," Trent said, and stepped back and away, shutting the front door. He thought better of it and pulled the door open again. "If that's all you came to say, consider it said." He cocked his head toward the front door, encouraging Gage to leave.

"Why won't you look at me?" Gage asked, stepping up on him, caging him between the front door and his body.

"I am looking at you," Trent said.

"You're looking at my nose," Gage said and lifted Trent's face with his finger under his chin. It forced Trent to lift his eyes and Gage narrowed his. "Have you been crying?"

"God, no! I just haven't slept in several days. I have a lot going on," Trent said as he wrenched his chin from Gage's grasp and looked away from the sexy compelling eyes that could hold him in their thrall. The pain in his heart crippled him from the lie he'd just told. This time he shut the door completely and scooted out from around Gage, but Gage stopped him.

"Why have you been crying?" Gage asked.

"I haven't, Gage. I have two children at the end of the school year. I have a business that's struggling, and the anniversary of my sister's death." *And a boyfriend, who isn't my boyfriend, like I knew he wouldn't be! And I fucking told you I loved you. How pathetic am I?* Trent averted his eyes again.

"Trent," Gage said, his voice pleading. Gage stepped in closer, if it were even possible for him to do so. Trent dodged the move and put distance between them by sidestepping Gage and walking into the living room. He needed space, actually he just needed Gage to leave and let him get back to recovering his life.

"Gage, please say what you came to say. It's late, I could use an early night."

"Well, I'm afraid that's the one thing that's probably not going to happen tonight, Trent. Can we go to your kitchen? I need to show you some things. I need the room," Gage said, coming to stand in the living room. Trent retreated back with every step Gage made toward him. It seemed Gage wanted to have every conversation with only a couple of inches between them. So much for those best laid plans. Trent couldn't bear to stand so close, breathing in Gage's cologne, watching those lips move, knowing he would never kiss them again.

Trent extended his arm as pain again shot through his heart at the thought of never again kissing Gage. The dull ache remained constant, but the painful sharp stabs kept coming, over and over, since Gage entered his house. He checked the urge to rub his heart.

Trent stepped back as Gage walked forward. He averted his eyes as Gage finally walked past him. Trent was done with the meaningful looks and the almost touches. As Gage placed his things on the kitchen table, Trent bypassed the table and went to the cabinet for a glass to get a drink of water. He didn't offer Gage anything. He watched the water from the faucet fill the glass, and drank it down like the shot of whiskey he wanted it to be. He stood at the sink until he heard the chair scrap across the floor.

Gage didn't say another word until he opened his laptop and placed a folder down in Trent's normal seat. Trent came to the table, but stayed standing until Gage finally spoke. "I understand I've hurt you, Trent, but please take a seat and let me explain. You've followed my career. You understand the reports I do. They aren't pretty and they aren't kind. I've been working this one, in this folder, for almost six years. It's the one I'm retiring on. You and I have talked about it. It's my last report, but what I haven't said to you... it's designed to be a going-out-in-a-blaze-of-glory kind of report."

Trent listened to him, let the words sink in, but he didn't sit. His focus stayed on Gage's nose or on the red file folder sitting in front of him, never back on Gage's face. For some reason, Gage felt the need to talk about his last project, when he'd guarded its secrecy to this point. Maybe Gage changed his mind about giving up his career, wanting to stay in the industry, but that didn't explain the intense anger or the lack of communication over the last few days. It didn't explain anything at all, because none of it had to do with Trent.

Trent let his eyes lift to the laptop sitting open, but the screen showed the desktop, nothing for him to see. Trent resisted the urge to run his hands over his face. With every passing second Gage stayed in his house, Trent's resolve weakened. He fought the desire to drop to his knees and beg Gage to give him one more chance. But Trent couldn't fix an undefined problem. Finally, Gage did something more than just look at him and reached forward to open the file in front of Trent.

"I need to warn you, some of these images are graphic, but they're necessary. And, Trent, I have never shared any of my cases with another outside of my employment since I started doing this. I'm asking for your confidence. I know it's not deserved, but please," Gage said, laying a hand on top of the open file.

"Is all this really necessary, right now? I get your career is important. I was a big fan, but it's not really a good time for me to go through all this," Trent said, hoping to get Gage out of his house sooner rather than later. Because the need to pick up Gage's hand and bring it to his lips nearly overwhelmed him.

"Baby, please just let me start from the beginning. You'll see soon enough." Gage scooted in closer to the table and began by turning over the first sheet of paper in the folder. A photo lay underneath. Trent saw several dead men lying around an exploded tank of some sort. Gage took the picture off the top and began to explain.

"This was the start of the Afghan war. I was there documenting everything, it's where I got my start. I took photos of everything I saw back then. I took this shot." He pointed to one photograph, and then moved it aside to point to another. "And then took this shot, all within a matter of an hour or so. You can see the time stamp documentation at the bottom of the photo. We were the first ones to come up on this scene. It was me and my crew. We didn't stay with field operations the way we were supposed to. Now look here, Trent. In this photo, you see six pair of downed boots. In this one, you see five. Not too abnormal, really, apparently someone didn't die, and escaped the scene. The problem, look at the wider view, there is no evidence that anyone with this degree of injury left the site."

Gage flipped photos as he spoke, every once in a while pulling a photo out, laying it above the red folder on the table. No explanation he gave was more than a bullet-pointed version and thankfully Gage kept this fast moving. Trent's mind was a little fried, but he followed, finally sitting down at the table, watching the things Gage pointed out for him to see.

"Now look at this one. Here I'm in Pakistan and it's the same type thing. Seventeen pairs of downed boots, and here in this photo, there are sixteen. Now look at this one, here I'm in Bosnia; it's the same thing. Now look back at these. Specifically at the soles of the boots gone missing in each shot they are different than the soles of the standard issue boots these soldiers were required to wear. This got me interested, so I began to dig. I looked at thousands of military photographer's photos taken all over the world. I found this same situation in twenty-three different photos and in every single case the boots that went missing were different than all the other boots in the photo... Make sense so far?" Gage asked.

"The one boot sole in all these pictures had the same tread design, but different than anyone else in the photo," Trent said, not looking away from the pictures, pretty amazed Gage found the pattern to begin with. Who would even think to scrutinize the photos that closely?

"Correct and I started to dig more. I found the design and maker of the boot. I found no government agency in the world bought this boot. This boot's an expensive, custom built boot. It's designed for hard wear and tear over any terrain. So what's it doing in each of these varied situations, every time there were casualties?" Gage asked.

"Now, Trent, before I turn this, let me tell you I got super lucky. I found a small photographer in the West Indies who had a similar photo as mine, but she took the shot with their faces up. It's gruesome, but look at the face I point out," Gage warned. Trent nodded before he turned the photo over. It showed several mutilated bodies and one which was whole, the body sprayed in blood. As Gage's finger moved to the whole man's face, Trent focused in on it, recognition instantaneous. His heart dropped to his feet. That man couldn't be Em's and Hunter's father. There had to be another explanation.

"Now based on these pictures, here and here, this man is wearing these boots," Gage said, and left it right there, not saying anything more.

"This looks like my children's father," Trent said, voluntarily lifting his eyes to Gage's for the first time that night.

"I know... that's why I freaked out on you on Sunday night," Gage said and sat back a little, giving Trent time to process everything. Trent took the time, looking at every picture again, then back at the face of the last photo. The time and date stamp at the bottom of the picture showed two years ago. Not possible. Aaron died four years ago.

"Gage, this can't be him. He's dead. Could it be a brother or relative?" Trent asked, lifting his eyes back to Gage's. Gage's silence said he had more to share.

"So he's not dead?" Trent asked; dread coursed through Trent's veins. Trent couldn't even fully wrap his mind around it all.

"Let me finish," Gage said, not answering any of Trent's questions.

"Then give me the more bullet-pointed version."

"After I identified him, I began searching for him. I found civilians who knew him in some of the worst parts of the world. Then I got lucky, one night in New Orleans, I stumbled on a drunk, talking a bunch of crap, but he knew this guy, a supposed family connection. I got a story and it's held together, but worse than I ever imagined at the time. He's a paid assassin, hired by just about anyone to kill just about anything. He's killed hundreds to thousands of innocent people, trafficked in drugs, sex, women, children, whatever the highest bidder needed, and he would change course in the middle of a job if someone paid him better."

"Trent, I've found him in Mexico. He's alive, but in hiding. His every movement is being tracked," Gage said. He turned over more pictures of the kid's dad, dressed as a monk with a large dark robe covering his head, but the eyes were there. Hunter looked so much like his father. Trent couldn't look at them anymore and lifted his eyes to the laptop in front of him. As he stared at it, the screen saver popped up with a picture of him in his tux at the grand opening. His brain struggled to digest it all and the slow steady pound of his heart wasn't helping his brain absorb everything fast enough. This wasn't the breakup speech he thought he was getting tonight. Though, it was that and so much more.

"So you're saying their dad is still alive and a paid assassin?" Trent finally asked, but his head rejected it just as quickly.

"Yes," Gage said. He leaned across the table, closer to Trent, getting back into his personal space again, and Trent sat back in his seat. Keeping a distance grew critical at this point if for no other reason than to ensure enough oxygen actually got to his brain.

"And you're sure it's the same person? He could have had a brother?" Trent asked.

"No, it's the same. I've spent the last two days researching, investigating, and testing the hypothesis. I didn't have this alias on him—the one he used with Lynn—but I have men there with him now. I have DNA on him and it matches the DNA found in a hairbrush on Em's dresser," Gage said.

"How accurate?" Trent asked. Gage flipped the DNA report over and the gravity of the situation fell in his lap with the numbers at the top of the page that screamed, '*Match!*'. There were pictures of him, his kids, and their father at different stages of their lives in the DNA report.

"Over ninety-nine percent accurate, Trent," Gage said.

"On both the kids?" Trent asked.

"Yes."

"Fuck, Gage, what does this mean?" Confusion clouded his mind. Nothing he came up with made any sense. But it all boiled down to his family being totally fucked. Gone was his need to save his self-respect. Now the biggest emotion pouring through called for him to protect Em and Hunter at all cost, and he wasn't sure it could be done or how to go about it.

"I don't know, I was hoping you could fill some of this in," Gage said, and he reached out to take his hand, but Trent shrugged it off, pushing back in his chair.

"I didn't know any of this," Trent said and began to absently run his hand over his chest, above his heart.

"How did your sister meet him?" Gage finally sat back some in his chair, giving him more room.

"Shit, Gage, I don't know. On a vacation I think. He was from here, but stationed in another country. He's of Middle Eastern decent I think, or one his parents were. Something like that... They met when Lynn and Sophia were on vacation during spring break, I think." Trent stumbled over his words trying to remember.

"Sophia was there when they met?" Gage asked.

"Yeah, I think so," Trent said.

"Did they live around here after they got together?" Gage asked.

"No, well Lynn did, but not in the beginning. I don't know all the details. I never liked him at all. I actually never met him face to face. I know they married right away after meeting each other. He didn't come home a lot. She got tired of being alone. When he did come home, he wasn't here more than a week. Maybe not even more than a week a year... Wait a minute, are you telling me you didn't know any of this when you met me? Or is this how I got the job in your gallery? Did you fucking come in my home, meet my kids, and fuck me to gather this information?" As he spoke, anger built inside him, his voice began to increase with each word.

"No, Trent! No, I was just as surprised and angry as you are right now when I saw the photo in Em's room. I wondered those same things about you, drawing me in," Gage said, holding his hands up, trying to calm the situation.

"Daddy, you're yelling," Hunter said. Em stood behind him in the entrance to the living room from the hall. Trent could see his precious children looking sleepy-eyed and disheveled from bed. They radiated uncertainty and didn't come any farther into the living room, staying in the safety of the hallway. They'd never shown fear of him, ever, but the raised voices clearly had them concerned.

"I'm sorry, guys. Go lay back down, it's okay. I'll be quieter," Trent said. He didn't get up, and Gage sat there with him, between him and his children, and the gravity of the situation fell hard on his shoulders. How would he protect them from all this? What would this mean to his family? And if he left Gage here in the kitchen alone would he be here when Trent returned? He needed all of the information the guy had before he walked out of their lives forever.

"I'm scared," Hunter said.

"Me too," Em agreed.

"There's nothing to be afraid of," Trent said and finally rose. He couldn't take the fear on their faces any longer.

"I've got them, Trent," Rhonny said, coming up the stairs. "Come on, guys, let Daddy talk to Gage. I'll stay with you."

"But, Rhonny, I had an accident," Em said.

"You did? It's okay. I'll take care of it in the morning. Let's get you clean pajamas. You can both come sleep with me," Rhonny said, pulling the pajamas up and over Em's head. She shooed them into the bathroom down the hall, looking over at Trent with worried eyes.

Trent watched the whole scene unfold in front of him, and for the first time ever, he didn't get involved. He was so unsure what to do. His instinct told him he should keep an eye on the person bringing all this crap down on his family until he had all the information. That gut feeling had him returning to his seat, Gage close by. At this point, Gage classified as the aggressor, and he understood killing the messenger wasn't necessary, but he didn't want Gage or any of this mess anywhere near his children.

Trent rose from his chair and paced the small area in front of the table, coming to stand in the entryway to the kitchen between Gage and the rest of the house. Aggression ate at his soul, and he focused in on Gage. He waited to hear Rhonny's bedroom door close before he stalked back to Gage. He braced one hand on the back of Gage's chair, the other on the table where his picture flashed every so often as a screen saver.

"Goddammit, Gage, you better tell me the fuckin' truth. Did you know he was the kid's father before the grand opening?" Trent growled the last words. If Gage had destroyed his life for this report... Damn it, he needed to hit something and if that something were Gage, so be it.

"No! On my soul, no," Gage said and didn't attempt to back away from him.

"So this is some giant coincidence?" Trent stayed there, leaning down in Gage's face.

"It's the conclusion I came to this afternoon," Gage said, nodding.

"How did you come to it?" Trent asked.

"My gut," Gage said, compassion in his eyes. Trent didn't expect compassion, and pity would have pissed him off.

"Why?" He stepped back a couple of feet from Gage, needing space.

"Because you're a good man, Trent. You have honor and integrity, and I've seen too much in my life. I know it can't be faked. You take care of these children, you give them everything you can, and feel blessed for the opportunity to provide for them." Gage's words took some of the steam out of the anger he held and it turned back to desolation inside his heart.

"I don't want them to ever know about this," he said, standing with his arms crossed over his chest, trying to keep himself together.

"Trent, I can't see how you can keep it from them." Trent stared at Gage, neither speaking again.

"If their father is still alive, it might threaten my adoption. What about their safety?" Trent said after a few minutes.

"I don't know. I'll provide an attorney for you. My guess, they'll want you all to go in the witness protection program. Trent, he's that bad of a guy. Another option's to let me keep you all safe, but I'm sure I'll be marked for exposing everything. I've never been in this situation. My reports were solely based on me before. My parents have personal security. I haven't had anyone I personally cared for before you. This list of Abdulla's buyers isn't pretty. They aren't going to wanna be exposed. But I can set you up somewhere remote. Keep you secure," Gage said. He rose to stand in front of Trent.

"Fuck, Gage," Trent said and lifted his hand to his chin, covering his mouth. Every possible outcome he could think of in this situation ended badly for his children.

"I know. I was thinking Sophia might be able to fill some of the holes in," Gage said. It took Trent several long minutes of staring at the computer screen, seeing his image smiling back at him, to finally respond by palming his phone and dialing Sophia. He put her on speaker so Gage could hear.

"How are you?" she asked, instead of hello.

"Not so good," Trent said and looked up at Gage.

"I know, babe, I'm really sorry Gage turned out to be such a fucktard. I so didn't see it coming," she said.

"Sophia, you're on speaker and Gage's here with me." There was silence on her end for a moment.

"Crap! I'm sorry, Trent, I didn't know," Sophia said in an explosion of words.

"No, it was deserved, Sophia. I'm sorry for the part I've played in this," Gage said.

"Sophia, can we come over? I know it's late, but there's a problem. I need you to help... Something about Lynn and the kids has come up," Trent asked, and they were again met with silence for several long moments.

"Is it about Aaron?" They were silent, looking at one another before they spoke.

"Yes," Gage finally said.

"Come now, I'll be waiting," Sophia said, and the phone disconnected.

Chapter 21

Gage called Hopkins, and within seconds, he materialized outside of Trent's house. Apparently, he'd been hiding in shadows for the last week, even before everything blew up on Sunday night. Trent never had any idea they were there. Hopkins agreed to stay in the house and keep an eye on everything while they met with Sophia. Rhonny came upstairs when Trent texted her. He filled her in on the basics, more of a need to know information of the moment. Rhonny looked scared, and at this point, Trent could do nothing to relieve her.

Against his better judgment, Trent rode with Gage in his Ferrari to Sophia's house, after giving him her address and letting GPS take them there, even though he knew a quicker, easier route. The ride was quiet and Trent sat with his hands in his lap. Every bit of their romantic trouble and the pain of lost love that he felt went to the wayside. The fear in his heart for his children became paramount.

Ever so often as he thought through everything, Trent would ask a question for clarity, but no matter how he spun it in his head, the resulting scenarios left him and his kids absolutely fucked. He'd never been in a situation like this before. It wasn't going to matter how hard he worked or how much money he threw at it, this was going to be beyond his control. His precious family, his sister's sweet children were going to be a target from this moment forward. He'd never feel truly safe again, which was the very best possible outcome of this dire circumstance.

Gage drove through Sophia's complex and Trent directed him to her townhome. It was late, well after ten at night, but her porch light stayed on and she stood out on the porch as their car pulled into her small driveway. There were no words said between them. She just looked at each one of them, then back at Trent, before giving an anguished look. She didn't reach out to him at all, but kept her arms crossed over her chest as if she held herself together and Trent knew those feelings too well. When they stepped inside and shut the door Trent started in on her immediately. The fear in his heart began to turn slightly angry again at the situation. Whatever Sophia hid, she should have told him before now.

"Why didn't you ever tell me?" Trent asked as he stepped inside.

"Trent, I don't really know anything. Lynn told me very little before she died and made me promise not to say anything unless it was needed," Sophia said, still clasping her arms around her chest.

"Let's go in and have a seat. Sophia we need to know everything you know about the children's father," Gage said from behind them both, encouraging them to move from the front door. Sophia walked into the living room where they all stayed standing. The tension so thick between them and Trent's heart began to pound. Any hope this might not be true diminished by the second. Serious fear began to build and Trent realized Sophia's confession could only add to this horror of a night.

"Where do you want me to start?"

"From the beginning of meeting him and work your way to the end," Gage said, he pulled out a pad and a pen from the file folder, and took a seat, balancing it all on his knee.

"Let's see, we met Aaron while we were on spring break in Cozumel. It had to be seven years ago, because Hunter just turned six. Trent, you all thought we were in Texas, but we changed it up some and kept it quiet. You and your mom would've worried. We met Aaron the first day we were there. Lynn fell immediately for him. Trent, they were love at first sight kind of stuff... He was stationed somewhere around there in the military and on leave. We were there a week and he spent the entire week with Lynn, every day and every night. They were so pretty together, everyone always stopped them to say what a nice couple they made. Toward the end of our spring break, I was alone all the time. It was sickening watching them, they really seemed in love. I know you don't want to hear this Trent, but he was Lynn's first and only. It had to be love. He couldn't be that good of an actor.

"Anyway, he was supposedly getting out of the military soon and during our last night there we all got completely wasted and woke up to them having been married in downtown Cozumel. I'm not sure the marriage was legal and binding, but nothing could convince Lynn of that. We had to leave, he had to go back too, and she turned up pregnant with Hunter. Trent, she was in love, but totally embarrassed, and I helped her hide it all from you guys. She only saw him two or three more times, ever, but they talked all the time. Every time they saw each other, it was like that with them. Real intense, but he would always up and leave, giving her a different excuse and be gone for a year at a time, sometimes longer. The last time he was in town, she got pregnant with Em. She sent him an email about it, the email he sent back was very sweet, a little cryptic, and he told her if anything happened to him there was an account with money in it.

"Then she got word of his death. It freaked her out a little bit. She did some research, tried to get benefits, but she found he wasn't ever listed as in the United States military, he didn't exist at all. And this account he set up for her in Switzerland had about half a million dollars in it." Sophia said it all still standing in the middle of the living room, her arms wrapped around her. Trent stood to her side, and she said it so quickly there wasn't any time for questions until Gage interrupted her.

"Do you have the account information?" Gage asked, looking up from his notes. "No, not anymore, let me finish. Now, I understand she knew there was a chance she would die giving birth. When she told me about the money, I thought she was just grieving Aaron. I didn't pay lots of attention to her, but she moved the money, cashed it in, and hid it away from the kids and you so there wouldn't be a tie back to you guys. She gave it to me. We put it in a bank safety deposit box because she wasn't sure where the money came from. She made me promise if anything happened to her, I would remove fifteen hundred a month and put it in an account for you, like it came from the government. She created an elaborate plan for it and it worked because you never touched the money, Trent. It just sits there. You never question it, or look at it."

"Do you have any of the emails or written documentation he sent her?" Gage asked, still bent over, writing.

"No, she got rid of it all before she died. She was scared, but she kept telling me she wasn't sure he was dead," Sophia said, looking at Trent.

"Why did she say that?" Trent asked before Gage could.

"I don't know, I think it was just a hunch. She would say they were too connected and sometimes she felt like she could sense him around," Sophia said.

"Did she see him, ever?" Gage asked.

"Not after he died, not that she ever told me," Sophia said.

"Did Lynn ever refer to him as anyone else?" Gage asked, looking up at Sophia, smiling at her. Trent knew he tried to make her feel comfortable, to help her remember things from back in the past, but he'd never seen Sophia look more nervous.

"No, not to me, but now you mention it, I remember a time early on when she was unpacking his things. She found a bunch of different passports, all with his picture. Back then, we thought he was some sort of secret agent spy for the government. Now, I'm guessing that wasn't the case. So I've told you what I know, tell me what's going?" Sophia asked. Trent began to speak, but Gage stopped him.

"Honey, we can't say right now, but we will soon. I promise," Gage said, rising.

"Trent, this money's yours, it's all yours. I always wanted her to just give it to you if something happened to her, but she didn't want you or the kids to know their dad wasn't what he seemed," Sophia said.

"Yeah, it's a little late for that," Trent said, running his hands over his face. He let out a pent up breath he didn't know he held.

"I get you can't tell me what's going on, but I can see on your face it's not good. I'm here for you. I'll do anything for you and the kids," Sophia said, coming up to him, wrapping her arms tightly around him. He hesitated a little, but finally enveloped her snugly back in his arms.

"Thank you, Sophia, I think it's about to get tough," Trent whispered into her hair.

"Trent..." Sophia started, but he stopped her.

"I'll tell you as soon as I can, and if the kids and I need to leave town, I'll call you as soon as I can. If we need to go, you have to promise to take care of Rhonny for me. Take the money and help her stay here as long as she needs to. Promise me, Sophia," Trent said, pulling back from the embrace, keeping his hands on her upper arms, looking at her hard. Willing her to understand the request and agree.

"Trent, this is sounding like an inevitability. You're scaring me a little. I want you and the kids in my life. I promised Lynn I would be here for them," Sophia said, wrapping her arms around his waist, drawing him for another hug.

"I know, Sophia, I swear I do, but I have to protect them, and this doesn't look good," he said, keeping her there tightly in the circle of his arms. Tears sprang to her eyes and she hugged him tighter. He could feel her begin to cry. Gage stayed at the edge of the sofa, watching them, but he stayed completely out of it.

"Trent, I love those kids. If you need to take them off, I'll go with you. You can't keep carrying the weight of the world on your shoulders alone. At some point it's got to get too heavy. Trent... don't be mad, but Rhonny told me some of your jobs canceled. You have all this money here. This could give you years without working."

"Look, Sophia, we have to go. I'll call you. Thank you for this information," Gage said. He stood by the front door, giving them as much space as he could to have this minute between them.

"I love you, Sophia. I couldn't have done this without you."

"You're such a brave, good man. Promise me, whatever happens, we're together," she said. He didn't promise her, but hugged her tight again and she cried in his arms. "You're scaring me, Trent."

"I'm scared too, but I have to go," Trent said, pulling from her arms. He didn't look back as Gage opened the door and they walked out together.

The drive back from Sophia's was the longest drive Gage had ever taken. This last twenty minutes felt more like five hours as his heart ached in his chest and fear settled in his belly. Watching Sophia hold Trent tore Gage up because, for the briefest of seconds, Trent let his guard down and held her tight, too tight, like she were a life preserver in the storm. A storm Gage caused. And despite everything he'd put on Trent tonight, he desperately wanted to be Trent's life jacket for the rest of their entire lives. Trent was so squarely inside Gage's heart. Nothing else mattered but this man sitting quietly beside him.

He knew of another option, one he hadn't let himself consider before now, but yet, somehow, predestined to happen since the first moment he met Trent. As he pulled from the highway, he reached down and tried to entwine their hands together. It wasn't fair of Gage, but he needed Trent's physical touch in order to consider the possibility of this last option.

Trent didn't seem in a giving mood. When he went to take his hand, Trent denied him. Trent never took his gaze from the side window, but refused his hand, instead linking his own hands together in his lap. Gage guessed he deserved it and if he were being honest, he would probably have done the same thing, but it didn't help the insanity of the thoughts going through his head.

He'd worked through it all in his mind, even this last unspeakable option, and now it was back to his heart. Not one of his feelings for Trent or the children had changed. Or maybe they had. The last few hours had strengthened the deep love he felt for this man beside him. He couldn't stand to see the hurt in Trent's eyes, and it pained him to know he'd put it there.

"I'm sorry for stepping away for a couple of days, but this is my life's work, Trent. You had a photo of one of the deadliest men in the world in your children's bedroom. I needed time to figure it out." Gage spoke as he drove, taking his eyes from the road every few seconds, glancing over at Trent to see his reaction. The man never so much as batted an eye.

"Now we've figured out who this guy is, we need to decide what the next step is for you and the children, and for us." Gage paused, giving Trent a chance to talk, but he stayed quiet, staring out the window.

"Please talk to me, Trent," Gage said, sighing when he was again met with silence. Tired of being ignored, Gage contemplated rounding the block one more time, forcing Trent to speak to him. Instead he pulled into Trent's driveway wanting no distraction as they talked, needing to work out a plan for their future.

"Goodbye, Gage," Trent said and was out of the door before Gage could put the car in park. The car door slammed hard. Trent took long strides, eating up the distance from the driveway to the front door.

"Wait a damn minute!" Gage yelled, tearing from the car toward Trent, but nothing stopped Trent. Gage ran the last few steps to get to the front door before Trent opened it.

"That's all you have to say to me: Goodbye, Gage?" Gage demanded from behind Trent, slapping his palm on the screen door to keep it closed as Trent went to open it.

"What the fuck else do you want me to say? Thank you for fucking me a few times before you screwed me in the ass with your last ever report on my children's father? Is that it? Is that what you want to hear?" Trent flipped around, raging at Gage who didn't step back, but kept Trent right there between him and the door, with the tables turned. Trent was completely in his personal space, bumping Gage in the chest.

"I didn't create this problem," Gage said back calmly, but firmly.

"No, but you're sure gonna bring it to a head, making sure the entire world knows," Trent raged back. They were nose to nose now, and Gage refused to move.

"This guy can't be allowed to go scot-free. Have you considered he might come after these kids? Fuck no, you haven't considered it. He's all holed up, getting his religion on. What happens when he decides he wants his babies back?" Gage said, in Trent's same tone.

"Fuck you! Don't you dare try to make yourself the hero here," Trent said. That one stung. Gage finally took that small step back, then another.

"If that's how you feel, go ahead inside then." Gage never experienced the depth of loss as those few words cost him. Everything in him screamed at him to make this right, but he didn't know what else to say and apparently Trent didn't either. Trent turned from him, fiddling with the key in the door. Gage could see Trent's hand shaking so badly he couldn't get the key in the lock. His head dipped forward, making a solid thump on the hard wood of the door. Trent cried and that did it for Gage. The love of his life was broken and crying, by his hand. The magnitude of the thought caused his heart to burst wide open. His own tears sprang to his eyes.

Gage carefully and tenderly came in behind Trent. He placed his hand over Trent's where he attempted to unlock the front door, and the other hand turned this exquisite man around to face him, bringing him in to cry on his shoulder.

"Baby, I'm so sorry," Gage said. Trent wrapped him in his arms, bringing Gage to him in a tight embrace. Trent's face lay buried in his neck and shoulder, the tears weren't stopping. "I'm sorry. I'll spend the rest of my life making this up to you. Shhh... I love you."

Trent stayed like this for several minutes until the tears slowed to a stop. Gage continued to hold Trent, never wanting to let him go. He stayed with his arms wrapped around this man, his hand resting along his neck, his fingers tangling in his hair, trying to give him any comfort he could. They stood alone in the dark, with the moonlight surrounding them. Gage knew his men were around watching this whole scene, but he didn't care, and he smiled when Trent wrapped himself tighter in the embrace.

"I'm sorry for what I said," Trent said into his neck.

"Me too," Gage whispered.

"I know this isn't your fault, you didn't do this," Trent said and laid his head on Gage's shoulder, still holding on tight.

"Trent..." Gage started.

"Shhh... You need to go take care of this. If you can, please call me once it's done. I'm gonna let the kids go to school, but bring them home early tomorrow. It'll give me some time to make arrangements. You're right; he could easily come after them. I didn't think about that," Trent said, finally rising.

"Trent, I love you, you know that, right? I meant everything I said to you." They were talking quietly together and Gage found he couldn't let Trent go. He got it wrong at Sophia's. It was Gage that wanted to hold this man so tightly he never lost track of him. It was time he fought for his future.

"Gage," Trent wouldn't look at him and didn't say it back.

"No, listen to me... I meant everything I said to you and even the things I've left unsaid. Trent, tell me the truth, did you mean what you said to me? Do you still love me or have I ruined everything?" Gage asked. Trent looked down, clearly weighing his options.

"It's a yes or no, babe," Gage said, ducking his head down, trying to make eye contact. It took a few minutes, but finally Trent looked up at him and rolled his eyes a little before he spoke.

"Yes, I do, Gage," Trent said, but he turned back to the door. Gage slid in behind him, keeping his arms around Trent.

"Good. Thank you," Gage said as relief swarmed him. No way could he live without this man in his arms. In such a short time Trent had become his everything, and because of it, this whole thing was going to play out differently than anyone could have planned. He wouldn't let Trent or Emmie and Hunter be hurt by this. He and he alone had the power to protect them, and honestly, he'd known from the minute he'd calmed down on Sunday night this would be his path. He'd tried valiantly to hang on to his goals, to the importance of his career, but after meeting Trent those things were less important to him than keeping this man in his arms safe and happy for the rest of their lives.

"Trent, kiss me one last time before I go." The front door opened and Gage watched his head of security exit through Trent's back door in the living room. Trent never said a word, he just turned around in the entryway, his face full of emotion, and he leaned in, slanting his mouth over Gage's. The swipe of his tongue thrust forward, and Gage opened for him, wrapping Trent in his arms, and swirled his tongue forward for the sweet kiss. There was no aggression in this kiss, no promises of a night of sex. It just held love and Gage never wanted it to end.

Trent moved his hands up to Gage's face and turned his head, deepening the kiss. Trent wrapped an arm around his neck and pressed him into the wall, consuming every part of him. This felt very much like the goodbye he knew Trent intended it to be. Gage lifted his arms, running them up and down Trent's back, and his heart again left his body, landing straight inside Trent's caring hands. The movement sealed the deal for him. He pulled from the kiss and kept Trent in his arms, but fished his phone from his pocket.

"Baby, I need to make a phone call in private," Gage whispered, his eyes still on Trent's now kiss swollen lips.

"You can call from my bedroom, or the garage, either would be the most private for you. I need to see if the kids are downstairs with Rhonny. Let me just make sure their doors are shut." Trent stepped back, averting his swollen red eyes, but Gage kept him close, not letting go of the hand that he clasped.

"I'll take care of this, Trent. You have to trust me." Trent didn't say anything, but his face said that trust would not come easily; it would take a long time to rebuild. That brand new protective mechanism that had spiked in Gage upon meeting this wonderful man roared to life at that look. His world tilted on its axis, and he wanted nothing more than to have Trent safe and in his arms for the rest of his life.

Trent stepped far enough away until he was able to look down the hall. Gage followed him, keeping their hands together, and they made their way to Trent's bedroom. Trent poked his head in the kids' bedrooms as he went, both were gone and he assumed still with Rhonny.

"Let me go check on them with Rhonny," Trent said, and Gage went into the bedroom. Trent quietly shut the door behind him. Gage waited until he heard Trent's footsteps retreat down the hall before he made the call he needed to make.

"I have something for you," he said into the phone to the groggy hello on the other end of the connection. He never took his eyes from the shut bedroom door, and he didn't let himself think of everything he gave up with this one phone call.

"It's one in the morning. Why can't you ever call at a decent hour, Synclair?"

"You need to get to Executive in Chicago before dawn. Call me before you land, I'll meet you at my gallery. It's the most private place. This is you and me and no one else, got it? But you'll need a field commander back at base ready to coordinate," Gage said, surprised at how good he felt with this decision. Trent wasn't going to understand it. The kiss they shared minutes ago was so final to the man he'd held in his arms.

"Wait, what?"

"You heard me," Gage said, a smile coming to his lips at the other person's confusion.

"Usually you have me playing catch up while you're making the military look like an ass." The statement caused a bigger smile to tear across his lips.

"Not this time."

"Why?"

"If you get moving, you can be here in five hours. It'll be easier to meet at the gallery. I'll be waiting. And in the end, this time you'll be saying, 'thank you, Gage.'" He laughed as he said the last part.

"Yeah, right, I'm not sure there's anything you can do to change my standard, you're a motherfucker, Gage," He heard the doubt in the voice over the line.

"You'll see." Gage disconnected the call and stayed standing, staring at the door, surprised there wasn't even a sense of loss at what he'd just done. It felt right. A smile touched his lips. He must be soundly and completely in love to do what he was about to do.

"They're in Rhonny's room. Did you make your call?" Trent said, coming back inside the bedroom. He shut the door behind him, but didn't set the lock and that made it clear he didn't think Gage planned to stay.

"I did. I have a couple of hours before I have to leave. You need to sleep, Trent." If Gage could get Trent to sleep, he could leave here in a couple of hours and still be there before General Porter could possibly arrive.

"I don't think I can," Trent said, coming to stand about a foot in front of Gage. He slid his hands in his jean pockets.

"Lay with me. Let me hold you," Gage said, moving to Trent who stayed rooted in his spot. Uncertainty played across Trent's face, and Gage ignored it. He couldn't tell him his plans, because he wasn't sure of them himself, but he did give a simple, "I've got an idea. You need to trust me, Trent. I'll keep you informed every step of the way, but you need to sleep. I need you fresh and alert on this deal."

Gage reached his hands out, needing to touch Trent like he needed to breathe. He began pulling Trent's shirt from his jeans. Trent followed suit, toeing off his shoes and unbuttoning his jeans. Neither said anything as they undressed him and Trent averted his eyes as he decided if his briefs would go, too.

"You're spectacular to look at, Trent. I don't know how you maintain this body, but you're hot as hell. Even under the weight of all this stress, I'm physically turned on by you. Let me make love to you tonight, baby," Gage said, moving closer to Trent, but he stepped back, and Gage wondered how his heart could hurt so badly at the move when it wasn't even in his chest any longer.

Trent didn't say a word as he walked over to the door, clicking the lock, and then to the nightstand, pulling a box of condoms out and a large bottle of lubricant. "I bought these this weekend when I thought I was gonna be having lots of sex in my near future. They'll be going to waste now. We might as well use them," Trent said casually and dropped his briefs to the floor.

Gage came up behind Trent, turning him around, drawing him into a kiss. One hand pulled at his own clothing, while the other stroked Trent's half aroused cock, bringing him fully to life. It took mere seconds for Gage to undress, and Trent broke from the kiss to open a condom. He pushed it down on Gage.

"Fuck me hard. Please? I need it hard, tonight, I can't take tender..." Trent whispered the words with a desperate edge filling his voice.

"Baby, you have to hear me. I'm going to do everything I can to make this right for you. I don't want to hurt you anymore," Gage said, holding him in place.

"I'm absolutely certain tomorrow I'm gonna regret this, but just fuck me hard, Gage. The harder, the better."

Gage flipped him around, not waiting until they were on the bed. Instead they were somewhere between the bed and the nightstand. Gage reached for the oil. He worked quickly, shoving two fingers inside Trent. Gage coated his own dick when Trent reached a hand around, pushed his fingers away from his ass and positioned Gage at his rim. Gage thrust his hips forward, driving his cock deep inside Trent, stretching him in one mind blowing thrust. Trent reared back with a deep, satisfying moan, growling from his chest. Trent braced himself on the headboard and nightstand, gripping both hard. The fact Trent stayed on his feet said a lot for his strength. Gage began pumping hard into Trent, slapping his balls against Trent's ass, dropping more oil on his fast moving cock.

"Harder," Trent growled out, and Gage gripped his hips, keeping him in place, pounding harder. The force of the fucking took his breath away and he liked it like this. The hot as hell experience pushed his orgasm closer. He drove faster, back and forth, digging his fingers into Trent's hips. He'd dreamed of Trent this way, he'd wanted him like this from the first moment he saw him. Gage reached his hand forward and knocked Trent's hand away from his own cock. He gripped it, stroking it hard in the rhythm his hips created. Barely a moment passed before Trent roared his release and Gage followed seconds later. It was fast, hard, and unbelievably gratifying.

Trent slumped over and Gage gripped his hips hard, keeping them upright. He needed a minute to gather himself, but Trent would have no part of it, his knees gave out and he fell to his side on the bed. Gage slipped out, but grabbed on to the nightstand, staying on his feet until he could fall across the end of the bed and not land on top of Trent.

"Jesus, Trent, that was completely unexpected." Gage's breathless comment met with the soft snoring of the man he loved. He gave himself another minute before he rose to get them both settled. He gathered his clothes to limit the wrinkles, knowing there wouldn't be time to change before he met General Porter. Gage intended to stay here as long as he possibly could. After he cleaned them up, he risked waking Trent to put him under the covers. Trent opened those red, swollen eyes to him and gave a small smile, pulling Gage down in bed with him. It felt like the most natural move in the world to have Trent's arm come out and hook around his waist, pulling him down in bed with him.

"I love you, baby," Gage whispered.

"I love you," Trent mumbled, back asleep within seconds. Gage laid there for several hours, holding Trent until his alarm alerted him of the time. It woke Trent, too. Gage dressed silently and Trent stayed where he lay, watching him dress, a look of resignation on his face. The thin summer blanket covered his legs and cock, but not his chest. Trent looked so good lying in that bed. Gage ran his fingers through his hair and walked back to the bed, bending down to place a chaste kiss on Trent's lips.

"Keep the kids home with you today, I don't know how long this will take. I'll call you as soon as I can." With that, Gage left.

Chapter 22

With barely enough time to run a comb through his hair and brush his teeth, Gage heard the buzzer sound below in the gallery. General Porter made record time in getting to Chicago. It was just turning six in the morning which did a lot to signify how important the government took his request, and they should. In the past, Gage made them run around chasing their asses on a couple of different reports he'd done. They needed to take him seriously.

He used the intercom to buzz him in and immediately took the stairs down two at a time. He forced himself to appear confident, easy going, and in control of this situation. Not showing the ball of nerves raging through his heart and head. Everything shifted inside him. He guessed his career never really meant too much to him. He never worried about it like he worried about Trent. Everything in him needed to make sure Trent and his babies were safe instead of finalizing the details on the raid for the last report of his life. Boy, Sid was seriously gonna be some kind of pissed off at him.

"Porter, thank you for coming so quickly," Gage said, striding through the gallery.

"I've learned my lesson. The place looks great, Synclair. I saw the photos of opening night. You've done well for yourself," the general said. As defense advisor to the president of the United States, Porter ranked rather high on the totem pole.

"Thank you. It's been a labor of love. Come in to my office, let's talk there. It's secure," Gage said, raising his hand toward the glass structure and walking toward the door. The entourage following behind Porter stopped at his raised hand. They stayed outside the office door as the men entered. Gage continued into the front office, the blinds to the front were partially open and he could see two armed military guards stationed out front, with four or five solid black SUVs parked right alongside the sidewalk.

The US military never did anything discreetly; the main reason they weren't included in any of his projects up until now. They wanted to make sure everyone in the neighborhood knew they were there. Gage pulled out a chair to the small conference table for Porter and circled around to the coffee station against the glass wall. His laptop and the file folder he'd showed Trent were sitting in front of Porter's seat. He'd removed all the evidence of Trent and the children, saving them for last, or not at all, depending on how this went down.

"I have to tell you, I'm honestly surprised. I knew you were cooking something up. You've been in Mexico twice in a matter of a few weeks, but I never expected you to call me in," he said, once the door closed, taking his seat.

"Things change, would you like some coffee?" Gage asked.

"Sure, but let's get down to it," the general said. Gage took the remote on the table and darkened the office walls, shutting them completely in. A knock came immediately from the office door, but Porter called out to let the guards by the door know there was no danger. Gage offered the first cup of coffee to the general, placing the cream and sugar on the table, and Gage took the second cup, keeping it black. He took a long drink of the steamy hot brew, gathering himself.

"I've prepared a folder for you. I'll ask you not to move forward on the information contained in this file until I've given you adequate background information. But first, I need some guarantees," Gage said, taking his seat at the table.

"I didn't expect anything less," he replied.

"I've come across an unexpected bump in the road in finalizing this report. There's an unexpected family involved. I can't find any connection at all with the suspect or the situation. They're as clueless to this as you, and I want them spared," Gage said, casually crossing one leg over the other and flicking a piece of dust off his slacks as he spoke. He hoped the movement hid the pounding of his heart.

"Well, of course, if it turns out they aren't involved, we would never—" Porter started.

"No, you misunderstand. To get my information on the front end, not the back end, I need the guarantee they will never be brought into any of this, no matter what. Their names will be stricken from my reports, never to enter back in. I need your guarantee," Gage said, looking the general straight in the eye while taking another long drink of the coffee. He kept his face passive and blank; he blinked. This was plan A, B, and C. All eggs in one basket to make sure Trent wasn't touched by any of this.

"All right, can you guarantee they absolutely weren't involved?" Porter said, leaning in, linking his fingers together on the table.

"Yes, I can."

"And if it turns out you're wrong?" Porter asked. A moment of silence followed where Gage just stared down the general.

"I still want them untouched," he said.

"Now, Synclair," Porter hedged.

"It's the deal. Your choice," Gage said. The general sat there, drumming his fingers on the table, looking at Gage, and he stared back passively watching the other man.

"And this report's worth that kind of unverified guarantee from our government?"

"Absolutely," Gage said, nodding.

"What if I don't give it?"

"I'll take this to Europe and move the family there. They'll do it in a heartbeat, and they're waiting now to be transported. I'm just giving my home team the first chance at doing the right thing," Gage said.

"Will you still do the report?" Porter asked and sat back in his seat.

"Not if we keep it here. I'm giving it to you to handle discreetly and confidentially. Which is what you want, you just don't know it yet," Gage said, still sitting in the same position as if he didn't have a care in the world.

"So you're giving up the report, turning it over to us, for the guarantee we won't involve one family?"

"Well, that's part one."

"What's the other?" Porter asked.

"You move in this morning to capture the suspect, and I want a meeting with him. You can be present, no one else," Gage said. The general sat silently thinking over it all, his eyes narrowed and he never let his gaze slip from Gage. Gage kept a tight rein on the emotions threatening to bubble free, offering nothing more than a return stare while drinking his coffee.

"Why are you doing this?"

"I'll give you a small amount of background after you agree." It took another few minutes before Porter spoke again.

"I want you for the next twenty-four hours in DC, available to us. Then I want you on call and on notice for the future until this is resolved."

"All right, do we have a deal?" Gage asked.

"Yes, against my better judgment, I'll agree," General Porter nodded.

"I want it from the top," Gage immediately said.

"My word's enough."

"I understand, but this is too important. I need it backed by the top," Gage said.

"It's seven in the fucking morning, Synclair. He's jogging." Gage sat there a minute and drained his coffee, staring again.

"Synclair, you're a trying, frustrating man," Porter said.

"Yeah, yeah, compliments won't help." Porter palmed his phone, calling the president. As the phone rang, Gage's heart began to pound. He was seconds from the final confirmation he needed to keep Trent and the children safe. As he watched the general on the phone, emotion rose to the surface. He hid the pounding of his heart and the deep breaths he took by rising to get another cup of coffee.

"Mr. President, I'm sorry to bother you this morning. I'm in Chicago with Gage Synclair. He has agreed to turn his next report over to us, step out of it completely, if we agree to keep an American family out of the case. He assures us there is no involvement on their part, and the case is big enough, we will want it regardless of their involvement," Porter said quickly into the phone while on speaker.

"General Porter, what did you decide?" the president asked.

"I agreed to his terms," he said, looking at Gage as he came back to the table.

"Then why are you calling me?" the president asked.

"Sir, he wants to hear it from you."

"Synclair, his word is my word. It's seven in the morning. You don't need to hear it from me."

"Sir," Gage said.

"Do not sir me. If he says it's a go, it's a go."

"Thank you," Gage said and finally smiled. The relief was too much to hide it anymore. The first part was complete. The second would begin soon and then Trent would be safe. Gage found himself saying a prayer of thanks as they finished the call.

"General, I want a report on my desk by eight. If Synclair's already this far in the game, I want whatever this is to be taken care of by ten, with a full briefing by eleven. I don't want this hanging over me today, got it?"

"Yes, sir." The phone disconnected. Gage slid the file folder closer and started from the beginning, explaining it all. It took forty-five minutes to get through it with all the forensic evidence tying Abdulla to every single case Gage brought to Porter. Gage started his laptop, showing all the bank accounts, video surveillance, and eye witness testimony of Abdulla being in every situation Gage connected him with. He also showed how Abdulla infiltrated the different government's military, gained access to the sites he targeted, and faked his own death time and time again. There were even links to his bombing plots in the United Kingdom and France with surveillance of him dropping packages along the way.

Porter stayed quiet, looking at the information, checking facts occasionally on the government laptop he'd brought into the office with him. After a time, Porter stopped Gage. "We need to know it all, but this is enough to bring him in. Where is he?"

"An abandoned mission in La Popa Basin, Mexico," Gage said.

"Why there?" Porter asked, and the question surprised Gage.

"Unsure, he hasn't left there for two months. He's staying quiet, it's reported he took a vow of silence," Gage said.

"Really?"

"So they're saying. We caught up with him the day he landed there. Up until then, we were always one step behind him," Gage said, sitting back in his seat.

"What was your plan going in? And how do we know your men?" Porter typed in his computer as he asked questions, Gage assumed preparing the briefing to the president, or perhaps getting the troops to the area. Who knew for sure; the man liked his mystery.

"My men will stand down if you're involved," Gage said. The general nodded. He typed on his computer for several minutes, and then fed paper into the machine, scanning Gage's work.

"Now, tell me about the family you're protecting while I'm awaiting confirmation the teams are being assembled," Porter said. Gage looked down, weighing his words, but the general stopped him.

"I need you to be honest with me. You have your guarantee, and it's off the record, but I need to know if anything comes up that implicates them or surprises us." Gage flipped his personal file folder around and turned several photos over until he got to one of Trent with the children standing in front of the gallery. It was a great shot. The kids and Trent faced the camera while talking to Sophia. They didn't know they were being photographed, and their beauty shone through in the candid nature. An all-American, home-grown beauty kind of shot. Gage stopped and looked at the picture for several moments before he spoke.

"You brought him to your opening?" Porter said. "Is that right?"

"Yes…?" Gage responded, his eyes snapped up.

"It was everywhere, plus I have to keep my eye on you, Synclair. We know you're working something. But did you know he was involved?" Porter said as he lifted the photo for a closer look. "Is he wearing a tool belt?"

"I didn't know of his involvement. It's a long story, but he didn't know either. He's the electrician on the gallery remodel. These are his sister's kids. The best I can tell, she didn't know, but they're both Abdulla's children. He wasn't around much. He died when Lynn got pregnant with Emalynn, the little girl in the picture."

"How did you meet him?"

"Like I said, he was the electrician on this remodel," Gage said, pulling the picture back in the file.

"You just randomly met him?" Porter asked.

"Yes." Gage nodded.

"You're giving up a lot here, Synclair, for someone you've known a few weeks."

"His sister died giving birth. He adopted the children and raised them virtually by himself. He's a good man, one I'm lucky to know. He doesn't deserve any of this," Gage said, closing his laptop and shoving the papers back in the files on the table. This part of the conversation took an awkward personal turn, one he wasn't sure he wanted to take.

"Does he know what you've given up?"

"No, but he will. I want him kept safe at all cost," Gage said, as the government computer dinged and Porter looked down.

"It looks like we're a go. You ready?" the general said, closing his laptop.

"Let me get my duffle."

Chapter 23

For the first time in Gage's life he took a backseat to the events unfolding around him. Gage stayed in the background, close to General Porter, answering questions as needed, but that became his entire roll in the capture of Ahmed Abdulla. The last six years of his life had been dedicated to apprehending Ahmed Abdulla. He'd spent hundreds of thousands of dollars to track every movement of the guy to this moment. Now, as the military worked, he stood back, watching, his arms crossed over his chest, his legs spread apart, his back straight, and his head held high. He watched everything going on around them.

From this side, it was interesting how the military worked. Gage had only watched them in panic mode after one of his reports, while they were playing catch up. Since he turned this all over to them before the report, he got to watch them work as a well-oiled machine, and he was honestly impressed as hell. They never faltered. There was no indecisiveness, just clear decision and immediate action by some of the best trained people he had ever seen.

They now stood in a makeshift command post, about an hour north of the infiltrated church. Gage watched all the video feeds from the ten or so LCD monitors stacked on top of one another against a wall. They were connected to video cameras, attached to helmets of the Special Forces teams currently raining down a bunch of whoop ass on the unsuspecting church. It looked like a bad ass, sci-fi, military based movie from where Gage stood, but the intel he'd shared had been dead on. They followed his maps and it didn't take much for them to know exactly how to proceed into the church yard.

The helicopters swooped in, troops descended from every direction, even those strategically hiding in the basin ridge area. Gage's men laid down their weapons, and everyone in the church compound surrendered to the forces. One of Gage's contacts had discovered weapons onsite only hours earlier, but they weren't used. Abdulla did the same as every other person in the compound and bent to his knees, spread out on the floor, and waited to be arrested. There was no fight against the incoming troops. Not one round of gunfire took place.

Gage watched as they took Abdulla into custody. He willingly put his hands behind his head and allowed himself to be cuffed. His ankles and wrist were chained and he was carried out of the compound to a waiting helicopter without one word said. Abdulla was the only one removed, and it didn't take long. Not more than a few minutes after landing were they circling back into the air with Abdulla in custody. And just like that, his last report completed, and he wasn't involved at all. It surprised him how okay he really was about it all. Now, he needed to get in front of the guy and make sure he never said a word about Emalynn and Hunter for the rest of his life, however long that may be.

"Synclair, thank you," the general said, and smacked him on the back with a good hard whack. "It went off exactly like you said. The information on the structure was dead on. Good job, son. Like you being on this side so much better!"

Gage stood there, his arms still crossed over his chest, watching the screens as the helicopters faded off into the sun and the on-ground troops faded back into the dense, dry forestry surrounding the old mission. It was a dusty, dry area in the middle of the morning, during the summer. It looked hot on the video and sweat trickled down Gage's back to prove the point. He wore his normal investigative attire: an old, worn T-shirt, and khaki walking shorts, and a bandana tied around his neck in easy reach to help keep the flying dust from his nose and mouth. His eyes never left the screen and he watched everything, making sure nothing happened to the helicopter until he couldn't see it any longer.

"Where are they taking him? You agreed to a meeting," Gage said as his eyes left the screen to focus on the general.

"El Paso. We'll leave in a few minutes. We need to get out of here." As he spoke, they folded the command center back up and had everything completely dismantled within minutes. The whole operation, from the time they'd landed in Mexico, had taken less than two hours.

As Gage took a step back and let everyone work, relief coursed through him. Relief the government agreed so easily to his terms, and relief that the capture ended successfully with no harm to his people. Funny, how a week and a half could change a person. He would have given them anything they asked in order to keep Trent safe. They had him by the balls and didn't even know it.

Gage took a moment, standing in the middle of the command center breakdown, to send a text to his head of security. The weak signal required he stand with his phone stuck in the air, but it finally went through. He used their code to let Hopkins know phase one completed with everyone intact, they were moving into phase two. He got an immediate text back assuring him Trent and the children were inside their home, safe and sound. Hopkins beefed up security surrounding the Cooper house in case Abdulla's apprehension triggered an attack on the family, but so far nothing had changed in the neighborhood, and again, staggering amounts of relief poured through him.

General Porter caught his attention signaling departure time. Gage followed the general to his jeep, where he was driven to a secret location. They left the region in a secure military airplane. Porter thrived in the environment, shedding the dignitary role and garbed in his fatigues. Seeing him from this side, Gage had a whole new respect for the man who seemed to crave being back in the trenches with his men.

Once they were in the air, he got a little bit better signal and finally received confirmation from Hopkins that all his men in the area were in retreat mode. The military had never beaten them to a target before. This was a first. They were retreating and regrouping, waiting to hear from him. Gage sat casually in the airplane, wondering what that conversation might be like. How could he tell these men who'd worked so hard for him, he'd abandoned the report for his boyfriend? A grin spread across his face at the thought, and he swiped his finger across the cell phone screen until Trent's photo came up. This particular picture never ceased to make him smile, and he thought about how in love he found himself with this wonderful man.

The plane ride to El Paso seemed to take longer than the extradition mission. Once landed, the entire team drove in caravan style to the secure location holding Abdulla. Dust and sand caked everything in this drought-ridden location. The farther they drove out of the city, the more tumbleweeds and dust bowl conditions they encountered. Porter spent his time studying the information Gage supplied them, occasionally asking a question, and Gage answered, but that was all he gave in the way of communication. His mind focused on exactly the best way to confront Abdulla. He'd decided hard and firm was the best approach. Abdulla needed to know he didn't mess around and he meant what he said.

As the detention center came into view, Gage watched the stark white building take shape in the distance. Gage took a minute and centered himself. He was going to have to look the devil of a man straight in the eye and intimidate him enough to make sure he never opened his mouth about Lynn, Hunter, or Em.

Guard shacks dotted the landscape around the highly secured detention center. Armed military guards patrolled both the grounds and the rooftops. Every few hundred feet there were elevated guard booths, high in the air, with assault-style weapons trained on the yard and the building. No one got in or out unless they were authorized to do so.

Gage's convoy entered through a remote location toward the back of the center. Even with the clear markings on the vehicles, no one was allowed entry without proper formal protocol taking place. Every one of their IDs were checked and scanned. They drove straight to the back of the facility, and used a private door to gain entrance. They held Abdulla in the maximum security portion of the center, but to Gage the entire place felt maximally secured. He couldn't see anyone making a step in the wrong direction without fearing for their lives. These guys weren't playing at all.

The deeper in the center they got, Gage watched the size of the officers grow. The military officers protecting Abdulla were massive and stood about every twenty or so feet, lining the stark white hallway. Gage was taken from security point to security point, ID'd the entire way. He stayed quiet, and the deeper he got in, the more glimpses he got of Abdulla sitting in a room from the many monitors stationed at the check points along the hall. Apparently they weren't taking any chances with Abdulla. He stayed under constant video surveillance. His arms and legs were still chained and the chains were locked to the floor where he sat.

"He hasn't said a word or resisted anything," a guard said to Gage who stood watching the LCD monitor outside the interrogation room Abdulla sat in.

"Nothing?" Porter asked.

"No, sir, not a word," the guard said.

"Has anyone tried to speak to him?" Porter asked.

"Yes, sir, his rights were read to him. He was told he is a prisoner of the United States, and he hasn't responded or said anything," the guard replied, handing them back their identification.

"He hasn't spoken in a month. It's the vow of silence," Gage added to the conversation.

"What's that all about?" Porter asked, staring at the screen now.

"I don't know. It was a surprise to us too. We found nothing that would have led him to this spiritual journey," Gage said, itching to get inside. The guard picked up his hand-held and began the steps to get General Porter and Gage inside the room. There was another long hall lined with armed guards and a massive set of doors locked from the outside, with two armed guards standing outside the doors.

"Then I doubt he'll say anything to you," Porter said as they walked toward the doors.

"I have to try," Gage said as they got to the doors.

"We need the video feed turned off," General Porter said to the men standing in front of the two massive doors.

"Sir, we can't, it's against policy," one of the two officers said, never looking at either one of them. "And, sir, civilians aren't allowed inside the room at any point."

"Young man, I do not need you to explain procedure to me. Turn the monitors off. Remove your men from the room, and that's an order from the President of the United States." There seemed to still be some hesitation which Gage found he appreciated. If they kept this attitude with Abdulla, he might not ever see the light of day again, which meant good things for Trent and the children.

"The order just came through. Sir, we would like to keep the monitors on, but the sound off in order to be available if you need us," a guard from behind a desk said as he came to the front of the desk. Porter looked over at Gage, and he nodded his approval.

"It's fine. Let's get this done," the general said.

"Yes, sir." The guard who kept them from the room dismantled the security of the door and opened it, allowing General Porter in first and then Gage. The room's dark gray steel walls were in complete contrast to the bright white of everything inside the building. A table stood in the middle of the room with two chairs on either side of it. Abdulla sat in one, chained to the floor. He no longer wore his robe, but sat in his own clothing of elastic waist cotton long shorts, and a tank top style undershirt. Without the hood, Gage could see Hunter more clearly in this man. He was dark headed and his face shaven. Even with the plastic surgery of the last few years, Abdulla was still a very handsome man. He could see how Lynn fell so hard for him. He just couldn't understand how he'd hidden the evil. It seemed to radiate from him as he sat staring at the wall in front of him.

When Gage got approval, he stepped farther inside the small room. The MP stationed at the door received his orders to leave, and with a look of uncertainty, he left, shutting General Porter and Gage inside the room with Abdulla. Porter stayed at the door, but Gage moved forward and walked a full circle around Abdulla. After a minute, he stopped in front of the guy and took the seat directly across from him, studying him closely. One thing about the way his reports played out, he rarely got this close up and personal with the suspects. This was different for him.

He took a minute to gather himself, but the entire time, he stared at Abdulla who wouldn't take his eyes off the wall behind Gage. After a minute he scooted into his line of sight, but even then, Abdulla wouldn't focus on him. His eyes were blank, staring at nothing.

"I'm going to cut straight to the root of my reason for being here, Ahmed Abdulla, aka Benito Bugiardini, aka Rennie Depaul, aka Aaron Adams, Emalynn and Hunter's biological sperm donor," Gage said, and paused as the full weight of Abdulla's gaze moved to Gage's eyes. He never said a word, but the stare spoke volumes as hate shot out at him. Gage stayed firm, unmoved by the evil glaring back at him and continued. "Yes, there we go, much better."

Gage let the words hang there a minute while he looked back at Abdulla before he continued. "Let me tell you how this is going to play out. You're never going to breathe a word about Lynn, Hunter, Emmie, Trent, or Sophia, and in return, I'm going to make sure those kids have functional, healthy lives, never knowing what their bio dad did to this world."

Gage leaned in across the table as Abdulla continued to stare at him, not saying a word. "Now, let me tell you what's going to happen if you decide to go against my request. Your days are numbered, that's not ever gonna change, but what can change is how these last few days of your life play out. Now, listen closely, you even say their names and General Porter's gonna give me a call, then I'm calling Karzai... Yeah, I can see by the look in your eyes, you know where this is going. They'll be made aware of your part in the massacre of their women, and those male children... I and I alone have the proof you orchestrated the violent attack against those children, even after you took their money to bomb the US Embassy in Afghanistan. Our military prisons are full of Taliban prisoners... Porter here is gonna make sure each of them has regular access to your chained up ass until the day you die. Got that?"

Silence. Abdulla stared back at him, his expression unchanging.

"You need to tell me you understand, and you need to know I'm not bluffing in the least," Gage said, his hands linked together on the table, his gaze never wavered as he spoke, but was met with more silence. They stared at each other for several minutes, before Gage grew outwardly disgusted. This must work. They had come so far, there were no other bargaining chips at his disposal. Gage needed to be able to tell Trent they were safe and mean it. But, then again why would he ever think this slime would grow a conscience and give Trent the peace he needed to get on with his life.

"You disgust me. I have no idea how those children could have turned out so precious coming from you. You need to hear me and hear me well. You keep your motherfucking mouth shut about them. I don't give a shit if you keep your mouth closed up tight about everything, but I'm telling you, this government, this prison, won't be able to stop the hell I'll rain down on your sorry ass if you breathe their names from this moment forward!" Gage stood, slamming his hand down on the table, trying to do anything to gain a reaction from Abdulla, but the man sat there silently staring at him. "You're a piece of sorry ass shit, you motherfucker. Let's go, Porter."

As Gage reached the door, Abdulla spoke quietly behind him, none of the hate in his gaze reaching his voice. It stopped Gage and Porter in their tracks. Abdulla's eyes were still on Gage when he turned back to the table. "My children have nothing to fear from me. Trent Cooper is a good man, raising my children as they should be raised. I've been watching. I've been watching you, Gage Synclair

Layne, as you have watched me. Know you have me to thank for his job in your gallery. As for the children, I don't want them to ever know of this. I want them to believe I was the soldier who died in war. That's my condition as to how this will play out." His accent was thick with Middle Eastern influence, and in a long line of mastered accents, Gage knew this was his real voice.

"You don't get a condition, but you're fortunate, they won't ever know because it would hurt them," Gage said, and Abdulla's eyes cut back to the wall in front of him, again giving his blank stare, saying nothing more. Gage stood there a minute more, letting all the little bombs Abdulla had dropped fill in the silence of his stare. Porter ushered him from the room.

"You can turn back on the audio portion of the feed," Porter said to the guard, as the other guard stepped back into the room.

"Just did, sir," the guard at the desk said. Porter's eyes stayed on Gage as he released a long breath he hadn't realized he was holding.

"You all right, Synclair?" Porter asked as they were escorted out the way they'd come in.

"Yeah, I guess. It's hard to hear the person I hate most in the world could possibly be the matchmaker, giving me the person I love most in the world... I need to get to a phone," Gage said, changing subjects, not welcoming any further conversation on the topic.

"This way," Porter said, allowing the discussion to drop. He was led to the administration area of the prison, to a small conference room. The light came on automatically as they walked in and Porter left Gage alone. "When you're done, open the door, but wait inside. I'm going down the hall to make some calls of my own. I'll be back to get you, then we're off to DC to present this case to legal."

Gage gave a nod and took a seat at the desk where a landline phone sat. He waited for the door to close with a solid click, offering him the moment of privacy he so desperately needed. The full weight of the moment settled in on Gage, and he took a deep breath, exhaling all the stress of the last few days out in a deep huff. It was over, well, almost over. He dreaded the idea of being at Washington's disposal for any reason. He knew this next twenty-four hours would suck no matter how he spun it. Regardless, Gage had pulled it off, and who would have thought he could? Wasn't that just a complete freaking surprise?

He grinned on a sigh of relief as he palmed his cell to get Trent's phone number. He'd gotten a commitment from Abdulla and the

United States government...*Wow*! And the case he'd spent the last six years working came to an end. Not with the bang he'd expected, but a small fizzle and for some reason he felt better about this case than any he'd worked before. Gage picked up the phone and dialed Trent's number.

"Coop Electric," Trent said.

"Baby," Gage paused. His voice sounded tired and drained even to him, and he was met with silence. What was with all the silence today? Trent didn't say anything and Gage looked down at the pad on the phone to see if the call was still connected. He tried again. "It's done."

"What does that mean?" Trent asked cautiously.

"It means he's in custody, and I've got an agreement with the government, as well as Abdulla, to remove you and the children from this," Gage said and waited for Trent's reaction.

"What?" Trent asked. Gage smiled at the disbelief he heard on the other end. He hadn't told Trent his plan because he didn't want to give him false hope, and seriously, who would have ever thought he could have pulled this off?

"It's been a long few hours. I've waited to call you until I had it confirmed from both sides. The president even verified it. I heard him say it myself."

"So the kids won't be brought into this?" Trent asked.

"No," Gage said. "We'll watch it, but they've given me their word."

"For sure?" Trent asked.

"Yes."

"Gage..." The relief in Trent voice caused Gage to smile and loosen his tight grip on the phone.

"I know," Gage said.

"Thank you."

"You're welcome, Trent," Gage said quietly back.

"I didn't even realize this was an option on the table. Gage... did you get your story?" Trent asked.

"No, I gave it up to get the agreement," Gage said. Trent was silent. "It's really okay, baby. You're more important than anything to

263

me. I want forever with you, and I can't have forever while jeopardizing everything you hold dear."

"I'm sorry... Are you okay?" Trent asked.

"No apologies, Trent. This was all my idea. I'm good, actually relieved. Wait a minute, you weren't saying I'm sorry because you don't feel the same way anymore?" Gage asked. His hands started to shake as he waited for Trent's answer.

"No, not at all," Trent said. Gage could hear the smile in his voice.

"Good!" And he looked up to the heavens and mouthed a quick thank you.

"When will you be home?" Trent asked.

"Not for a while. I agreed to fly to Washington DC. I'm theirs for at least the next twenty-four hours, and then I'll be back."

"I'm in serious shock here, Gage. You spoke to him?" Trent asked.

"Yes, I did. It was hard; he's gone religious or something. He's taken a vow of silence, but he did speak about the kids and about you too, nothing else. It was about three or four sentences. The main points are you have nothing to fear from him and you're raising the children as they should be raised. You're a good man, per him."

"Really?" Trent asked.

"Yes, that and he knew you were working at the gallery," Gage added.

"So he has been watching like Lynn thought?"

"Yeah, looks like it."

"Thank you, Gage. I'm sorry you gave up your story, but thank you for keeping Emalynn and Hunter safe," Trent said, his voice sincere and quiet. Gage could hear the relief with each word spoken.

"No thanks necessary, Trent. I'm glad it worked out. I didn't have a backup plan."

"I'm still so shocked. I thought the kids and I would be on the run. I was afraid the adoption would be overturned or the kids would be a target for retaliation... Gage, I really thought we would be on the run..." Trent let it all tumble out, and Gage smiled, knowing his words were finally sinking in.

"On the run with me! We're a team, Trent. I have to go, though. When I get back, we need to talk. If it's okay, I'll come by there first," Gage said.

"Please do. And it's safe for the kids to be at school now? We can go on with our lives? I can start looking for new business, now?" Trent fired off the questions, back to back, not giving Gage time to answer any of them.

"Yeah, I forgot about that. Sophia mentioned it last night, and I meant to ask you. Trent, you promised to tell me if anything happened as a result of coming with me to the opening. I'll transfer money into your account when I get cell signal again, and I'll call vendor relations at Layne and get you set up by the end of the day. They'll get you working tomorrow. You don't need to worry about any of it. That should be the least of your worries right now," Gage said, pulling the calendar of his phone up to schedule a reminder to do all those things. His brain was fried, his adrenaline high ebbing. He didn't want to forget because he knew Trent would never remind him.

"Gage, I'll figure it out myself. You gave us back our safety; it's more than enough. You don't even know my bank information," Trent said, but Gage stopped him by spouting off the name of his bank and his account number.

"What else do you want to know about you? I told you I pulled your complete background information. Babe, I don't want to argue right now. I love you, just let me have this one without a fight. Layne will have enough work for you to run five crews, I promise. It's gonna be fine and you deserve it. You do outstanding work."

"Thank you," Trent simply said.

"I love you, Trent. Stop saying thank you," Gage said, not wanting the gratitude, just the love.

"I love you, Gage."

Chapter 24

The grill sizzled with burgers and hot dogs adding to the celebration going on in Trent's backyard. Gage was due home at some point today. They wanted to surprise him with a small party in the backyard. Gage stayed in Washington DC a day longer than expected, tying up the loose ends of the case and being at their disposal for any questions. As of now, the only words Abdulla uttered were those he'd said to Gage, but true to their word, the case the government built kept him and the kids completely out of it. Gage truly saved his family.

Sophia lay on the deck, tanning her winter white body. Gage's mom cooked inside, putting together some sort of dip she'd brought which was supposed to be Gage's favorite. Rhonny laid in about the same position as Sophia, but floating on a blowup raft in the freshly filled swimming pool. Gary and his father were in the water with Trent's kids who splashed and played in their inner tubes and arm floaties. Gage's parents brought a couple of the grandchildren along to play with Em and Hunter and they were all splashing around in the pool. The radio played in the background on the local pop-rock station, not that anyone could hear it over all the squealing coming from Em and Mirabella every time they got splashed. The meat was done, but no one seemed quite ready to eat yet, hoping Gage would get there soon.

Trent checked the cooler he kept outside, the ice held up even in the summer sun, keeping the drinks, the potato salad, and mayo all cool inside. The table looked ready; disposable plates, napkins, bags of chips all ready to open. Everything looked perfect. They were waiting to see if Gage could make it home before too much longer. He loved the thought Gage might make this a home. They hadn't discussed it, but it felt natural for Gage to be considered part of the family here.

Trent grabbed his shirt from the hem, lifting it up and over his head, tossing it aside. He kicked his sandals off to land in the same general direction as the shirt, leaving him in his long brightly-colored swim trunks. A glance down at his chest revealed he was pretty winter white himself, and he chuckled. He had decided to relieve Gary of the kids, maybe dump Rhonny into the pool when he got the chance, but before his decision moved toward action, a car pulled to the back of the driveway, straight past the fence he'd left open. Gage's driver came into view through the windshield. Gage was home.

The moment the car stopped, Gage stepped out from the backseat, and the kids went nuts cheering for him. Trent changed direction, swiveling on his heels, and a smile spread across his face as he walked over to Gage. Trent didn't think Gage could look any sexier than he did wearing his khaki work shorts and an old T-shirt with his duffle slung over his shoulder. He shut the car door without a backward glance, and the driver began to back down the drive. Gage called out and waved to the children, before walking to meet Trent.

"I told him I was staying, I hope it's okay," Gage said loudly, still several steps from Trent.

Trent could hear Sophia and Rhonny corralling the kids, keeping them from darting forward. He appreciated the minute they gave him. Gage looked tired, his eyes red, and his usually perfect blond hair needed a good brushing, but he was still the most handsome man on the planet. Trent walked straight to him, gathering Gage in his arms, and kissed him with everything inside him. Every bit of love, compassion, and appreciation pouring from his heart into the kiss. Gage seemed surprised at first and it took him a minute to catch-up, but he dropped his duffle bag and slid his hand up to Trent's face, turning him to deepen the kiss. It took a minute to register the cheers and laughter going on behind him. He finally broke from the kiss, slowly opening his eyes to meet those of the man in his arms, but Gage's eyes were still closed.

"I was worried it still wouldn't have been enough to keep you with me. I can see I might be wrong. Tell me I'm wrong," Gage said and finally opened his eyes. Trent smiled watching all the emotion playing out on Gage's face.

"You're here for as long as you want to be," Trent said and kissed Gage softy on the lips, letting it linger until Gage pulled away.

"I want forever," Gage said, watching Trent closely. The uncertainty was back, but it was just like Gage to run head first in and ask questions later.

"Then it will be forever," Trent simply said, no doubt or hesitation in the words because he meant them.

"Good, it's exactly what I want." Gage wrapped Trent tighter to him.

"Thank you, for saving our lives," Trent said, keeping Gage in the circle of his arms. They stood toe to toe, chest to chest. The personal space Gage always breached now seemed right to have him there. Trent wanted him this close forever.

"Thank you, for saving my life." Gage said. Hunter bounced at their feet which meant Em was close behind. Trent bent down, scooping up Hunter in his arms. Gage ruffled Hunter's wet head and scooped Em up in his arms. She wrapped her arm around Gage's neck and kissed his cheek.

"What's that for?" Gage asked.

"Daddy said you helped us real much. Thank you," Em said and gave a big nod.

"Thank you," Hunter said too, sliding his free arm around Gage and they stood there a minute in a small group hug." I think this is about the best moment of my life," Gage said, the emotion of the moment landed in Trent's heart, and he leaned in, capturing Gage's lips in a slow, chaste kiss, before he turned and kissed Hunter's forehead and met Em with her lips puckered up for a big wet kiss.

"I love you, guys," Gage said, looking back and forth between Em and Hunter.

"We love you," Em said, looking at Hunter, who nodded, smiling at Gage.

"You two are wet and you got Gage all wet. Go get ready to eat. The hamburgers are ready." They both placed the kids on the ground. Trent leaned down and grabbed Gage's duffle, slinging it over his shoulder and wrapped an arm around Gage as he turned back to the waiting crowd for the first time. Sophia, Rhonny, Gary, and Gage's parents had given them a few minutes, staying on the porch, but they appeared ready to greet Gage home and start the party. Gage and Trent walked forward, arm in arm.

"Gary spending lots of time here?" Gage whispered.

"Pretty much," Trent answered.

"I can see why. She's beautiful," Gage said, giving Trent a sideways glance.

"He seems to think so." Trent smiled, enjoying the closeness.

Sophia got to them first, giving Gage a hug. Tears were in Sophia's eyes as she kissed Gage's cheek and whispered a simple thank you to him. Rhonny came in second with her hug and hushed gratitude. Gage's mom waited until the girls had moved away before embracing her son, holding him the longest. The love she felt for her son was evident in her expression, and it had Trent smiling to know there were people out there that cared for his Gage as much as he did. Trent stepped away, giving them room, and left the small circle to get the kids' lunch started. He pulled four hamburgers off the grill and began preparing their plates, with Em, Hunter and the others taking their place at the picnic table under the patio.

"Is this new?" Gage asked from behind Trent with one hand on the table. His other hand came to rest on Trent's back and then ran forward over the muscles on his stomach. "I love this six pack thing you have going on here."

"Thank you," Trent grinned, giving Gage another simple kiss. "I had nervous energy and built the table yesterday."

"Do you have an extra pair of swim trunks for me?"

"They're in my bathroom already, the farthest door leads in there, but if you need to sleep, we can be quiet."

"No way," Gage said. "I'm so celebrating with you guys!"

Gage leaned down and opened the cooler, pulling four water bottles for the children, placing them on the table. Trent finished their plates and opened a bag of chips, doling them out between the kids.

"I'll be back. I'm going to change, don't do too much without me," Gage said, Trent watched him walk away with his duffle over his shoulder. As Gage got to the bathroom door, he turned back to Trent and gave him a smile and a wink. He mouthed the words Trent felt so deep in his heart, *"I love you,"* before disappearing inside.

Epilogue

"My daddy just got married," Em said, her legs kicking back and forth under the wood bench where she sat, located directly across from the judge's quarters. She worked at making her new pretty pink dress float out, then land again around her feet.

"Well, that's exciting," an older woman, who sat beside Em said somewhat disinterestedly.

"Em, you aren't supposed to talk to strangers," Hunter said, scolding Em. He sat casually next to Rhonny. He was well past the excitement of wearing his new suit, now just tired of its restrictions. Rhonny carried his jacket, he'd abandoned it well over an hour ago, and he slowly worked the tie knot loose, his dress shirt hung partially untucked in the back.

"Hunter, it's okay, we're all here with her," Rhonny said, tucking his shirt back into his pants. "Em's just excited."

"We're going on a honeymoon tomorrow for my birthday," Em told the lady next to her, sticking her tongue out at Hunter after she said it which got an immediate snap of the fingers from Rhonny.

"Emalynn, you know better than…" Rhonny started but got interrupted.

"Em, it's not just for you, it's for Daddy and Gage and me, too," Hunter said, scolding Em, again.

"Daddy said it was for my birthday, and for the adoption, and for the celebration. That's why we're going to Disney World!" Em said angrily to Hunter, forgetting all about the woman next to her. She turned five tomorrow and no longer put up with anything Hunter dished out.

"Guys, stop! No fighting here," Rhonny said quietly, but firmly.

"Hunter, come sit by me," Gary said from beside Rhonny. "It won't be too much longer and they'll let us back in there to watch them sign the papers."

Hunter did what Gary asked, and they all scooted down a little to make room on the bench for Hunter at the other end. Gage's parents sat on the other side of the hall along with all of Gage's other brothers and sisters and their spouses. Sophia was there, typing away on her smart phone, updating Facebook with the events of the day. It started with Trent and Gage getting married in a civil ceremony, and now they were waiting for the judge to finish with them, and the adoption to be finalized. The door opened to the judge's office, and Gage stood there, pretty much looking like a Prada male model, smiling big. He looked so happy, as though he could barely contain it.

"Come on in, we're ready," Gage said, and he walked across the hall to pick Em up, and took Hunter's hand in his. "You guys ready?"

"Yep," Em said, hooking her little arm around his neck, in what had become her signature move with Gage.

"Yes," Hunter said, still working at the knot at his neck. "You tied this tight, Gage."

"It's supposed to be tight, son. Come on, just a few more minutes and I'll untie it, okay?"

"Okay," Hunter said with a little whine as they walked back into the judge's office. Gage went to his seat across from Trent, but kept the kids in his lap. He helped Hunter onto one knee, and placed Em on another. His family stood back in the back along with Rhonny and Sophia who already snapped photos.

"Okay, guys, it's time for your dad and I to sign the papers. You still want me to be your father, right?" Gage asked, and both the children nodded, their eyes big with excitement.

"Do we need to sign it? I've been practicing writing my name just in case," Em whispered loudly into Gage's ear. Everyone chuckled and smiled at her sweet thought.

"I do believe we will need your signature Emalynn," the judge said. "And you, Hunter, are you ready to sign?"

"Yes, ma'am," Hunter said, taking it all very seriously. The judge met his agreement with a nod and started the formal process of signing all the paperwork. Trent signed everything first, and encouraged the kids over to him so Gage could sign it, but Gage would have none of it. He kept the kids in his arms, where he wanted them, and signed the paperwork with them right there. The judge opened a back page of the document and drew two lines across the bottom.

The judge smiled at both kids and took on an official tone as she asked, "Now, you understand, this means Gage becomes your father? Are you sure you are both good with everything this means?"

They both nodded enthusiastically, and Em confirmed her nod by tightening the hook of her arm around his neck. Hunter leaned over the desk and signed his name first, and then Em wrote her first name out letter by letter. When she was done, she turned back to Gage's mother with a giant smile on her face. "Now you're my gammie, for real!"

"I'm so glad I am, honey" his mother said, tears finally spilling over.

"All right then, let me sign it, and it's official." The judge signed the paperwork. When she closed the file, the room erupted in applause and congratulations.

Gage held on to the kids, and Trent moved in, hugging and kissing them all. They stayed together several moments before they turned to their family. Gage's family came over, hugging the children. Em and Hunter were long past calling his family gammie, grandpa, aunt, and uncle. Rhonny hugged them both too. Sophia stood to the side, waiting her turn, tears rolling down her face.

Trent came to her first, hugging her tightly. Gage's mom and dad took ahold of Em and Hunter, while Gage went to Trent, wrapping Sophia and Trent in his arms.

"Lynn would be so proud right now. I know she's here. I know it! And she would just be so proud," Sophia said, hugging Gage's neck tightly.

"I want her to be proud, she has two incredible children and a brother I can't live without," Gage whispered, tears clogging his throat as he released Sophia to step back.

"You two are the incredible ones," she said. Gage stayed quiet, holding Trent close. Rhonny came in for a hug, and the kids bounded forward, getting in the middle of it. After a minute, Hunter finally broke free, tapped Gage's arm to get his undivided attention, and asked the biggest question on his mind.

"Can we take my tie off now?"

The End

About this Author

Best Selling Author Kindle Alexander is an innovative writer, and a genre-crosser who writes classic fantasy, romance, suspense, and erotica in both the male/male and male/female genres.

Send me a quick email and let me know what you thought of *The Current Between Us* to kindle@kindlealexander.com. For more information on future works and links to my social networking pages (come friend request me!) check out the website at www.kindlealexander.com.

If you loved *The Current Between Us*, then you won't want to miss Kindle Alexander's bestselling novels:

Texas Pride
Up in Arms

Coming In September: *Double Full*

Reader Comments

Texas Pride

"I have a severe case of book hangover. Seriously readers – you need to read this book. Ten stars for me!" — **Foxylutely* Blog*

"The end of this book was so well done!" —*Shh Mom's Reading*

"Definitely a great read...I didn't want this sweet story to end."
—*Author Christi Snow*

"Recommend this to those who love cowboys and movie stars ...and a very happy ending." —*Mmgoodbookreviews*

"I highly recommend it." —*Samantha, passionate books*

"I would DEFINITELY like this to be a series...hint hint to Kindle Alexander!!!" —*Brenda, Twinsie Talk Book Review*

Up in Arms

"*Up in Arms* is a compelling, fascinating drama that honestly explores the conflict of love in the military without taking away from an enchanting romance." —*Joyfully Reviewed*

"This story not only follows these men's love affair, which is sweet and sexy, but we also see the aftermath of how they deal with tragedy. I love these boys, how they interact, how they over come, how one of them blushes *sigh*." —*The Bitches of Eastwick*

"This is a tender love story.... She taps all the sensory elements that binds a romance reader to the narrative, characters, conflicts and resolutions." —*Blackraven's Reviews*

Check out these title from friends of Kindle Alexander:
Tyrian's Mist by VL Moon
Grand Slam by JT Cheyanne
For a love of a God by VL Moon and JT Cheyanne

29695706R00160

Made in the USA
San Bernardino, CA
29 January 2016